THE TRIAL OF LESTER CHAN

MARTIN WILSON

Matador
9 Priory Business Park,
Wistow Road, Kibworth Beauchamp,
Leicestershire, LE8 0RX
Tel: 0116 279 2299
Email: books@troubador.co.uk
Web: www.troubador.co.uk/matador
Twitter: @matadorbooks

ISBN 978 1838591 700

British Library Cataloguing in Publication Data.
A catalogue record for this book is available from the British Library.

Printed and bound in Great Britain by 4edge Limited
Typeset in 11pt Aobe Garamond Pro by Troubador Publishing Ltd, Leicester, UK

Matador is an imprint of Troubador Publishing Ltd

For Martha Kate whose name links four generations.

A letter of credit is a document provided by a bank which guarantees that a seller will be paid on time and in the full amount agreed between the seller and the purchaser. If the purchaser defaults or for any reason does not make payment in full the bank is obligated to pay the full amount or any outstanding balance to the seller. Until the sale is complete, the bank has title over the goods which are the subject of the contract between the vendor and the purchaser. If the purchaser cannot or for any other reason does not reimburse the bank, the bank can legally seize the goods in order to protect its own position. A letter of credit transaction presupposes that there is an underlying and genuine sale and purchase of commodities.

Martin's International Dictionary of Finance, 17th Edition

What the fuck is all that about?

Australian lawyer in the Commercial Crimes Unit of the Legal Department of the Government of the Hong Kong Special Administrative Region

PART ONE

陳

1

So, here he was again. Sitting at the table in the kitchen, staring at the tea stain that he had made days, weeks, months ago. Of course, it was only four days since she had left. But it was four days in a row that he had woken, alone, in their bedroom, and four evenings when he had come back from the pub, destroyed a ready-meal in the microwave and sat, a bottle of red wine at the side of his plate, forking frozen brown lumps from the scalding, runny sauce and wondering whether he would be able to stay awake long enough to call her at a decent time, allowing for the eight hour time difference.

He looked at the kitchen clock. Quarter to six. Quarter to two in the morning in Hong Kong. She would be fast asleep now, those soft, innocent, gentle breaths that, in his insomnia, he would lie and listen to. Those slight shudders as she rolled towards him when he stretched out his hand to her. If he had a quick Scotch now before going out and perhaps another, or maybe a beer at The Unicorn, he could waste an hour or so before coming back to his empty home

to have something to eat, watch some mindless crap on the television whilst drifting in and out of consciousness and, somehow, keep going until it was quarter to midnight, when she would be up and waiting for his call. She would still be drowsy from her long and deep sleep. He would, he knew, be mildly incoherent from fatigue and drink. But still, they would be able to talk.

The visit not been, he conceded, an unmitigated success. A Chinese family, coming for a couple of weeks to see their married daughter in Cheltenham when none of them had set foot outside Hong Kong before was always going to be a risky proposition. And when their daughter was married to a *Yinggwok Gweilo*, an Englishman who was much older than her, the fact that he had brought face to the family by his being a solicitor, albeit now retired, was not enough to make them feel at ease in such foreign surroundings. So it was not altogether surprising that they had cut short their holiday and that Winnie had been persuaded to go back with them for a while.

He looked out of the kitchen window. A light drizzle was falling. Enough to put off walking to the pub. But if he started on a Scotch now, he might want another at home and then be stuck in for the evening. What was a little rain? He needed some company, even if it was the old soaks who leant against the bar and the pond life who played the gaming machines; even if there was no-one else but the landlord, that oleaginous fake.

He switched on the hall light, grabbed a coat from the stand and locked up. He had not gone far before he realised that it was anything but a drizzle. The rain was coming down hard, and by the time he reached the door of The

4

Unicorn he could feel the wet on the back of his neck and the soles of his feet.

'Good evening, good evening, good evening,' the landlord called to him. 'Another fine night. Seems to have kept my regulars away. You're the first one here.'

Frank Grinder glanced around the empty pub. Hell, it was going to be an evening of anecdotes from behind the bar. And did he really think that he was a regular? He supposed that, coming four evenings in a row, it was not an unreasonable assumption.

'And what will it be this evening? Your fancy as per usual, the Gold Cup bitter, or some other tempting tincture, perhaps?'

'Just a pint of bitter, please,' he said. And a large strychnine for yourself, he thought.

As the landlord pulled the beer handle he turned towards Frank. 'I gather your wife has gone back to… Singapore, is it?' He gave him a studied look of sympathy. 'Mine left two years ago. Probably much the same reason – cultural differences and too big an age gap.'

He assumes that she's a mail-order bride, thought Frank. Of course, he is just the sort of oaf who would.

'It's Hong Kong, actually. And she hasn't left me. Well, just for a holiday with her family.'

The landlord smiled, conspiratorially, to show that he understood the excuse. Frank caught his breath and felt the ire rising in his throat.

'And I am going out to join her as soon as I can get away,' he added to his own surprise, and took his beer to a table as far away from the bar as he could.

'Of course, you used to live there, didn't you?' mine host called over to him. 'Is that where you met her?'

Bur Frank was thinking about what he had just said. It more or less made sense; and even if it did not, it was what he knew he wanted. He would suggest it to Winnie when they spoke later. He drank his beer in silence. There was no need to talk to the few people, all of them men, damp stragglers who had come into the bar. No need – nor, now, the slightest inclination.

He finished his drink, got up and, ignoring the landlord, set off into the rain.

As soon as he had got through the doorway he checked the time. It would be three in the morning over there. He pulled off his wet coat, slung it over the banister finial, went into the lounge, poured himself a Scotch and sat on the settee. There really wasn't any good reason why he should stay here on his own. Winnie had not asked him to go back with her, probably, he hoped, because her parents' apartment high up in a tower block in Yuen Long, in the New Territories, was so small with barely enough room for her to stay in; but was there, possibly, a chance that she wanted to get away from him for a bit, to get back to a completely Cantonese environment, where she could eat and talk and laugh noisily without the inhibition that his presence might create? It was odd that she hadn't even suggested that he might like to join her, had not raised the possibility and given him the chance to demur. Maybe she did need to be away from him for a while. Maybe she was not happy with the way things were. She had never given any sign of that; but she was very attractive and the appeal of marrying a mature solicitor, and her boss, might have worn off.

His glass was already empty. He poured another, much larger this time, and assuaged his conscience by taking it into the kitchen and topping it up with tap water before bringing it back to the lounge. She couldn't possibly have met someone else, not here at home. But that was it, Hong Kong was her home: her family was there, living and dead. It had not previously occurred to him that she might be disturbed by being so far away from the graves of her ancestors, not being able to visit the cemetery and to take part, with her relatives, in the *Ching Ming* grave-sweeping ceremony every year. However Westernised she may have seemed, it was always there, beneath the surface. In every temple in Hong Kong, young people in jeans and designer sunglasses, with the latest smart phones, could be seen lighting incense and supplicating before some god or other and shaking *chim* sticks out of their pots so that they could take them to the resident fortune-teller for an interpretation of their future. And she was not much different from them; she looked so attractive in jeans and a cotton shirt that so suited her slim, firm body; indeed, when she wore her hair in a ponytail, she could easily pass for someone in her twenties.

He looked at his watch and then at his glass; there was hardly anything left. He must have drunk it quickly. Perhaps there was time for another small measure, and then he ought to get through the tedium of making himself some supper. It was still only half past seven; definitely time for a quick one. He might see if the *News* was on. He refilled his tumbler, zapped the television into life and sat back down on the settee.

He realised, when he woke, that it was dark outside and the rain was streaking heavily down the windows. For a moment he panicked, but saw that he had been asleep for only an hour and a half. Nine o'clock here; four there. She would be fast asleep in a small bed in a cramped room with scarcely enough space for her clothes, let alone her suitcases, in an overcrowded flat. Was she dreaming of him, perhaps? Did she think of him before she went to sleep?

His head was beginning to throb and his mouth was dry. He must get himself something to eat, he knew, even though he really would prefer to sink into his own bed and try to sleep till morning. He went into the kitchen. He could not face another microwave calamity; and although he knew that there was still a rump steak in the fridge, the thought of frying it with some mushrooms or tomatoes, even if he had some, and peeling and cooking potatoes was too daunting. There was also some bacon. A bacon and egg sandwich, that would do. And some mustard to make it taste of something other than grease. And a glass of that Chilean Merlot that he had opened yesterday.

He took a long drink of tap water and set to work. Within minutes he had dropped a rasher on the floor and knocked an egg into the sink, where its shell cracked and the yoke began to seep into the plughole. Another egg and the rest of the pack of bacon were spluttering in the frying pan when he noticed smoke coming from the toaster. He leapt and pressed the eject button. Two thin slices of smouldering charcoal jumped onto the work surface. He opened the bread bin; there was nothing in it apart from the plastic remains of wrappers and some fairly large crumbs.

There was some crispbread in the pantry and a packet of rice. He realised now that he was quite hungry. Crispbread wouldn't hack it. He would have to boil some rice. Bacon, egg and rice, that could be interesting but perhaps not the mustard. Soya sauce, that would do. He tipped some rice into a saucepan, filled it near to the brim with water and put it on the gas. As he did so, he noticed that the frying pan was giving off a cloud of pungent steam and that the egg had turned solid and coalesced with the bacon, which had gone black at the edges. He moved the pan, and as he flinched from the searing handle he knocked over the glass of red wine that he had forgotten he had left beside the cooker. The flame under the rice went out and a smell of gas came from underneath the saucepan. He slopped the pan onto another ring and tried to relight the burner. It clicked a lot but would not come to life. He tried the one that he had moved the pan to, but he must have drenched that, too, with the rice water. He moved both it and the saucepan off the cooker and could see that he had flooded the whole of the top. Shit, he had put the frying pan on the kitchen table without thinking; he shifted it and saw an ominous round scorch mark on its surface. He put the saucepan in the sink.

He refilled the glass and contemplated the mess. There was no point in trying to clear up now. That could wait until tomorrow. The immediate problem was food. He peered into the rice pan: it was still not properly cooked, and he remembered stories of Japanese soldiers torturing prisoners of war by making them eat half-boiled rice. He poked around with a fork; the grains were small and hard. In fact, there was a more immediate problem, as the smell of gas was getting stronger. He turned the two knobs to shut off the supply and opened the kitchen window. A gust of wind and rain blew in, knocking the china jar which held Winnie's spatulas into the sink. Shards of pottery embedded themselves into the now coagulating egg.

It would all have to wait. Was it too late to go out for something to eat? The local corner shop would be closed by now, and he did not care for the idea of walking fifteen minutes in this weather to the nearest fish and chip shop. And he had had too much to drink to drive. So they would have to manage without his custom. Just top up the glass of red and be inventive.

He took out the pack of Ryvita again, crumbled a few slices into the frying pan, got what was left of the block of Cheddar cheese from the fridge, cut off a few lumps from the cracked and dried edge, dropped them in, scraped the solidified scab from the bottom of the pan and turned the whole lot onto a plate. It was disgusting, but it went some way to filling him. It certainly smothered the desire to eat. The overwhelming sensation was of salt. Perhaps mustard or soya sauce or both might have helped. He finished the glass of wine and ate an apple to try to take the taste away. It was nearly ten. Less than two hours now. He made a cup of instant coffee. But perhaps he should set the alarm on his smart phone just in case he nodded off again. He went back into the lounge. The television was still on. An incomprehensible quiz show. He changed channels to a cookery programme. What could there be for him to learn?

He startled awake. His first thought was that she had called him but then he recognised the alarm tone. His mouth was dry and his heart thumping. It was a just past quarter to midnight. He went back into the kitchen, took a swig of water from the tumbler in the sink and pressed the stored number on the phone on the wall to call her mobile. As he waited for the connection he could still feel the beat beneath his shirt pocket. He thought he could also hear it. Would it be audible on the phone? A few clicks, silence and then the dial tone. The connection had failed. The thumping got louder as he tried again. This time it was ringing, curiously the same over all those thousands of miles as the sound you got when you called a number in the UK. That, and the square three-pin 13-amp plugs, links to the British legacy. She answered on the second ring: she was waiting for him.

'Hello, darling, it's Frank.'

'Oh, I know it's you. I know your ring.'

'I didn't wake you?'

'No, you silly man. I had been awake. I wait for you.'

'Do you love me?'

'You know I do. Why you ask? You done something wrong?'

'Of course not.' Not unless you counted the destruction in the kitchen and the damage to his liver. 'I just miss you so much and wanted to know.'

'I miss you, F'ank, but I can't come home yet. Too many family things.'

Home, she called England home. Why did he let worry get on top of him?

'F'ank, I had been thinking. Are you very busy? Do you have many things to do?'

'No, why?' He did not want to tell her how he spent most of his days trying to find things to do and to stretch them out when he did.

'Well, you know you like Hong Kong. Because, I cannot come back yet.'

Because, the Cantonese prefix to something that you are not going to want to hear.

'Because, I can't come back, but you can, maybe, come here. *Mummiah* and *Daddiah* home is very small, but maybe, if you come, how about we can hire a serviced apartment in Jung Wan or Tung Lo Wan, you know, I mean, Central or Causeway Bay. I know you have lots to do and you are a very important man, but maybe you have a holiday here and we can be together and I can still see my family, but not live in their house, I mean flat, and you could see some friends, and the weather is very good here, very sunny, and maybe you could go horseracing, you probably still a member of that Club, and we could go to Macau…'

'Winnie.'

'What? Is it I ask too much?'

'No, Winnie, you don't ask too much, but you do talk too much. Will you just listen for a moment?'

2

At a quarter to eight the alarm clock went off in the bedroom of Charles Hartington Munsonby, golfer, and partner in the firm of Chan, Yeung, Munsonby & Lam, Solicitors and Notaries of Admiralty District, Hong Kong. At a quarter to nine, he emerged from the lift of the Skywards Gardens apartment block in Robinson Road, Mid-Levels and, puffing slightly, strode with his golf bag slung over his shoulder to his Mercedes sports car.

At nine-thirty he drove onto the car park of the Lung Yeuk Tau golf course in the New Territories. As he climbed out of the air-conditioned interior he felt the late summer heat strike him like a hot towel. He was conscious, also, of a slight discomfort in his right arm, probably caused by sleeping too heavily on that side.

At nine-forty-five, now wearing spiked shoes, he was on the driving range attempting alternate shots with his wood and his number seven iron. The exercises seemed to have relieved the ache and he continued practising for a quarter of an hour.

At ten o'clock Munsonby walked to the first tee. His two golfing partners were already there and he greeted them with a nod and a brief exchange of words. He could just see the flag on the par three green. He took a couple of practice swings with his wood and then squared up and struck the ball with a gratifying thwack. It sailed in a long, graceful arc towards the hole. His satisfaction was soon somewhat diminished because, at three minutes past ten, he realised that he was lying on his back on the grass and that someone was shouting to call for a doctor.

Frank Grinder could not get to sleep. After he had finished talking to Winnie and had put the phone down he had gone into the kitchen to see if it was in as bad a state as he thought it would be. It was worse, and the smell of burned egg mixed with spilled wine was nauseating. There was nothing he could usefully do that night, apart from drinking a couple of large tumblers of tap water, so he went into the bathroom and brushed his teeth. My God, he looked dreadful. A ravaged old man with crumbs of cheese stuck to the side of his mouth. He would have a proper shower tomorrow and try to restrict his intake of alcohol.

The glow that he had felt when he realised how much Winnie wanted him to join her was still there when he got into bed but it was now mixed with anxiety about how much he had to do before he left. Frank had committed himself to flying out the day after tomorrow, but as he lay in bed he realised how much that would entail. Air tickets, a hotel for him – or them – to stay in until he could find a serviced apartment which was available on a very short lease, letting his few friends here in Cheltenham know that he would be away, cancelling appointments, although how many and what they were he was too groggy to be sure of, stopping the papers, making sure that he had enough Hong Kong dollars to get him from the airport, letting the bank and the credit card people know that he would be using his cards in Asia and, of course, trying to clean up after his attempts at cooking. As he lay in bed with all these thoughts tumbling through his mind he began to feel the sensation around his breast that reminded him of his life before Winnie – the heartburn which was the product of too much alcohol and hastily eaten meals. He sat up, belched, and tried to wriggle himself into a comfortable position and then realised that he very much needed to pee.

By the time that he got back into bed he was wide awake. He turned on the bedside light, put on his glasses and opened the novel that he had been trying to read on the previous few nights. It was hopeless: at the end of every paragraph he had taken nothing in as his eyes automatically scanned the words. The story was not sufficiently gripping to compete with the thoughts that kept running through his mind. He put the book back and switched off the light. At least if he lay in bed for an hour or two and rested his body it might be of some benefit. He would just have to have an early night tomorrow. For the time being he would try not to add worrying about insomnia to all his other problems and he would try to relax, even though sleep seemed impossible to achieve.

He woke to a sunny morning with the light streaming through the gap where he had not closed the curtains properly. His head was unexpectedly clear and, although his mouth was bitter and dry, he felt that he could tackle the kitchen after a cup or two of coffee and then get on to his computer to start making bookings. He looked at the bedside clock. It was already gone nine. Four o'clock in the afternoon in Hong Kong. He wondered whether she would be in if he tried to call her. He could try her mobile if she wasn't and, anyway, it would be better to do that than risk the phone being answered by her parents who sometimes understood English and sometimes did not. But perhaps he should wait until he had some news for her.

At five that afternoon, in Hong Kong, the Court of the Honourable Mr Justice Brett O'Brien rose. The judge bowed, acknowledged the obsequious bows of junior counsel and the curt nods of the more senior barristers and waited for his clerk to open the door behind him. He strode down the corridor towards his room, pulling off his wig as he went. It had been a very warm day in court; the air-conditioning seemed not to be functioning properly and the day's list had been piecemeal and unsatisfying. A few pleas of guilty, in none of which were the reports ready, a couple of applications to vary terms of bail, three approvals of the terms of settlement in claims for damages for personal injury where the plaintiffs were minors and an extraordinarily long-winded application to adjourn the date of a murder trial on the grounds that the defence had not yet received the reports from their forensic scientist. Try as he might, and did, to indicate that he could see no possible reason to refuse the application, that it would be wrong and patently appealable to force the trial to go on when the defence was not ready, that as the prosecution did not oppose the application there was no reason to pursue prolix and detailed grounds, and that it was already past the usual end of the court day, there was no stopping defence counsel, a superannuated, somewhat portly Chinese barrister who was standing in for the chap whose case this was, and who plainly relished what was, evidently, the rare opportunity to appear in the High Court. After a few tentative attempts to shut him up, which had resulted in a counterpoint of unnecessary explanations, the judge had resigned himself to the conclusion that the more he tried to shorten proceedings the longer they were taking and so he sat glumly waiting for counsel to draw breath long enough for him to insert his ruling that the application was granted. Several opportunities had seemed to present themselves, but he had been too slow off the mark and the peroration had continued. Then, in mid-sentence, the barrister had turned to his instructing solicitor, who was sitting behind him, apparently to ask for some documents.

'Excuse me, my Lord…' he said. 'Application granted, and I adjourn this case for mention in two weeks from today,' replied O'Brien. 'Bail refused. We shall now rise.'

'My Lord,' said counsel, 'I have further submissions to make.'

'Are they about bail?'

'No, my Lord, I am not instructed to ask for bail. My client is realistic enough to know that he would not get bail.'

'Well, you've won your application for an adjournment. What more do you want?' the judge's New South Wales accent becoming more marked with his exasperation.

'My Lord, with the greatest of respect, and if your Lordship pleases, I have more points to make.'

'Well, I don't please.'

'I am sorry, my Lord, I don't follow.'

'I'm sorry too, that you don't. I am rising.'

'But, my Lord, my client wants…'

'Tough,' the judge had said as he stood up.

Nor had the air-conditioning in his room yet been fixed, and the smell of stale bookshelves and bureaucracy hit him as he opened the door. He pulled off his judicial wig and loosened the stud of his plastic wing collar. The front of his neck was sore and he could feel the damp beginning to run down the inside of his shirt. What a day it had been: largely pointless and culminating in that last episode of forensic fuckwittery. He unzipped his gown and sat at his desk.

It was odd that there were no files on it. Normally Henry, his clerk, would have the papers for tomorrow's list waiting for him, so that he could run his eyes over them before taking them home. It looked like the end of a perfect day: the Judiciary office had cocked up, there would be minions scurrying from floor to floor in the High Court building and he would have to wait on in his room until they had managed to sort out his work for the following day. The last time that had happened, he had had to wait for well over an hour; but at least, on that occasion, the aircon had been working. He moved to the easy chair in the corner of the room and closed his eyes. As he did so, there was a faint tap and the door opened softly.

'My Lord, I am sorry to disturb your thinking.'

'Ah, Henry,' said the judge, 'Come in. Oh, you are in.'

He was usually pleased to see his clerk. Quietly efficient was how he would have described him. In fact, he often did. And with a courteous, smiling manner. Reassuringly unflappable. Except that he was not carrying any papers for the judge.

'Henry, this is too bad. Listing seems to have messed it up, again. Am I going to have to wait here until they have managed to sort out my cases for tomorrow? Have you any idea how long they will be? I have an appointment at six this evening.' His clerk didn't need to know that it was with a cold glass of Philippines lager in the Long Bar at the Club. 'And Maintenance has still not fixed the air-conditioning. It's stifling in here.'

'Yes, I can see, my Lord. I spoke to them again this afternoon when you were in court, and they promised that they would fix it before you had come back,' said the clerk.

'Well, they haven't. And I have got to wait in this…er… fug.'

'I am sorry; are you displeased with me?'

'Oh no, not with you. Why? Oh, I see. I said "fug", you know, unpleasant atmosphere.'

A half smile formed on Henry's face. O'Brien wondered why. Was it relief, or amusement?

'I can, for the moment, do nothing about the fuck, my Lord. I think that the Maintenance had gone home now. Also, the Listing.'

'What? So what am I to do about tomorrow's work?'

'Nothing.' The smile remained. 'They have run out of work for you for tomorrow. All the cases before the other judges are running on, and we do not want to start a new trial on a Friday, so nothing was listed. Except a mention in a fraud trial.'

'What case is that?' asked the judge.

'Oh, it is a new one. I know only that it is a letter of credit fraud.'

'Well, where are the papers?'

'They do not appear to be ready yet. It seems the defence solicitors have instructed a London QC, and the Hong Kong Bar Association has only today indicated that they do not oppose the application for his admission to the local Bar. So it is just a mention tomorrow to let the court know the position. So you will not need papers. '

'And when is this listed for?

'Ten o'clock, my Lord.'

'And can you promise me that there will be no surprises: nothing added to my list at the last moment?'

'Yes, I think so.'

This, thought O'Brien, sounds like the early start of a nice weekend.

3

The sky had turned to a leaden grey when he emerged from the tube station and lugged his bags up the stone steps into Temple Place. In the wheeled case were his wig and gown, his folding lectern and his copy of the latest edition of *Archbold's Criminal Pleading, Evidence and Practice*, the increasingly expensive and weighty practitioner's bible. In the other was the bulky brief in the murder trial that he had concluded that morning in Sheffield and which his instructing solicitor's clerk had neglected to take back with him after they had come up from the cells, having advised the client that the chances of a successful appeal were, at most, slim.

All the way back on the train he had been conscious of an increasing feeling of gloom or dissatisfaction; he wasn't sure he could distinguish between them. It was not just that he had lost the case; after nine years in silk, as a Queen's Counsel and, for many years before that, as a junior, he had plenty of experience of winning and losing. Nor was there any self-recrimination about his performance. He was generally his own fiercest critic (at least, he hoped so); he had read the papers thoroughly and did not think that he had missed any good points in cross-examination or in his closing speech. It had been a very strong case against his client, who had only made it stronger when he gave evidence. But still there was that ineluctable sense that all was not well. Perhaps he was tired; it had certainly not been easy to sleep in the dismal hotel which was all that he could reasonably run to on Legal Aid rates. Perhaps he had never quite got used to the personal impact of seeing someone whom he had been defending, whoever he was and whatever he had done, being sent down for life. Perhaps it was the weather.

By the time he got to the top of the steps it had started to rain. There was a telescopic umbrella in his briefcase, but he would not have been able to hold it up and carry his cases at the same time. He had no coat. Taxis were always scarce when it was raining, and he could hardly justify the expense for such a short journey to his chambers in Queen's Bench Row.

As he got to the doorway of the 17th-century building that housed his chambers he glanced at the list of names on the board outside. It had become almost a self-mocking ritual to check that his had not been taken down in his absence from London. It was still there: Jonathan Savage QC, seventh down from the Head of Chambers, a heavyweight commercial silk who had probably not had to address a jury in his life and who certainly would not have just travelled standard class from Sheffield if, in the unlikely event, he had ever been there. He was getting on a bit now and it was rumoured that he might have missed the chance of the High Court bench, although the truth probably was that he would not have considered that a knighthood and a pension would justify such a shuddering drop in his income.

Jonathan looked up at the security camera and waited for a moment, then put down his briefcase on the wet pavement and tapped out the code on the panel beside the door. It buzzed and swung open, revealing a wooden boarded floor and a dark oak staircase which smelled of wax polish and school. In an alcove to the left of the stairs, behind a waist-high partition, sat Debbie, this month's pretty, vacuous, smiling, school-leaver receptionist-cum-tea maker.

'Hello, Mr Sandwich,' she said. 'I saw you struggling.'

'The door release button not working?'

'I dunno; was I supposed to let you in?'

'Well, it might have helped,' said Jonathan. But what was the point of saying more; long before she had learned what to do, she would have been replaced by another seventeen-year-old who would probably call everyone by their first name. He lugged his cases up the stairs, dropped them in the small room which he shared with two other members of chambers and walked along the corridor to the clerks' room.

'How did you get on, sir?' Eric, the senior clerk, was thin, grey-haired and approaching retirement. He had been a barrister's clerk since he was fifteen, had seen pupils in chambers end up as Lords Justice of Appeal and could no more address even the most junior barrister by anything other than "sir" or, just possibly, his surname than he could arrive anywhere late. He wore half-moon, gold-rimmed glasses that lent an avuncular air which was only occasionally justified. He stood up between his chair and his desk.

'We went down, I'm afraid,' said Jonathan. 'The client was all right, in fact he seemed quite grateful for my efforts, but the bloody solicitor's clerk disappeared and I had to bring all the papers back with me. Could you get them sent back to Sheffield?'

'Of course.'

'And what's next week looking like?'

'The armed robbery in Chelmsford has gone off, I'm afraid. Apparently, the co-defendant has gone sick and the judge has ordered it to be taken out of the list.'

'That was supposed to last the week, wasn't it? And I've spent hours reading the brief. It will be just my luck that it will be put back in when I am doing something else and I'll have to return it. Legal Aid rates are bad enough, but not getting paid for the work that you've done is depressing. But I should be used to it by now. Anything for the week after?'

'Well, sir, until half an hour ago I was going to say there was not. You are going to have to return the Chelmsford case, though.'

'How so? We can't yet know when it will be relisted.'

'Because I have just had a telephone call from Arthur at Seven Bradford Row.'

Savage, of course, knew that set. Very high-powered, with lots of QCs.

'He is having to return a leading brief for Mr Gresham Nutworthy who has had to go into… ahem, a clinic.'

'The booze has caught up with him at last?'

'Arthur was not specific. But he said that none of his silks were available or were of sufficient seniority.'

'What do you mean, of sufficient seniority? A QC is a QC. No-one takes silk unless he is very experienced at the Bar.'

'The lay client insists that the silk who defends him must be of at least eight years' standing. Apparently, eight is an important number.'

'I'm sorry, I don't follow this. The solicitor selects the barrister. The lay client can't pick and choose on the basis of seniority. Legal Aid isn't that accommodating.'

'This isn't such a case, Mr Savage.'

'What, it's a privately paying client?'

'Yes, sir; and because you are over eight years in silk, I suggested your name, Arthur gave me the name of the instructing solicitors, I have emailed them your details and, rather to my surprise, considering the hour, they have already responded.'

'But it's only just gone four. Why were you surprised?'

'Oh, I'm sorry, sir, I forgot to mention. They are in Hong Kong. They are happy for you to replace Mr Nutworthy; they believe that the lay client will agree as neither your current age nor your year of birth contain the number four, although he is in custody and they will have to wait until tomorrow before they can see him; but they have worked on the assumption that he will agree and so they have already emailed an application to the court and the local Bar for your admission.'

'What, you mean that the trial is in Hong Kong?' asked a stunned Jonathan.

'Yes, sir, the solicitors, the lay client, the judge, the trial, everything. Of course, we shall have to expect a renegotiation of the fee, as you don't quite have Mr Nutworthy's reputation. But it will, I am sure, still be very substantial.'

'And what sort of case is this?'

'Fraud. I think it is called "a letter of credit" fraud. Something to do with banking.'

Oh Christ! thought Jonathan. 'Oh good,' he said. 'So, what's next?'

'If all goes well,' replied Eric, 'the papers will be sent here for you to read them, and then you will fly to Hong Kong for consultations with the solicitors and the client. Depending when it is fixed to start, you may have to stay there until the trial starts. I believe that the estimated length is six weeks.'

Jonathan gulped. 'Look, Eric, I don't mean to sound ungrateful. I appreciate everything that you have done for me, I really do. And who would not want a case in an exotic jurisdiction? But, frankly, I don't think that, at present, my bank balance would stretch to a long-haul flight, let alone a prolonged stay in a hotel. I believe it is pretty expensive out there.'

'You need have no concerns on that score, sir,' said Eric, who could, probably, have funded the flight and hotel from his personal account several times over. 'As you know, my previous set of chambers had several members who had overseas practices. It is usual for first class or business air fares and all accommodation to be paid for by the client. Arthur confirms that that was going to be the arrangement for Mr Nutworthy and I see no reason why it should not apply to you if you take over the case.'

'Business class will do,' said a relieved Savage.

4

Saturday in the Commercial Crimes Unit of the Prosecutions Division of the Department of Justice of the Hong Kong Special Administrative Region of the People's Republic of China was, in spite of sounding like the product of Franz Kafka's imagination, a very casual arrangement. Staff came in for the morning only, dressed in jeans and tee shirts, and the balance of work and chat tipped towards the latter and so it was normally something to look forward to on Friday.

However, this Saturday morning Graham Truckett, a Grade Four member of the division and one of several others of that rank, arrived in a foul mood. He would, normally, forget that he had an obligation to put in an appearance at work on the following morning and, like many of his other Antipodean colleagues, be in the habit of treating Friday evening as the end of the working week, meeting each other and members of the local Bar for drinks at Mortimer's Bar in Admiralty, and absorbing large quantities of beer in a process akin to osmosis, before going on, still suited and tied, to less sedate establishments in Lan Kwai

Fong, Wanchai or Causeway Bay, and sometimes to all of them. However, last night he seemed to have accidentally advanced time by one day and to have exceeded his normal weekend intake and could not now remember where they had ended up, or whether he had eaten any supper or how he had got back to his government flat in Mid-Levels, let alone got out of the lift at the correct floor and staggered into his own bed, as he must have done, having woken in it, alone and still in his work suit, when the bastard alarm clock had screamed its unwelcome call at him. It was ironic, he reflected, that as a school kid he had been taught that the word "Antipodes" came from the early maps when strange creatures were depicted as inhabiting the furthest reaches of the southern hemisphere with their faces in their chests and their feet turned backwards; this morning he felt as if it were his head which was on the wrong way round.

He had had to wait a long time for a lift to the ninth floor. Two of them were out of order and the crowd round the others seemed to push him further back the longer he waited. The irritating custom of repeatedly pressing at the call button, when it was lit and indicating that the lift was on its way, as if frantic jabbing would make it come quicker or emptier, was, this morning, infuriating. Nor did the Hong Kong habit of pressing the "Close Door" button as soon as they stepped inside improve things as, several times, he had been shut out just as he approached and had had to wait and watch the signs to see which was likely to arrive next. When he, eventually, did manage to crush in, it was obvious that the air-conditioning was not working and it was stifling. It stopped at every floor for just long enough for a few passengers to squeeze their way out before

28

the man standing closest to the control panel, who was evidently fulfilling a childhood ambition to be a lift driver, closed the doors behind them, ignoring the people who were approaching and trying to get in.

The doors of several offices which he passed along the corridor were open, revealing, in various states of sprawl, some of the people with whom he had, or thought he had, been drinking last night. A few looked up and groaned a greeting.

'Emily.' He looked into the cubby-hole room that was his secretary's realm. 'Do you think you could be a love and bring me a black coffee? No need to go out for it; from the kitchen will do.'

'Yes, Mr Truckett, I will do. You want it on your desk?'

'Yes please, like usual.'

'Because…I think not so much room on your desk.'

'Why not? I cleared all my files yesterday.'

'Because, Mr Soh, he came in early.'

'Which Mr Soh? Wesley, in the room next to mine? What does he want? Some advice?'

'No, Mr William Soh, the Director of Public Prosecutions. He had come in yesterday evening after you had left and again this morning before you had arrive and he want to talk to you about the case papers.'

'What papers?'

'Oh, because, first thing, the messengers had come with a trolley from the police. Well, maybe few pieces of trolleys, and they put the boxes of papers on your desk.'

'Why on my desk? Why couldn't they just leave them on the floor?'

'Also, they did.'

'What!'

'And against the wall. But I had said they must not block your window. Must have some light.'

'Oh, shit! I'm sorry, Emily. Ah, look, no wuckers, I'll start looking at them later. Forget the coffee, I'll just go out for one.'

'No, Mr Truckett, better I bring to you. Mr Soh wants to talk about the case this morning.'

Graham slunk the short distance along the corridor to his office. The desk was covered with pink-covered files, the familiar reports of the Hong Kong Police Commercial Crimes Bureau, and piles of cardboard bankers' boxes, which he knew were filled with statements and copies of documents, lined the walls. He gulped and the throb at the front of his head worsened. There was no possibility of starting to look at them today; he had better see what the Director wanted.

His phone was just visible in a small island of space on his desk top. He picked it up and called Emily.

'Would you tell Mr Soh's secretary that I'm on my way down to see him.'

陳

William Soh Tak-man presented a contrastingly elegant figure as he rose to greet him.

'I am sorry to trouble you, Graham,' he said. 'Please sit down. Would you like some coffee or a Chinese tea, perhaps?' and he motioned Truckett to the chair on the other side of his enormous, empty desk.

'Ah, no thanks. A glass of water, perhaps.'

'Let me get straight to the point. Have you seen the papers in your room?'

'Well, I've glanced at them, but I can't pretend I've read them all yet, William.'

The irony was not lost on the Director, nor the familiarity. Nor Truckett's sprawling posture. He said, 'I assume that they have come as something of a surprise to you.'

'A surprise is putting it quite mildly, mate,' he replied, thinking that a pants-stainer would have been nearer the mark.

'Yes, I know that as a Grade Four prosecutor you wouldn't normally expect something of this size. But I think that you are on the path to becoming a Senior Assistant and, in fact, I can foresee you eventually taking silk and becoming a Senior Counsel in the not too distant future. And you would have my support for that course and that could possibly lead to your becoming a Queen's Counsel if you returned to practice in Victoria – I think they have reinstated the title there, haven't they? – but I digress. So, this would be very good experience for you. And the fact is, those in the Department to whom I would, normally, have considered allocating this case are all already tied up with existing cases. Of course, in these circumstances, I would have considered briefing an SC from the private Bar but I have recently received a directive from the Secretary for Justice. As you probably know, questions have been raised in the Legislative Council about the cost of administering the Department of Justice and, in a nutshell, he has asked me to cut down on the cost of sending cases out on *fiat*. I find it very difficult to do that, given the restricted size of our complement, and we have, as you know, more cases going on in the District Court than we have people sufficiently experienced to present them and so I have been compelled to brief out. The situation with jury trials in the High Court is not so bad, but even so, we only have a limited pool of people in-house who are strong enough to take them. So, it struck me that the next long prosecution case had better be kept within the Department. And this is it.'

'Well, could we at least get a leader from the private Bar?' asked Truckett, knowing, of course, what the answer would be. His head was still pounding.

'No, Graham,' replied Soh. 'That would defeat the whole object. You know how expensive an SC would be for us. And I am quite sure that you are more than up to the job. Although, perhaps not this morning,' he added.

Truckett said nothing. A sensation of nausea was rising up and he was not sure whether it was from last night's overindulgence or from panic.

'I will ensure, however,' continued the DPP, 'that you have a competent junior to assist you but, obviously, it must be someone from within the Department. Have you any preferences?'

'Not really,' said Graham, glumly.

'Good, then perhaps we can ask Lee Sit-ming.'

'Sorry, never heard of the bloke.'

'It's not a bloke. It's Pammy Lee.'

'I still don't know who you mean.'

'No, perhaps not. She's quite new to the Department. Quite young. Very nice. Very pretty.'

'Is she any good, William?'

'Frankly, I have no idea. But she is the only one we can spare, Graham, particularly as I am taking you off any other work that comes in and that, of course, has a trickle-down effect so that everyone of your grade and below will have to take up the slack.'

'Oh, I see.' He could not think of anything else to say. He was now feeling quite sick. He straightened and got up from his chair.

'Before you leave: did your glance at the papers get you so far as to see who the accused is?'

'No, not really. Well, not at all. Who is he?'

'It's Chan Wai-king. Lester Chan.'

'What, the…'

'Yes, the Jewellery King.'

'The one who is always in his own television advertisements, boasting about how cheap his stuff is. Always smiling. Lots of teeth and dyed hair.'

The Director's hand involuntarily went to the back of his head where his hair had recently been retouched to black.

'Yes, him. It's a letter of credit fraud. It seems that he has more interests than just jewellery. And he has already instructed a London Queen's Counsel. But don't worry; you'll have plenty of time to master the papers. The trial has just been put off and there's no date yet.'

'Trial? I thought all those papers had come in from the police and that they would want some advice on the preliminary charges and, perhaps, the evidence.'

'No, that's been done. Alfred Mak,' he said, referring to a Senior ADPP, Grade One, 'has seen to all that. Didn't I mention to you that it would have been his case? Did you know he has resigned? No? Well, he said that he has decided to run a restaurant in Vancouver. A very strange decision.'

'Emily told me that the papers had been brought in from Police HQ, so I assumed that I would just start reading them at...' he checked himself from saying ...at my usual leisurely pace.

'Oh, that,' said the Director. 'They were being stored at the police station, that's all. We had to put them somewhere as we wanted Alfred's room back and he left so suddenly that he didn't make any arrangements for the papers to be passed on. It is all very odd. You know, I can't think what could have driven him to do such a thing.'

'Ah look,' said Graham, 'I'm not feeling too sharp. Maybe I should go out for a breath of fresh air. If you don't mind, I think that I'll tie up the loose ends of some other matters when I come back. I'll come in early on Monday morning and start going through the files. And perhaps I'll have a word with, er...'

'Pammy Lee. Yes, that's alright,' answered the Director, smiling at Truckett. 'There's no point in trying to concentrate when you are, shall we say, unwell. I should think that a couple of aspirin and some coffee might help.'

5

As the plane continued its descent, Frank Grinder experienced a familiar frisson of... What was it? Excitement or anticipation; he was not sure. It was quite some time since he and Winnie had left and he had so easily assumed his life in Cheltenham which seemed, so satisfyingly, to replace and contrast with his former working days, and yet here he was, eager to identify the first recognisable landmarks. Seated beside a port window he could see, through the thinning cloud and far below, shipping and islands and high-rise buildings but nothing that he knew or that struck a chord. They were too high and this still must be mainland China. There was a huge delta, probably the Pearl River, and then that must be Shenzhen, which had already begun to grow furiously outwards and upwards well before they had left. And then the aircraft, now much lower, was flying over Lantau Island in Hong Kong territory and commencing a slow curl so that it disappeared under the wing and out and over the New Territories, and dipping more, and there, now, was the unmistakeable profile of Hong Kong Island with towering buildings, some of which had not been there when he left, some even on land which not been there but which had since been reclaimed from the sea, projecting into the narrowing stretch of water between Hong Kong and the Kowloon Peninsula. He could just catch the distinctive shape of the island of Cheung Chau, and there was the familiar power station on Lamma, and down towards Lantau again and they were landing, three hundred tons of 747 touching the concrete with scarcely a bump, and the urgent scream of the engines in reverse thrust and the easy miracle of the transition from being airborne to coasting at what seemed to be a sedate pace with the engines hushed and the air-conditioning once again audible.

He knew at once that he was glad to be back, after all, and a rush of memories came to him: old friends; hiking on some of the islands which they had just flown over; the smell of that enticing mixture of cooking and traffic fumes; dropping in at some of the clubs of which he used to be a member; the megaphone of Cantonese chatter; to eat and eat; to stroll around the shopping malls, constantly astonished by the variety, quantity and price of super-luxury clothes, jewellery and shoes; taking the Star Ferry across the harbour or joining the throng of tourists on the Peak Tram and strolling the circuit at the top; meeting for lunch in one of the many superb hotels. But now he could do so with the added pleasure that, unlike most of the others in business class, he had no office to go back to, no transactions to complete nor clients to call or be called by. And, of course, there was Winnie, his warm, attentive, pretty wife who, he hoped, would be waiting for him in the arrivals hall.

陳

There she was, waving excitedly, as he pushed his trolley through the huge, glass automatic doors. Waving and jumping like an uninhibited little girl. They embraced, she, enthusiastically, talking all the time, he, with the reserve that came from a consciousness of the disparity in their height, age, ethnicity and demeanour which always hovered just above the surface when they were together in public. He disentangled himself from her arms and gently pulled her to one side to stop her seizing hold of the bar of his luggage trolley and pushing it for him.

'So, you had miss me?' she asked him, a skittish smile beneath her lovely eyes and pageboy haircut. 'Or that you can't cook and had to come to me?'

'Of course I missed you, Winnie. That's why I came out. It's just wonderful to be with you.'

And then he noticed that Rambo was there also. Wong Chi-king, her younger brother, who had managed to get himself into so much trouble during her family's recent visit to England. He was walking towards them, eating a hamburger from a paper napkin, a greasy grin on his face.

'I thought that we might have some time on our own before we go to your family's apartment,' muttered Frank, not trying very hard to hide his disappointment.

'We will. I have a surprise. But because Younger Brother want to come to greet you.'

'Hello, old boy,' shouted Rambo, extending his free hand.

'Where did you pick that up?' muttered Frank. Had he been watching old black-and-white films on television?

'Er, hello, Rambo. How are you?'

'I'm mighty fine.' Perhaps it was black-and-white cowboy films. 'You are most certainly looking great, my man.' And he slapped Grinder on his shoulder, leaving a faint, oily mark on his lapel.

'It's good of you to come to meet me,' lied Frank. 'Have you driven here?'

At least that would save the bother of getting a taxi.

'No, didn't Older Sister tell you? I lost my licence last month. Over the limit. No, we came on the Airport Express. Return ticket, so we go back that way, also. Old chap.'

So, possibly, it was Ealing Comedies. It was hard not to like Rambo. His baseball cap at a rakish angle, he was openness itself. At times crass and flashy, always at war with the conservative values of his parents, often lazy, but engagingly upbeat; however, Frank, tired and in need of a shower and some time with his wife, could easily have managed without him, just at the moment.

'Don't blame Winnie,' Rambo said. 'It was my idea to come. I wanted to see you again, you old fart.' So, perhaps not Ealing. 'But you don't put me up… I mean, put up with me for long. I get off at Kowloon Station and go home.'

'Aren't we going with you?'

'No,' Winnie interjected before Rambo could reply, 'I think I tell you already.'

Rambo took hold of the grab bar.

'Let me push this,' he said. 'An old man like you shouldn't…'

'Listen, Rambo,' said Frank, amused in spite of himself, 'I want to get one thing clear.'

'You did already,' Rambo interrupted. 'When we were in England. After I got arrested. But you won't change me, old fruit.'

'Rambo?'

'What?'

'Have you been watching much television since you got back to Hong Kong?'

'Yes, I have. The Movie Channel. They are running a lot of old British films. I had been watching as many as I can. You had, maybe, noticed that my English is improve.'

'Well, I noticed something. It's certainly different.'

'Oh smashing,' grinned Rambo. 'Jolly good!'

'And Rambo?'

'What, old fellow?'

'Do you mind if I talk to Winnie? She *is* my wife, and we haven't seen each other for…'

'Plenty of time for that,' replied the younger brother. 'After Kowloon Station.'

Grinder look puzzled but said nothing.

The Airport Express glided up to the platform. Rambo pushed the trolley to the glass doors and, when they swished open, loaded Frank's cases in. There were recorded announcements in Cantonese, Putonghua and English and, almost noiselessly, the train started off. Within minutes they were at Tsing Yi Station. Rambo, who was sitting behind Frank and Winnie and had not stopped showing off his newly acquired idioms of the Forties and Fifties, leaned forward and struck him on the shoulder.

'Kowloon next,' he said.

'I know, I used to live here,' Grinder retorted.

'I just thought I remind you. Because maybe you had forgotten, old bean.'

'Well, I haven't.'

Frank squeezed Winnie's hand and wondered whether they would ever have any chance to be alone before the onslaught of the rest of her family. He looked at her face and tried to interpret what lay behind her slight smile. As the disembodied voice said, 'Gow Lung…Jiu Long…Kowloon,' Rambo got up and hit Frank on the shoulder again.

'Cheerio, then, you two lovebirds. I'll be seeing you,' and, looking back with a simian grin, Rambo pushed to the front of the queue by the door.

'Don't we get out here?' Frank asked.

'No,' said Winnie. 'Because too much family in *Mummiah-Daddiah* house, I had book us an apartment like I said. More better for us there.'

'Where?'

'Ginn Nei Dei *Sing*.'

'Where's that?'

'You know, Ginn Nei Dei.'

'That must be the Chinese name. Say it in English.'

'I did say.'

'No.'

'Yes. Ginn…Nei…Dei,' she replied patiently, as if talking to a toddler. 'That is English.'

'Doesn't sound like English to me. What's the Cantonese name?'

'I told you. Ginneidei *Sing*.'

'It sounds exactly the same to me.'

'It is. Same in English, same in Chinese.'

'Oh, alright. Why there?' Grinder could still not place it.

'Because it is not too very far from MTR station at Sheung Wan. And it has good view of the harbour. And you can see Naahm Nga Dou, you know, what you call Lamma Island, with the electricity chimneys.'

In spite of his tiredness and the onset of jet lag, Frank created a map of Hong Kong in his mind. As they weren't getting off at Kowloon they must be going under the harbour to Hong Kong Station. On Hong Kong Island the Mass Transit Railway ran along the northern side. Sheung Wan was, at least for now, the last stop on the western end of the line, and so, to be close to it and able to see the power station on Lamma Island, it would have to be…

'Do you mean Kennedy Town?' he exclaimed.

'Yes. That's what I say. Ginneidei. Except *Sing* is town.'

'Oh, great!'

'It's a nice apartment. One bedroom, so Rambo can't come and stay with us. Nor anyone.'

'Even better.'

'And I had put a bottle of *wai si gei* in it already. And six pieces of bottle of *bei jau*. *Sam Lik* from *Mah Nei Lai*, that you like.'

Frank recognised these once familiar words: whisky and San Miguel beer, brewed in Manila.

'Better still.'

'I not get you wine. You choose more better than me. I thought of getting you *hung jau*, red wine like you always drink, but I don't want to buy the wrong one.'

'Darling Winnie, a cold beer will be just what I want when I get in. You are wonderful. You think of everything. And you have the loveliest face I have ever seen.'

She smiled demurely.

'Oh, and yesterday, when I had been to the apartment, and then was in Chung Wan…'

'Central?'

'…Yes, I saw Mr Yeung Chi-hang the solicitor.'

'What, Billy Yeung, my old partner, when it was Chan, Grinder, Yeung & Lam? You know, when you used to work for me. Of course, it's not called that now, I believe. Not since they took in that pompous fool, Charlie Monsonby. I wonder how they're getting on with him. I must say, I always had a soft spot for Billy Yeung. I hope that Monsonby isn't throwing his weight around. How is Billy, did he say?'

'She is fine.'

Frank tried to suppress his laugh. Winnie could never quite get her head around English personal pronouns, not surprisingly, as they did not exist in Cantonese; it wasn't her fault, but it still was very funny.

'Yes, and I told Yeung Chi-hang you were coming to Hong Kong. And she said that he would be very happy to have dinner with you and so I had gave her the phone number of the apartment. I did not give him your cell phone number because I think that you will get a small one with a SIM card just for Hong Kong. That's more cheaper.'

'Yes, you're right. I'll get one tomorrow.'

6

The flat was really very nice. On the small side, with just one bedroom, as Winnie had said, but it had a proper bathroom with a real bath and shower, and there was a small kitchen and quite a decent-sized lounge with a dining area at one end and a large, green-tinted picture window at the other, framing a view of Kowloon across the bustling harbour and the smoke stacks on Lamma Island off to the left. On the fifteenth floor, they were high enough not to be overly troubled by the noise of traffic on Victoria Road. The furniture was functional rather than aesthetic, but it was clean and looked new and was not untypical of serviced apartments all over Hong Kong.

Frank lugged his bags into the bedroom, took off his jacket and kicked his loafers under the bed. He went into the lounge; Winnie was sitting on the settee and had put a chilled glass on the side table in front of her, but waiting for him. He sank down beside her, put his hand on her thigh and reached for the beer. He sighed contentedly, a pleasant fatigue sweeping over him.

'Winnie, you're such a marvel. This flat is just right and I have got all that I could possibly want just now: you beside me, and a glass of cold beer in my hand. When I've had a shower, shall we go and get something to eat? Hello, what's that light flashing on the phone?'

'Maybe you leave it, F'ank.'

'Yes, I don't want to be bothered now. But maybe it's important. It must be a message and it might be from your family. It can't be for me. Nobody knows I am here. Perhaps you had better see what it is. But will you tell them that I'm too tired to go out tonight and probably will be tomorrow as well?'

Winnie got up and went to the phone.

'No, F'ank, it's a message for you. You had better to listen.'

Wearily, Grinder hauled himself up and went to her.

'Just press 1,' she said.

Frank listened. A faint, slightly metallic recording came to him.

'Hello, Frank Grinder. This is Billy Yeung. I met your wife and she told me that you were about to arrive in Hong Kong. I would like to give you dinner as soon as we can arrange it. But first of all, there is something important. We need your help on a little matter because something urgent has come up. So, could you call me on my cell phone? Or at the office? The number is the same as when you were here. My cell phone is…' and he gave his number, too fast for Grinder to pick it up or write it down. 'So, call me, please.' And the message ended with a click.

'Oh God,' said Frank, suddenly feeling utterly exhausted. 'Billy Yeung wants me to talk to him. Said something about helping him, but I'm retired and I've come here for a holiday with you. I don't want to do any work. It's too late to call him at the office, they'll have gone home by now. He gave me his mobile phone number, but he went so fast, or I'm so slow, that I couldn't catch it and, anyway, I didn't have a pen and paper. I suppose I could replay the message, but I'm so tired.'

'9614 6216,' said Winnie.

'What?'

'That's his number. 9614 6216.'

'How do you know that?'

'Because I was a very good secretary.'

'Yes, I know you were. But I didn't see you write it down. How could you remember it?'

'Because I am very efficient.'

'Yes, but you hardly listened to the message. How could you get it? You're not, by any chance, just making the number up, are you?'

'No. It is right number.'

'Well, I don't get it.'

'So, maybe I pretend that I have special power. Or maybe I tell you the truth.'

'Which is?'

'I wrote it down when she gave it to me yesterday. And put paper by the phone.'

'Well, I think you do have special powers. You knew what I wanted to drink. You can read my mind.'

'Oh, that,' she smiled. 'I thought that you are too tired. Maybe later, after we eat.'

'But I am supposed to call Billy.'

'I read your mind and then I give you orders. Call him tomorrow.'

7

Monday morning found Graham Truckett feeling more up to the challenge. He had been for a walk on the Peak yesterday morning; it was one of those days when the air was clear and bright, the breeze blowing the pollution back towards China, leaving the surface of the harbour dancing and sparkling. He had limited himself yesterday evening to a couple of beers in Mortimer's, had had a modest and early meal and had gone back home to watch a film and was in bed by 10pm. Entering the Department of Justice building in a dark suit and tie instead of the stained slacks and open shirt that he had worn on Saturday morning somehow seemed to invigorate him, and he thought that perhaps nausea had made it all look worse than it really was. He expected that the piles and boxes of papers would not seem so daunting when he came back into the office; but no, they seemed to have grown. They certainly looked different. He wondered whether someone had been in over the weekend and added to them or whether they had reproduced as – was it amoebas? – some creatures were supposed to do by subdividing themselves. A sensation, part numbness part panic, descended on him. He wondered whether a coffee and a doughnut at the Ocean Coffee Shop would help; possibly it might make him feel more nourished but it would not, he conceded, make the papers diminish. He knew he was merely indulging in displacement activity, in the fantasy that if he gave himself some time he would be able to come at the problem with more energy. No, there was nothing for it: he would have to make a start. At least he could justify having a coffee at his desk. He rang his secretary.

'Emily, could you bring me a black coffee, please. And also, would you see if Miss Lee, Pammy Lee, is available as I would like to talk to her.'

'Yes, Mr Truckett. I did already.'

'What, you've made the coffee?'

'No, I already call Lee Sit-ming. She is here with me. I know that you would want to speak to her.'

'How did you know?'

'Because I saw the boxes.'

Graham, puzzled, said, 'Oh. Ask her to come to my office please.' He took his jacket off and put it on the back of his chair.

As the Director had said, Pammy Lee was very pretty. Tall and slim, with a pair of large, dark blue-framed glasses that gave her a studious appearance whilst emphasising her small features, she wore a cream silk shirt and a pale grey skirt. Truckett glanced down and saw that there were food stains on the front of his trousers and hoped that she wouldn't notice them. Perhaps he should have also checked his shirt this morning; there might be sweat marks under the sleeves. He tried to keep his arms close to his chest. She put her cup of coffee on the desk in front of him and, still clutching a slim file, went to the other chair in the room.

'Hello, Pammy. I am afraid that we have a lot of work ahead of us. These are the case papers we have been landed with. It's a fraud case.'

'Yes, I know.' Her English suggested an overseas education. Possibly Australia, more probably the UK.

'I came in yesterday evening and started looking at them.'

'Really? On a Sunday? How long were you here?'

'Not long… well, a few hours.'

'Well, that's er…impressive.'

'Maybe so.'

'I don't suppose you could have got very far into them. Were you able to get any idea of what it's all about?'

'Not much. Only that it involves allegations of false letters of credit. Six of them. To do with the apparent purchase of various commodities from overseas traders. Using a chain of nominee companies. A couple of banks in Hong Kong and several overseas. All of them traceable to Chan Wai-king, Lester. And it's a conspiracy to defraud over a period of about six months in the middle of the year before last. With some supporting evidence relating to other questionable transactions which we might be able to get in under the Similar Fact rules. Most of the witnesses are reliable, either because they are independent of Chan or the employees have been immunised.'

'What, protected from flu or something?' Truckett wondered why he still came out with that old chestnut. It probably wasn't funny the first time he said it. Was he trying to establish some sort of joking mastery or was it a defence in the face of his embarrassment? His head was beginning to throb again.

'No, it means that they have been given an immunity against prosecution if they agree to give evidence, so long as their evidence is true. But you are, perhaps, joking. Yes, you know what it means, of course.' Her dark eyes sparkled as she smiled and half-lowered her head.

'So, what were these commodities? The Director told me that it isn't jewellery, I think.'

'Oh, various. I know there is some rolled steel involved, but I didn't have time to examine all the documentary exhibits yesterday. You see, I was only here for part of the time. I had to have dinner with my family. And play mah-jong. And then I came back to the office for a bit. Otherwise I might have been able to do a better job. I am sorry.'

'Oh, you did pretty well,' conceded Truckett, aghast at his own contrasting ineptitude. 'And just so we can make sure that we are singing from the same hymn sheet…'

'I am sorry, but I don't think I understand what you mean.'

'To make sure we are thinking along the same lines, just give me some idea of what you think a letter of credit fraud is. Sit down, and I'll make a note of what you say.'

Pammy looked puzzled but she sat in the chair opposite Graham's desk as he requested.

'Perhaps I am wrong, but I thought that a letter of credit could mean only one thing. I did not know that there could be more than one interpretation.'

'Oh yes,' lied Truckett. 'I have come across several different versions. But rather than wasting time with my explaining them to you, just you let me know what you think they are.'

'Well,' said Pammy, 'it is to do with banks. Always.'

'Yes, and?'

'It is to do with trading between companies in different countries.'

'Always?'

'Usually.'

'That's right,' said Graham, hoping that he was emanating the air of a genial schoolmaster.

'And it is a way for a seller of merchandise to have the confidence that he will receive full payment when he is trading with a party who he does not know well or who is in a different jurisdiction.' Her tone was even and measured despite her concern that this senior *gweilo* was testing her to see whether she was good enough to be his junior in such a big case. But what different versions were there? She only knew of one. Perhaps he meant differing ways of doing it. It would help if she had some more time to do some research. She might even have a word with one of the other government counsel on her floor.

'And what about the way that the fraud is carried out?'

Pammy pulled down the hem of her skirt and slid one leg over the other. She noticed that, so far, he had not taken any notes.

'Please,' she said, 'perhaps, maybe, it would be better if I wrote something down. Then I will not miss anything. Do you think that would be alright?'

'Sure. What a good idea. And if you could try to fit it to what you have seen so far about the facts of this case that would, er… that would save us having to discuss theoretical possibilities and we can then concentrate on the real issues. But look, don't put yourself under too much pressure. If you can come up with something in a day or two, that should be fine. In the meantime, I'll start going through the police report, if there is one.'

'Yes, there is. I had a look at it yesterday. But I did not have time to read it all.'

'No, of course not.'

What a nice man, she thought. He seems very understanding and patient in spite of my inexperience and his seniority. And he is so polite.

What great legs, he thought. And, obviously, very bright. Certainly seems to know her way round commercial crime.

'But look, Pammy, I think it is important that we get to know each other a bit 'cause, er… I think we are going to work well together. Let's go down to Ocean Coffee in Pacific Place and I'll buy you a latte or something. I could do with a coffee myself.'

'I would like that very much. But have you got the time?'

'I find that you can get a lot accomplished over a coffee. Workwise, I mean. And it's really very stuffy in here this morning, don't you think?'

She said nothing, but stood up.

'Emily,' he called, 'Miss Lee and I are just going out for a bit. To Ocean. Not out to Ocean Park for the day; just for a coffee downstairs.' Embarrassing all three of them by his clumsiness, he led Pammy out of his beige office, into the beige corridor and across to the beige lift lobby.

8

Grinder knew there would be no point in calling Billy Yeung before eleven in the morning. A man of regular habits, he would look into the office every morning not long after his secretary had arrived, check that there was nothing really urgent to attend to, his classification of urgency excluding anything less than the collapse of the building or the firm, and then slip out to the Luk Yee teahouse in Wellington Street to be insulted by the waiters and to take in a sufficient quantity of dim sum and strong, dark *Pu-erh* tea in order to sustain himself back at work until a respectable time would arrive for him to go out to lunch. Another of his routines was to leave his mobile telephone on his desk when he was taking this snack, confident that a messenger would be sent the short distance from the office in the event of a real emergency occurring. So, having slept in, taken a shower in the sleek, gleaming bathroom of their temporary home and sat with Winnie for breakfast for the first time in what seemed an aeon, Frank picked up the *South China Morning Post* which she had arranged to be delivered and glanced through the headlines.

He had always enjoyed the correspondence column for its quirky combination of the momentous and the utterly trivial. Sure enough, there was a letter making a good point about climate change and another dealing with the risk to Hong Kong's status as a world-class financial centre posed by the lack of native English-speaking teachers, a problem, he mused, which was longstanding, as Winnie had picked up some bad habits from her Hong Kong-born teacher whereas her younger brother had been taught by an English lady schoolteacher; and then there was a complaint about a dead mouse near the Tak Man Street stop for the 6A green Public Light Bus, the writer observing that it had been there for more than two days and that the relevant authority should deal with it as it was not a nice thing to look at. Not very nice for the mouse, either, thought Frank. He looked at his watch; it was now eleven fifteen. Probably safe to call Billy.

He tried the mobile phone number. It rang for a couple of times and then there was a pause, a click and then a voice which was, patently, not that of the senior partner of Chan, Yeung, Munsonby & Lam, Solicitors and Notaries.

'*Wai…Yeung Sin-san bei-syu.*' A young woman by the sound of it.

'Sorry, er… I must have the wrong number.'

'Oh, no. Yes. This is Mr Yeung's secretary.'

'Thank you. Is Mr Yeung in the office?'

'No, he had not come back yet.'

'Oh, has he been in this morning?' Frank wondered whether his old friend had changed his lifestyle and started the day in the office at a more conventional time.

'I just tell you. He has not come back.'

'Where's he been?'

53

'At home. Sleeping.'

'What, you mean he has been in to the office and then gone back to bed? Is he ill?'

'No. I think he is very well.'

A pause.

'He looked well. Did not say that he was ill.'

'Well, why has he had to go back home? Did he tell you?'

'No, I said he has not come back. From yesterday evening, when he left.'

'Oh, you mean he has not yet come in today.'

'I already tell you he had not come back.' There was just a trace of exasperation in her voice.

'I would like to speak to him. Can you ask him to call me when he gets in…er…comes back?'

'No need. He already left you a message.'

'But I haven't told you who I am.'

'He said I should expect a call from a *nau Gweilo*… an angry foreigner, Mr Grinder.'

'Oh, thanks,' said Frank, taken aback.

'He will meet you in the Oyster Bar at the Island Paradise Hotel, in Admiralty. You know where it is?'

'Yes,' replied Frank, bemused yet again by the ability of Hong Kong Chinese to read your mind. Or was it arrogance, an assumption that he would respond to the request to get in touch as soon as he could?

'What time?'

The Island Paradise was a slightly old-fashioned example of Hong Kong opulence, just short of the edge of ostentation.

There were newer, trendier bars in recently built or refurbished hotels on both Hong Kong and Kowloon sides, but when the Island Paradise had opened in the early nineteen nineties it had plainly been intended as standard bearer of flamboyance. Enormous crystal chandeliers shimmered from the lofty ceiling of the entrance hall, and a wide, curving staircase with a polished elm handrail swept up to the first floor. Giant chinoiserie tapestries hung from every available wall down to the thick, soft, royal blue carpeting. The huge plate-glass entrance doors were permanently manned by bellboys in pale grey uniforms with matching pillbox hats. Outside, two white-uniformed Sikhs ushered visitors across the pavement and, once inside, morning-suited attendants directed them to the bars and restaurants or to the long, mahogany reception and concierge counters which took up one end. The rest of the lobby was scattered with glass-topped tables and impossibly heavy and heavily-cushioned chairs. The Oyster Bar was on the same level, past the lift lobby and down a corridor, the sides of which were lined with large, decorated porcelain pots on rosewood stands. As he approached the doorway, Frank passed tiers of bottles of aged clarets and burgundies lying just sufficiently elevated so that you could see the labels and be impressed, overwhelmed, daunted or whatever the intention was.

As soon as he was inside he could see that it had not changed since he was last there. A long bar in the middle of the room and tables all around the edge. A huge selection of wines and spirits at wildly exaggerated prices and a range of bar food which consisted of almost every delicacy imaginable except, curiously, oysters. He glanced around but could not find Yeung, so he let the stately, white-jacketed maître d' guide him to a table. This was what Frank had not wanted to happen: it was not that he dreaded paying the prices on the menu if he ordered a drink for himself but that he knew Billy would expect him to start before he got there and would insist on paying the whole bill at the end. That was the way it was done here, but Frank had never quite got used to the idea that munificence without the slightest reservation was the norm; he may have lived for many years in Hong Kong but he remained an unreconstructed Englishman.

He sank into the depths of the cushioned chair and picked up a thick, embossed bar menu. There were little pots of strange, green peanuts on the table. Playing for time, as he could sense a waiter hovering nearby, he took several and inelegantly tried to stuff them into his mouth without dropping any. They had a mildly peppery taste, with a faint background of mustard. The texture was pleasantly crisp on the outside until he bit into the buttery centres, a very satisfying combination. He had just started on another handful when his head seemed to explode. Gasping, coughing and choking all at once, his eyes and nose streaming, one word came to the surface of his olfactory memory – *Wasabi* – and he cursed himself for forgetting that the swankier the bar, the more impossible were the snacks. The waiter had gone but reappeared with a carafe of iced water and a tumbler and, averting his eyes, left them, wordlessly, on the table. Grinder tried to thank him but could do no more than nod his appreciation through his splutters. As the sensory volcano began to subside he wriggled his handkerchief from his trouser pocket, took off his horn-rimmed glasses and mopped the tears from face so that he could try to read the menu. As the text swam into sight, so also did a feeling of gratitude that any observer, particularly the maître d', would assume that he was simply reacting to the wasabi and not to the prices. Had he misread them through his watery eyes? No, he hadn't. HK$1,680 for a bottle of Johnny Walker Black Label; that was, he calculated, about £140. And there was a whisky, a blend, not even a single malt, and what at first he thought was, by comparison, the reasonable price of HK$750, or £62, was not for a bottle but a glass. He rubbed his rheumy eyes with his handkerchief and felt a tap on the shoulder.

'Frank, old chap! How are you?'

Billy Yeung seemed not to have changed at all in the years since he had seen him at the farewell banquet given by the firm just before he left Hong Kong. Dapper, beautifully suited and with a thick silk tie, its perfect dimple just below the knot, he looked anywhere between thirty-five and fifty, although Frank knew that he must be touching sixty by now. He sat down next to him on the banquette so that they were both facing the bar, and beckoned the waiter over.

'Two glasses of Dom Perignon.' He pronounced it "Perry On". Frank wondered why Billy's type always spoke to Chinese waiters in smart restaurants in English. Was it for courtesy to him and other *gweilos* or was it to impress in some way? He suspected that if he had not been there Yeung would still have used English.

'It's very good to see you again, Frank.'

'And you.'

'How is your wife?'

'Winnie?'

'That's the one I had in mind.'

'Oh, she's fine. She's back in Hong Kong for a holiday. But of course you knew that.'

'Yes, she looked very well when I saw her the day before yesterday. *Ho leng*...I think you know what that means.'

'Very attractive.'

'Yes.' Not for the first time, Frank wondered whether Yeung fancied Winnie. He had been very keen that she should join the firm as a secretary when, together, they had interviewed her however many years ago it was. She was, indeed, a very pretty girl.

The waiter slid up to their table and silently put the champagne in front of them.

'Maybe you had better take them away and bring a bottle instead,' said Yeung.

'Of the same?'

'Yes, of course.'

The waiter picked them up and returned moments later with two new flutes. Seconds later, there was a silver ice bucket on the table with the distinctive neck of the Dom Perignon emerging from it. He carefully filled each glass and was gone.

'I should have asked you, Frank, whether you are all right for time.'

'Yes, Billy, I've got a couple of hours. But isn't this going some, a whole bottle of champagne before lunch? Are you trying to soften me up for something?'

'Of course not, Frank. I just wanted to see you again after all this time. I am so glad you have come back, even though Winnie said you weren't planning to stay too long. Well, maybe also I am softening you a little bit.'

Had Winnie really told him that? He couldn't recall discussing with her how long he would stay.

'Come on, Billy, let's get to the point. What is it you want to talk about?'

'But first, you must let me know what you think of this champagne. I don't have your knowledge of wine but I believe this is a good one, isn't it?'

Frank took a sip and tried not to reveal that, since he had ceased to earn big dollars and pay very low taxes, his drinks ranged from supermarket whisky to special offers on wine, via the occasional pint of bitter in The Unicorn.

'It's excellent. Beautifully creamy. Nicely small bubbles. What vintage is it?' That should be enough to impress or, more importantly, allow Billy the satisfaction of giving Frank some face.

'Oh. I forgot to ask about the vintage.' He leant forward and pulled the bottle from the dripping ice.

'It's 2004. Is that all right or would you like me to change it for another one?'

'No, of course not,' said Frank, recalling his recent £5.99 bottle of Chilean red. 'It's absolutely fine. Thank you. A really good year. One of the best.' He hoped that that might be right, but he knew that it really didn't matter in the course of the unspoken ritual they were both observing.

'So come on, Billy, what is the real reason you wanted to see me?'

'I told you. I wanted the pleasure of meeting you again. That is the main reason.'

'And the other? I am assuming that there is only one other.'

'Yes, of course. As I have said, I very much wanted to resume our friendship and to see how you are now that you have been retired and living in the UK for a while. I have so much been looking forward to chatting with you since your wife told me that you were here.'

'Yes, and I too have been looking forward to seeing you.'

'Yes. It is so pleasant sitting here with you, Frank.'

'Yes.'

'And chatting.'

'Yes.'

'No doubt we shall talk about old times and I will let you catch up on the news.'

'Yes. That would be good. But what news would that be, Billy?'

'Oh, just general things. You know, who is doing what. Who has died. Who the latest appointments are. And so on.'

'Billy, I know you. Don't forget that we were partners in the firm for years. What are you getting at?'

'Oh, nothing special. Except, you know about Charlie Munsonby, I suppose.'

'No, what about him?' Just in time, Frank restrained himself from characterising him as that pompous, snobbish fart.

'Did you not know?'

'Know what?' He hadn't been appointed the first solicitor High Court judge, had he? God, he would be impossible, as well as incompetent.

'Well, he was playing golf a short time ago.'

'Nothing new in that. He was always taking the afternoon off to go up to that golf club at Leung something or other.'

'Lung Yeuk Tau. It's in the New Territories. Apparently, it's a very good course. Yes, he did go there rather a lot,' Billy added.

60

'And?'

'He died. He had a heart attack just as he was about to start a game.'

'My God,' said Frank, relieved that he had kept his acidulous thoughts to himself. 'I'm very sorry to hear that. He wasn't married, was he?'

'No. Still a bachelor.'

'Well, that's something I suppose. No grieving widow.'

There was silence for a few moments while, in their separate ways, Grinder and Yeung wondered why he had said that.

'Billy,' he continued, 'you didn't really invite me to lunch just to tell me that, did you?'

'In part, yes,' replied Yeung. 'But let us order some food first. I really am glad to have you back in Hong Kong, you know, and I want you to have lunch with me. And then I tell you.' He raised his hand and clicked his fingers. A different waiter materialised instantly at the table with food menus and hovered attentively, half-bending, while they considered them.

'Are the portions still as big as I remember them?' Frank asked Billy.

'Oh, about the same. Nothing special.'

'Well, Winnie will be cooking tonight, I expect,' said Frank. 'I'll just have the risotto of scallops, prawns and lobster. That will be pretty filling, I expect.'

'Yes,' said Billy. 'I'll just have the same, I think, and,' looking again at the menu, 'the Wagyu beef ribs with duck liver. That does come with vegetables?' he asked the waiter.

'Yes, sir, pan-fried potatoes, mushrooms and snow peas.'

'Good, that will be fine. I must leave room for dessert.'

The waiter evaporated and Frank and Billy glanced at each other, Grinder contemplating how much the Chinese eat, Yeung mystified by how little Westerners do.

Within moments, one waiter was topping up their glasses and another was bringing the plates of risotto.

'Shall we order some wine to go with our food?' suggested Billy.

'No, thank you, not for me. But you go ahead if you want some.' Frank, more by instinct than judgment, knew that he had better try to keep a clearish head. He took a forkful of risotto. It was, of course, delicious.

'Come on, Billy. This isn't about Charlie, is it?'

'Well, yes it is. It's because of his, um… passing that I want to see you. Are you sure that you would not want a glass of wine? They have an excellent Puligny Montrachet here. It would go so well with our first course.'

'Not for me, Billy, thank you. But please order some for yourself if you want to.' Frank had noticed it on the wine list, at HK$1,650. About £140. He hoped that that was for a bottle, not for a glass.

'No, it would not be polite for me to drink while my guest watched,' smiled Billy. 'And I must keep a clear head.' He beckoned to the waiter to refill their champagne.

'So, you are enjoying your retirement, I hope,' he continued.

'Very much.'

'But surely you must sometimes get bored.'

'Not really,' said Frank. 'And even if I did, I would balance that against the sheer pleasure of not having to go to work.'

'But a man of your intelligence and great experience must sometimes feel the need to use your brain.' Frank noticed that he did not place the qualifying adjective before "intelligence".

'Well, I do miss earning the big bucks,' he replied. 'But then, that's what you prepare for when you are earning.' Did he notice a brief smile pass across Yeung's face? A moment, almost of panic, struck him.

'But what has this got to do with Munsonby?'

Billy Yeung put down his fork and leant back in the settee. He picked up his glass, sat forward and extended it towards Frank in a toasting gesture. Grinder realised that he was expected to reciprocate, and clinked his against Yeung's.

'It's great to have you back, Frank. It will be just like our old time.'

'It's very good to see you, too, Billy.' What was this all about?

Yeung put down his glass and pronged a forkful of lobster.

'I hope you like the food, Frank. It's very good, is it not? A good choice by you. You are always good at choosing Western dishes.'

'Thank you, it's excellent. And thanks for the compliment. But, Billy, what do you want?'

'I don't want anything. Well, not much. So, you are here for a holiday?'

'Yes, I told you.'

'How long for?'

'I haven't decided. It's open-ended. Winnie has got us a serviced apartment in Kennedy Town. And I don't yet know how long she is intending to stay.'

'That's good.'

'What is? Kennedy Town?'

'No, it is good that you haven't yet fixed your return flight. And Kennedy Town is good. Also, very convenient for Central and Admiralty. On the MTR it is only a short distance from the office and the High Court. A couple of stops.'

'I know that, Billy.' The sense of trepidation was increasing.

'Yes, of course you do.' Yeung took another forkful and then some champagne.

'Billy, what are you getting at? And when are you going to tell me what this has got to do with Charles Munsonby?'

'Well, he died.'

'Yes, I know. You told me that.' And he added, because he thought he should, 'It's very sad.'

'Yes. It is. He will be missed in the office. He was in the middle of a big case. Not so much in the middle. He had just taken it on. Very good for our firm. A very big client. Big name. Very big fees. And we are not such a big firm. So there is no-one else who has the time or is sufficiently senior to handle it. And client insists that it is handled by a *gweilo* solicitor.'

'That sounds rather racist,' said Frank. 'Is he a Westerner, a *gweilo*? I thought that that sort of attitude had disappeared.'

'No, no. He is Chinese. Hong Kong now but from the Chui Chow region of Guangdong, you know, Canton.'

'I seem to recall that Chui Chow men have the reputation of being domineering.'

'In this case, it is certainly true,' said Billy, a rueful look troubling his normally placid face.

'Why does he insist on a *gweilo*. There are several good, experienced solicitors in the firm, not the least being you, Billy. Who is the client? Can you tell me?'

'Yes, of course. It is Chan Wai-king. Lester Chan, the jewellery tycoon.'

'Wow!' said Frank. 'That really is a feather in your cap.'

'I am sorry, I don't understand you.'

'I mean, it is very prestigious for the firm to have a client like that. If you don't mind my asking, why didn't he use one of the really big firms like Richards Risk or Charles, Jane & Egg?'

'It seems that he met Charlie Munsonby at the golf club. He was impressed with his grey hair.'

'His hair?'

'Yes, he said that as this is such a serious case, he must have a grey-haired *gweilo*.'

'Why?'

'Because he believes that he would have influence with the police. And the prosecution. And the judge.'

The purpose of the invitation to lunch was beginning to emerge. 'And, with Charlie gone, you have no senior Westerner solicitor in the firm,' observed Frank, and he added, 'and so I suppose that you are likely to lose the client to another firm that has.'

'That is so. Chan has expressed his unhappiness at the death of Mr Munsonby but I believe that he was thinking more of himself than of our poor colleague.'

Billy Yeung paused, as if contemplating the problem for the first time. He lifted his glass again and moved it slightly towards Frank, who pretended not to have seen.

'Unless…' he continued, and raised his glass again.

'Unless what, Billy?' Grinder wanted to sound steely, but it was not easy. He was a guest, he had become mellowed by the champagne and, above all, there was, on Billy's face, the look of a lost, bewildered little boy. A sense of inevitability came upon him.

'Because, if you were to take over the case from where Charlie left it, I know that the client would be very pleased.'

'But, Billy, you said something about the police and the prosecution. This is a criminal case, isn't it?'

'Well, yes, it is. He's charged with letter of credit frauds.'

'You are well aware that I have no idea whatsoever about criminal law. I did learn a bit about it when I was at university, but I didn't even study it for the solicitors' exams. I have always been involved with commercial law and property. You know that's all I did all those years when we worked together. And a bit of banking.'

'But this is about letters of credit. That's banking.'

'Yes, but it's fraud. I wouldn't recognise a criminal case if it jumped out of the bushes and bit my arse.'

'No, but I didn't say it was an assault case,' replied a puzzled Yeung. 'Perhaps I didn't explain myself correctly.'

'You did. Perfectly. What I meant is that I don't know the faintest thing about criminal procedure and evidence, only that they are different from civil cases.'

'But you don't have to know. We have instructed very good counsel, DS Ng; do you know him? Dempsey Ng.'

'No. I haven't heard of him.'

'Oh, he's very experienced in criminal cases. Very. Yes, very.'

Grinder's suspicions were aroused by these repeated assurances. 'How senior in call is he?'

'Oh, about twenty-five years; maybe twenty-eight.'

'It's surprising that I haven't heard of him if he's been at the Bar that long. I thought I knew most of the well-established barristers from before I retired. Can you describe him for me? He's obviously Chinese. How old is he?'

'I just told you.'

'No you didn't.'

'Yes I did. I said he was twenty-eight years old. About. Maybe thirty.'

'What!'

'What's the matter, Frank?'

'I can't look after a big-shot client in a case where I don't know the first thing about it and leave it all to a baby barrister.'

Billy saw his advantage and went for it straight away.

'But you would feel able to take it over if we had instructed a more senior barrister?'

'Probably,' Frank conceded.

'Well, we have. Not just a more senior barrister, but leading counsel. A silk.'

'Oh, I see.'

'And not just a silk. A London QC. We have already got permission from the High Court for his admission.'

'Oh, really. Who is that?'

'Very famous London QC.'

'Who?'

'Very experienced in big criminal cases.'

'Tell me who it is, Billy.'

'He was in the Worthington trial. And in that match-fixing case.'

'Billy, come on…'

'Well, we got Gresham Nutworthy.'

'Wow,' said Frank, now deeply impressed. 'The client is prepared to pay for him? He's very famous. Been in a lot of major cases in England. Getting a little long in the tooth, perhaps, but quite a star.'

'Sorry, Frank. I had not notice his teeth.' Billy was showing a just perceptible sign of agitation. 'But I saw from the picture on the website of his chambers that he had long earlobes. That is very propitious.'

'So, still the man to have on your side,' said Frank.

'Yes, we instructed him. Because…'

Oh shit, thought Frank, what's about to prick the bubble?

'Because…he got taken ill and so we have obtained another.'

'Who?'

'Jonathan Savage QC, from London.'

'Never heard of him,' replied Frank, but he knew full well that the die was cast. Nevertheless, he persisted.

'But what makes you think that the client will accept me as the solicitor in the case? He socialised with Charlie and knew the man. I am a complete stranger to him and, if he bothers to make any enquiries, which I'm sure he will, he will realise that not only do I have no experience of criminal cases but also that I am not even in practice anymore.'

'Don't worry about that,' replied Yeung. 'I arranged for you to be readmitted by the High Court. The hearing is tomorrow. It is a formality.'

Frank wondered how, at the same time, he could be flabbergasted but not surprised.

'OK,' he said. 'But what about the client accepting me?'

Billy Yeung gazed at him, as if he were examining his face for some blemish.

'No need to worry. You have the right ears. And with your grey hair and big glasses you are the right sort of *gweilo* for him.'

'And what about my total ignorance of this area of the law?'

'No matter. That would not bother the client.'

They finished the meal, talking of other things. Billy Yeung had got what he wanted and Frank saw, with resignation, that his fate had been decided even before he had arrived at the Oyster Bar. He knew there were some details to be cleared up: how much he would be paid, whether he would have his own office, when he would have a chance to look at the papers, whether this young chap, Dempsey Ng, would be able to fill him in about the case without his having to do much reading himself. But that could all wait, because Billy had succeeded in the purpose of the lunch. Frank had not agreed to anything but he knew that, nevertheless, he had committed himself. Yeung raised his hand slightly and made a writing gesture in the air. The waiter appeared immediately with a bill and a credit card reader. Frank tried not to look at the total, but the several red hundred dollar bills which Billy left as a tip confirmed that it must be huge.

'Thank you, Billy. That was very generous of you,' said Grinder, although he suspected that the bill would find its way onto the next fee note sent to Lester Chan.

'You're welcome,' replied Yeung. 'I call you tomorrow after the application. No need for you to attend. It will be granted. And I forgot to tell you, the trial is listed already for the end of next month and is estimated to last twelve weeks. But I have told the first QC's clerk less than that because I had not wanted to put him off doing the case. It was the client's instruction to tell him that. Just so you know.'

陳

He got back to the apartment in Kennedy Town by mid-afternoon. The concierge, sitting behind his desk, unlocked the glass entrance doors and Frank pushed them open and went into the reception hall. Only as he got into the lift did it occur to him that the concierge already knew who he was and had let him in without questioning him. But he could not remember seeing the man before; indeed, there had been a young woman on duty when he had arrived with Winnie yesterday and she had been there when he left that morning to go into town. How did the man know who he was? It was one of those Hong Kong mysteries that he used to encounter so regularly.

Winnie was not in when he let himself into the flat. Possibly she was visiting her family, or playing mah-jong, or both. The place was completely quiet, except for the hum of the air-conditioning and the sound of traffic below. He sank into an armchair in the lounge, suddenly overcome with weariness.

He woke to the sound of the front door being opened. Winnie came into the lounge carrying a "ParknShop" plastic bag straining with groceries. She went over to him and gently kissed his forehead.

'I'm sorry. I must have fallen asleep.' He struggled himself upright in the chair and adjusted his glasses.

'Yes, I know. I thought that you would.'

'It takes a while to get over jet lag,' he said.

'Yes, and to get over lunch with Yeung Chi-hang. I know you would have too much wine.'

'I didn't.'

She patted him on the head and smiled at him like an indulgent mother.

'I know more better. But was it good to see him again?'

'Yes, very. But I'm afraid I've rather landed myself into something. Look, Winnie, I know that you only wanted to come back for a holiday with your family, didn't you?'

She nodded.

'Well, it might be a bit longer than the couple of weeks that you thought of. I seem to have agreed to do some work for my old firm while I am in Hong Kong. And it could take two months or three. Or even four. I feel awful because I should have spoken to you first. But you're right, there was quite a lot to drink at lunch and I must have got carried away. Of course, we'll get a decent amount of money from it, but Hong Kong is not your home now and you would probably have wanted to get back to Cheltenham. Honestly, love, I don't quite see how it happened, because I can't remember actually saying that I would help Billy out, but I must have done so, somehow. He was pretty desperate and I can't go back on my word. But I really do feel bad about not checking with you first.'

'Do you like this flat that I got for us?' Her question made him wonder whether she had taken in what he had just said. 'I had put some nice flowers on the table. Did you see them?'

'Yes, no, I mean, I didn't notice the flowers before, but it is a very nice apartment. Very comfortable.'

'Good, because I went to the agent this morning when you were having lunch. I had extend the lease for another six months.'

PART TWO

9

The roaring thrust of the huge aeroplane's engines as it swept along the wet runway pushed Jonathan Savage firmly into the depths of the generous seat. Raindrops streaked diagonally across the window adding a magical dimension to the lights busily twinkling and flashing in the dark. Barely perceptibly, the ground slid away and downwards, and they were climbing and veering, leaving behind the vast airport and its illuminated buildings and the headlights on the motorway and the now tiny airliners queuing for take-off.

He watched until they had climbed into the low cloud bank and then settled back. The cabin lights came on and the stewardesses began their routine fussing: drawing across the curtain that separated his cabin from first class and its, presumably, superior lavatories, and opening and shutting cupboards and compartments in the galley. They had changed from the caps and uniforms they had been wearing to greet the passengers and were now in some sort of sophisticated pinny, like nannies ready to serve food and drink to unpredictable children. An agreeable sense of weariness was beginning to steal over him, possibly the result of his having experienced a couple of hours and some red wine in the business class lounge. Perhaps he should have heeded the advice to go easy on alcohol before flying.

This was all unfamiliar, part of a series of new experiences. He had never before known the calm leisure of an airline lounge nor the luxury of a business class flight. Nor had he travelled on such a long haul flight, New York having been the furthest that he had achieved; so it was axiomatic that he had never been to the Far East. In fact, he had not previously seen so many Chinese as there were in the airport terminal, waiting to board his flight. A sense of comfort settled over him, but at the same time there was an underlying, uneasy feeling. Was he up to a case of this magnitude? From what he had heard, only very well-known and well-established London silks were normally instructed in cases in Hong Kong, or in Singapore for that matter. But here he was, he had to admit, at best a middle-ranking QC whom few people would have heard of outside his own Circuit, used to a professional diet of murder, rape and assorted blood-and-guts trials, possibly thought of as an efficient cross-examiner and closing-speech maker and about to take on the defence in a case involving banking and all sorts of commercial activities with which he was only passingly acquainted. He could see why old Nutworthy had originally been instructed: he had been in some of the major fraud trials of the last ten or so years. The Worthington trial, and Associated Provincial, and the Bank of the Americas case. Everyone knew him; indeed, it was common knowledge in the Inns of Court that he now spent more time in the courts in Hong Kong and other overseas jurisdictions than in England. And there were several other QCs who had that sort of reputation and experience. A cold shuddering thought struck him: what if one of them had been instructed to lead for the prosecution in this case?

There was some consolation in the fact that he was not flying out for the trial. Not that he could put that off for long but, for the time being, there was some breathing space; this was going to be a short trip so that he could meet the client, his instructing solicitor and his junior. Strange name that, Dempsey Ng. He wondered how you pronounced it. In fact, both names were odd. How did you get to be christened Dempsey? One thing he was certain of was that the third criminal clerk in his chambers had not got it right when he told him that there had been a phone call from a "Mr Not Guilty". When there had been a follow-up call from Hong Kong from someone saying that he was to be his junior in the forthcoming trial, he hadn't caught the surname properly; Dempsey, he had understood, but the rest of the name sounded like a short hum. What was it that he had wanted? Oh, yes, to let him know that the application for his temporary admission to the local Bar was unopposed and that the High Court had granted it.

The illuminated seat-belt signs went off and Jonathan pressed the button to ease his seat back. They were well above the clouds now and the black expanse below was broken by clusters of tiny lights from towns and villages in an unidentifiable country. He wished he had checked the route beforehand. Was this France below them? What countries would they be passing over? Then he remembered that there might be a flight-path programme and, after a certain amount of fiddling around with buttons and tapping the screen in front of him, up it came. They were over Denmark and heading towards the Baltic and Russia. He had had no idea that the route would take him so far north. This was quite exciting but, in spite of that, the unexpected drowsiness was still surrounding him.

'Champagne, Mr Savage?'

'Oh…er…yes, please.'

He sat up as the stewardess leant over him and, from a recess beside his armrest, clicked a small shelf into place. She put a paper coaster and a tiny foil bag of nuts on it and then there was a glass of sparkling enticement in front of him. Well, perhaps just this glass and then he could drink water for the rest of the flight. She smiled at him gently, perhaps sensing that he was not a seasoned business class traveller, and moved down the aisle with her tray. Jonathan drank the champagne quickly – well, it was not a particularly big glass – and was wondering whether it would be appropriate to ask for a refill when she came back to his seat and topped it up again. He looked out at the night-clad land below the window.

'Another glass of champagne?'

Glass? he thought as he took it. Yes, this was glass and flute-shaped; not one of those squeezable plastic tumblers half full of the caustic red he usually had – and had to pay extra for – on his usual no-frill flights to the warmer regions of Europe with his wife and the boys. And why "no frills"? How did a frill acquire a connotation of luxury? He hadn't noticed any frilly parts of the cabin in which he was sitting now. Why didn't they call cheap flights "no service" or, for that matter, just "cheap flights"? And this could be called a "service and sleek flight". Although he wasn't so sure, nor did he particularly care, about what happened at the back of the plane. And there must be a more polished service beyond the curtains, through which he had caught a glimpse of Mount Olympus, to deserve a special nomenclature, such as...

'I see that you appreciate our house champagne, Mr Savage.' The stewardess had appeared at his side again. 'Would you like a refill? Although we will be bringing round the wine selection shortly. And here is today's menu for the flight.'

He took the stiff grey fold-over and held out his glass again. The slip of white paper inside showed a choice which he found difficult to make up his mind about. He wondered whether he would be required to say now or whether he could decide when the trolley came round. Did they need advance notice so that they could prepare it especially for him? Was there a kitchen on the plane, or perhaps three kitchens, one of them cooking pots of gruel for economy class...?

He opened his eyes, aware that there was a trolley at his side, with a male steward standing behind it. His hair was cut very short, almost shaved, in a line above the ears, and a small, slicked quiff rose from the front of his scalp. He was perspiring slightly in his tight red waistcoat. Jonathan caught a faint, fragrant aroma as he leant in to take the empty glass and asked him whether he had made a decision on the main course, and bent over again to unfold the tray further until it became a platform for the embroidered cloth cover, in the same grey as the menu folder, and upon which he, almost with one movement, placed the tray. Smoked salmon and cream cheese glowed on white china, with a small bowl of vegetable salad beside it. He asked Jonathan to choose his white wine for the first course and said that he would bring the wine trolley round again with the next. Was this smiling explanation an indulgence because he, too, could detect the smell of a first-time business class traveller?

The earlier sense of panic seemed to have evaporated. There wouldn't be any immediate problem. This was a sort of test run, not the trial itself. He could wing it this time; find his feet and have time to absorb the brief. This should be not much different from getting to grips with any other fraud trial; just a bit more complicated, perhaps, and in unfamiliar surroundings. He had done it before, although nothing quite like this.

The main course had arrived. Beef with duchesse potatoes. He had considered an oriental option but there would be plenty of time and opportunities to try that in the next few days, he supposed. It was the stewardess again.

'Would you prefer to have red wine now?' Her smile was really engaging even though it was probably not genuine. 'Have you looked at the wine selection?' and she gave him a larger grey folder. 'I can recommend the Rhone.'

'Have you tried it, or are you just trying to get rid of it?' He regretted his gaucheness even as he said it and wondered whether his voice sounded a bit strange, a bit slurred.

'Oh, I've certainly tried it. We are all encouraged to try the wines at our briefing sessions.' Her smile was unwavering.

'Thank you, then that's what I'll have.'

He eased the seat forward a little and settled down to his meal, with his earphones on. He played with the screen until he had worked out how to bring up the film selection, lost it again, and after a couple more tries found a newly released thriller that he had been meaning to go to see. He did not notice the tray being removed or the cabin lights dimming and woke with a stiff neck and a sore throat.

'Would you like some fruit juice?' The steward was back, like a mother hen fussing over her brood. Jonathan croaked a yes. As he took it, the steward asked him if he would prefer to lie flat and pressed a button on the armrest. The seat made no noise above the constant hum of the engines and the whooshing of the air-conditioning as it eased Jonathan into an almost horizontal position; and he was asleep again.

Several hours later he woke to the sound of clattering in the galley behind the curtain and the smell of food and to the realisation that the cabin lights were now on, his head was throbbing and his bladder was painfully full. He was not at all sure what the procedure was: would he miss breakfast if he was in the lavatory? Would the plane start to land before he got there? Why had he not exercised some restraint? He unclipped his seat belt (which he did not remember buckling on before he went to sleep) and dragged himself upwards. The illuminated sign showed that there was a loo free and he lumbered towards it. Had he really managed to go all this time without needing to pee? He pushed opened the door and went in, swaying. It was probably safer to sit. But nothing happened. He was bursting, but in this claustrophobic and pressurised compartment it was as if a bung had been jammed in. Nausea was overlaid with a moment of alarm and then relief as he began to empty. This is quite a learning experience, he thought, what the hell am I doing here? And realised that he was saying it aloud.

It had not occurred to him that Eric had not told him whether any arrangements had been made to collect him from the airport, but now, as he was directed by a marshal to one of the long shuffling queues of incoming travellers in the immigration hall, he did not know what to expect. He knew that a room had been booked for him at the Majestic Harbour Hotel, that was all.

He was now at the front of the queue, standing behind the yellow line. A severe-looking, blue-uniformed immigration officer in his glass-topped compartment was examining the passport of a young man in scruffy jeans and with a faded and stained green canvas haversack, incongruous in the gleaming, antiseptic surroundings. Wordlessly, he slid it through an opening at the side of the window and beckoned Jonathan forward. He took out his passport and removed the landing card which he had filled in as the plane was descending, opened it at the page with his photograph and assumed the same ingratiating smile of so many people in the presence of an austere authority figure, as if this might somehow smooth away any possible obstacles. The officer stared hard at his face and began, slowly, to turn the pages. He looked at Jonathan again and then at the white slip of paper, the so-called card.

'So, you are staying at the Majestic Harbour?'

'Yes.' Jonathan just resisted adding 'sir'.

'For how long?'

'A few days, six, I think.'

'What is the reason for your visit? A holiday?'

The officer's identity tag displayed his photograph and his name: Wong Man-kin.

'No, for work.'

'What sort of work?' His expression seemed to Jonathan to harden slightly.

'I'm a QC…a lawyer, that is, a barrister.'

'You don't have a work permit.'

Jonathan was gripped by a chilling panic. He felt, suddenly, very tired.

'I wasn't told that I needed one, er, Mr Kin. I mean, Mr Wong.' The officer shook his head briefly with a clear implication that this was not anyone else's fault but his own. He flicked through the pages again as if searching in case a permit had been inserted somewhere. He said nothing.

'What happens if I haven't got one?'

'Then you cannot enter the HKSAR.'

'Sorry?'

'Without a permit you cannot enter the Hong Kong Special Administrative Region for work. You will have to leave.'

A sudden, desperate light pierced the gloom in Savage's head.

'Does it make any difference,' he asked, 'that I am not going to appear in court? I am merely going to have meetings with my client. Like a businessman meeting a customer, I suppose.'

The officer riffled through the pages again and slowly examined the landing card, as if a clue might be found there. He looked up again.

'You wait a moment,' he said and slid from his seat, opened the door in the glass compartment and, with the passport in his hand, went behind a partition wall.

Jonathan leaned on the counter. His head was muzzy and throbbing and his legs ached. Was his flu-like feeling the onset of jet lag? Limbo: that was the word he was searching for. He was stuck in a place from which he could neither advance nor retreat. The minutes limped by and he was increasingly aware of the people behind him; self-consciously, he refrained from turning to look at the queue, or to seek sympathy with an exaggerated gesture, raised eyebrows and a look which said 'Officialdom, huh?' He half-wanted to do so, but he was too tired to perform and, anyway, it was his fault: he should have checked before he took the flight.

A male Australian voice behind:

'Looks like they've caught an illegal. Probably a North Korean with no papers.'

There was a guffaw from more than one voice and a waft of alcohol.

Time passed without passing. The attempt at humour behind him had given way to silence and then groans and muttered tut-tutting. He half-turned to see whether there might be any sympathy but was met with baleful looks and averted eyes. He turned back towards the glass and heard another irritated voice, this time English, say that he was going to join another queue. He looked round again and saw that the adjacent lines were rapidly filling with the arrival of more passengers from incoming flights. The queue behind him was now very long. He caught the eye of the Australian, shrugged and inclined his head sideways with a hands apart gesture, hoping to elicit some commiseration. The man behind him stared and shook his head in a markedly unsympathetic manner.

He heard the door of the glass compartment opening. The officer climbed back onto his seat.

'Yes, no need for a work permit. Not if you just talk to your client. But make sure you get one if you go to court. Have a nice stay in Hong Kong.' Was it possible that a smile briefly appeared? He slid the passport through the opening and waved a relieved Jonathan through.

'Thank you very much, sir.'

'You're welcome.'

'At fucking last,' said a voice from behind.

The huge size of the terminal was even more apparent in the baggage reclaim hall. Sunlight streamed through the curved transparent roof and he could see high hills through the glass walls. He had not realised that there were green-covered peaks here. He looked at the overhead display and found the baggage belt for his flight. A few cases were circulating on it and, occasionally, a piece of luggage or a heavily wrapped parcel disgorged from one of the two openings at either end. Only a few passengers were standing nearby and he did not recognise any of them from his flight. He was just about to go check that he was at the right place, when he saw that his bag was coming towards him. He hoisted it off the conveyor and onto a trolley and made for the customs check, where he passed straight through and out into the enormous arrivals hall, where there were more giant glass walls, an ancient biplane suspended from somewhere, shops, cafés and a thousand people.

He searched for a sign to show him where the taxis were. He had read that the Airport Express train was very good but, for the time being at least, he wanted to use the minimum of effort. He just wanted to get to his hotel and have a bath. He couldn't see where to go for the taxis; the feeling of wooziness had come back. He looked for an information desk.

'Jonathan Savage QC?'

'Yes.'

A Chinese man, aged no more than thirty, rimless glasses and a very smart, dark-grey suit, was at his side, extending his hand.

'Hello. I am Dempsey Ng. I heard from the solicitors that no arrangements had been made to meet you, so I decided to come myself. This your first time in Hong Kong?'

'Yes.'

'I was starting to worry. Your plane landed on time. I thought, maybe, you had got lost.'

'No, I was delayed at Immigration. They thought I needed a work permit.'

'No need yet. The solicitors will sort it out while you are here. You only need it for court appearances. You need temporary admission to the HK Bar to see clients here but that has been done. I appeared for you on the application. You're in. You remember, I called to tell you.'

'Thank you. And thank you very much for meeting me. I must admit that I am feeling a bit confused after the long flight. And there are so many people in here.'

'Well, there are a lot of people in a small place. Seven million now.'

'It feels that most of them are here, at the airport. But thank you, again, for coming. Can you show me where to go for a taxi?'

'No need. We go in my car. My driver is waiting.'

Bewildered by the, mostly Chinese, constantly moving throng, Jonathan followed Dempsey past the Airport Express counter, hotel desks, coffee bars, a McDonald's, a pharmacy, bookshops, what looked like – yes it was – a

Chinese medicine shop, the sign for the taxi queue, ATM machines, vast arrivals and departures screens, passengers pushing overloaded luggage trolleys, signs pointing down corridors to lavatories, a sign for coaches to the mainland, another bidding "Welcome to Asia's World City", benches with sitting, sprawling and sleeping people, escalators, huge electronic advertisements for watches and perfume, the Golden Crystal restaurant, bronze sculptures, people looking round them with mobile phones held to their ears. Suddenly they were on a sort of bridge, still in the terminal but crossing what seemed to be a huge terminal below them, and through sliding glass doors and out into hot sunshine.

'Wait a minute,' said Dempsey and spoke into his mobile phone. A moment later, a large black car slid up to the pavement and the driver got out, took the trolley from Savage and loaded the case into the boot.

'You sit in the back. I will sit next to the driver.'

Jonathan got in. He wondered how he could describe how he was feeling. Tired, certainly. In need of a shower, probably. Headachy, unquestionably. But this sense of not actually being a part of what was going on around him was something he had not experienced before. He knew that at half past two in the afternoon, here, it was still only half past seven in the morning in London; he thought that was right, as British Summer Time had kicked in a couple of days ago, but he found doing a simple mathematical calculation to be very, very difficult. But it wasn't the time difference; that might explain it a bit, but this was something entirely different. Nor was it the unfamiliarity of hearing Cantonese spoken in the car, the driver possibly asking his boss something and the staccato, strangely intoned reply. No, it was as if he was observing rather than experiencing what was happening to him. Disorientation, that's what it was, except how could he be disoriented when he was in the Orient? That wasn't funny, not even to himself. Dempsey Ng was talking to him, half turning with his right arm over the back of his seat. The car had started moving smoothly away from the kerb. The driver was now silent.

'I'm sorry. I didn't catch what you said.'

'I said we are taking you straight to your hotel.'

'Oh, that's very good of you, er, thank you.'

Why had Ng said that? Where else could they have been going? He had just landed after a twelve hour flight. No use trying to puzzle it out. He looked out of the window; they were leaving the airport and were on a dual carriageway. On one side there were steep-sided hills, probably the same ones he has seen from inside the terminal. On the other a town of high-rise buildings, the tallest he had ever seen, on improbably narrow bases.

'This is Tung Chung,' said Dempsey.

'Oh?'

'Yes, it was built for the airport. In the early 1990s it was still a little village. For fishermen.'

Jonathan summoned up the energy to ask a polite question.

'When was the airport opened?

'In 1998. The year after the changeover.'

'What, all these towers were built in a few years?'

'Not just the town. The whole airport. Even the land that it is standing on was built into the sea. And this road. And the bridges and the railway connection.'

Pride was evident in his voice.

'Well, it certainly is impressive.'

'You are going to like it, I think.'

Dempsey Ng turned back and said something to the driver.

'*M'hai.*'

He twisted towards Jonathan again.

'My driver says he doesn't think that the traffic will be too bad if we take the Western Harbour tunnel.'

'Oh.' What other response was there? God, he was feeling tired.

There was now sea on the left-hand side, and tugs towing heavily laden lighters. Across the water he could see more hills and more clusters of high-rises.

'Is that China over there?' he asked.

'No, that is still Hong Kong territory. Not the mainland. That is NT, New Territories. The town you can see is Tuen Mun.'

'I thought you said that was the place we just passed. By the airport.'

'No. That was Tung Chung. This is Tuen Mun. Quite different, you see. And now we are getting closer to the other side, so that is Siu Lam and then Tsing Lung Tau. All different places. '

Jonathan's head was spinning. A hackneyed expression, he thought, but it seemed it was actually happening to him. He closed his eyes and there was some relief.

'You are tired?'

'Yes, I am rather.'

'Don't worry. It won't be too long. Look, we are now leaving Lantau Island.'

They were on a bridge, its cable-support stays fanning out from huge concrete aitches. Another one veered off to the left and, ahead of them, an even bigger one appeared.

'This is Kap Shui Mun Bridge. It takes us to Ma Wan Island. The next one is Tsing Ma. That joins Ma Wan with Tsing Yi. Then we will be on Kowloon-side and take the tunnel to Hong Kong Island.'

The names: they were impossible. Was he supposed to try to remember them?

'Listen, I talk too much, maybe. Perhaps you want to sleep.'

They were now going over the next suspension bridge, astonishingly bigger than the last, its span seeming to go on endlessly.

'No, no. It's very interesting, seeing all this.'

He wasn't just being polite. He had never been anywhere like this. They crossed the bridge and, to the right, they were passing giant gantries and stacks of multi-coloured shipping containers, with the exotic names of their lines, spreading towards the black water that he could just glimpse on that side. A line of lorries was on that side of the dual carriageway, green with strutted canvas canopies and with two large Chinese characters painted in white on their sides. They had a ramshackle, curiously dated look, like something you would see in black-and-white photographs of pre-war China, which contrasted with the towering apartment blocks and dramatic civil engineering all around him.

'Impressive, isn't it?' said Dempsey.

'It certainly is, and I wouldn't want to be asleep and miss it. I'll have a rest when I get to the hotel.'

Dempsey looked at him, smiled slightly and turned to face the front again. He said something to the driver, who laughed.

In spite of himself, Jonathan felt his eyelids beginning to droop. When he woke, they were going through a long tunnel. Traffic was streaming through beside them. Then they were out into the daylight, driving with the water on the right and tall buildings on the other side of the harbour, with eagle-like birds hovering and swooping, and then into a canyon of skyscrapers. At ground level, he caught sight of restaurants, a multi-layered car park, entrances to office blocks.

'We are now on Hong Kong side.' Dempsey had turned back to him, his arm again over the seat. 'A few minutes to the hotel.'

Traffic was building up and they were slowing down. In the right-hand lane, there were red Toyotas with silver roofs and Chinese characters on the doors. They must be taxis.

'Those are taxis,' said Dempsey. 'Red means Hong Kong and Kowloon. Green for the New Territories. On Lantau they are blue.'

'Oh.' Jonathan hoped that he sounded interested. His eyes were feeling gritty and he was becoming aware that his bladder was filling again.

The traffic had come to a standstill. Chinese faces everywhere. No Europeans at the wheel of any nearby cars. More luxury models than he had ever seen on a street. Mercedes, Jaguar, Lexus; many of them black and gleaming. An open-sided covered footbridge crossed the road, with streams of people on it, all with jet-black hair. Double-decker buses with Chinese writing. The car moved forward again, slowly, passing a building, a bit shorter than the others, that looked like a stubby, inverted pencil, its point at the bottom spreading outwards and then upwards.

'That is the garrison of the PLA,' said Dempsey. 'Before 1997 it was the British Army HQ. We still call it the Prince of Wales Building, though they eventually changed the name. We are now in Admiralty District.'

'Oh, really,' replied Jonathan as if that meant something to him.

'So, your hotel is also in Admiralty.'

They passed more enormous, glittering buildings and then, suddenly, the car veered and swung onto a curving road that took them over the road which they had just left and onto the forecourt of the Majestic Harbour Hotel. The driver got out and opened the door for Jonathan. Dempsey got out as well and waited until the driver took the luggage from the boot. Within the blink of an eye, a white-uniformed bellhop had come out of the hotel, gathered up the cases and disappeared inside with them. Jonathan went to shake Dempsey's hand.

'Thank you. I very much appreciate your doing this. I must admit that I was a bit worried about finding my way from the airport. So, will you be in touch with me?'

'No, no. I come inside with you.'

Together, they walked into the most stylish lobby Jonathan had ever seen. He was aware of huge, painted columns and leather settees. At the far end was a bar area, with glass-topped wooden tables and bergère chairs. He went up to the reception desk. A row of morning-suited, smiling hotel employees stood on the other side. Instinctively, he approached the one European face.

'Good afternoon,' he said. 'My name's Savage and I believe that a reservation has been made for me.'

'Yes, sir.' He tapped the computer keyboard. 'Here it is. It's been made in the name of your company, Chan, Yeung, Munsonby & Lam.'

In spite of, or perhaps because of, his exhaustion, Savage corrected him.

'No, it's not my company. They are a firm of solicitors. I am a barrister. A QC.'

'Yes, of course, sir. The room has been booked for you, on the executive floor. So, if I may just have your signature here, and if I may take the details of your passport, thank you. Here is your key, Mr Savage. Your luggage will be sent up to your room. And please remember to insert your key into the slot in the lift; otherwise it will not take you above the restaurant level.'

He slid across a small cardboard folder with the room number written on the outside and containing a credit card sized oblong of black plastic, which Jonathan assumed must be the key. He took it and turned to say goodbye to Dempsey but his junior was walking towards the lift lobby.

'I will go up with you.'

'There's no need,' replied Jonathan. What there was a need for was a pee, and perhaps something more.

Dempsey had started to jab at the lift button. Jonathan noticed that it was illuminated and wondered why he was doing it. The lift came, and Dempsey took the black key from him, put it in the slot and pressed the button for the fifty-ninth floor. He gave the card back to Jonathan as the lift whooshed upwards. There was scarcely time to take in the ornate interior, depictions of golden dragons and landscapes with oriental figures, before they had arrived. Jonathan stepped out, his head reeling, and Dempsey followed him. He wondered how, politely, he could get him to go; making conversation was becoming increasingly difficult. All he wanted was to use all the facilities in the bathroom and to lie on a bed for an hour. He found the sign indicating the corridor which matched his room number and moved along the plush carpet. Dempsey followed him and then was at the door before he could get there. Taking the key from Jonathan's hand, he slid it into its slot and released the lock, gesturing with a sweep of his hand and a slight bow for him to go first.

The room seemed full of people, all men, mostly in dark suits and all talking. One of them came forward and shook his hand.

'I am Billy Yeung, from your instructing solicitors,' he said. 'This is Hector Lee, our managing clerk.'

He too came forward and took Jonathan's hand. He realised that there were, in fact, only three of them and Dempsey. The other, shorter man was wearing a windcheater and trainers. No attempt was made to introduce him and a resentful stubbornness made him want to ask who he was and what he was doing in his bedroom. Come to that, what were any of them doing there? Before he could do so, the man calling himself Billy said something in Cantonese and the small man left, without looking at him.

'Who was that?'

'Oh, just my messenger. He brought some papers for you.' Billy indicated a large, cardboard banker's box on the floor by the wall. 'Did you have a good flight?'

'Pretty good thanks. But, I hope you don't mind, I am very much in need of a shower. So, are we meeting tomorrow?

What are the arrangements?' Jonathan could hardly get his words into lucid sentences.

'We have a meeting with client tomorrow. You know he is in custody? Yes, well, we go over to Stanley Prison. In the morning. I will collect you from the hotel at seven-thirty. But perhaps you have your shower now and Dempsey Ng and Hector and I will wait here and then we can discuss the case over dinner. We can talk about the bail application then.'

'Oh,' said Jonathan, trying to take all that in whilst conscious that if he did not get into the privacy of the bathroom soon he might start his first evening in Hong Kong by wetting himself. Or worse. 'Shall I meet you downstairs in, say, half an hour? I noticed that there was a bar in the hall…er…the lobby.'

'No, no,' said Yeung. 'We will wait for you here in the room.'

In spite of his exhaustion, Savage knew that he had to exert some authority, or try to, at least. He was, after all, a London QC who had been brought into the case to lead the team. That is why silks were called leaders. He must lead.

'No, that is not a very good idea.' He was surprised by the firmness of his voice. 'I must have a shower, now, and then I will need to change. When my luggage comes up, I will have to unpack and to find some clean clothes. Also, I don't feel very comfortable using the, er, facilities with anyone other than my wife in the next room. So I will meet you in the bar in, let's say, forty-five minutes. Please.'

Ng and Yeung exchanged puzzled glances. Then Billy said, 'I told Dempsey that you were what we wanted for this case. Very strong.'

'Good,' said Jonathan. 'I might be in a better position to talk to you when I am fresher.'

He was about to add a request for a large whisky, with ice, to be waiting for him but thought that that might be going too far.

'OK,' said Billy. 'See you downstairs. Would you like me to order you a Scotch on the rocks?'

'How did you know?'

'That is what Frank Grinder usually wants.'

'Who's he?'

'An English solicitor.'

Jonathan no longer had any time to enquire further. He quickly moved into the bathroom and locked the door. As he sat on the lavatory he heard the room door shutting. His relief was indescribable.

10

The weekend started early for Mr Justice O'Brien. The mention that had been listed for Friday morning had been so brief as to have passed almost without notice. He had been told by defence counsel, the very pleasant Dempsey Ng, that their London QC was in the air on his way to Hong Kong and that it was difficult to make any assessment of the real length of the case or to do anything else meaningful until he had arrived, so the application was that the mention hearing be adjourned for at least seven days. A very pretty young woman from the Department of Justice, whom the judge did not recall having seen before, had risen, said in a tremulous voice that she had no objection and hastily resumed her seat. Who was he to argue with common sense? So, by five past ten he was taking off his judicial robes and removing his warm, stiff wing collar. When Henry came in to ask whether he would wait in his chambers until Monday's papers came in or have them sent to his home, he had replied: neither. This was going to be a rare occasion when he would have a couple of days without case papers to read, and he told his clerk that he would come in a little early on Monday and see what was what. So would Henry be kind enough to call his driver and tell him to be ready to take him home as soon as he had had a cup of coffee.

He and his wife lived in that Hong Kong rarity: a house. Whilst probably ninety-five per cent of the population made their homes in flats of varying degrees of space and luxury, some living in cramped shoe boxes in towering, almost contiguous high-rises whilst others were accommodated in relatively spacious apartments, they had the use of a residence in Jamaica Gardens, small and semi-detached, but a real house with two floors and a private paved area at the back. It was in a row of identical houses, all owned by the HKSAR government and all lived in by members of the higher judiciary and their families, so that neighbourly chats tended towards the mono-topical end of the spectrum of conversation, but it, like the car and the driver, was included in the expat package, and part of its attraction was they did not need to buy or rent accommodation in Hong Kong or to sell his house in the suburbs of Sydney; which was just as well as Sharon seemed to be spending more and more time there, apparently checking on it and visiting old friends. This time her reason was the approach of the Hong Kong summer and the need to make sure that the spacious gardens and the swimming pool were ready for the coming New South Wales winter; not that he could remember anything that needed doing at this time of year, but that was Sharon's department, not his.

The backyard – you couldn't really call it a garden as the only things that grew in it were a couple of hoyas struggling up against the wall of the house and a few osmanthus plants in dark brown, glazed pots which formed a border with the much better-tended garden of old Squires, next door – was big enough for some outdoor furniture: a glass-topped rattan table and six chairs, a couple of rather faded sun loungers and a decent-sized barbeque for those, now rare, occasions when they had a few people over for drinks and a meal.

When he got home there had been a moment of uncertainty. What was he going to do with himself? Mid-morning he would normally have been hard at it in court; if not in the middle of a trial, he would be going through the packed Friday list of applications, pleas of guilty and sentencing, approvals of settlements in civil actions, the unintended consequence of his having achieved a reputation for briskness that the Judiciary Administration seemed to favour over the careful thoroughness of some of the other High Court judges. O'Brien liked speed because he liked things to move on – an early end to the working day being a constant target – but the result was that his Friday list would usually be loaded with enough cases to overwhelm the more painstaking of his fellow judges. And if, by some happy chance, he had been given a shorter Friday list which he had been able to crack through with plenty of time to spare, he would then be sitting in his room in the court building reading the witness statements for the next trial; or medical reports; or written arguments on points of law; or applications for leave to appeal against conviction or sentence, or sometimes both, as a preliminary step before a case which had been tried by another judge could be considered by the Court of Appeal; or, possibly, trying to get to grips with less familiar aspects of his work, like the increasing number of applications for judicial review, or skimming through newly released judgments of the Court of Appeal and the Court of Final Appeal (that coven of self-regarding, out-of-touch pseudo-Justinians); or, if he had nothing else to do, reading recent sentencing guidelines.

But now, in the quiet house, he was experiencing a break in routine which made his own home seem strangely remote. The daily cleaner had gone, presumably back to her own home, wherever that was. Sharon had insisted that they did not employ a Filipina live-in help, ostensibly because it allowed her to parade her social conscience and expatiate on the evil of taking a well-educated woman away from her husband and children to come to a life of domestic drudgery in Hong Kong; but the real reason was, more likely, that she had been able to take on, from the family of a judge who was going back to retirement in England, that rare status symbol: an old-fashioned and decrepit Chinese *amah* who was one of the last to wear the uniform of black trousers and a white tunic. So instead of the house being looked after by a hard-working, obliging youngish, Catholic woman with a Spanish name and sing-song English, there were the brief visitations of an elderly, unsmiling harridan who, in spite of being able to communicate only in staccato grunts, was able to make her disapproval of the O'Brien family perfectly clear. Why was that? Was it because they had no children for her to pursue her traditional calling? Or that they were not as nice to work for as her previous employers? Frankly, Brett did not care very much as long as he was not home when Mrs Ma was there.

He was about to change out of his dark suit and take off his formal shirt and tie when the thought struck him that he might go back into Central and have lunch in the Club. All members of the higher judiciary belonged to it, housed in a prominent modern building standing on the site of what had been, many years ago and before land reclamation and the urge to demolish and reconstruct vertically, a beautiful, white, colonnaded building on the water's edge. He often went there for lunch in the bar or in its two, practically identical, formal restaurants where, for an hour or so, you could forget that you were in Hong Kong, or indeed anywhere in the East. He also regularly went for a drink after work and occasionally would take friends to dinner. Sharon seemed to love the sense of being at the centre of power there. But he realised that he hardly went in the evenings when she was not around and now wondered whether he really wanted to go back, specially to meet the same people and have the same conversations. Sometimes, he reflected, an interruption in routine makes you ask yourself what you really want: forces you to distinguish between habit and desire.

He looked out of the lounge window. There at the front was the grey, government-owned Toyota still parked with the engine running, with Wing, the driver, sitting patiently at the wheel. O'Brien was struck by the recurring question: who was controlling whom? Was it a legacy of colonial days, the Chinese servant ready for the whim of his master? Or was it that the driver had decided that Brett ought to go back into Admiralty on a working morning and was merely waiting for his judge to come to the same conclusion? He came out of the house, locked the door and got into the back of the car.

'Back into town, please,' he said. 'But not to the Law Courts. Take me straight to the Club.'

'OK, Mr Judge.'

In the mirror, Brett thought he could see the curl of a smirk.

The Chummery Bar was almost empty when O'Brien got there. Two earnest-looking Chinese were at a table in the corner, immaculate in dark suits, bright white shirts and perfectly knotted silk ties. He had not noticed either of them before. They seemed to be breaking a club rule by discussing business in the bar, for they were speaking so quietly that he could hear nothing but an English-language hum. On a stool, up against the counter, a solitary figure, with grey hair and heavy-framed spectacles, was nursing a half-pint of beer. He was reading a folded-up copy of the *South China Morning Post* and making half-suppressed snorting noises. Brett took a stool a respectable, non-intrusive distance away, but still close enough to see that the source of amusement was the correspondence page. He could not remember having seen anything particularly funny when he glanced through it in his room that morning.

There was something familiar about the chap, even though, with his elbow on the bar, his open hand supporting his head hid most of his face.

'Good God,' said Brett. 'It's Grinder!'

Frank turned in surprise.

'Why, hello, Brett.'

'What in hell are you doing here? I thought you had retired and gone back to the UK. You married that very pretty local girl, didn't you? Wasn't she your secretary? And took her back.'

'Well, I have…I did. But Winnie is over here seeing relatives and I have, somehow or other, got myself caught up in some work for my old firm.'

'What,' asked O'Brien, 'was amusing you so much?'

'When?'

'In the paper.'

'Oh, that. Well, it's just that I've been away from Hong Kong for a few years but, with all the new land reclamation and the new buildings on them, and everything else, some things never change. There were some pretty high-minded expressions of opinion in the letters page about democracy and PRC interference today, and amongst them was someone writing to support whoever had written in yesterday complaining about a dead mouse at a bus stop. In fact, he – I assume that it was a man – went into so much detail that it was longer than a letter suggesting a solution to the Middle East problem. And there is another longish one, look, here it is, about a ticket machine at North Point Station being out of order. One machine amongst probably dozens.'

He slid the newspaper along the bar.

'No need,' said O'Brien. 'I looked at the paper this morning. I see your point: it's a touch incongruous, isn't it? I suppose I am so used to it that it doesn't register anymore.'

'And I suppose that I have been away long enough for it to strike me. Can I get you a drink?'

'Yes, that would be very nice. But are you able to?'

Frank glanced down at the sleeve of his well-worn suit.

'Do I look that impoverished?'

'Ah, Christ, no. That's not what I meant. Are you permitted to buy a drink? Club rules.'

'Oh, I see. Well, yes. For some reason, the committee offered to convert me to overseas membership when I left. Not sure why. I must have got the chairman pissed or something. Anyway, I took it up, possibly because I thought that I might be back sooner than this. So, what will you have?'

'A Crown Lager, please. Makes me think of home. Sharon's down there at the moment. God knows what she does there. So, tell me more about the work you're doing here.'

'Well, there's not much to tell. It seems to be a criminal case, a fraud of some kind. Not really my area of work when I was in practice but I think that I'm in it because of, er… I'm probably in it, mostly, to babysit the London silk who is coming out. I genuinely don't yet know much about it. I got suckered into it only yesterday when I met one of my former partners for lunch.'

'I think we'd better stop there,' said the judge. 'I know I've got a trial coming up with an English QC. I don't know anything about it, either. Probably nothing to do with your case. But best to be on the safe side.'

'Understood,' Frank replied. 'Let's talk about anything apart from work. That would suit me. Do you fancy some lunch here? It's been a long time since I had old-fashioned English food. You don't seem to be able to get it in England now: anything but. It's not too early for you, is it? Do you have to get back to court?'

'No, I'm a free man now, till Monday. It would be great to have lunch and catch up with your news.'

The soporific ambience of the Blue Room was partly the product of thick carpets, across which reverential waiters ushered rubber-tyred trolleys laden with meat puddings and large joints of beef and lamb. In subdued and solicitous tones they enquired of the members and their guests whether the heaped pyramids on their plates were quite sufficient and backed away with quiet expressions of profound gratitude, as if some service, beyond any possibility of adequate reciprocation, had been rendered to them. 'Thank you, thank so much, sir,' they murmured as they retrieved a fallen linen napkin or a dropped silver fork and replaced them on the table; and the diners tuned into the environment with muted, somewhat sluggish talk, or periods when there was no conversation at all. But it was the food itself which was the principal cause; its quality was so high that it tended to direct the mind of the eater to it and to nothing else. There was also the quantity which, coupled with the Club's very drinkable clarets and burgundies, made for companiable taciturnity rather than sparkling expression of original thought.

When they were finishing their coffees, Frank asked whether he had any papers to read for the coming week.

'No, like I told you, nothing. No work, no wife, no commitments for the whole weekend.'

'Isn't that a bit difficult for you?' Frank recalled the often empty weekends in Hong Kong before he had fallen for Winnie and the recent few days when she had come back ahead of him.

'Well, it's unusual, certainly, because when Sharon's away I normally spend quite a bit of time working in my chambers, reading case papers and drafting judgments and so on. But I don't think it's going to be difficult. I might go to a movie. I might go downstairs and have a game of billiards. I'll certainly get some sleep in. What about you, have you got any plans for the rest of the day?'

'Oh, me? I'm going to get off home. Did I mention that Winnie has got us a great little apartment in Kennedy Town? She'll probably be back from visiting her parents fairly soon. So I think I'd better be off now.'

They went through the usual pirouette about who was going to sign the bill. Frank won by a whisker, reminding the judge that it was he who had suggested lunching together, and he signalled the waiter to come over. They said their goodbyes and Frank left the building and caught a taxi from the rank outside. O'Brien went back to the bar.

His first idea was to have a brandy. Full of red meat and Eton Mess and red burgundy, his black coffee had done no more than create an exigent, dark yearning for something to follow it, but there were far more members there now and he suspected that several among them would be only too pleased to witness a judge succumbing to the tongue-loosening effect of too much drink. Some, in the past, had behaved incautiously at the Club, and he had seen the mortification of a servant, on the instructions of the manager, refusing to serve a District Court judge who had tumbled his last whisky down his shirtfront and was slurring demands for a replacement. The last thing that Brett wanted was a reputation as a lunch time soak, and one drink too many might set some gleeful tongues in motion. He wouldn't mind a crack at a seat in the Court of Appeal; he knew he was well-regarded, for his efficiency if for nothing else, but you didn't get there by making incautious witticisms in public or by falling asleep during the day. He did not, for a moment, suppose that a decent glass of brandy would be beyond his capacity – he was from NSW, after all – but not here and not now.

The steward was hovering by his table and he ordered another cup of coffee. With the coffee came his neighbour, Mr Justice Squires. Desiccated by years in the legal service of an expiring empire and wearing a perpetual expression as if in bemusement that he had, somehow, seen himself promoted in Hong Kong through the magistracy to the District Court and then to the High Court; and, as far as the local bench and Bar were concerned, a bafflement which was entirely justified.

'Oh, er, may I join you?' He took a seat across the table from O'Brien.

'Ah, hello Dennis. Please do.' He was going to add "mate" for the sole purpose of ruffling his stuffiness, not because, by any measure, he came under the radar of mateship. 'But I ought to tell you that I'm not staying long,' he added, having just that instant decided to leave. 'I've already had my lunch.'

Squires's face fell. He probably had no inkling that his reputation for indecision and incompetence was matched by that for parsimony and readiness to accept the hospitality of others.

'Oh dear. I was going to suggest lunch in the Snooker Bar. I might just go down now and have a sandwich and see who else might be there. I don't think I have that much time, anyhow, as I am sitting again this afternoon.'

That wouldn't have stopped the old sod from cadging a decent lunch off me, thought Brett, even if he is pressed for time. It was odd how quickly freeloaders can get through food and drink.

'But I am very glad to see you, now, er, Brett,' he continued. 'In fact, I came over to the Club especially to find you or, er, perhaps someone like you. I mean to say, of course, there's no-one quite like you, but someone who might fit into your category.'

This is intriguing, thought Brett. My category? Does that mean Antipodean? Or someone younger than him? In which case the whole of the membership would slip in perfectly, and probably the staff, with the possible exception of old Ho, the doorman, who, because of certain physical similarities, was rumoured to be about the same age as a Galapagos giant tortoise.

'I'm all ears,' said Brett.

'What? Oh yes.' Squires fell into a reverie.

Brett wondered whether he was having some sort of quiet seizure or whether he had merely expired. He rattled his spoon against the side of his coffee cup.

'Oh yes,' repeated Squires. 'What was I saying?'

'You said something about my being in a category. I have to admit that I'm not entirely following your drift.'

The old judge looked down and then towards the ceiling, as if searching for an answer to a conundrum that Brett had posed. The aura of perplexity seemed to intensify.

'Oh yes, that's it!'

'What is?'

'Um, well, you see, I've been invited on a junk trip for Sunday, and that sort of thing, well, it isn't really my cup of tea. And I don't think my wife would be too keen.'

O'Brien tried to imagine Mrs Squires, an old biddy from an impecunious family of faded gentry, perched in her tweed skirt and woollen cardigan, knees pressed tightly together and desperate for a cup of weak tea, on the deck of a pleasure boat as a mixed party of Aussies, Kiwis and Brits loudly boozed their way through the East Lamma Channel towards a makeshift restaurant on some outlying island. No, he could not see her doing that, nor her husband. He also wondered whether the fear of being expected to contribute a few bottles of wine and a six-pack of beer might have dampened any flicker of interest.

'I told my host that I was not available on Sunday and he very kindly told me that I could invite someone else in my place. And I immediately thought of you.'

Or of my category, thought Brett.

'So, if you aren't doing anything else on Sunday, perhaps you would like to take my place.'

'Brilliant,' replied Brett, 'I'm free and would have been at a loose end, with Sharon away in Oz.' He did not add that a Sunday, when Squires would be notable for his absence rather than as a wraith-like presence across the garden hedge, had a distinct appeal. 'I would love to go. Whose boat is it?'

'Actually, it belongs to a man called Law. He's in the property business.'

'Common Law or Chinese Law?'

'Sorry, I don't follow. Of, yes, yes, he's Chinese. His name is Law something something. I can't remember what. Oh yes, he's called KC Law. But it wasn't he who asked me: it was one of his other guests. You probably know him. Actually, he was appearing in a case before me until yesterday, when it finished. Apparently, there may be several members of the Bar, and possibly some other judges, although I don't know who.'

'And who is this chap?'

'What chap?'

'The one who asked you to invite me.'

'Stratford, I think that's his name.'

'What, do you mean Gerry Stratford, that guy from New Zealand? The Kiwi with the good-looking Filipina girlfriend always in tow?'

'Yes, I have heard that he has a very beautiful companion. But I've never seen her.'

'Funny chap, though, that Stratford,' said O'Brien. 'How did he get on in front of you?'

'Nothing special. What do you mean, Brett?'

'I've heard that he has a reputation for being very clever but sometimes he gets too close to his client.'

'I don't know about that. I haven't heard. I wasn't conscious of any impropriety in this last trial. I know he has quite a lot of work for big clients. He has appeared in front of me a couple of times in the past for that jewellery tycoon, Chan something or other.'

'Anyway,' said Brett, rising from his seat, 'it sounds good. Thanks very much. Where and when?'

'Where and when what?'

That's impressive, thought Brett. Three interrogative words in a four word sentence. 'Where and when do I meet them?'

'Oh, yes, well I was told that it would be Aberdeen Boat Club at ten-thirty. On Sunday.'

11

Saturday seemed to pass O'Brien by. He had answered the personal correspondence which had been nagging at him to be dealt with. He had replaced the faintly mildewed lining paper in his shirt drawer and fixed the loose bracket in the downstairs lavatory. He had carried a glass, and then another, of wine into the garden and sat looking at the huge, motionless banana spider that had recently taken up residence in the spindly bauhinia trees that separated their garden from Squires's. He had, for a moment, considered taking the latest edition of the *Hong Kong Law Journal* out with him but had easily rejected the idea as he wanted to savour his self-indulgence; contemplating the spider as it hung in the centre of its web watching him was far more rewarding than reading academic commentaries on the latest judgments of the Court of Appeal.

He had waited until it was nearly six in the evening in Sydney before telephoning Sharon and, acknowledging guilt at his relief when there was no answer, had left a message on her voicemail promising to call back tomorrow. After he had hung up it occurred to him that something had changed: she had replaced his voice with a bright and cheery recording of her own.

Saturday was not one of Mrs Ma's days and he had had the kitchen to himself. He had made himself a cheese sandwich and poured another glass of wine. He had thought of trying to call home again but easily persuaded himself that it was pointless: if Sharon was out earlier then she was probably with friends for the whole evening. No, this was going to be an untroubled afternoon with enough time to watch a couple of downloaded movies.

Saturday for Jonathan Savage was not so pleasant. After he had, at last, showered and changed on the previous evening and had gone to join them for what turned out to be several drinks in the lobby bar of the hotel, Billy Yeung had suggested taking him and Dempsey Ng and Hector Lee to a traditional Cantonese restaurant for dinner – 'Not so far, you are probably tired' – and, overcome by exhaustion and courtesy, he had not put up any opposition. They had squashed into a taxi, and he swam through the rest of the evening in a blur of half-understood conversation, greasy portions of duck and many other dishes which he could not identify, noise all around him and the impression that he was the only man not wearing a business suit. He had never seen so many Chinese people together in one place nor heard such loud conversation from all around. Mechanically, he had accepted the wine that was proffered throughout the meal. And, somehow, he was in a taxi, trying to make sense of the crowded, brightly lit streets that surged outside, and then he was back at the hotel. He had fumbled through his pockets for the key and the thin cardboard folder that had the number of his room on it. His brain seemed to be revolving inside his head as he lurched along the corridor from the lift until he found his door. Somehow, he had succeeded in getting undressed and into bed and had fallen immediately into a deep sleep until a terrible thirst and a pounding head had woken him at, as he could see from the bedside clock, one-thirty in the morning. He had found the light switch and a bottle of water and then lain between long periods of anxious wakefulness and short periods of shallow sleep until the telephone rang and woke him.

He could see that light was slipping in between the curtains. He picked up the phone.

'Hello, yes, who is it?'

'It's Billy. Billy Yeung. I'm in the lobby.'

'Why?'

Surely he hadn't come into the hotel after dropping him off in the taxi. Oh God, please, not another drink.

'Why? Because it is seven-thirty. I have come to collect you to take you to see client.'

'Oh, shit! Sorry. I mean, give me ten minutes and I'll be down. Sorry, I forgot to set the alarm.'

'I think I must teach you a Chinese expression. *Mho man tai.*'

'What's that mean?'

'It means don't worry. So, I will wait for you.'

That's very decent, thought Jonathan, as he reproved himself for making such a bad start. He brushed his teeth, shaved quickly and didn't bother to shower. He had no time to sort out his clothes so put on what he had dropped on the floor beside the bed. And so, with gritty eyes, a faint aroma of stale sweat and refluxed duck, and a jet lagged sense of disconnection, he grabbed his briefcase and went down in the lift to meet the new Hong Kong day and the most important case he had ever worked on.

Billy Yeung was in a beautifully cut sports jacket and slacks. Jonathan, who had not been able to find his tie on the floor by his bed, was relieved to see that he was not wearing one but was aware of the contrast with his own dishevelment.

'We take a taxi to Stanley and then meet Dempsey Ng at the prison.'

The feeling of fatigue was unlike anything Jonathan had ever known. It was as if he had flu, with his head floating and a sense of detachment; again he seemed to be a witness to events rather than being part of them. He was also conscious of a sense of alarm; he had been flown out at great expense to lead the defence of a wealthy, and possibly prominent, businessman but he could not even remember the name of his instructing solicitor, nor even his junior, in spite of it having just been mentioned.

The solicitor was talking to him.

'Client very much wants to meet you.'

'I'm sorry. I haven't had a chance to study the papers. I won't be able to discuss much about the case with him.' It sounded to him like the voice of someone else.

'No, WK Chan just wants to meet you. He is very glad to have a London silk. Very proud. And he will probably want to look at your ears.'

'I'm sorry. I don't think I heard you properly; I'm still jet lagged, I think. Did you say my ears?'

'Yes, WK will want to look at your earlobes.'

'Oh.' There was no other possible response and he could not summon the energy to take the matter further.

They got into a taxi outside the entrance to the hotel and Billy Yeung barked something to the driver, who immediately lurched off at high speed, leaving Jonathan struggling to find the socket for his seat belt as they swerved and jerked along the road from the hotel, across a main road and onto a flyover.

Apart from noticing that it didn't seem to be particularly oriental, it was impossible for Jonathan to observe the scene outside the cab. There were double-decker buses and a lot of advertisements in English, mostly for very expensive watches and clothes. But he could not fail to take in the scruffy interior. For one thing, the driver had four – no, there were five – mobile phones, three loose on the dashboard, one clipped into a socket attached to an air vent and one attached to his ear. He seemed to be receiving calls and hollering back to at least three of them at the same time; there was loud Canto pop music and a constant, monotonous chanting voice coming from somewhere inside the car. On the inside of the windscreen were two small gold-coloured figurines in traditional dress, one of a woman with an elaborate hair-covering, the other a fiercely moustachioed grimacing man with a scarlet face. Beside them was one of those inane, smiley cat-like creatures, standing upright with its left arm waving, the sort of thing that he had seen in the windows of Chinese-themed shops in England. Every so often, the driver would pause his shouted conversations and appear to listen respectfully to the chanting.

Jonathan was aware that Yeung was smiling beside him.

'I think that you are not used to Hong Kong taxis.'

'No, although we did go in one yesterday evening, I think.'

'But all the same, it is a change from London cabs, isn't it? Very different, I think.'

The biggest difference, thought Jonathan, is that you don't feel terrified in a London taxi, but he could not say that.

'It is certainly much noisier,' he replied. 'Tell me, what are those little statues? Are they gods of some sort?'

'They are. The man is Kwan Tai, very military. The other is Tin Hau, the Queen of Heaven. Probably it means that the driver comes from a fishing clan.'

'Does that mean he is a Buddhist?'

'No, possibly a Taoist. Or an animist. Or all three. Or none,' replied the solicitor.

Jonathan feared that he might embark on an exegesis of Eastern religions, which could be interesting if he were alert enough to take it in. So he deflected him with another question.

'So, is that chanting that he is listening to some sort of prayer?'

'What chanting?'

'That man's voice that seems to becoming from the radio that has been playing since we got into the cab.'

'No, no, those are the current prices. What he is reciting now is the futures market. Before that it was precious metals. *Kam Ngang*, gold and silver, is a religion here in Hong Kong, I suppose you could say.'

They were now on a dual carriageway. Jonathan caught a glimpse of the harbour before the cab swung onto a slip road and through a canyon between high-rise buildings. There was a sudden expanse of green grass between them, on the left.

'That is Happy Valley Racecourse,' Billy Yeung said.

Then they were in a tunnel through high hills and out into an altogether different landscape. Although the wide road stretched ahead of them towards what appeared to be toll booths, there were green hills and no longer any tall blocks. They passed through the tolls and swung to the left and, suddenly, there was the sparkling blue sea, with beaches and curved yellow booms floating offshore. On the other side of the road was a golf course and what looked like apartment complexes. Back towards the sea, Jonathan caught glimpses of villas perched among the greenery. It all had a vaguely familiar feel, reminiscent of the French Mediterranean coast.

He began to feel more awake. At least, he thought, he was able to hold a lucid conversation with Billy Yeung.

'I had no idea that Hong Kong was like this.'

'No, many *gweilo* say that. It reminds you, perhaps, of the South of France.'

'Yes, a bit. Have you been there?'

'Yes, of course. My daughters are at CLC and I take them on holiday.'

'Oh really?' said Jonathan, wondering what on earth CLC was. Was it in France? Yeung seemed to assume that he would know, and he did not want to expose his ignorance any more than was necessary. He tried another tack.

'How many daughters do you have?'

'Two. One is fourteen and one sixteen.'

So it must be a school. Perhaps one of the Cs was for "college". College for Lawyers' Children, perhaps. No, that was unlikely. Central London College – that was more like it – probably one of the many institutions whose titles are the most impressive thing about them. He recalled from a fraud trial he had once been in how they had aimed at foreign students who (or whose parents, more often) were enticed by the connotation of dreaming spires to pay very large fees to be taught in a large room above a launderette in Cowley. He was surprised that someone as seemingly astute as Yeung should have fallen for that, but he was conscious that he had much to learn about Hong Kong; apparent sophistication might mask ingenuousness.

'How do your daughters like living in London?' Jonathan asked.

'They don't live in London. I don't think that they have ever been there. Except at Heathrow.'

His gaze rested on Jonathan a little longer than was necessary.

'I'm sorry, I must have misheard you. I thought you said that they were, er, somewhere in London.'

'No,' replied Yeung slowly. 'I said that they are at CLC. Cheltenham Ladies College. Perhaps you do not know of it.'

'Oh, I see. Of course I do.' Know of it, yes, but never before met anyone who could afford to send his daughter there. Two daughters, in fact.

'I thought you meant the Central London College. A very good school,' he continued, floundering. 'I have heard very good reports of it.'

'Really?' said Yeung. 'That is not a school I know of.'

Jonathan had thought that his jet lag was lifting, but he realised that he was still struggling to think clearly. He could not continue praising this fictitious institution.

'How far are we now from the prison?' he asked.

'We turn soon and go through Stanley village and the prison is a few minutes further on.'

Jonathan nodded sagely, relieved to have deflected the conversation from English schools. He looked out of the window at the passing seascape. There were coves edged by steep, green hills and across the water he could see the misty outline of islands. A huge container ship, making its imperceptible way, dominated the middle distance. His head was throbbing again but he could not remember when that had started. He felt in pockets for some Panadol, but there was none; anyway, he had no water. He was also feeling quite sick. This was not the best way to meet his client.

The taxi lurched into a sharp right-hand bend and began to career downhill, past more villas set back in subtropical gardens and into what appeared to be a small town. There was a bus stand on the left, and as they came to a halt at a set of traffic lights a group of discordantly dressed and mostly European-looking people streamed across the road in front of them towards what seemed to be clothing stalls in front of tin shacks.

'They are early customers going to Stanley Market,' Billy explained. 'You should go there. Pick up a bargain for your wife. Copy handbags, perhaps.'

Jonathan grunted in what he hoped sounded like an expression of interest. The taxi started up again and they were driving out among lush greenery with occasional glimpses of the sea. The tanker seemed not to have moved.

And then there was a long, high, grey security wall with a two-storey gatehouse set into it. The taxi pulled up outside the entrance and Yeung stretched across to pay the driver.

Jonathan sat there for a moment wondering vaguely how they were going to get back and, more urgently, how he was going to get out, as his legs seemed to have lost the ability to move. By an effort of will and concentration he opened the door and swung himself into the heat of the morning. He staggered slightly and hoped that Billy Yeung had not seen him; but the solicitor was walking towards the entrance of the prison and to a sign above it with large Chinese characters and, in smaller English writing, "Stanley Prison". Jonathan followed him and saw, to the left of the gate, another sign "Hong Kong Correctional Services Department. The Government of the Hong Kong Special Administrative Region". He thought he had heard of that term before – didn't they call prisons correctional facilities in the USA? – but had not expected it in a former British colony with a legacy of British institutions. His mind was wandering into the puzzling nature of euphemisms when he became aware that he was standing alone, for the taxi had driven off, and Yeung was beckoning him. A figure, dressed like Yeung, was standing beside him; he seemed familiar. Oh shit, thought Savage, it's my junior and I can't remember his name.

'So, you are ready to meet the client?'

'Er, yes.'

'You will find him an unusual man, I think. Full of energy. Very positive about his situation. But he will probably ask you a lot of questions.'

God, what was the lay client's name? He had forgotten that, too. How was he going to talk to him without remembering something as simple as that? He was beginning to feel nauseous again.

'Look, um, er,' he began, 'I, I'm feeling quite tired still and I don't think I can say very much to, er…'

Dempsey smiled sympathetically.

'I understand. You are still jet lagged. I suffer when I travel to the UK or the States. I think, perhaps, that you cannot remember the client's name.'

'No, you're right.'

'He is called Chan Wai-king. Lester Chan. Or WK Chan, sometimes.'

'Oh, thanks for reminding me.'

'And I am Ng Dim-si. Dempsey.'

'Oh, what? No, I remembered your name. Dempsey.'

Billy Yeung had been talking at the intercom beside the main doors and a wicket gate opened. He beckoned to Jonathan and all three walked through.

What happened next unfolded in a daze of disconnection. Jonathan was aware of being asked by a uniformed officer for his identity card, hearing Dempsey speaking in Cantonese and then to him in English, and having to repeat the request for his passport; of assuming that he had not brought it out with him but finding it in the inside pocket of his jacket; of following behind the other two as they were led through a series of locked doors into the open air and a sort of square, the centre of which looked like a basketball court enclosed by a high, chain-link fence; of seeing prisoners in brown shirts and shorts and wearing some sort of flip-flops; of being back inside again and walking through a long corridor with doors on each side, and then into a small room with a metal table and four plastic chairs and a wire-reinforced glass window set in the door. The officer withdrew and they all sat down. Dempsey Ng and Billy Yeung opened their briefcases and took out papers and writing pads. Jonathan realised that he did not have even a pen with him. As they waited, the other two chatted in Chinese, and Jonathan struggled to stay awake.

Then the door opened and in came a Chinese man dressed in the same uniform as the other prisoners and carrying under his arm a box file and several bulky manila envelopes. He looked as if he was in his mid-forties, with strands of grey appearing below a mass of unnaturally black hair,and gold-rimmed glasses. Revealing bright white protruding teeth, he smiled at Yeung and Ng who had risen to greet him and stretched his hand over the table to Savage. He spoke briefly to the other two, and even through his befuddlement Jonathan could appreciate the demeanour of command, of someone who was used to giving and not receiving orders, an air which was unaffected by his current predicament. He rose and took the hand.

'I am Chan Wai-king. You should call me Lester. I hope that you had a good flight and you are not now tired. It is very good of you to come to see me. There are some things I wish to talk to you about. I realise that you have not had the papers very long but you are London QC and very clever. I hear that you have won many cases. So this will be another one. Please sit down.'

'Mr Chan…'

'No, you must call me Lester. Or some people call me WK.'

'Mr Chan…'

'Lester.'

'Mr Chan, I make it my practice never to call a client by his Christian, er, his first name.'

'Chan is my first name.'

'Sorry?'

'Chan. I am Chan Wai-king. Chan is my family name.'

'Yes, I know that. I mean, perhaps, I do not call my client by his personal name. You are Mr Chan to me and I am Mr Savage to you.'

Billy and Dempsey glanced at each other uncomfortably.

'And why is that?' asked Chan.

'Because, Mr Chan, ours is a professional relationship. I would hope that we will come to like each other but this is a criminal charge that you are facing and there will be a trial before a judge and jury. It would be extremely damaging to your cause if the jury were to get the impression that we are friends and that that is why I am advancing the case on your behalf rather than because I am presenting an impartial and logical destruction of the prosecution's evidence and arguments.' Thank heavens he could remember his stock response to clients who tried to become too close. In fact, coming out with it made him feel a little more alert.

'In fact,' he continued, 'I have seen defendants giving evidence and, in court, accidentally referring to their counsel by their, er, personal names. It completely destroys the impression of dispassionate advocacy, that is to say, it makes it look as if the barrister is speaking up as a friend rather than as objectively presenting the case. We must not let that happen. Do you understand?'

'Yes.'

'So, we are Mr Chan and Mr Savage. Clear?'

The other two spoke hurriedly, and worriedly, in Cantonese. Jonathan was conscious that Lester Chan was staring hard at his face – at either side of his face – and he resisted the temptation to touch his ears. A broad grin spread across Chan's face.

'You impress me, Mr Savage. We will win this case together. Now, I want to discuss it with you.' He put the box file on the table and went to open one of the envelopes.

'Mr Chan, you know that I arrived in Hong Kong only yesterday. I am still very tired. More importantly, I have not yet had a chance to get to grips with the case papers. I know that my junior and the solicitor, that is, Mr Yeung and Mr Dempsey, are very good and will give me all the help in preparing for your trial but I am not yet in a position to discuss it. The most I can do now is discuss your bail application. One of the grounds, I would suggest, is the practical difficulties in having case consultations with me in these restricted surroundings and, I imagine, in the short period we are allowed for discussion. So, we can do that now unless there is anything in these documents of yours which you want to mention to them while they are here.'

Chan was still staring at him, his smile still there.

'Yes, there are some things I want to talk about to Mr Solicitor and Mr Barrister. We will perhaps do it in Chinese. Will be quicker.'

'Quite.'

There then began a vigorous exchange between the other three. Jonathan felt his momentary revival ebbing away as he listened to the unfamiliar, staccato cadences interspersed with words and phrases that he could understand: High Court, *habeas corpus*, director of public prosecutions, letters of credit, bill of lading, charter party and, several times, presumption. Lester Chan took several photocopied documents from the envelopes and the box file and slid them across the table to Dempsey Ng who, even in his state of incomprehension, Jonathan could see was not giving them his full attention as he slipped them into his briefcase. From time to time the discussion seemed to become heated, although he could not discount the possibility that it might just be the way of the language. Chan, certainly, spoke very loudly and gesticulated quite a lot, occasionally changing his demeanour and flashing a conspiratorial smile at the uncomprehending Savage.

There was a sharp knock on the door and an officer's face appeared through the wire-meshed glass. He held up his hand and tapped his wristwatch.

'You see?' said Billy Yeung. 'You are right. They do not allow enough time to see the client and to take his instructions. We have to go now.'

Jonathan snapped himself awake. 'Right. We will definitely use that as one of the grounds for the bail application. In the meantime, Mr Chan, I would like you to concentrate on preparing a list for me of all the personal reasons why being in custody awaiting your trial is a particular hardship for you. And I would appreciate from you, Mr, er, Dempsey, your assessment of the main points we can advance in support of the application.'

'I will tell you what the main points are,' said Chan.

'Thank you. Please put down everything that you can think of. Too much information is better than too little.' As soon as he said that, Jonathan had the feeling that he would regret it later.

They all rose.

'Until we next meet,' said Jonathan.

'Thank you, thank you,' said Chan.

The officer came in. He spoke abruptly to Chan, plainly telling him to sit down, and escorted the three lawyers out.

As soon as he was outside the interview room, and the solicitor and the junior were having an animated conversation in Chinese, Jonathan descended back into jet lag. Everything again seemed to be happening to someone else, as if he were a detached and exhausted observer. He was aware, once more, of the unlocking of doors, of being in the open air and then back inside a building, of uniformed Correctional Services officers speaking to the other two, of being given back his passport which he had not realised had been taken from him earlier, and then there he was, outside the gate and standing in the sunshine. He thought that he knew the name of his hotel, but had no idea whether a taxi driver would understand what he was saying. Then he fumbled through his pockets to try to find the card which, he seemed to recall, he had been given by the concierge. But where would he get a taxi? There didn't seem to be any near the prison. He wondered whether Billy Yeung would be able to call for one. He realised that Dempsey was talking to him.

'Oh, sorry, er, I didn't catch what you said. I was thinking of something else.'

'I asked you whether you were going on to somewhere else from here or whether you would like me to take you back to your hotel. My driver is just bringing the car round.'

Going somewhere else? Where? What could he have in mind?

'Oh, no,' he replied with relief. 'I'm not going anywhere. Just back to the hotel. That's very kind of you.'

'I thought, maybe, you would like to do some shopping in Stanley Market. Very good place for presents. Copy handbags, silk ties, luggage. How about pearls for your wife?'

There was nothing, absolutely nothing, that Jonathan less wanted to do, except perhaps to have to read documents. The only things he really wanted were to have a shower and to get back into bed. The very thought reminded him how grimily tired he was.

'No, no, no. I don't want to go shopping now. I need to get back to the hotel.'

'Yes, of course,' interjected Billy Yeung. 'You want to start going through those papers I had sent to your hotel yesterday. That is right, isn't it?'

'Oh, yes, er, certainly.' Jonathan swayed slightly. 'Yes, I probably will, after I have had a rest. And a coffee. I didn't get any breakfast,' he added, and thought that this might sound a touch resentful, but so what? The solicitor had put him in this position, arranging a conference at that hour the day after he had flown six thousand miles.

'Oh,' said Billy. 'No breakfast.' He shook his head. 'Then I must take you out to lunch. We do that in Central. And we can talk about this morning's meeting with the client.'

'No,' said Savage as firmly as he could muster. 'Just back to the hotel. Thank you.'

陳

For Frank Grinder, it was a pretty good day. He had been called by Billy Yeung on the previous afternoon telling him that a legal visit had been arranged for the morning at

Stanley Prison where he was to meet Lester Chan for the first time and also the London silk. An hour or so later, Billy had rung him again and told him that there had been a change of plan. As Dempsey Ng would also be there, that would make four lawyers at the meeting. Billy began to explain the problem.

'The client, he is very superstitious. Four is not a good number because, in Cantonese, it is *sei*. And that sounds very much like…'

'I know,' Frank interrupted, 'it is the same as the word for death.'

'No, it is not the same. Death is *sei*.'

'Sounds the same to me.'

'No, different. Four is *sei*; *sei* is death.'

Oh God, thought Frank, who had never got his mind round the differing tones of the language. Or even the fact that it wasn't referred to as a language but a dialect of Chinese. He wasn't in the mood for the impenetrable.

'Well, I know from what Winnie has told me that that is the reason why four is considered to be an unlucky number.'

'Your wife is right. And what is important is that it matters to Chan, the client.'

'Yes, of course,' said Frank, who was beginning to see the advantage.

'So, I must be there. And the junior counsel, who knows the client and the facts of the case. And, of course, must London QC be there because the client wants to see him. And to look at his ears.'

'Of course.'

'So, if you come to the meeting as well, that will make four lawyers. I know that you are very keen to meet client, but he would not be happy with four there. Of course, if you insist to come I can bring my managing clerk, Hector, along as well to make it five, but then would be a lot of people in a small room, isn't it?'

'Oh, it's a shame but I understand, so I won't insist,' said Frank, trying to suppress the smile in his voice.

'Thank you very much, Frank.'

'You're welcome,' he replied.

'So, I will call you later tomorrow to tell you how the meeting went and whether Chan likes Mr Savage.'

'Better call me on my mobile as I may be out and about tomorrow.'

So, that morning, as they were having breakfast, Frank smiled at Winnie and said:

'You know that I have somehow got myself committed to doing some work while we are in Hong Kong.'

'Yes, you already tell me.'

'And you remember how I used to have to go into the office most Saturdays.'

'Yes, I expect it. You work very hard, F'ank, for a *gweilo*.'

'Well, this isn't one of them. I thought I had to go to a meeting in Stanley Prison today, but now I don't.'

'I know.'

'Know what? That I had to go to work?'

'No, I know that you don't have to.'

'How on earth do you know that?'

'Because I hear you on the phone talking to Mr Yeung Chi-hang last night. You were talking about *sei*. So, I know you were discussing about unlucky number. So I think that, maybe, he was telling you not to go. Because Chan Wai-king is very famous for being superstitious.'

'Hang on, how did you know that it was Lester Chan? Chan Wai-king? I don't think I ever told you who we are acting for, did I?'

'No, you did never tell me.'

'Then, how do you know?'

'Because Yeung Chi-hang told me.'

'When?'

'Oh, maybe before you come to Hong Kong. Maybe when he ask me to ask you to call him.'

Grinder scrutinised the innocent expression on his wife's face.

'But how did you work out that my talking about the meaning of *sei* meant that I wouldn't have to go to work today?'

'Well, what else could it mean?'

He continued to stare at her. Goodness, she was pretty. But her expression gave nothing away. Was that slight smile an indication that she was teasing him? He gave up.

'OK, so what would you like to do today?'

'Well, I already saw my parents yesterday. How about we go to see them again today and play mah-jong with them?'

She was certainly teasing now.

'Oh, I would love that, as you know.' Two could play at this game. 'But let's do something different, but equally nice. What would you like to do? Apart from shopping.'

'Anything you want to do.'

'Except shopping?'

'No shopping.'

'So,' she said thoughtfully, 'how about maybe you choose.'

'No, I want you to choose.'

'No, you. Because I like shopping. So, better you choose.'

'No, I want you... Oh, for heaven's sake. Are you sure you don't want to...?'

'F'ank, my choice is that you choose.'

'Right, well, do they still have that row of seafood restaurants on the waterfront at Lamma Island?'

'Yes, I think. I had not been since you were here before. You mean at Sok Kwu Wan village?'

'I think that's what it's called,' he replied. He decided not to add that in his younger, expat days its ungazetted name was "Hepatitis Row".

'Well, why don't we take a ferry to the other village...?'

'Yeung Shue Wan.'

'Yes, that's it, and walk across the island and get the ferry back from there after lunch.'

'Yes, that would be good. We go hiking.'

'Well, it's only about an hour's walk, as I remember it.'

'Hour's walk is a hike. Better we take some supplies. I bought a shoulder sack yesterday.'

Winnie went into the kitchen and came out with a brand-new, green rucksack. It still had its price label. It was bulging.

'And I put in some supplies. Water, some fruit, chocolate, two towels, some bitter melon candy – very, very good for the heat – some hats, sun oil, some paper tissues packs, some oranges...'

'That's the fruit?'

'No, as well as fruits.'

'Winnie,' Frank asked suspiciously, 'you seemed very well-prepared. Why is that?'

'Because maybe I knew that you would let me choose.'

Frank surrendered the conversation in bafflement.

The taxi pulled up at the Outlying District piers as people were starting to hurry towards the gate for Lamma Island. Frank leant forward and gave a couple of notes to the astonished driver and pulled open the door.

'Have you got some change for the ferry?' he asked Winnie.

'No need, I had already bought Octopus cards. Take yours.'

They ran to the barrier, touched the cards against the reader and got to the big metal gate just as it was opening. Winnie was ahead of him now as she nudged and pushed and nudged her way through the crowded ramp and onto the gangplank of the ferry. Her rucksack swung dangerously as she charged onto the boat and up the companionway into the air-conditioned "deluxe" cabin. Frank would have preferred to sit on one of the battered plastic chairs on the afterdeck but he knew better than to argue with his wife for whom chilled air and reasonable proximity to the noodle counter were infinitely preferable to a view of the islands and hills. Winnie found a couple of seats towards the back, where cold gusts blew on them from an overhead grille. Not for the first time, Frank wondered why it was that Hong Kong Chinese complained about, and swaddled themselves against, the slightest drop in temperature when they were outside but seemed happy with a much colder atmosphere as long as it was inside a building.

A whistle blew and with a gust of black diesel smoke the ferry backed away from the pier and swung into the harbour. Another belch of smoke and they were making way, the whole ship shuddering and rattling with the turning of the engines. The skyscrapers of Hong Kong Island slid past on the port side and within minutes Winnie was asleep, her head resting on Frank's shoulder. He looked around the cabin; at least half of the passengers were slumbering, some with their heads back and mouths open, others down with their arms crossed on the tables. The rest shouted into mobile phones or at their companions or opened their bags and took out snacks and soft drinks. A couple of mothers wiped the backs of their children's heads with flannels and gave them little cartons of soya milk as if they were already in need of sustenance to counter the heat of the day outside. He began to slip into a comfortable recall of the familiar sounds and smells and noise of a ferry crossing, and he closed his eyes.

There was a loud, crackling noise and a recorded tannoy voice spoke in Cantonese, then Putonghua then English. He could not understand any of the Mandarin but, as always when he heard it, thought what a perfect language it was in which to give orders. He had picked out some of the words in Cantonese but knew the tenor of the announcement because it was always the same and followed by the same message in English, alerting passengers to the presence of life jackets, warning them not to spit or to gamble and identifying the ordinances under which dire penalties would be inflicted if they did so, and then wishing them an enjoyable trip. Winnie had not stirred during this interruption but remained sleeping like a child. Frank stroked her head with his free hand and shivered in the cold.

They were now passing an island with an area sectioned off by a high mesh fence, containing a couple of single-storey buildings. A few young men in brown prison uniforms were sitting on a bench. No sign of any guards. They passed into the East Lamma Channel. Enormous container ships in the middle distance, seemingly motionless except for the evidence of their bow waves. High-speed jet ferries, standing out of the water on their stilt-like foils, plied the route to and from Macau, a few fishermen's sampans rocking in the swell, bigger fishing boats coming away from Aberdeen Harbour on their way to attempt to satisfy the Hong Kong Chinese craving for fresh fish, and then the chimneys of the power station on Lamma Island slid into view above the hills. Frank had a strong urge to go outside, onto the stern deck and into the warmth of the sun; he would have loved to have watched the shipping and to have seen what changes had been made to the waterfront since he had last taken a ferry, but he could not bring himself to disturb his young wife. Almost as if sensing his thoughts, she snuggled her head deeper into the side of his neck. Now most of the other passengers were asleep, impervious to the refrigeration. One or two wandered back from the food vending machines with cans and cartons of drinks and packets of chemically enriched carbohydrates. He closed his eyes in the vain hope of passing some time asleep.

The rumbling pitch of the engine altered and he saw that they were very close to the island, steering to port. There was another crackle and an announcement. Even had he not been able to remember its thanks to the passengers for travelling with Hong Kong Ferries, as if they had any other choice, and the stern admonition to remain seated until the boat had docked, he would have guessed at its meaning as, almost to a man, the occupants of the saloon leapt to their feet and swayed and stumbled towards the stairway leading to the lower deck. By the time he and Winnie joined the end of the queue the steps were crowded with loudly chattering, mobile phone examining, eating passengers. Somehow, two or three tiny, elderly ladies, whom he had seen at the start of the journey being carefully assisted to their seats by solicitous younger relatives, had got themselves to the front of the crowd and were already at the bottom of the staircase.

They were slowing down now. The captain somehow seemed to make the boat go sideways towards the jetty. Warps were thrown ashore, there was shouting from watermen in their old-fashioned, faded blue uniforms, a whistle shrieked and the gangplanks were lowered with a crash; and a surge as several hundred tightly packed people all struggled to be the first off the boat. Frank, an irredeemable Englishman, tried to let them all go ahead of him. Winnie, once again a local, dragged him along until he realised that they were now in front of some of the people whom they had been behind. There was a palpable air of excitement.

Off the gangplank and onto the sloping walkway, Winnie dodged between aged grandparents, over laden trolley-pushers, dawdling young couples and the occasional *gweilo*, Frank following as best as he could until they were in the open air with the sea on either side of the ferry pier and houses on the hillside ahead of them. The first restaurants came into view along the concrete path. Most of the passengers hurried towards them for emergency sustenance after the forty-five minute sea crossing. Once they had walked past the tables stacked with bamboo dim sum steamers and bowls of rice,

Frank remembered how quiet Lamma was. He and Winnie were now strolling side by side through the lanes of Yeung Shue Wan village, past grocery stores, more restaurants, bars catering for the ageing remnants of the Western hippie community which had once lived and smoked pot on the island, and out into the countryside, banana trees right up to the edge of the path and thick, glossy vegetation rich with the sounds and stings of insects.

They walked on, passing a ramshackle stall selling bowls of what he remembered as the best bean curd in the world, sweetened with treacle-like cane syrup, but he did not want to stop and spoil his pathetic occidental appetite. He wondered, though, whether she was in need of something, but before he could ask, she answered him.

'No, F'ank, we don't stop here. Very dirty.'

Before he could protest that he had, many times in the past, sat on the little, faded plastic stools and eaten the *dofu* with never any unfortunate consequences and that, in fact, he remembered that it was a very effective gut-liner, she had plunged on ahead of him and was following the signs for the beach.

She was sitting on a rock when he caught up. Beside her she had spread a large towel on which there were a bottle of chilled water, a can of San Miguel – 'I know you need to have a beer because you must be very thirsty' – a packet of crisps, another packet of beef jerky, two apples and an orange.

'The water is for me,' she explained.

Frank sat down beside Winnie, slightly higher on the hard, sloping surface, his feet on the sand. The sky was clear and blue and, in the sea, children shrieked and splashed under the watchful gaze of their parents and of a lifeguard perched on his platform like an umpire at Wimbledon. Two or three grown-up swimmers struck out for the confining yellow boom of the shark net. Winnie opened the can of beer and passed it to him.

'So, maybe we sit here for a bit,' she announced.

He nodded his consent, content.

'And maybe you tell me now what you are doing. What is it, your work with Yeung Chi-hang?'

'Didn't he tell you when he spoke to you? You seemed to know more about it than I did.'

'No, he tell me only that he want you to call him. And then you meet him for lunch and then you tell me that we are going to stay longer in Hong Kong than you had thought we should. And I think Mr Billy had mention Chan Wai-king also. And this morning you talk about Stanley Prison. But otherwise, I know nothing about what you are doing.'

'And you can't guess?'

'No. How could I?'

'Because you pick everything up. You are always ahead of the game.'

'What game?'

'Oh, I'm sorry, I meant that you are very clever and you always work out what is happening. And,' he added, 'you are very, very pretty as well as clever.'

She snuggled up to him and tried to lean her head on his shoulder, but missed and nudged his upper arm. Beer slopped into his lap.

'Now look what you've done. It looks like I've wet myself.'

'No, it was your fault.'

'How's that?'

'Because you don't tell me anything about your work and then say nice things to me. So you make me spill your beer.'

'Well, look, I am going to have to sit here in the sun until my trousers dry off. So I might as well tell you what I know.'

'OK.'

'Which is practically nothing. Lester Chan has been charged with fraud on some banks.'

'So the banks are suing him?'

'No, this is a criminal trial, not a civil one. It is the Hong Kong government, the Department of Justice, that is bringing the case.'

'So, what is the difference?'

'Well, it will be tried in the High Court before a judge and a jury. And if he loses, he won't have to pay damages, but he will go to prison, I expect. Although he may have to pay as well. I'm really not sure of the procedure.'

'So, it is about banks,' Winnie said. 'You are very good on banks. You did many cases about banks when I had worked for you.'

'Yes, but this is different, it's a criminal case. I don't know anything about criminal law. It's what's called a letter of credit fraud. Do you want me to explain what a letter of credit is?'

Winnie glanced down. The wet patch was still showing.

'No, so perhaps we talk about something else,' she replied. 'So, how come Billy Yeung want you to do the work?'

'Well, extraordinary as it may seem, Lester Chan wants someone of my description on his defence team. Someone who looks like me.'

'You mean very, very handsome?'

'No, a *gweilo* with grey hair. Do you remember Charles Munsonby who used to be a partner in the firm?'

'I think so. You and him were the only Western men.'

'Yes. Well, he was acting for Chan, that is, looking after the case. But he died.'

'Who died?'

'Well, it wouldn't be Lester Chan, would it? Otherwise there'd be no case.'

'Could be many men. Could be him. Could be Mr Yeung Chi-hang. Could be Mr Charles. Why are you snappy with me? I ask you a sensible question.'

'Well, it isn't me. And Lester Chan is still alive and you heard me speaking to Billy Yeung yesterday evening.'

'So it is her.'

'What "her"?'

'It is Mr Charles. She had died.'

'Yes and no.'

'What do you mean?' Winnie was perplexed.

'Yes, it was Charles Monsonby who died. No, it is "he" not "she". I know there are no male and females pronouns in Cantonese, but I thought that by now you would remember that a man is "he" and also...' But he did not think he should also lecture her on the tenses. Now was not the time to expound on the difference between the perfect and the pluperfect.

'Is your fault. You snap at me and I am confused.'

'I'm sorry, darling, I was trying to help you.'

'It had not seem like it.'

'Well, Charles Monsonby died suddenly and for various reasons, Chan wanted another *gweilo* solicitor of, let's say,

139

mature years to be in the case. Billy has too much on his plate, that is, he is too busy with other work.'

'And he is very lazy, I think,' Winnie interjected.

'Well, perhaps a little of that also.'

'But if you don't know criminal law, how are you going to look after his case?'

'That's a very good point and I asked Billy the same thing. But this is a very big case and they have got in two barristers, one a QC from London and the other a young Hong Kong barrister and they will deal with it. So I am not certain what my role will be. But there has to be a solicitor in the case. And that's going to be me. I will give what help I can, but I am in it because I fit the description.'

'And because you are very handsome.' So peace was restored.

They sat looking out to sea for a while. Winnie had now opened the dried beef and was taking delicate nibbles from the corners, chewing contemplatively.

'I don't know how you can eat that stuff,' Frank said. 'The last time, the only time, I tried it, it almost took my teeth out. And it's so salty.'

'But it's not proper food. It just keeps me going till before we eat our lunch.'

'Does that mean you are hungry?'

'Always.'

'Then perhaps we had better get going. The sun's high in the sky now and it's getting hot and we've got that steep part to climb.'

They walked along the beach and back onto the track, Grinder insouciantly carrying his cap in front of the damp patch. By the time he had struggled up to the pagoda, just before the path's descent, he was short of breath. He put his cap back on, partly because he was worried about the sun on his bald patch and partly because the beer stain had been subsumed by his perspiration. He was uncomfortably sticky; Winnie looked as cool as she had on the ferry and was still chewing.

'Can we stop and sit in here?' he panted.

'Yes, OK, but not long. I want to get some food.'

They remained in the shade, under the curving, green-glazed roof of the pagoda, until his heart stopped thumping against his ribs, gazing at a fishing boat appearing slowly from behind the power station.

'OK, I'm ready to go.' They set off on the blissfully downhill path, leaving the sight of the sea on the right and walking beside thick hillside vegetation. Soon, on the other side of the path, a cove came into view, and across it, a line of single-storey shed-like buildings. In the middle of the bay, flat, open, wooden squares floated, tended by the fish farmers in their sampans.

'Sok Kwu Wan,' said Frank. 'It hasn't changed a bit, as far as I can see.'

Winnie's pace had quickened.

'I am very, very hungry,' she explained. 'I had eaten nothing since breakfast.'

'Well, you had a pretty big breakfast. You had about six slices of toast and butter with your boiled eggs. And a banana. And a milkshake.'

'Yes, but that was not proper food. That was what you eat. I need *sik fan*. Chinese food.'

'Well, from what I remember, you'll get plenty of it.'

They descended to the shoreline and walked across a bridge to the little temple at the edge of the village.

'Wait a minute.' Winnie disappeared through the open door. Frank paused outside. He could see her putting some coins into a box and removing a handful of incense sticks which she lit at the brazier by the entrance. She knelt on a cushion in front of a table laden with offerings of fruit and oil, facing the fierce-looking plaster gods in glass cases behind it. She bowed three times and then stood and, with her head inclined, waved the smoke towards the deities. She stuck the smouldering sticks into a sand-filled stone bowl and turned back to Frank.

'So now I've fed the gods, so we can eat.'

They walked on into the line of restaurants whose canopies joined each other creating an unintended covered walkway. On the waterside of the path were tables and chairs, on the other were tanks of fish, refrigerated cabinets of wine and beer and behind them the gloomy recesses from which waiters in jeans and tee shirts scurried bearing plates of food and in which, presumably, were the kitchens.

One they came to called itself, proudly but fallaciously, The Lamma Marriott. Further down, other restaurants bore the names of well-known hotels with which they had not the slightest connection. The owner stood by the fish tanks, encouraging them to sit down. It was more than an exhortation: he blocked their path.

'This looks alright,' said Frank, slightly ashamed at his lack of courage. 'Quite a few customers here. And they've all got food in front of them, which is a good sign.'

'Yes, it's OK. They are all the same, I think,' Winnie replied. 'And I walked far enough.'

They sat at a table on the water's edge. Below them two sampans rubbed gently against the side of a dilapidated motorboat, its engine cowling open as if waiting for someone to come and breathe life into it. Iridescent, oily water swished in the bilges. A plastic bag with the Chanel logo lay incongruously on the wooden thwart.

Winnie ordered and within minutes their food started to arrive: plates of pepper squid; clams in black bean sauce; glistening, green *gai lan,* its stem and leaves studded with garlic; a whole steamed garoupa cooked with scallion, garlic and ginger; shredded chilli chicken; a large bowl of *yeung chau fan,* the irresistible Cantonese fried rice.

'Stop, stop,' said Frank. 'You've ordered too much.'

'Because, I am very hungry and you are a big man. Only one more dish to come.'

'What's that?'

'Your favourite.'

'And what might that be?' he smiled.

'You are a *gweilo* and all *gweilo* like it.'

'Well, tell me.'

'It is sweet and sour pork.'

'But you are always telling me that it isn't a genuine Chinese dish. You said that it was invented in England for the take-away market.'

'Yes but you like it. And you may be a Westerner but you're my special *gweilo* and I want you to have what you want.'

'Winnie, I can't remember ever having seen you eat it. Do you like it?'

'Of course, that's why I told the man to bring it. But I blame you to him.'

Frank had, almost without noticing, emptied his large bottle of chilled Tsing Tao beer.

'I am going to order another. Would you like to have some? I had forgotten how good it is on a hot, thirsty day like this. And it's perfect with the food.'

'No, no, I just have tea. Well, maybe a Coke.'

One of the imponderables in life, he reflected. They cook and appreciate – indeed, it was often the main topic of conversation – the most scrumptious food on the planet, painstakingly balancing flavours and textures and colours, *yin* and *yang*, fish and meat and fowl, and even try to ensure that the total of the dishes amounts to a propitious number; and yet, so often, they are ready to accompany it with inappropriate drinks: revoltingly sweet colas and other fizzy drinks or, in the case of big shots, and he suspected that Billy Yeung might fall into this category, tumblers of vintage Grande Champagne cognac with chunks of ice floating in them.

With his third bottle of beer, the meal was ending. A pleasant stupor was beginning to overcome him, so Frank called for the bill, which arrived almost immediately. The restaurant had filled up, and the waiters, carrying several plates at once, bustled between tables of noisily laughing families. The owner was obviously happy that they were going to leave and make room for the chance of more custom, more profit, a more secure old age. Frank glanced at the figure at the bottom of the scrawled scrap of paper and left three, red HK$100 notes on the table. That was fantastic value, he thought, about twenty-two pounds, and he told the owner to keep the change. His response was a deep bow of gratitude, although whether it was an acknowledgement of his munificence or relief that this would not have to go through the books nor come into the purview of the Inland Revenue Department was not altogether clear.

They walked along the alleyway, ignoring the pleas from all the other restaurants to take a seat and enjoy the best food, and onto the concrete finger that led to the other ferry terminal. A boat was just pulling in. Frank took Winnie's hand.

'That's a bit of luck,' he said as they joined the queue. 'You know, darling, this has been the most wonderful day.'

12

'Oh, shit!'

Graham Truckett rolled over in his crumpled sheets and looked at the clock on his bedside table. He had forgotten to set the alarm. He wouldn't normally have done so for a Sunday morning, but he had bumped into Gerry Stratford at The Old China Hand in Lockhart Road the previous evening and, over a few beers, had let himself be persuaded that today was not a day for working. He had, after all, spent most of the week trying to get the boxes and files in some sort of order and had had occasional meetings with Pammy who seemed to be getting to grips with the case rather better than he was. He easily persuaded himself that he would be much fresher and more able to try to get himself into the documents in the coming week if he spent the day in the fresh air; and, by something of a fortunate coincidence, Gerry had the use of a junk and said that he would be very glad if he joined him and a few other mates on it. Graham could not remember whose boat it was or who the others were, or even if he had been told. But he had agreed and was pretty certain that they were to meet at the Aberdeen Sailing Club on the south side of the island at ten-thirty. It was now almost nine-forty-five.

He could hear the telephone ringing as he was in the shower. It stopped just as he got out and grabbed his towelling robe. If it's important, it'll ring again, he thought. Just as he started to brush his teeth, it did. He expected it was Stratford leaving it late before telling him the trip was off; after all, he wasn't particularly a friend and the bonhomie of the evening before had probably dissipated at about the same rate as the alcohol had metabolised. Graham didn't mind too much; these trips always seemed better the night before than on the actual day, and the incubus of a sense of work panic was beginning to make itself felt.

'Yep.'

'Mr Truckett?' It was a woman's voice.

'Yep.'

'I hope that I don't disturb you.' A young woman, by the sound of it.

'No. Who is that?'

'It's Lee Sit-ming.'

'Who?'

'It's Pammy. Pammy Lee.'

'Ah, Pammy. How are you?' The sound of her voice brought back the image of that very good-looking face.

'I am very well, thank you.'

'That's good. I'm glad to hear it.' He adjusted the bathrobe with his free hand.

'That is very kind of you, Mr Truckett.'

'Ah look, Pammy, please call me Graham. We're colleagues.'

'Yes, alright Mr… Graham.'

He wondered whether he ought to suggest that they meet for lunch, or perhaps brunch somewhere, though most Chinese, he knew, spent Sundays with their families, usually several generations at the same restaurant table. Maybe it would be pushing his luck at this early stage.

'I wondered if we could meet today,' she continued.

'Ah, that would be great, really great.' His robe had slipped undone again.

'Yes, because there is much we have to discuss about the case of Chan Wai-king. I have been doing more work yesterday and I have begun to produce some schedules which I would like to go through with you.'

'Oh. Yeah, er, as I say, that would have been great. But I can't manage it today. I've got, er, a family commitment. Can't get out of that.'

'No, of course not.'

'But I have been looking at the papers. In fact, I have been going through them for a while this morning. I was just taking a break and making myself a coffee when you called. I didn't get out of the kitchen in time when you called before. It was you who called, wasn't it?'

'Yes, I tried calling you a few times before you answered.'

'Funny that, I didn't hear but the once. Must be something wrong with the phone. Or the line. I'll get on to the company.' He had better stop lying; that was no way to treat this woman. 'I'll have to stop work soon, anyway. I have arranged to meet my, er, uncle. Anything else?'

'No, I am sorry to have disturbed your working.'

'No worries. It's a pleasure to talk to you.' At least that last bit was true. 'See you in the office tomorrow, Pammy.'

'Yes, I will be in early.' Graham had guessed as much.

'OK, see you then. Have a good Sunday.'

It was now ten o'clock. He pulled on a pair of jeans and the long-sleeved white shirt he had been wearing the night before, conscious of a faint odour of dried sweat wafting from it. In the bottom of his wardrobe there was a pile of shoes in which, somewhere, was a pair of deck shoes which he always wore when out on a boat. One of them had floated to near the top, but he could not see its twin. He couldn't go onto someone's deck in the black leather brogues he had worn every day for the last week. Where the hell was it? He scattered the whole pile onto the carpet, surprised at how many pairs there were, some of which he could scarcely recognise. No sign of the other but there were two battered, stained, once-white trainers that he sometimes used on hiking trails and, rarely, at the gym; they would have to do but, shit, one of them was missing its lace. He yanked out the lace from one of the brogues and, with clumsy fingers, fed it through the empty eyelets. He wished he knew for certain what time they were supposed to meet; he wished he had Stratford's phone number or even his email address; above all, he wished that he had had the coffee that he had lied about.

He grabbed the single apple from the fruit bowl in the kitchen and, whilst looking round for his wallet and mobile phone, took a bite from it. That would have to do as a breath-freshener and breakfast. Where were his keys? They weren't on the work surface where he normally slung them when he came in late to his flat. The idea crossed his mind that he might slam the door to as he left and then, when he came back, tell the doorman that he had locked himself out, but there they were, hanging from the keyhole on the inside of the door. And with one lace trailing and the back of his shirt out, he ran into the lift lobby and pressed the button. The indicator above the door lit up, showing that it was at the top, the 26th floor. He pressed again and it started its slow, rumbling descent through the eight floors above him. When it reached his level, it did not stop but went to the 15th, where it remained, seemingly forever. He pressed again and it started to move down until it reached the ground floor. If there was anyone in it, he appeared to be taking a very long time to leave, as the light remained on "G" and did not respond to his increasingly frantic percussion. Then it showed the 2nd floor and, agonisingly slowly, the 3rd and 4th until it reached the 18th. He took a step forward but the lift did not stop and went crawling its way back to the top, where it remained, asleep and unresponsive.

He ran round to the other side of the lobby and pushed open the service door. Why were so many of these blocks where the government owned apartments in such a crap state of repair? He wondered whether it was a reflection of the disdain with which his position within the Department of Justice was regarded by the accommodation allocation officer, or whether it was because expatriate housing was slipping into a decline after the 1997 handover of Hong Kong, with more locals being given government jobs. The staircase was concrete, dismal and airless and smelled of warm damp. Grey light filtered through the small, grimy windows on the walls of the levels between each dismal flight. Running down them as fast as he could, he began to experience an unpleasant sensation of vertigo and had to pause to recover before starting again, slowly and more sensibly and increasingly sure that he would miss the boat. It dawned on him, as he went down, that there was no indication of what floor he was at. Not only did that mean that he did not know what progress he was making but, when he thought about it, he could not remember seeing a service door on the ground floor. What if there wasn't one and he carried on until he was in the basement? He wished he had said no to Gerry last night: he could by now be showered and shaved and going off to meet Pammy.

He tried a few more flights but now both panic and dizziness were combining and he shoved open the next door that he came to. Back in a lift lobby and he was only on the 14th floor.Even assuming that superstition might have eliminated the 13th and 4th, there was still an impossible way to go. And then he heard a rumbling sound and realised the lift was moving. It was two floors above him. He leapt at the button and, in true Hong Kong style, jabbed at it repeatedly and, to his amazement, the indicator showed his floor and the door opened. He got in and was assailed by the odour of cooked food. That might explain the problem earlier: one of the tenants was having a delivery – a large one by the smell of it, probably for a family get-together – and had held the doors open so that the steamers and pots and polystyrene containers could be offloaded from the van and into the lift, and had somehow contrived to work the lift so that there was no risk of anyone else getting his hands on any of it before it reached, presumably, the top floor. So, in an atmosphere considerably more fragrant than he, Graham Truckett continued his descent to the lobby.

Green and red Public Light minibuses often stopped outside his building and some of them went to Aberdeen.

It would be too much to hope for that there would be one drawing up as he emerged, and he was right. Not a sign of one. He waited for a moment, wondering what best to do. If only he could call Stratford and tell him he would be late, or even that he wouldn't be able to manage it. He wished he knew who else might be going on the trip, as there was chance that he might have a number to at least be able to pass on a message. As he stood there, weighing whether it would be worth waiting for a PLB, a taxi swerved in, making him jump back, and let out a Chinese couple who went into the building, perhaps guests at the party. Graham put his hand up and the driver opened the door. He looked about eighty-five and wore thick, round, smeary glasses. He had on a grubby white tee shirt over which a green jade pendant hung on a tarnished chain. Probably he had borrowed his son's, or possibly his grandson's, cab for a bit of weekend unregistered moonlighting, thought the prosecutor. He stared at Graham curiously, perhaps for the first time encountering a *gweilo* more scruffy than he, but said nothing.

'*Heunggongjai Yauteng Woowie,*' said Graham deliberately. It never took long for unattached expats in the Justice Department to learn the words for "yacht club", nor that *Heunggong* was where the name "Hong Kong" came from, nor that *Heunggongjai* was where it all had started, what was sycophantically named "Aberdeen" after some English lord.

The driver said nothing, but continued to stare at him as he got into the back seat.

'*Heunggongjai,*' Graham repeated, '*Yauteng Woowie.*'

Still nothing.

'Shit,' thought Graham before realising that he was saying it aloud. 'What am I going to do?'

He tried again.

'*Heung-gong-jai, m'goi.*' Nothing to be lost by saying please. '*Yau-teng-woo…*'

'Yes,' said the driver. 'I understand you perfectly. I am so sorry if I seemed impolite. It is just that one so rarely hears a *gweilo*, I'm sorry, I mean a Westerner, try Cantonese, and good Cantonese at that. Mind you, it's not that I am used to taxi passengers. This isn't my usual job. My nephew is sick and I am helping him out for the day. I think that he has a flu, at least that's what he says. So, you want to go to the Aberdeen Yacht Club?'

'It's the Aberdeen Sailing Club, actually.'

'Oh, I see. Actually, you said "yacht club"; the sailing club is different. Quite nearby, but it is a different organisation. Rather more downmarket, if you don't mind my saying so. Still, I am sure that you will have a good time. It's beautiful weather for a day on the water, if that's what you are going to do.'

'Yes, I am, if we get there in time. I am afraid I've left it a bit late. It's a good job you pointed out the difference. What is, or was, your line of work, by the way?'

'Oh, I'm still working. I'm a bank manager, but I had better not say where as I don't think that the shareholders would approve of my part-timing. Don't worry, we'll get you there soon. There's not too much traffic. I've just come from the south side.'

And with a screech of tyres and a scream of the engine, they were off.

The entrance to the Aberdeen Sailing Club was through a gap in an off-white wall. Beside it a number of small industrial units sprawled in a confusion of broken-down lorries, stacks of cardboard boxes and wooden shipping pallets. Once through, the taxi stopped at a pair of tall, black, metal gates. They were open.

'Are you not going to drive through?' asked Graham.

'No, I think it better if I stop here and let you out.'

'It would be more convenient to me if you went down the driveway to the club entrance. And there might be a fare for you to pick up.'

'Yes, possibly so. But rather less convenient for me if I were to be seen by any of my clients or superiors at the wheel of a cab. I rather think that some of them might be at the club. Some might even be on the same boat as you. So, if you don't mind, you can pay me now and I will not linger.'

Graham scrabbled in his pocket for some notes and hauled himself out as he handed them to the driver, who immediately reverted to the persona of an ancient cabbie.

'Fangyou. Fangyou ver' much,' he called out of the window. 'How abou', maybe, I see you later? You want pick up?'

Graham did not reply but ran down the tarmac roadway, through the car park and up the steps to the front door.

Gerry Stratford was waiting in the lobby. He wore neatly-pressed white Bermuda shorts, a pastel-blue polo shirt and tan deck shoes. He was holding a cap with the club logo embroidered on the peak. He stared, briefly, at Graham's attire.

'Hello, mate. I thought you weren't coming. Thought perhaps you'd forgotten our chat last night. We are all here and were just about to give up on you. They're in the bar. I said I'd wait by the door for another five. Come on through.'

He led him into the front bar. Through the windows Graham caught a glimpse of the masts of sailing yachts and the brown varnished superstructure of pleasure junks, some of them with slim women in shorts and halter tops and men dressed like Stratford, drinks in their hands, posing on their sun decks as if they were already out at sea.

A group of people were sitting at a round table.

'Here he is,' said Stratford. 'Lucky bugger. I told him we were just about to go off without him. Do you know everybody? Probably not.' He paused and looked round. 'You know Brett O'Brien, of course.'

The judge rose slightly and smiled at Graham.

'His wife's not here. Back in Oz, I think.'

O'Brien nodded.

'This is KC, KC Law. I'm sure you've heard of him even if you haven't met him before.'

'No, I haven't. How do you do? I mean, I've read about you, of course, but I don't think we've met before.'

Slim and immaculately dressed in a blue blazer with gold buttons and beige chinos, in his fifties, Mr Law extended his hand.

'KC owns the boat. He's not coming out with us today. He's got business to attend to. But he has very kindly let us use it. You probably think you owe me a favour, don't you, KC? Mind you, I did get a bloody good result for you in front of that old fart Squires. Oh, I'm sorry, Brett. Er, your Lordship.'

There was a restrained laugh round the table in which neither the judge nor KC Law joined.

'This lady is KC's wife. I don't think she's coming either.' A svelte Chinese lady with a powerful diamond necklace and matching ring looked up at Graham. Indeterminable age but probably much the same as that of her husband.

'No, of course not. I will stay with KC. I hate that boat of his.'

'This is Rosetta, she's with me.' A stunning young woman flashed a smile at Graham, shining black hair, perfect white teeth and dark eyes beneath long lashes. Probably a Filipina with a large dollop of Spanish blood, he thought. She was wearing a pair of immaculately pressed white trousers and a tee shirt with "Maid in Manila" printed across her chest. He realised that he was staring at the outline of her bra and snapped himself back to Stratford.

Sitting at a table which was pushed up close was another couple in their forties. They were both in the weekend-on-a-boat casual uniform. Both fair-haired. Graham had the feeling that he had seen them before somewhere and that they were Brits.

'Do you know the Cockcrofts?' asked Stratford.

They looked at each other with the embarrassed half smiles of people who couldn't remember someone's name or even if they had met. The man half rose, just like the judge had done.

'I think we've met. I'm David and this is my wife, Sandy.'

'You're not at the local Bar?' Graham asked.

'No, I'm a solicitor.'

'Not just any solicitor,' interjected Stratford. 'He's Magic Circle. He's a partner in Luck &Egg. He instructed me in that case for KC.'

There was a moment's hesitation; David Cockcroft and KC Law exchanged glances.

'Sandy is a lawyer, too. Works for a different firm, though.'

'I imagine that you're in a different area of practice from me,' said Graham. 'I'm with the DoJ. Prosecutions Division.'

'Yes, Gerry filled us in whilst we were waiting for you.'

'Listen,' said Graham, addressing everybody, 'I am so sorry about that. I could make up an excuse but the truth is that I overslept. I was on the razzle last night.'

'Yeah, well, you don't look as if you allowed yourself much time to get ready for today.' Stratford smiled, but his barb hit home. 'Come on then, let's get going. Oh, I forgot to say, there's another couple but they are already on the boat. They said they would prefer to catch some rays to hanging around waiting in the clubhouse. You probably know them, Graham. They're at the Bar. Couple of crackers. Such a bloody waste.'

'You don't mean…Liz and Charlie?'

'Yep, that's them. Right, shall we go? Thanks again, KC.'

Law and his wife remained sitting.

'It is my pleasure, Gerry,' he said. 'I hope that you have an enjoyable and profitable day.'

Just for a moment Stratford looked aside.

'I won't be here when you get back,' continued Law. 'And I don't think it is necessary for me to come down to the boat with you. I have given Ming, my boatman, his instructions. He knows where to take you and when to return. I hope that one of you speaks some Cantonese as he doesn't know any English at all. Perhaps, though, you ought to check the fridge and the cool box before you start off, Gerry. Make sure he has got on board all the food and drink that I told him to buy for the trip. I have given him the money and he is trustworthy, but he's getting on and doesn't always remember everything. My wife and I will wait here for a while just in case you need me to come down and talk to him. I will assume, if you haven't come back in, say, twenty minutes, that all is well. And so, if I don't see you, I wish you all a very happy and, er, satisfactory excursion.' He seemed to be looking at Brett O'Brien in particular as he said this.

With a murmur of thanks, the others stood and filed out of the bar and down to the water's edge. Up against the landing stage, with its engine quietly pulsing, was an immaculate, teak, clinker-built junk. This glistening boat was designed and built for pleasure and for entertaining guests; although its square, raised stern gave a nod to the traditional working boats of the South China Sea, it had as little correspondence with them as its owner had with the Tanka fishermen in domed bamboo hats who lived and raised their families on the bobbing sampans which floated in the waters nearby. Standing on the foredeck and clinging onto the painter which he had passed through the mooring ring was the oldest man Graham had ever seen. His spindle arms poked through the apertures of an oily singlet, revealing a glimpse of a skinny chest and a large, black wart from which sprouted dozens of long, grey hairs. The stub of a cigarette smouldered from the centre of his mouth. He staggered slightly with the impact of every new shoe stepping through the gap in the taffrail and down onto the deck.

Graham held back to allow the rest of the party to board. His attention was caught by a loud scream of laughter. Sitting on the coach roof, above the wheelhouse, were two young women whom he recognised as very junior members of the private Bar and had seen in the lobby of the High Court and in the lawyers' canteen, although never before dressed like this. He had heard rumours that they were a couple; but they were very good-looking in their bikini tops and tight shorts. They were also, obviously, already squiffy, with an empty wine bottle rolling in front of them.

'Hi, you two,' he called to them. 'It's Liz and Charlie, isn't it? I'm Graham.'

'We know who you are, you prick. You're the demon prosecutor of the Legal Department,' screeched Liz or Charlie.

'Yeah, and you're a fuckwit,' laughed Liz or Charlie, sitting up to stare at him.

'And look at the way you're dressed!' shouted one of them. 'Is that a new trend, odd laces in your trainers? They are yours, I suppose. They're not exhibits from a murder trial, are they? Looks as if someone was wearing them to dispose of a corpse. Or were they the victim's?'

This might not be such a great day, he thought as he followed the last of the group onto the boat.

As he stepped down onto the deck the boatman looked at him through watery eyes and released the rope, slinging it untidily onto the gunwale so that the end trailed into the oily water.

'You must be Ming,' said Graham, pointlessly. 'Good morning, er, *jho san.*'

The boatman stared at him, then muttered something incomprehensible, spat the cigarette over the side and shuffled in his battered flip-flops into the wheelhouse. Feeling that he had exhausted all possible pleasantries, Graham turned to the rest of the party, all of whom had taken up their positions on the padded benches along the sides of the cockpit, apart from the two girls. Stratford was standing and filling glasses with white wine which he handed round to the others. He noticed that the judge was the first to be served.

There was a judder as Ming rammed the engine into reverse and then another as he swung the boat forward and away from the dock. Graham hastily took a seat beside Sandy Cockcroft, who winced involuntarily and edged closer to her husband.

'No, don't sit there, mate,' said Stratford. 'Come and sit next to Rosetta. I've kept a place for you.'

Rosetta crossed one perfect leg over the other and beamed at him. She slid along the seat and patted the space beside her.

'Please, you come here,' she said. 'Gerry, he tol' mee about you.' An enticing smell of perfume and sun oil came off her as he lurched across the cockpit towards her. He gratefully accepted an offer of a beer from Stratford as he squeezed in beside the gorgeous Filipina. He was aware that she was staring at him and still smiling, but was she in fact suppressing laughter? His appearance – shabby, unkempt, unshaven and, yes, a bit whiffy – was such a contrast with these gleaming, groomed high-flyers.

'I'm sorry about the way I'm dressed,' he said, turning to meet her gaze. 'To be honest, I had a pretty late night and overslept and I'm embarrassed that I didn't put on some more suitable clothes.' But what smarter clothes? He didn't own a single item that even approached the stylishness of the rest of the boat party. Even the judge was looking sporty and dapper. I must, he thought, look pretty shonky.

Rosetta lowered her eyes briefly, seemingly taken aback at having been caught staring at him.

'No, no,' she said. 'I was not lookeen at your clothes. They are pretty OK. No, I was admiring your face. You have a good profile. Very handsome, to mee.'

What the hell is going on? Stratford is a big bloke, thought Graham. He could floor, well, deck him if he wanted to and he certainly had a reputation for aggression in court. He wasn't going to like his girlfriend giving him the come-on but he just smiled at Rosetta and reached over to pat her on the knee.

'Here, mate,' he said, 'let me get you another beer.'

Graham's throat had been so dry that he had scarcely noticed that he had already finished the chilled bottle of VB, or indeed that it was VB, a beer brewed in Melbourne in his home state.

'Yes, please. That certainly slipped down well. Best breakfast known to mankind. Is there any more of it? Otherwise I don't mind something local. I hadn't realised I was so thirsty.'

'Yep, there's plenty. I made sure we were well stocked up with the essentials of life and I thought you would like to have some Victoria Bitter, seeing that you're from there.' He turned back into the cabin and opened the ice chest. Looking over his shoulder he said, 'Actually, there's something that I want to have a word with you about, Graham.'

The Cockcrofts stood up. 'I think we'll go up onto the sundeck,' said David. 'Come on, Sandy. It looks as if these two are going to start some barrister talk.'

'I think I'll join you.' Brett O'Brien stood up and followed them along the gunwale and up to where the, now quieter, girls were sitting.

Stratford came back with a couple of bottles and gave one to Truckett before sitting in the space across from where the solicitors had been sitting. 'Cheers,' he said and leant forward with his elbow on his bare knee, stroking his jaw, as if deep in thought.

'I heard that you've got the Lester Chan case,' he said quietly.

'Well, yes, in the sense that no-one else in the Department has it now. It was Alfred Mak's but he seems to have run away to Canada, so it's just me and a girl called Pammy Lee, whom I'm leading. I was only given it last week. Why? Are you in it?'

'No, no, it's not my case,' replied Stratford, perhaps a little too hurriedly. 'I gather they've instructed some poncey London silk and that guy Dempsey Ng. It's just that I know old Lester.'

'Do you? Having you been buying jewellery for Rosetta?'

Although she continued to smile at him, almost as if she were acting a part, her expression did not change and she showed no sign of being interested in the question or, indeed, the answer.

'No,' Stratford replied, 'of course not. I've appeared for him in the past in a couple of civil cases. He's a great mate of KC Law's; you know, the chap who owns this junk. I've had dinner with him a couple of times.'

'Who, Law?'

'No, well yes, I have had dinner with KC, but I mean with Lester Chan. He's a pretty sound sort of guy.'

'Gerry, why are you telling me this?'

'It's just that I don't like to see a decent bloke put through the mill and, from what I've gathered, he's got a pretty good defence. Or, at least, you've got a pretty weak case against him.'

Graham could feel the blood surging to his face. Suddenly, he was wide awake.

'I've got no idea what the strength of the case is,' he said. 'All I know is that the Police Commercial Crimes Bureau seems to have done mountains of work on it. I told you that I've only recently been given it and I haven't yet had much chance to get into it. I don't yet really know what it's about, other than it's a letter of credit fraud. Tell me,' he continued, putting the bottle on the bench beside him and looking fixedly at Stratford, 'is this why you invited me on this trip?'

'No, of course not; I only bumped into you last night by accident. You're not suggesting that I went looking for you, are you?'

'It's hardly a secret that I go to The Old China Hand most Saturday evenings.'

'Well, I wasn't looking for you, but when I saw you I thought I would ask you to join us. Don't get upset, Graham. I asked you because I like you and know that you are good in a party...'

'I can't think why; we've hardly spent any time socialising with each other...'

'True, but I know you've got the reputation for being a good bloke. Look, don't get upset. I'm sorry if I have somehow given you the wrong impression. I was only making chit-chat. Let's not talk about it anymore.'

'OK,' said Graham. 'Let's not.'

He picked up the bottle. Rosetta's smile was unchanged, as if it had been cemented onto her face. He took a swig.

'But...' said Stratford, pensively.

'But what?'

'It's just that, from what both KC and old Lester have told me, Lester would be very relieved if the weak case against him were dropped before it got very much further down the line. Of course, I know you can't make a decision or advise the DPP before you've had a chance to go through the papers and weighed it all up. But I'm just saying that I know that he would be *very* grateful. He's a generous man.'

Without a word, Graham got up and looked over the side. They were well underway now and there was no chance of persuading the old boatman to go back to the dockside even in the unlikely event of making him understand what he wanted. He turned back to Stratford.

'You can tell your girlfriend that she can stop grinning at me now,' he said and went up to join the others on the deck.

'Christ, you look as if you've seen a ghost,' said Liz or Charlie. 'Here, have a swig of this,' and she proffered the neck of a bottle of wine from which she had been drinking. 'It probably won't actually make you look any better, but the more I drink the better you seem.'

'Oh, for God's sake, shut up,' Graham retorted.

'Oh, what's got into him?' said Charlie or Liz. They were sitting so close to each other that there could be no mistaking their relationship. Or they were very drunk. Or probably both.

'Probably it's the wrong time of the month for him.' They both screamed with laughter and one of them repeated it.

Graham went round in front of the wheelhouse. Through the window Ming stared at him angrily and gestured for him to get out of the way. Graham moved to the side and climbed onto the roof. The judge was up there, sitting with his back against the life rail, a glass of wine in his hand. No-one else.

'Hello, Graham,' he said. 'It's great being on the water, isn't it? On a clear day like this, heading away from Aberdeen towards the islands, there aren't many better places than Hong Kong.'

Truckett sat down beside him.

'Judge,' he started.

'Call me Brett, please.'

'OK. Er, Brett, there's something that I need to talk to you about.'

'Is it about those two girls? You're not shocked, are you?'

'No, not all. They can do what they want, although I wish that women weren't so noisy when they're drunk.'

'No, but they do seem to have started early, don't they? But they'll calm down, I'm sure, or fall asleep.'

'Yeah, probably.'

'So, what do you want to tell me? Or ask me?'

13

It was still only just after 11am when Jonathan Savage got back to his hotel room, or so his wristwatch told him. He knew that it was some time in the early hours of the morning back in England, but he was too tired to make even that simple calculation. He had managed to shake Dempsey off in the lobby and had gone up in the lift on his own, swaying and woozy as it sped upwards, the illuminated floor numbers flashing past until it reached the fifty-ninth.

He put his briefcase down on the floor of his room, glancing at the large cardboard box that had been put beside his suitcase, pulled off his shoes and lay down on the bed. The silence was blissful; the hum of the air-conditioning and the sound of traffic far below provided a soothing background to the palpable absence of voices, of people talking to him and of the need to make replies or, indeed, to say anything.

He knew that he must not go to sleep but try, somehow, to connect to local time. Perhaps if he went for a stroll and tried to shut out all thought of the case and the strange circumstances that had brought him here he might be able to acclimatise. If he could keep going until, say, nine in the evening, he would be able to go to bed and perhaps have a largely uninterrupted sleep. So, just a short rest now with his head on the pillow and his gritty eyes closed.

There was a muffled chiming sound and then a gentle tapping on the door: he had, of course, forgotten to hang the "Do Not Disturb" sign outside the door. Come to think of it, he hadn't noticed one in the room, which was surprising for a hotel of this quality. The tapping continued, and then a discreet voice.

'Room service. This is room service.'

He had not ordered anything. He knew that.

'Hang on a moment, I'm just coming.' He shuffled over to the door and half-opened it.

'Thank you, sir. I am sorry to disturb you,' said a young man in uniform with some sort of trolley behind him.

'I didn't ask for anything,' said Jonathan, as politely as he could manage. 'And nor do I want anything. I was having a rest. I only got in last evening.'

'I am so sorry for the inconveniences, sir. But I had come to change your fruit.'

He slipped into the room carrying a large bowl filled with apples, oranges, bananas and, on top, a large, puce object with scaly skin from which stubby, green leaves emerged. For the first time Jonathan noticed an identical fruit bowl on a table by the window. The attendant removed it and replaced it with the bowl he had just brought in. He bowed his way backwards towards the door.

'Thank you, sir. Have a nice day.'

'One moment, before you go. It's my fault for not putting it on outside, but where is the "Don't Disturb" sign? I don't seem to have one. Where is it?'

'No, sir, there is no piece of sign. You should press the switch,' and he indicated the faintly illuminated buttons beside the door. 'This one to keep out,' and he pressed the red one, 'and this one to come in.' He pressed green.

'But maybe better I leave it on red.'

'Thank you.'

'Is there anything else, sir?'

Jonathan felt confusion and slight embarrassment. Probably every luxury hotel in the world had this sort of arrangement, and he had revealed his lack of familiarity with them.

'No, thank you very much.'

'And *thank* you, sir.'

'Thank you.'

'You're welcome.'

'Thank you.'

The smiling young man obviously had better things to do than this gavotte of endless courtesies. He slid backwards through the doorway.

'Thank you very, very much, sir,' he said firmly and pulled the door closed behind him.

Jonathan felt more awake. Perhaps he would feel even better if he took the shower he had missed earlier. And perhaps a coffee somewhere. And some fresh air.

He came down in the lift, not invigorated but certainly cleaner than when he had gone up. He had unpacked and managed to find a short-sleeved shirt and a pair of casual trousers, and the simple act of changing into clean clothes had had something of a refreshing effect. As the door opened at the lobby level he thought he might even be able to face Billy Yeung or Dempsey but, to his relief, they were not there. He went over to the concierge desk A European in a morning suit was behind it.

'Is there anywhere nearby where I might get a breath of fresh air?'

'Well, we are in Hong Kong, sir, so normally I would say no.' He was English and Jonathan felt comforted by that.

'But it is a clear and sunny day, so I would suggest Hong Kong Park. It's only a short walk from here, sir, just past the Paradise Hotel and then you will see the High Court Building and the park is just beyond that. You will probably want to know where the High Court is, anyway.'

'Well, yes, but how on earth did you know that?'

'We try to keep our eye on things, Mr Savage. That way we can be of assistance to our clients.'

'And I wouldn't mind getting a coffee.'

'Yes, sir, I will order one for you.'

'No, not here. I think I need to get out for a bit.'

'Oh, you'll find lots of coffee shops in this part of town. There are some in Pacific Place, or just outside.'

'Pacific Place. Where's that?'

'It's the shopping mall below the hotel, sir. If you take the lift down to the lowest level you will come out on the top floor. Some lovely shops there.'

A fifty-something-storey hotel sitting on top of a multi-storey shopping mall. This was really something. But not shopping. Not now.

'Is there anywhere where I can sit outside and have a coffee?'

'Yes, sir. There's one in the park or, if you go out of the hotel and turn right, go down the first escalator and then step off to your left and down the steps and then turn right and keep on the right towards the glass doors leading into the office block, you will find a café there with some outside tables.'

'Er, I think the park will do. Thank you.'

It was, indeed, clear, sunny and very hot as Jonathan walked out of the hotel, past the escalators and across the forecourt of the Paradise. He had never seen so many Bentleys in one place; it was as if the hotel owned a fleet of them. Then a tall office building clad in light grey tiles, and he crossed a short road which led to a turning circle with a fountain in the middle with a glimpse of the harbour behind it. At the end of the road there was another multi-storey building, vaguely similar to the one he had just passed. He could see large glass doors and people carrying packages coming out. He walked a bit closer and could see a sign above the entrance. Chinese characters at the top and, in English, "The High Court". So this was where the trial would be. He was tempted, for a moment, to go through the glass doors but it was a Saturday morning, there would probably be nothing to see and above all there was the need for coffee. Still, perhaps on the way back, he might look in.

From where he stood he could see the entrance to the park. He walked on and there in front of him was a restaurant with a terrace and outside tables shaded by giant umbrellas. He took a seat and immediately a waitress was at his side. She was oriental but somehow did not look Chinese: her skin was darker and eyes rounder, Jonathan thought.

'Er, do you speak English?'

'Of course.' The woman's singsong accent was quite different from that of the people he had heard so far, Dempsey and Yeung, Lester Chan and the room attendant.

'Sorry. I'm new in Hong Kong and didn't know if everyone spoke English.'

'They don't. Loss don't. But Eengleesh is my national language. Or one of the-em.'

'Where do you come from, then?' Jonathan wasn't sure if he was being rude by asking her.

'I am from Manila, the Pilipee-eens. So, what can I get you?'

'I'd like a coffee.' Then he realised that he did not want one. He was very hot and his throat dry and scratchy.

'No, actually I'd like a beer.' He looked at his watch. It was now eleven-thirty. That wasn't too irregular; he had had beers on holiday at that sort of time.

'What kind of bee-eer would you like? We have different sorts. Local, international.'

'Anything. What would you recommend?'

'Of course I would suggest Pilipeeno San Miguel.'

'Then that's what I'll have.'

He stretched his legs out and leant back in the chair. For the first time since he arrived he was enjoying himself. He watched people coming in and out of the park. Mostly Chinese, but quite a few Europeans and Indians. He caught occasional snatches of an American accent. His eyelids began to droop and he snapped himself awake just as the waitress came back to the table with a pint of beer, glistening with condensation. He had not appreciated quite how dehydrated he was.

It was delicious. It was salvation. It was gone. He had drunk it all.

'You want one more?' The girl was back at his table.

'No thanks.' But why not? It might help him get over his jet lag. You never knew.

'Yes please, I will.'

He drank the next one more judiciously, taking sips, watching people and luxuriating in the thought that he knew nobody in Hong Kong and nobody knew him. He could sit there for as long, or short, a time as he wanted and could spend the rest of the day on his own. He did not even begin to think what he would do tomorrow, Sunday. He supposed that if he slept properly tonight, he might look at the documents that had been sent to his room. But, for now, nothing mattered very much.

When he had paid for the drinks, feeling better but still too befuddled to be able to work out what HK$130 converted to, he left the bar and wandered into the park proper. It was an oasis of foliage and water surrounded by skyscrapers. The sun now felt pleasantly warm on his face and his throat was no longer like sandpaper. He sat down on a bench facing a small lake and watched the people going along the path in front of it. Many of them had huge cameras and crouched to capture the plants along the water's edge. There were several, resembling the waitress, in charge of small children, some Chinese, some European, wielding very expensive-looking pushchairs; a couple of groups of elderly people, all wearing badges, followed what looked like tour guides flourishing aloft sticks with paper signs on them. On the next bench, a boy and girl in school uniform sat close and gazed into each other's spectacles. Then, to his surprise, a bride in a white wedding dress and, presumably, her bridegroom in an ill-fitting suit with a giant posy in his buttonhole walked past him and paused, or rather posed, by the lake as another young man knelt and photographed them. The bride was elaborately made-up, somewhat overdone, he thought, for such a pretty girl. They went to a bench for more pictures and as she sat down the hem of her lacy gown rose up and revealed a pair of white trainers.

They moved on, stopping at intervals for more photos, and out of his view. Shortly afterwards another bride, with similar thick lipstick and face powder, appeared, accompanied by a young man in what appeared to be a morning suit except that is was made from some very shiny electric-blue material. He was wearing a ruffled shirt and a black bowtie. They stopped at the same place and another photographer fussed them into exaggeratedly loving positions. They went over to the same bench and, once again, a fascinated Jonathan saw that she was wearing trainers, only these sparkled with glitter. When they had gone he looked towards the lake again. On the rocks at its edge, turtles or terrapins, he was not sure which, basked motionless in the sun, some small ones on the backs of bigger ones.

Then there was a swish of a white dress, and another bride walked past, holding the hand of her groom. He was wearing a dinner jacket but otherwise seemed indistinguishable from the other two. He was intrigued to see that they stopped at the same spot; a man carrying a tripod and an outsize camera came half-running towards them, erected his equipment and started taking pictures. As he watched them to see if they too would move over to the same bench, he became aware that someone was sitting next to him.

'It's because there is a marriage registry in the park. But most of them haven't got married today.'

He turned. It was Dempsey Ng.

'No, they already got married, perhaps last week. They get dressed up again to take photos.'

Jonathan was as much surprised by the manifestation of his junior as by what he had told him.

'Are you serious? This isn't part of the ceremony?'

'No, after they got married they would go for a celebration meal in a hotel or a restaurant. So, their guests would be waiting. Also, the bride probably is hungry. So they don't want to waste time, and they come back for the pictures, near where the wedding was. This is a good place for the photos. Very beautiful, would you say?'

'I certainly would. Frankly, I'm astonished that they managed to preserve this bit of countryside when Hong Kong grew around it. It's a perfect place, with lakes and, look, there's a waterfall over there. How did they persuade the authorities to retain it and not to build over it?'

'Yes, it is a very nice place, but it's all man-made.'

'What?!'

'Yes, all the rocks have been brought here and the lakes dug. And the waterfall is pumped.'

Jonathan, in silence, looked around him. Yes, on closer inspection it did have something artificial about it. He also noticed, for the first time, that the park was quite high off the ground. He had assumed that, because there were buildings behind which were higher, it lay naturally on the slope, but he could see now that this was not so.

'All the same, it's very impressive and convincing,' he said. 'It must have taken a long time to create it.'

'No, maybe not so much,' replied Dempsey.

The both sat, contemplating the terrapins. No more brides came past.

'Dempsey,' said Jonathan, 'is it a coincidence that you happen to be here, in the park, sitting next to me?'

'No.'

'I thought not. But how did you find me?'

'Well, as your Mr Sherlock Holmes would say, "by elementary deduction".'

Did he ever say that? Jonathan was pretty familiar with Conan Doyle but he did not think he had ever come across that phrase. But it really didn't matter. He was more concerned about what might follow.

'After you told me that you didn't want to go shopping *and* that you did not want lunch, I thought maybe he is tired. Maybe still suffering from jet lag. So I thought perhaps you would take a rest and then have some fresh air. And this is the nearest fresh air that you can come to from your hotel. So I looked for you here and found you.'

'Well,' said Jonathan, somewhat perplexed, 'why did you come looking for me? I am alright, you know,' he added, 'just jet lagged, as you say.'

'Yes, I know,' said Dempsey, 'I always get jet lag when I fly from the UK back here. It's much worse coming this way. Sometimes it takes me almost one week to get over.'

Jonathan groaned inwardly. He was going to be here for only about a week; would the whole time be spent feeling like this?

'But sometimes it is less and it is good that you are getting some fresh air. But lunch would be better for you. It is now lunchtime, or soon will be.'

'Oh, that is very considerate of you and I am flattered that you worked out where I was and came to find me. But I won't bother with lunch. I'm feeling a lot better than I did but I'm really not hungry.' Something told Jonathan that talking about lunch was not the main purpose of his junior tracking him down.

'Not hungry? How can that be?' asked Dempsey in astonishment. 'Look at the time – it is twenty past twelve. Everyone is hungry then. Although I have heard that some *gweilo*, I am sorry, I mean Westerners, don't always eat much at lunchtime.'

'It's probably just that I am tired, and also my body clock hasn't yet tuned into Hong Kong time. It thinks it's the early hours of the morning.'

'But everybody gets hungry when they are tired! Not you? But if you say so.'

'I do,' replied Jonathan, thinking another display of firmness was needed. 'But thank you for worrying about me.'

'OK,' Dempsey said. 'Because that was not my main reason for coming to find you.'

Jonathan's heart sank. Just at the moment, he did not want to hear, think or talk about the case, or the bail application, or the client. Or anything, for that matter.

'No, I just wanted to tell you that I spoke to Yeung Chi-hang after I took you back to the hotel and…'

'Who's that?'

'Our instructing solicitor. Billy.'

'Oh, of course.'

'And he confirmed that client said he was impressed with you and is very pleased that you are leading his defence in this case. He said that he thinks you were very firm. He told us so when the guards were making us stop the conference, and he has managed to call Yeung Chi-hang later and he repeated the same thing to him.'

'Oh, thank you. That's very good to know. I always try to establish a good relationship with my clients.'

'Also, he has confidence in your earlobes.'

'Well,' said Jonathan, relieved that that was all that Dempsey wanted to talk about to him, 'I suppose that's good to know. Thank you for coming over here to tell me that.'

'You're welcome.'

Jonathan looked towards the lake again. A young couple were standing on a white bridge that he had not noticed before, taking photographs of each other on their smart phones. This really was a very attractive place and it suited his mood and tiredness and the gentle daze that the beer seemed to have brought on.

'It's lovely here, isn't it?' he said.

'Yes, it is; and also as the table I booked is not until one o'clock, perhaps we can have half an hour to talk about the case.'

'Alright,' Jonathan surrendered, taking a wistful look around him. 'Where do want to go?' Thirty minutes shouldn't be too difficult, he thought, and then perhaps I can come back to the park.

'Oh, we talk here.'

This was the first time that Jonathan had held a case conference on a bench in a park. Normally, they would be in his room in his chambers, sitting at his desk with a window onto Queen's Bench Row as the background, whilst his instructing solicitor, his junior counsel and the lay client sat on chairs of varying degrees of comfort and went through the defence case with him; or, when he was leading for the prosecution, with an earnest senior police officer, always exceptionally well up with the evidence, and a usually less well-informed case officer from the Crown Prosecution Service. Sometimes he would have to go through a prolonged and convoluted procedure in a high-security prison before getting to a claustrophobic interview room where his client would be ushered in, preceded by a strong smell of carbolic and tobacco smoke. Often during a trial, he would talk to the person whom he was defending in the atrium of a law court building, if on bail, or in the cells if not, snatching what little time there was before the court sat, or after it rose and before the vans arrived to collect the prisoners and return them to their sometimes not so temporary abodes. Occasionally, now the rules of professional conduct had been relaxed, he would meet the client in a provincial solicitor's office and feel uncomfortable at being asked to sit at a desk whilst its rightful occupant perched on a chair beside it. But never before had he sat discussing a case on a hot day in the open air near a man-made waterfall as a procession of brides and grooms went past. Perhaps that was how things were done here. He knew, of course, that Hong Kong followed the Common Law system and they wore wigs and gowns in court and made much use of English case law, but so much that he had already experienced was very different from what he was used to; he had better start adapting to the unfamiliar.

Nor had he ever felt so weary and less up to listening to an account of a case, particularly about fraud and letters of credit and banking. It was a sunny Saturday late morning, he had had a couple of unaccustomed early beers and he was just beginning, for the first time since his arrival, to feel a degree of contentment and normality returning and he did not want to spoil it.

'There's not much time for a chat,' he said. 'Let's not bother with the facts of the case. Let's just discuss the bail application.'

'I already prepared a list of points,' said Ng. 'For you to look at.'

'When?'

'When what?'

'When did you prepare it.'

'I went back to my chambers after I left you at your hotel. I did it then. When you were resting.'

'What, on a Saturday morning?' Jonathan had had to work on many weekends, but only when it was necessary. This was hardly urgent.

'Because I always work on a Saturday morning. It is a good time for making lists.'

'So, you have made a list for me? That's very good of you.' As Dempsey was reaching into a briefcase that Jonathan had not noticed before, he added, 'Let me guess what's in it. Don't take it out yet.' His junior shut the case.

'First, let's see, this morning, that conditions in the prison and the limited time they allow for legal visits make it impossible to take instructions fully in a complex case such as this.

'Second, that the client has no previous convictions – I assume that that's the case – and is, therefore, a man of good character.

'Third, that he has businesses and properties in Hong Kong – I think that you said it was jewellery shops – and, I assume, his own home is here so that he has every incentive to remain in the jurisdiction and not to jump bail.

'Fourth, he has substantial deposits in Hong Kong-based banks and would not want to risk having his accounts frozen.

'Fifth, the prosecution case against him is, on paper at least, not so strong that it is inevitable that a jury will convict him. Of course, I don't yet know the strength of their case, but at this stage we can safely assume that neither does the judge, and it is always worth putting that ground forward in support of a bail application. In fact, it is very rare for a fraud trial to seem, at the beginning, to be cut and dried, at least not to a judge who hasn't yet had a chance to go through the statements and documents. It would be different, I suppose, if the client had made a full, written confession to the investigating officers: he hasn't done that, has he?'

'Oh, no,' Dempsey Ng replied hurriedly. 'Chan Wai-king would never do that. He never has in the past.'

'Good, so we can argue that it would be wrong in principle for him to spend any more time in custody when there is at least the possibility of his being acquitted of all the charges.

'Six, that even were he to be convicted on some or even all the charges, it would not mean an inevitable sentence of immediate imprisonment. Although, did I catch what you said correctly? Did you say he has not made admissions in the past? Does that mean he has previous convictions?'

'He has been charged before. But only once did it come to court, and that time the jury couldn't agree, and then...'

he paused, 'and then, on the retrial, many of the witnesses had left Hong Kong. And so he was let go.'

'Well, perhaps that point may not be so strong. The judge will probably know about that. But it is still worth a punt.'

'Excuse me?'

'Still worth putting it forward.'

'So, that point is called a punt?'

'No, it's… Oh, never mind. The seventh, er, submission should be that the practice nowadays, at least in England, is that there is a presumption in favour of granting bail before a trial. And the prosecution cannot rebut that presumption. I suppose that the courts in Hong Kong are still influenced by what goes on in England?'

'Yes, but not so much as they used to be.'

'OK, but we'll still put it forward. The eighth point is that he has no property or residence outside Hong Kong, if that's the case.'

'I think so.'

'Nine, that his wife and children – if he is married and has a family –all live here, and that he has a sick and aged mother and they all depend on him.' Jonathan was amused by the growing look of admiration on his junior's face; and then, slightly alarmed, he added, 'That's only to go in if it's true.'

Dempsey now looked crestfallen.

'Have I guessed correctly?'

'Yes, except about the mother. I do not know if he has a mother. Shall we put in that she is ill?'

'Only if it's true. But we can certainly make the point about his having family here. Are there any others in the list that you have made?'

Dempsey brightened. 'No. No other. It shows that the solicitor was right to get you to do the case. Very experienced and very quick to grasp everything.'

Jonathan wondered whether he knew that the solicitor had gone for Gresham Nutworthy and that it was only by chance that he was now in the case. He guessed that he did know and was now being polite, if not obsequious. Probably best not to say anything.

'Because you have dealt with everything possible about the bail application,' Dempsey continued, 'we can now talk about the facts of the case and the evidence.'

And that, thought Jonathan, will teach me not to show off how clever and experienced I am; particularly as he had no confidence that either was true.

And so, for twenty minutes or more, the eager junior talked of bills of lading, charter parties, back-to-back letters of credit, corresponding banks, LIBOR and HIBOR, rolled steel, uncured timber, porcelain electrodes, dockside securities for loans and the names of financial institutions that Jonathan had never heard of. What on earth was the Chemical Bank? And all those banks with Chinese names which he could not begin to retain in his memory.

'Thank you. That's very helpful,' he lied at the end of the dissertation. 'It will help me when I *start* reading the case papers.' He hoped that Ng had picked up the emphasis on "start". 'But look, it's almost one o'clock. Didn't you say that you've got a table booked somewhere?'

'Yes, I did. I have.' He indicated the restaurant that Jonathan had come from. 'I booked because I thought it is more convenient. In the park. I called them when I was in my chambers. I made a reservation for two.'

'Well then, you had better go to meet your guest.'

'I have met. You are the guest.'

'But you didn't know for sure that I would be here,' Jonathan began, without having any idea where this was leading. But then he said, 'Look, I am a bit hungry now, after all, and I'd better eat something. I suppose the jet lag is just beginning to wear off. I don't feel quite so dazed as I was.'

Dempsey's smile was both disarming and flattering.

'But,' said Jonathan, 'you must let me pay.'

'No, no. That is not how we do things in Hong Kong. You are our guest here. And besides,' he added with a smirk, 'our top rate of income tax is fifteen per cent. Yours is, I think, higher.'

'Oh, alright, this time. And thank you. But let's not talk any more about the case; I want to appreciate my lunch.'

'No,' replied Dempsey. 'How about, after we have had lunch, I let you go back to your hotel for a sleep. And maybe you take tomorrow off for some shopping. I am meeting my family as it will be Sunday, so I cannot see you until, perhaps, the evening. But perhaps it is better that we meet again on Monday morning.'

With a wave of relief Jonathan realised that he was now looking forward to lunch with Dempsey.

'No, Monday morning is fine. I can't monopolise all of your time. And it will give me a chance to start to look through the papers that are in the hotel, the ones that I think you sent me. Or perhaps it was Mr Yeung.'

'I can see why you are such a forceful advocate and such a famous QC.'

14

'So, what's bothering you?'

Brett O'Brien could tell from the troubled look on Graham's face that this was not going to be a polite social enquiry, such as an invitation for lunch at the Cricket Club.

The junk was now approaching Lamma. Solitary fishermen in domed straw hats dangled lines from their sampans into the calm, limpid water, occasional wavelets and the wake from small boats broke the surface, sparkling in the reflection of the clear, hot sunshine. It was an unusually beautiful day. O'Brien slid further along the empty bench towards the stern and into the shade of a temporary awning. He beckoned Graham to come and sit opposite him. Raucous shrieking from the coach roof was proof that the party was now under its well-oiled way. The Cockcrofts had abandoned dignity and self-importance, and glimpses of their limbs showed that they were dancing wildly and erratically on the foredeck to the sound of, but not quite in sync with, the rock music that was blaring from unseen speakers. Stratford and Rosetta were out of sight, but her screeching laughs and shouts of 'No, Gerry' left little doubt about what he was doing to her.

O'Brien threw the dregs of his wine over the side, went into the wheelhouse and took a bottle of San Mig from the ice chest, squeezed it into an esky and sat back down.

'You don't seem to be in the party spirit,' he said. 'I must admit it's a bit too boisterous for my liking. Do you know those two girls? They seem to have it in for you.'

'Yes, I know them, unfortunately. Have you come across them before?'

'I think so. One or other of them has appeared in some minor matter before me, I'm pretty sure. Perhaps both have, I can't remember. Are they a couple, by any chance?'

'Yes, it's common knowledge at the Bar. Bloody shame, in a way, if you ask me, although I wouldn't dare say that to them.'

'No, perhaps best not to,' said the judge. 'Is it them that you want to talk to me about? Frankly, I wouldn't let it worry you if I were you. They were probably pretty smashed before they got on the boat; it's just the booze talking or, rather, screaming.'

'No, I'm not bothered about them, Judge. They're just a couple of noisy ladettes. As a matter of fact, they're normally quite nice, if a bit unconventional. Yeah, I agree with you, they're well tanked up.'

'So, what's the matter, then?' O'Brien had met Graham a few times on social occasions and he had been in a couple of trials in front of him. He regarded him as a decent operator, his somewhat shambolic manner belying an astute intelligence. He had always seemed to be a fair-minded prosecutor, unlike one or two of the lawyers at the Department of Justice. He also seemed keen to get a trial moving and over with, a trait that the judge found very creditable.

'Well,' said Graham, 'this is a bit awkward.' He paused and seemed to examine his eccentric shoelaces.

'Come and sit next to me,' said O'Brien. 'We appear to have this part of the boat to ourselves, but it's best not to be overheard. I don't suppose the boatman can understand.'

Ming turned back from the wheel and stared at them. His unblinking, watery gaze gave nothing away. He muttered something, incomprehensible but suggestive of malice, and then resumed steering the junk closer to the island.

'It's like this, Judge.'

'I told you to call me Brett, please. We know each other well enough and this is a social occasion.'

Graham considered for a moment the hierarchy of address, inherited no doubt from English practice and colonial days: "my Lord" in court; "Judge" if you were a member of the Bar meeting outside of court or in the judge's chambers; first names if you were on close enough terms. Just like you referred to your opponent in court as "my learned friend" even if your private description of him might be "that stupid bastard".

'Ah, thanks, er, Brett. No worries. As I say, it's awkward and I hope that you won't mind my mentioning it.'

'Well, I won't know until you tell me what it is, will I?'

Graham paused again and O'Brien waited patiently.

'Well,' he continued at last, 'I have recently taken over the prosecution of a pretty big fraud case.'

'I see.'

'Yeah, it was Alfred Mak's. You probably know him. Senior Assistant Director of Public Prosecutions at the Department of Justice. Well, he seems to have chucked it. Left the Legal Department. Left Hong Kong. Running a restaurant somewhere, I think. And I've been landed with it.'

'I can't discuss a case with you; I might be trying it. Unless you know that someone else is, but even then…'

'No, I don't yet know who's going to hear it. But it will be in the High Court, so it could be you. It's too big for the District Court. But it's not the trial that's worrying me. Although, to be fair, it *is* worrying me because it's huge. I've never seen so many case papers in my life.'

'Have you got a leader?'

'No, the DPP won't let me have one, even though there is one for the defence. I've got a junior instead, a pretty bright girl.' Pretty and bright, he reflected.

'Well, what's it about?'

'I don't really know yet. I'm going to start on the files tomorrow morning. I couldn't begin to talk about the case itself, even if it were possible to talk to you about it, which it isn't, is it?'

'No, of course not. So, that being clear, what's the matter, then?'

'Well, I don't know if I'm right or wrong.'

Graham hesitated.

'It may well be that I've got hold of the wrong end of the stick, particularly as I'm not feeling too sharp this morning. But…'

'But what?'

'Ah, er, Brett, it looks as if – even though I've only just been handed the case – as if the defendant and his friends already know that I'm prosecuting it.'

'Well, that's alright, isn't it? They were bound to find out sooner or later.'

'Yes, that's right: sooner or later. But the question is: how did they know so soon? William Soh only told me about the case a week ago. And I've been so scared of it that I haven't mentioned it to anyone else apart, that is, from Pammy, my junior.'

'Ah look, don't worry about it,' said the judge. 'I think you're reading too much into it. You know how quickly gossip travels in Hong Kong.'

'Yes, but it's not just that, Judge, er, Brett, although it is pretty puzzling.'

'Well, what is it, then?' There was an unintended note of sharpness in O'Brien's question.

'OK, here goes. I think that an attempt may have just been made to bribe me.'

'What! What do you mean by "just"? Today? By someone on this boat?'

'Yes, sort of.'

'Who by?'

'Well, it seems that that chap, KC Law – you know, the owner of this boat – it seems that he is a friend of the man I am prosecuting, and I now think that that may be the reason why I was invited to come on this trip. I've never met him before; in fact, I don't think I'd ever heard of him before today.'

'He's pretty well-known, I believe, although I'd not met him before today. Actually, it wasn't he who invited me. I got the invitation second-hand. So, if you didn't know him, I assume that your invitation didn't come from him either.'

'No, it was Gerry Stratford. He bumped into me last night at a bar. The Old China Hand in Wanchai. That's where I usually go on Saturday nights and meet some mates. Do you know it?'

'Yes, I used to go there sometimes when I was at the Bar. Before I took this job and had to start being careful about where I might be seen,' Brett half-smiled.

'Anyway, Gerry was there and he told me that he was coming on the trip today and suggested that I might like to come along. He said the owner would be pleased to see me. Actually, I'm not all that keen on this sort of thing, but I was a bit pissed, I suppose, and I agreed. Although I had forgotten all about it until the alarm went off this morning.'

'Well, what are you worrying about?' asked Brett. 'I know that Stratford's a bit of an oddball and has a reputation for keeping some dubious company, but if it was he who asked you to come it sounds normal enough to me. Come to think of it, I seem to recall that my invitation originated from Stratford as well. But it's not as if he deliberately made contact with you...or are you suggesting that there might be something more?'

Graham was silent for a short time. The implication of what he was about to say was very serious and, if he was not right, it could be defamatory. After a while, he answered.

'Aw, maybe I've got it all wrong. Maybe I'm too quick to jump to the wrong conclusion.'

'Listen, Graham. I know you. You're a pretty sound bloke. You had better tell me everything. It will go no further unless you want it to.'

'Are you sure, Judge?'

'Absolutely sure.'

'Right. Well. It's this: it wasn't KC Law who said anything to me. We hardly spoke to each other at the yacht club. Nor did I speak to his wife or she to me. It was Gerry Stratford. It seems as though he is close to Law and, as far as I can make out, also to the accused in my case. I think he may have acted for him in the past. But he's not in this trial.'

'Oh,' said Brett pensively. 'I think that I can see where you're coming from. Did he say anything about your case?'

'Yes. He told me that he knew I was in charge of the prosecution, which, as I say, came as a bit of a surprise to me.'

'And?'

'And he told me that the case against Chan wasn't strong; I think that he said that the evidence was weak, though how on earth he knows that, I cannot imagine.'

'Probably just bluff,' suggested O'Brien.

'And he implied – no, actually, he said – that Chan would be very grateful if the case was dropped. What he did imply, I think, was a bribe because he said that both Chan and Law would be grateful if the case were to be stopped and that Chan was a generous man and would show his appreciation.'

'That sounds like a bribe to me,' said O'Brien. 'Hang on, did you say that the man's name was Chan?'

'Yes, Lester Chan.'

'And is this a letter of credit fraud with a London QC coming out for his defence?'

'Yep. It is. I think…'

'Stop now, Graham.'

'I'm sorry. I thought you said that…'

'You must stop. I think I will be trying the case!'

'Oh shit. I'm sorry. It didn't occur to me that you might be the judge in the trial. I shouldn't have mentioned it. Honestly, Judge, I didn't know.'

'No, of course you didn't. It's not your fault. But what do you want to do?'

'I don't really know. I can't hand the case over to someone else in the Legal Department. William Soh made it pretty clear that there was no-one else to do it. Do you think that, after what I've just said, you should remove yourself from the trial?'

O'Brien considered the suggestion briefly.

'How could I?' he said. 'The Judiciary Administration has allocated it to me, and if I now said that I couldn't try it there would be questions. I would be asked why not and I can't make up false excuses. Apart from anything else, it would be thought that I was ducking out of a difficult case and, to say the least, that wouldn't look too good. If I explained what you have just told me it would go as far as the Chief Justice, who would probably want to refer it to the DPP and the police or the Independent Commission Against Corruption. You might then become a witness and it would make your position as prosecutor in the case difficult, if not impossible.'

'What do you suggest I do, then?' asked Graham unhappily.

'I'm not making a suggestion; it's more than that. You and I must do absolutely nothing. Stratford isn't appearing in the trial, from what you've said. And also, from what you said, he did not actually go so far as to offer you a bribe. It could be said that he did no more than pass on his inappropriate concern for a client – a former client – and simply expressed the expectation that the man would be happy if the case against him were to be dropped. It is *just* possible that that is what he meant, though that is probably a naive take on what he was doing.'

'Yes, I know what you mean,' Graham said.

'It's a difficult position for you and for me. But from what you've told me there probably wouldn't be a strong case, just on that, to justify either criminal charges or referral to the Bar Council for disciplinary proceedings against him. So, bearing in mind that doing anything at all would result in a monumental fuck-up with nothing gained, what we do is nothing. And we *say* nothing, except…'

'Except what?'

'Except we both treat that Kiwi shit with maximum circumspection in the future.'

Graham nodded.

'And,' continued the judge, 'as far as I am concerned, not to hold it against this Chan fellow. It's not impossible that he didn't know about this approach and that it was Stratford who initiated it in the hope of raising his own stock and, possibly, of getting some sort of reward out of it.'

Graham could see the sense of all that.

'So, this conversation ends here. You were quite right to raise it with me, but it ends now. Let's get back to the party.'

15

It really was a lovely apartment. It had plainly been recently redecorated in very pleasing shades of pale blue and grey, and the furniture was comfortably up to date. The long window in the sitting room, tinted the faint green-blue which so many of the new domestic tower blocks favoured, looked over the harbour, or as much of it as could be seen between the buildings on the waterfront; but the gaps were wide enough for Frank to be able to watch the shipping heading out towards the Lamma Channel and to be able to see the distant hills in the New Territories dominating the skyline above the townships of Tuen Mun and Tsuen Wan and onto the border with mainland China. The morning sky was as clear as it had been yesterday. The sound of Winnie tinkering in the kitchen somehow added to his sense of contentment following that perfect day.

He picked up the colour supplement of the *Sunday Morning Post*. Nothing had changed; it was full of advertisements for seriously overpriced wristwatches and other luxury items: jewellery, perfume, as well as top-end department stores and investment properties in London, Canada, Australia and Shenzhen; and in between them, hyperbolic features on the latest trends in fashion and food and travel. There were also a few more serious articles, taken from the pages of mostly British broadsheets. It was strange, he reflected, what still persisted from the colonial period: the legal system; the general use of British spelling; the structure of the Legislative Council; the largely unchanged police uniforms and ranks; driving on the left; double-decker buses; and this keen interest in British football, politics and news media. What he could do with, to complete his Sunday morning well-being, was a...

The door to the kitchen opened and Winnie came through with a steaming mug of coffee and a warm croissant. Where on earth had she got that from? There was even a dab of jam on the side of the plate.

'So,' she said, 'you need breakfast before you think where we go to for our lunch. I got a machine for the coffee, so I make it how you like it. Not so much milk.' She pronounced it almost like the Cantonese *kah-vay.* 'If you want another kwassong, I have it. I bought it this morning.'

'When? I didn't know you'd gone out.'

'When you were in the shower, cleaning. There is new Western bakery near the building. It was one of the reasons I had chose this apartment. So you could have the breakfast you like.'

'Winnie.'

'What?'

'Have I ever told you that I love you?'

'So many times, but more is good.'

She went back to the kitchen and continued to bustle. Frank took his breakfast to the dining table and spread out the main section of the newspaper. He turned briefly through the pages devoted to events on the mainland and went to the world news, sipping his coffee which, as he knew it would be, was just as he liked it. What more could he want on this lovely morning?

The telephone rang and he went over to the corner table to answer it.

'Hello.'

'Hello, you old nutcase. How are you doing, my very dear chap? Is everything toodle-pip for you today?'

'Rambo, is that you?'

'Right on, old bean.'

'Hang on a minute.'

'Winnie,' he called, 'it's for you. It's your brother.'

'Wait on, wait on,' came the voice from the receiver, 'it's you I want, not *Chi-fa*, Older Sister.'

'Why don't you want to talk to Winnie, to your sister?'

'I do, I do, but not now. In fact, matey, I had hope that you would pick up the phone because I not want her to know.'

'Know what?'

'Know what. Know that. Know which I am about to talk to you.'

'Sorry, Rambo, you're losing me.' Frank's peace of mind was beginning, he knew, to evaporate. Then a thought struck him.

'Look, Rambo, you're not in trouble again, are you?'

'What do you mean "again"?' Even over the telephone he sounded affronted.

'You haven't forgotten, have you, the mess you got into with my nephew, Alistair? The mess that you got *him* into? When you were in England? When you were both arrested?'

'Oh, that teeny thing? That was not much to make a fuss about. Old chap.'

'Not much to make a fuss about?!' exploded Frank. 'It caused me, and your sister, and your mother for that matter, a hell of a lot of bother. Don't you remember that I had to drive down to Weston-super-Mare police station to persuade the officer not to bring charges against both of you for criminal damage? You do recall, I hope,' he added icily, 'that you got my naive nephew horribly drunk. And that you compelled me to drive down to Weston in the company of that stultifying prig, his father. And that you cost me a great deal of money compensating the owner of the amusement arcade. And that my mother-in-law – your mother – has never forgiven me and still thinks that, somehow or other, I was responsible for her innocent son being arrested. Innocent? Hah! What about the fact that you came to visit Winnie and me in England only because you had been thrown out of your college in Hong Kong?'

Frank stopped and took a breath, for he was conscious that the sounds coming from the kitchen had stopped and that Winnie might be listening to see why he was shouting. He did not want to upset her. There was silence at the other end.

'Rambo, are you still there?'

'Yes, of course.'

'You're not saying anything. That's unusual for you.'

'I was waiting for you to finish, old fruit. I had want to let you get the hairs off your chest.'

In spite of himself, Frank could not help smiling.

'You're mixing up two expressions. And while we're at it, would you mind dropping this "old fruit" and "old bean" business? It's very dated and it's getting a bit annoying.'

'But as I told you, I had been watching a lot of old British films on the telly to improve my English. Why so many are not in colour?'

'Look, never mind about old films; let's get back to the reason for your wanting to speak to me. You still haven't answered my question: are you in any sort of trouble?'

'Of course not.' Rambo sounded as if the very suggestion was absurd. 'I just want your advices on something…'

'And you promise me that you're not in any sort of trouble with the police?' Frank tried to moderate his voice: there was still silence from the kitchen.

'No, I said to you that I was not.'

'And nor with anybody else?'

'No.'

'You're not involved with the Triads, are you?' Frank joked, but as soon as he said it he realised his misjudgement. You never could be certain what Rambo might, in his rather touching but false bravado, get up to or claim to be connected with.

'What's a triad?'

'Oh, come on, Rambo. You know perfectly well. You know, the 14K and Sun Yee On.'

'Oh, them. Of course I am not involved.' Rambo sounded, this time, genuinely shocked.

'Sorry, I shouldn't have suggested it. Come on, tell my why you called.'

'Because I am thinking of going into business.'

'You? You've never done a day's work in your life.' Again, he regretted it.

There was silence at the other end. Had he gone too far this time? He really ought to try to control his brusqueness. For all his affectation of what he believed to be American dress style or British conversation, Rambo was Chinese and had almost certainly been brought up not to be sarcastic or overly direct and, above all, not to make other people lose face, and that was what Frank had just done to him. He would never, he reflected, have spoken like that to any other member of his wife's family, and now he had done so to the only one of Winnie's relatives who seemed to look up to him and, as now, appeared genuinely to value his opinion and seek his advice. Although Rambo could often be irritating, and occasionally infuriating; although he was often misguided – as in the personal name he had chosen for himself – he was also engaging and eager to please and, above all, young.

Still silence.

'Rambo.'

'Yes, *Dai Lo*…Older Brother.'

'Rambo, look, I'm sorry for what I said. I apologise.'

'No.'

'What, you don't accept my apology?'

'No, I don't accept it because no need to. So you do not be sorry.'

'I'm sorry…I mean, say again. Are you accepting my apology or not?'

'Because, no apologies. No need for sorry. Because you are right. I had never worked. I was at school, then college, then not. But I had not ever a job.'

'That's very decent of you, Rambo,' replied a relieved Frank. 'But I am still sorry that I…' He recalled the current *Chinglish* usage that he had seen in the *South China Morning Post* in a report of a trial in which a judge had had a go at the police. 'I'm sorry that I scolded you.'

Rambo's tone palpably lightened.

'So, I can still call you "old bean"?'

'No, not that, I really do advise you not to try to talk like anyone in a black-and-white film. Just be natural. Be yourself.' He, fortunately, refrained from adding: Perhaps it would be better if you tried to be someone other than yourself.

'So, how should I talk? Can you teach me?'

'Look, Rambo, we're getting off the point again.'

'Oh, that is true. You are a very wise old *gweilo*.'

'Thanks for that… I think,' said Frank. 'Now, tell me what this is all about.'

Rambo drew a breath so loudly that it could be heard over the phone.

'*Wah*, it is good to talk to you. You had been right: I never work since college and got chuck out because I never work at college either. And because of some other things also. I had thought I must now start to work. I would like to be a great lawyer like you, but no college degree, so I cannot do. Also doctor I cannot do. I think maybe I went into government.'

'What, you… a politician?'

'No, not that. Work for government. Like in Inland Revenue or Agriculture Departments. Or something. But so boring! Perhaps maybe tourism or the airport, but still, I think, without college degree they would not want me.'

'What course were you taking at college before you, er, left?'

'Business studies. Everyone in Hong Kong does business studies. Well, lots do. Then I thought,' he continued, 'maybe I should go into hotel trade.'

'That sounds like a good idea.'

In spite of himself, Frank was beginning to be impressed that a change of course from fecklessness was on the horizon.

'Yes, it was. Although, because when first I look it up online I saw that it is called "hospitality" and I thought maybe it was to do with operations and sick people and I cannot be a doctor. But then I had learn that it meant restaurants and hotels, and perhaps restaurants in hotels, so that was no good.'

'Why not? It sounds to me like a good career move. Particularly in Hong Kong, where there are so many.'

'*Aieeyah*, so many and such good foods! That is why I cannot do it.'

'Why, can't you cook? I don't suppose you've ever had to learn. But it's not all about cooking. There are plenty of hotel jobs that don't involve working in the kitchen. And people often start at the bottom in the hotel trade and work themselves up to very good positions, I believe.'

'No, I know that. They can see I could not cook. But suppose they make me work in the restaurant as a waiter. Or have to take up room service food to people's bedrooms. I cannot do that at all.'

'I'm not following you, Rambo.'

'Because they make me carry food on plates and I am always very hungry and maybe I am tempted to eat some.

So they sack me. So that would stop me getting a job at another hotel.'

Frank could see the force in that, perplexing and illogical though it might seem to someone who did not know his brother-in-law.

'So, that puts hotels and restaurants off the list, then,' he said.

'*Wha!*, you follow very quick. So, not lawyer or doctor and not work in government or hostility industry. Not police because I had been arrested in the UK. I thought also how about driving instructor? But I had not learn to drive. Cannot be soldier because Hong Kong doesn't have an army.'

'So that's the hostility industry off the list,' said Frank

'No, Frank, I already said I cannot work in hotel.'

'So you did.'

'Therefore,' Rambo continued, 'I tell myself that it must be business. I must start a business. That is, by the way, old chap, I mean Frank, what I had study at college, but I already tell you that.'

'That sounds a good idea,' said Frank. 'But I have to say that it's not as easy as all that. You need capital, you need a project – something that the business is all about – and you need a business plan. Also, unless you already have particular skill or experience that you can exploit on your own, you would need a partner, someone to go into business with.'

'Yes, I already got all that. Well, some of it.'

'How come? I wasn't aware that you had an expertise or experience.'

'Because when I get chuck out of college I had not been the only one. It seemed that the college was having a clean brush and they wanted to make room for some more students, mostly from the PRC because they all got plenty of money now, and so they got rid of some of the…'

'The lazy ones?' Couldn't Grinder have put it more tactfully? Too late now.

'Yes, that's it. So also my friend got chuck out. And I met him this week and he said "How about maybe we go into business together?" It was his idea.'

'Doing what?' Frank was intrigued.

'You know, having an office and a secretary. And wearing suit and tie.'

'No, I meant what would your business do?'

'Oh, I see. Yes, we would sell watches. But not clocks; nobody buys clocks anymore because they all keep their smart phones by the bed. But most people wear wristwatches. Very cool.'

'But what made you think of watches?'

'My friend, he already buys and sells watches. But not clocks. He goes over the border to Shenzhen and buys lots of watches. He gets them very, very cheap and sells them in Hong Kong at much more expensive.'

'Where does he sell them? Does he have a shop? It sounds a bit surprising if he's recently out of college like you.'

'No, no shop. He sells them here and there. To people. Sometimes he takes them with him when he goes on trips abroad. In the bottom of his suitcase. In a special box. That is his experience.'

'I think I see what you are talking about,' said Frank, amused in spite of himself. 'And I'm not sure that I want to know any more about it. But that's a long way from running a business. Is what he is proposing to you a proper business venture?'

'Yes, it is proper. It is not selling from a suitcase.'

'Well it would probably take quite a lot of money to start up. And, if you don't mind my saying so, but it's only fair that I do, I very much doubt that a bank would be prepared to advance you a sufficient loan on the basis of your previous experience or that of your friend. It seems to me that neither of you having any relevant experience and, even if you had, the bank would want to have some sizeable security and, as far as I am aware, you haven't any. It's not as if your family is wealthy and could act as guarantors.'

A chilling thought came to Frank's mind.

'Is that, by any chance, why you phoned me, Rambo? Look, much as I like you and we are, I suppose, family, I am retired now and not in a position to act as a guarantor for a loan. Anyway, I'm only here temporarily and Winnie and I will go back to England when this bit of work that has landed on me has finished. I very much doubt whether a bank, whether it's HSBC or the Wing Lung Bank, would be prepared to accept a non-resident as a guarantor. And you have nothing to offer as collateral, have you? You don't have a home of your own and I could not advise your parents to risk their flat in the New Territories, and you wouldn't want them to do that, would you? Actually, I believe that they don't own it, they rent it; isn't that right?'

'No, they do not own.'

'So,' continued Frank, 'you can see the difficulties, I hope.'

'Yes, but that is not a difficulties. No need to borrow money. My friend has a lot of money.'

'What, from bringing watches over the border?'

'A bit. But not so much. His daddy had always give him a lot and would be pleased to see him start in business. But because his daddy say he would not help him unless he has business partner to share – what had he call it? – the responsibility. He is a very rich man, the daddy, and very good at business.'

'He sounds very sensible; that is just the advice that I would give. It doesn't matter that the business partner cannot put in much money: that is something to work out, sorting out the partnership agreement or the share-holding if it is to be a limited company. The one who puts in the most money usually draws the bigger income and has a greater holding in the assets and a greater share in the value of the company itself; but I think it is very sound advice for the father to tell your friend that he must go into business with at least one other partner, to share the work and the decisions and, as he rightly calls it, the responsibility. Running any sort of business can be very difficult and, as they say, two heads are better than one. In fact, for a small concern I think that two is the right number. Sometimes three can make for two ganging up on the other one, and any more than three could make it unwieldy and, in fact, unprofitable for a small start-up like you are suggesting.'

'Yes,' said Rambo after a moment's apparent reflection, 'I see what you say. You are a real top man in advising.'

'Never mind the flattery, Rambo. I just think that your friend's father sounds intelligent and practical. You know, I am beginning to warm to this idea of yours. I must admit that it sounded crazy at first, but this could be the making of you. But you would have to apply yourself, I mean that you would have to work very, very hard and – how can I put it? – change your ways. Be serious about it and accept that you must be committed to it. No more time-wasting. Do you understand what I mean? No more watching television in the afternoon, for example.'

'Yes, I know what you mean. I already had thought that I must grow up. Work hard and make money.'

'Rambo,' said Frank, 'I am so pleased to hear it. I've always been fond of you but you have, I must admit, often worried your older sister and me.'

'Yes, I understand that must be.'

'So, I think that it is very good news that you are getting down to work at last. Tell me, would your friend's father be prepared to act as a guarantor, you understand what I mean, to agree with the bank that he, or his company, will compensate the bank if you don't keep up with your payments on the loan? That would be essential for you to be able to start a business. You must have working capital and you would also need an arrangement whereby you could draw down additional money if, for instance, a good opportunity presented itself for you to be able to buy a substantial amount of profitable merchandise. So you would need both some money to get the business started and what's called a "facility" so that you could borrow more at very short notice.'

Frank Grinder had the impression that they had been cut off. There was unusual silence.

'Rambo, are you still there? Are you listening? Would your friend's father be prepared to back his son and you in that way?'

A pause, then Rambo spoke.

'Oh yes. My friend's father is very rich. And a big businessman. He already had explain to my friend and told him he would help. The father is very experienced.'

'Well, that's great. Obviously, I would need to know more details and see what the sums involved are likely to be and also have some written evidence of his willingness to act as a guarantor. But congratulations, Rambo, I think that you are maybe on to something. What's your friend's name, by the way? Perhaps we can invite him over here for a drink. Has Winnie met him?'

'No, because I think that she had not met him. His name is Chan Sik-lung. English name, Sicky Chan.'

'No, I don't think you've mentioned him before. I think I would have remembered that name. Who's his father? Might I have heard of him?'

'Oh yes, very famous man. He is Chan Wai-king.'

'Chan Wai-king? Hang on, that name rings a bell,' said Frank.

Winnie came through the kitchen door.

'Chan Wai-king is who you call Lester Chan. He is the man you not go to see yesterday,' she said.

'Oh shit!' said Grinder.

16

Jonathan Savage had slept throughout most of the night and had woken on Sunday morning feeling much better and definitely ready for some breakfast. The bewildering array of multinational dishes on the buffet had for a moment made him regret not having chosen something simple from the menu when the waiter came to take his order; he could not work out the correct precedence and whether he should start or end with the lavish display of exotic fruits. Nor did he want to reveal his inexperience by trying oriental and occidental in the wrong order. As he hesitated, a young couple, talking animatedly in Japanese, walked away to their table, each carrying a plate laden with scrambled eggs, Danish pastries, sashimi, slices of watermelon and pineapple, pork sausages, smoked salmon, cheese and a hillock of noodles. So he just plunged in and picked at what he fancied.

Once he got back to his room he remembered his promise to Dempsey to start on the papers. He looked out at the restricted view of the harbour, mostly blocked by glass-covered tower blocks across the plaza many floors below.

In fact, he had a better indirect view of the water and the activity of the boats on it by looking at the reflection in the buildings opposite. It was fascinating but he was not here on holiday and had to make a start. Using the knife from the fruit bowl he slit open the first of the boxes, and then thought it best to do the same to the others. There seemed to be more than he recalled seeing yesterday. Could more have been delivered when he was sleeping?

The boxes were all numbered and there were six of them. He opened the first and pulled out the contents. They seemed to be witness statements in English and Chinese, which came as a bit of a relief as he would not be expected to read them all. The next box also, and the next. The other three all contained what appeared to be copies of exhibits. Some were in English, some in Chinese, some in a mixture of both, and all were, at first glance, incomprehensible. Jonathan had heard of bills of lading but had not before come face to face with one; that he knew that that was what they were was only because their headings said so. He saw that in amongst these arcane documents were letters: correspondence from and to banks and other financial institutions. He tried to make sense of some of them which appeared to be instructions to remit money or applications to extend loans. Fortunately, many of these documents, although with headings in English, were written in Chinese. Some of them had annotations in English handwriting, but even those he could read were meaningless to him. He realised that he had not got over his jetlag; the effort of trying to distil some sort of narrative from these papers resulted only in making his head swim with frustration. He simply could not begin to work out what this case was about. He searched through them trying to find something that looked different from the others: a police report or an outline of the case from the instructing solicitors or from his junior, or anything meaningful that might help him start to read in. There was nothing. It was Sunday, he was tired in a way he had never experienced before and he knew that if he started to go through the witness statements and the exhibits, without anything to guide him in to give him an indication of what the case was about and let him know what he should be looking for, he would be doing nothing more than killing time.

He thought of calling the number on the card which, when they had first met, Dempsey had proffered to him with both hands. But he remembered that he had said he would be meeting his family and it would, plainly, be wrong to disturb him. And it was not Dempsey who had suggested that Jonathan work on the papers in his hotel room; on the contrary, he had rather given the impression that he should take the day off. No doubt, somewhere, there would be an outline of the prosecution's case which he could get his teeth into, but it was not here and there was nothing that he could usefully do until he had seen it. So, with a sense of relief, tinged by only a modicum of guilt, he had put the papers back into their boxes, left his room and walked out of the front doors of the hotel to explore Hong Kong.

When he got back to his room there was a note pushed under his door, a message. It read: *Please come to my chambers at 10.00 Monday, tomorrow. Rooms 8 to 12, 16/F, Tower Two, Tiger Centre, Admiralty. Is near your hotel. May have good news.*

陳

The concierge pointed out the towers. You could see them from the lobby, but seeing them and getting to them were not the same. After repeated directions, the concierge had feared losing, literally, a guest and called a uniformed bellboy over; and he accompanied Jonathan down by lift to the top floor of the shopping centre that lay below the hotel, across to a glassed-in walkway that went over a busy dual carriageway and emerged into another shopping mall, and to the end of that and into the huge, marble-lined atrium of the Tiger Centre. Indicating the lifts for Tower Two he left Jonathan with a deep bow, seemingly unembarrassed by the incongruity of his white uniform and gold-edged pillbox hat amongst the crowd of business-dressed and busy Chinese and European denizens of the building.

There were six shining steel doors in the lift lobby. With a loud ping, the door nearest to him slid open and ten or so people emerged from the brightly lit, mirrored interior, all talking, either to each other or into mobile phones. Jonathan got in, followed by several others. The lift started to ascend and he looked, in vain, for the button for the 16th floor. The red illuminated sign above the door said "20" and then "21". The lift stopped and a young woman got out. Then "23", and two men and another woman left. Then "25" and the last passenger, a young woman. He was alone and it was still going up. Where was button he wanted? "30", and another woman got in and the lift started to go down. It did not stop until it had reached the lobby, where the woman got out. Just as more people started to enter he thought that it would be better if he left as well and tried to take stock of the situation.

He got out just as the door was starting to close. The woman was standing there, waiting.

'You're new here?' She was European and had an American accent. Smartly dressed and carrying a briefcase.

'Er, yes. I've only been in Hong Kong for a couple of days.'

'Yes, I thought so. You're not the first to have trouble with the elevators here. Where did you want to go?'

'Dempsey Ng's chambers.'

'Never heard of him. I meant what floor do you want?'

'Oh, 16th, I think. Yes the 16th.'

'You got into the wrong one. Look above the door.'

He did so. It indicated 20 to 39.

'You want that one.'

Gold letters on the door to the left read '2 to 19'.

'Thank you very much.'

'It's a pleasure,' she said. 'You're not the first I've helped and you won't be the last. Impressive, isn't it?'

'It certainly is,' replied Jonathan, thinking what a contrast this huge commercial edifice was to his own chambers, situated in a row of Georgian three-storey buildings in a street entirely occupied by barristers and solicitors.

He entered the correct lift, alone and able to take in the luxury of the interior. Thick carpeting and sculpted wood around the mirrors. He got out at the 16th floor and Dempsey was waiting for him. He was about to ask how he knew but shelved the question; he had already realised that there were too many imponderables. His junior led him along to a glass door into a pleasingly familiar corridor lined with shelves of bound volumes of law reports.

'This is my room,' he said. 'Tea or coffee?'

'No thanks, I've just had breakfast.'

The room was unexpectedly small. Most if it was taken up with an outsized desk. There was a chair behind it and another in the corner. The rest of the floor space was piled with boxes, similar to those in the hotel room but, Jonathan noticed, far more of them.

'So, what's the good news?'

'Billy Yeung called me. He said that your work permit will be ready today, this morning. So no need for you to go straight home. You can appear in the bail application. Which is good because I am not sure that you should have seen the client in Stanley Prison before you had the visa. But no matter because Billy Yeung says that it will be backdated.'

'Is that proper? And how can that be done?'

'First question: I don't know. Second question: Billy Yeung can do anything.'

'Hang on a moment. Are you saying that I am now instructed in the bail application before I go back to England?'

'Yes, don't worry, the fee will be agreed by your clerk. I am sure that it will be a good one.'

'I'm not worried about the fee. What I *am* worried about is that I don't know the first thing about the case,' Jonathan said, and then, seeing the shadow of a pained look, added, 'Apart of course from what you told me on Saturday morning.'

'Yes, but what you said that morning showed that you were very familiar with the facts. You seemed to know everything for the application.'

'Dempsey, how could I be? I wasn't sent any papers in London and all that I have are in the boxes that were sent to my hotel.'

'But you read them?'

'That's something I wanted to mention to you. Some of the papers are in English and some in Chinese or a mixture of both. I can't read Chinese.'

'No, probably not.'

'So I don't know if any of the papers that are written in English are translations of the Chinese documents.'

'Probably not.'

'And I admit that I was still pretty tired when I started to look at them, but I confess that I couldn't make head nor tail of them.'

'Probably not.' This response was both puzzling and a touch annoying.

'I couldn't find any written instructions from the solicitors or anything else, like an outline of the prosecution case, which would have helped me to get an idea of what the case is about and what I was supposed to be looking for.'

'No, I think that there is not one in the boxes.'

'So, in your opinion, was there any purpose in sending those boxes to my hotel?'

'Probably not. Actually, not at all.'

'Then why were they sent?'

'It would have been because of Chan Wai-king. Client is a very powerful man and he pays big fees. Yeung Chi-hang, Billy, does what he asks if he can do it properly. One of the things that the client got Billy to do was to make a hopeless approach to the Department of Justice trying to persuade them that there was not enough evidence in the case and that the charge should be dropped. I was instructed by Billy to draft the letter. This happens in Hong Kong sometimes, but these submissions hardly ever get anywhere. I know that client wanted you to have some papers to look at when you got here. In fact, when he heard that I was going to meet you at the airport he wanted me to take some documents for you to read on the way to the hotel. I told him yes, but I could not inflict that on you. Please don't tell him that I didn't.'

'No, of course I won't. That was very thoughtful of you. But who decided which documents to send to the hotel? Are they the only papers in the case?'

'Oh no, there are many, many more boxes. You will see them all eventually. It would have been Yeung who chose the boxes. I think that he does not expect you to read them yet. Just a sample so that client is satisfied.'

'Well, I must say that's a relief. Will I see any explanatory note or report before the bail hearing so that I can know enough about the facts of the case before making the application?'

'Probably not. In fact, definitely not. The bail application is listed for two-thirty this afternoon.'

A cold shudder shook Jonathan; he hoped that his junior had not noticed. He was, he told himself, a Queen's Counsel brought over from London, and control and authority were expected of him. Then a thought came like a ray of sunshine.

'But I was not expecting to appear in court this time. I had no work permit when I left England. So I haven't brought my robes. I am right, aren't I, that barristers and judges wear the same wigs and gowns here as they do in English courts? But I can't borrow yours as I am a silk and you're not.'

'No need. No robes. Billy Yeung has spoken to the Judiciary Administrator. The hearing will be in court but will be treated as in the judge's chambers, so no robes. Just your suit and tie as you are wearing now.'

Jonathan involuntarily fingered his tie which he had bought at The Accessory Rail while waiting for his flight and contrasted it with Dempsey's plumply knotted, shimmering neckwear. His suit was still looking crumpled and he thought that he should have had it pressed by the hotel yesterday. Too late now, he supposed.

'But what am I supposed to say in support of the application for bail? I don't have any instructions. Is it too late to arrange another visit to the prison so that I can get some information from Mr Chan?' This was despair.

'No, no. That cannot be done. We would need to give Correctional Services Department twenty-four hours' notice. Unless the court makes an order.'

'Well, we might have to apply to adjourn the hearing.'

'Probably not. Instructing solicitor would lose face. He made a special effort to get the hearing for while you are here and he made even more effort for your employment visa from the Department of Immigration.'

'Alright,' Savage replied grimly. 'I accept that we can't put off the hearing, that I shall be making the application, that there will be no opportunity beforehand to take instructions from the client as to his personal circumstances and that I do not know the first thing about the charges, the facts, the evidence or the strength of the prosecution's case let alone what our defence is. The only thing that I can I think of is to present the points that I mentioned to you when we met in that park on Saturday morning. So, let's just sit here and see if I can remember them all and you can make a note of them.'

'No need,' said Dempsey Ng.

'What do you mean, "no need"?' Jonathan was aware that his irritation may have resulted from a combination of fatigue and panic, but he had not expected to be contradicted over such a straightforward decision. 'Of course we need to.'

'Because there is no need. I have already done it.'

'How come?'

'Because after we had lunch in the park I came straight back here and made a note of everything that you told me about the grounds for the application.'

'That's very impressive. But are you sure that you remembered everything I said, er, we discussed?'

'I think so. I wrote it up on my computer.'

Dempsey opened a file on his desk and passed some sheets of paper across. Jonathan read through them. All the points seemed to be there; he even thought that he recognised his own style. Certainly there were some turns of phrase which he had used in court in the past.

'This is astonishing, Dempsey. What a useful, no, impressive, junior you are going to be in this case. I must admit that I had no idea you would go back to your chambers after lunch. It was the weekend, after all. I know that Hong Kong Chinese have a reputation for hard work but this, well...'

He looked again at the note that Dempsey had made.

'Yes, all the points are there. But I recall that we had quite a decent lunch and we took some time over it. You were very generous. And didn't you have a couple of glasses of wine? I know that I had a beer or two. How on earth could you remember all that so accurately?'

'Because, I had my mobile phone on record mode all the time when you were talking. I wanted to learn from you.'

How could I be angry when it is put like that? Jonathan thought.

'So, what are we going to do for the rest of the morning? Have you got other work to do? I could come back after lunch?'

'No, no,' said Dempsey. 'While you are in Hong Kong I work only on this case. What would you like me to do?'

This is a time for frankness, thought Jonathan.

'You know, on Saturday morning, when you were telling me about the case.'

'Yes.'

'Well, I realised afterwards that I didn't seem to have taken much in. I was still pretty tired, from the flight.' He did not think it wise to mention the refreshment he had taken.

'It is common. Jet lag makes everyone forgetful. Very hard to concentrate then.'

'So, suppose we spend the rest of this morning with you going through all that again and, this time, as we are sitting down, I'll make a note.'

And so, with a markedly improved alertness, Jonathan listened as his junior talked and, in spite of his continuing, but he hoped concealed, unfamiliarity with many of the commercial and banking expressions, he began to discern some sort of picture emerging from the mists and to understand something of the allegations Chan was facing. He knew that, five minutes after the end of Dempsey's peroration, he would probably not be able to remember a single detail without looking at what he had written down. He knew that he would have to go on-line as soon as he was able to do so, in privacy, and try to find out what some of the terms meant; he might even have to buy a dictionary of banking and commerce when he got back to London. He was aware that he would, almost certainly, have to affect an understanding and to nod wisely during the coming days; but at least he was beginning to have a glimmering of what the case was about. Dempsey seemed to have finished so Jonathan took a long shot.

'So, in essence, the issue is one of dishonesty, I would say. From what you say, or rather from what I have gathered, perhaps incorrectly, the client does not dispute much of the evidence. The question will be what interpretation should be put on his actions. Was his intention to defraud – by the current definition of the law – or did he lack the element of dishonesty which the prosecution must prove? So it's relatively simple.'

Dempsey was silent for a moment, fiddling with the papers on his desk. Hell, thought Jonathan, I've blown it. I've just demonstrated that I have not understood anything he said. He could see that his junior was trying to think of a way of telling him so without causing him embarrassment. He would have to report back to the solicitors that the London leading counsel was completely out of his depth. He supposed that they would still pay for his return flight.

'*Wah!*' said Dempsey, looking straight at Jonathan. 'You are some top QC! Without even reading the papers you got the whole point of the case. The client will be very, very happy. I will print another copy of the note I made of what you said in the park. Perhaps you would like to have it so you can use it in court this afternoon.'

'An excellent idea,' replied a relieved Jonathan. 'Look, it's almost midday. I think I'll go back to the hotel and freshen up before this afternoon.' And possibly buy a better tie, he thought.

'But we have lunch together?' said Dempsey. 'I could take you for some dim sum. I already booked a table.'

'Sorry, but I don't think I will. I'll probably just have a salad in my room or possibly just some fruit juice. I never eat much if I am going to be on my feet in court.'

The junior looked at him with a mixture of disappointment, bewilderment and concern. 'But how can you go into court without eating?' he asked. 'You may get faint. I think a lunch would be good for you.'

Time to assert authority again. 'No,' said Jonathan firmly. 'I am never hungry when I'm about to perform. If you are free, perhaps we can have dinner together this evening. And you must let me pay. But no lunch.'

Dempsey, mystified, gave in. 'So, if you come back here at two o'clock I can show you where is the court.'

17

The High Court of Hong Kong was unlike any court Jonathan had seen before. An off-white, twenty-storey building, recognisable now as the tower he had seen when he was having too many beers in the park. A fountain played in the middle of a red brick roundabout in the space in front of the doors, at which a succession of silver-roofed red taxis pulled up and deposited litigants, lawyers, witnesses and defendants on bail; except for those wearing court jackets and wing collars with white cotton bands, it was impossible to tell who was who. Dempsey opened one of the glass doors and ushered him through into a crowded atrium, one side of which was the lift lobby where the now familiar queues waited by the lift entrances. A persistent electronic peal heralded the arrival of each one and there was a scramble as the passengers pushed in, unconcerned with the attempts of those trying to get out. Jonathan followed as Dempsey forced his way in and stretched over to press the button for the seventeenth floor.

'Crowded, huh?' Dempsey said.

Jonathan nodded. Conversation seemed inappropriate with so many faces pressed close to them. Stopping at every floor, the lift eventually arrived at their floor.

'OK, so we get out here.'

Dempsey went first and Jonathan squeezed apologetically after him and into a wide lobby with huge windows on one side through which was a view of the harbour and construction machinery working on an area of land reclamation. Opposite him were pine-clad walls, with double doors set into them; above them, in English and Chinese, were the numbers of the courts into which they led. A sensation of confusion hit him, caused by unfamiliarity with the surroundings or the remnants of jet lag or the lift ride, he didn't know which. He noticed a very attractive young Chinese woman standing by one of the black benches in the centre of the hall and, at the other end, the familiar face of Billy Yeung, his instructing solicitor, who was talking to a grey-haired European man with heavy-rimmed spectacles. Dempsey guided him over to them.

'Mr Savage,' Billy greeted him. 'How are you today? I hope that you have been able to have a rest since we last met. Are you over your jet lag?'

'Yes, I think so. Probably I am. It's all a bit of a new experience to me.' Instinct told him to say no more.

'Mr Savage, I would like to introduce you to one of our former partners who will be helping with the case. This is Mr Grinder.'

'Please call me Frank.' They shook hands.

'Oh, yes, and call me Jonathan. You too, er, Billy.' He was not sure of the protocol but the easy manner of Grinder suggested a familiarity with local custom that he ought to follow.

'Actually, I've been brought into this case for reasons that I can't altogether understand. It's true that I was a partner in the firm but I retired a while ago and went back to England. I only came out here because my wife wanted to visit her relatives. And crime was not my area of law; I did commercial work. I don't know how much help I am going to be to you.'

Dempsey and Billy were conversing in Cantonese, and Grinder was talking to him quietly enough for them not to be able to hear what he was saying.

'Oh I'm sure you'll be a great help,' Jonathan said, taken aback. No solicitor had ever said anything like that to him before. 'Your knowledge of commerce and, er, banking will be invaluable.'

'I hope so, but I have my doubts. Do you know anything about the case yet?'

'No, not really. I haven't had a chance to read the papers.'

'Like me,' replied Frank. 'Let's hope it's not too obvious to the client.' He gave Jonathan a wry, sympathetic smile.

Dempsey Ng turned back to Jonathan.

'Let me introduce you to our opponents,' he said, and led him towards the Chinese woman. Standing next to her was a man in his late thirties or early forties. He was wearing a crumpled dark suit and his brown hair looked unbrushed. Jonathan had not noticed him earlier.

'Hello, Graham,' Dempsey said. 'Thank you for your message. I had not known until then that you were prosecuting our case; otherwise I may have been in touch with you. This is Mr Jonathan Savage, our London QC.'

'How are you, mate?' said Graham. Jonathan thought at first that this was addressed to his junior but then saw that the Australian was extending his hand to him. Mate? They had never met and Savage doubted he had even heard of him.

'Oh, you're talking to me?' Realising how pompous he must have sounded, he added, 'Actually I'm pretty well. Probably still a bit jet lagged. But thank you for enquiring.'

'My name's Graham Truckett. I'm with the DoJ.'

'The Department of Justice,' explained Dempsey.

'Yep, and I'm leading for the prosecution. I've just been landed with it. And this young lady is my junior, Pammy Lee.'

'Yes, I am Lee Sit-ming, Pammy.'

'Hello,' said Dempsey. 'I don't think we've met before.'

'No, I think that maybe we have not. I have not been in the Department for very long. But of course I have heard of you, Mr Ng. You are very well-known.'

'Don't call me Mr Ng. I am Ng Dim-si, so you should call me Dempsey, please. You must not be formal.'

Pammy lowered her eyes as if she had been rebuked.

'So,' said Jonathan to Truckett, 'you're the prosecution team, then.' He hoped that he sounded friendly, and was going to add that he did not yet know the first thing about the case, but thought better of it.

'Have you got an estimate for the length of the trial?' he asked, instead.

'Nope, mate. No yet. I haven't much idea about it yet. Have you?'

'No, not really.' Jonathan was unsure of the question he was answering. Best leave it at that.

'I think that I had better have a word with my instructing solicitors,' and he turned away, with Dempsey following him.

223

Brett O'Brien had lunched in the judges' dining room and, as a consequence, taken the narrow judicial lift to his chambers in a less than satisfied mood.

Henry was waiting for him.

'Good afternoon, my Lord. I have the papers for the bail application this afternoon. It concerns the famous Chan Wai-king.'

'Famous? I've not heard of him. Or her.'

'That is his Chinese name. You may know him as Lester Chan. He appears on television advertising his jewellery shops. He is, I think, a rude man.'

'Oh, I know who you mean. Always wears a bow tie. Sells flashy stuff.'

'Yes, my Lord. Do you remember last week I mention a case where the defence had a London QC? This is it. So, this afternoon it is the application for bail. The London QC is here.'

'Is that the case where there was a short mention on Friday morning?'

'Yes.'

'But I thought they said they weren't ready and that he had not yet been admitted for the trial.'

'It seems, my Lord, that events had move. And now he is here. But without his robes, so the Judiciary Administrator had said no need.'

'Hang on a moment, isn't it up to the judge to say whether or not robes are to be worn?'

'Yes. But robes are not worn in hearings in chambers. You do not, ever.'

'Well, is this hearing going to be in chambers?'

'Yes, but in the courtroom.'

Brett decided to pursue this no further. What difference did it make if it was in court or in chambers or in the public lavatory?

'So, I am to go into court in my ordinary suit and treat the hearing as if it is not in public?'

'My Lord is very wise,' replied Henry without betraying a flicker of what he meant.

'So, who is this QC?'

'He is from London. In England. In the UK.'

'What's his name?'

The judge's clerk glanced at the file.

'Is Mr Savage. Mr Jonathan Savage.'

'Never heard of him.'

'No, my Lord, this is his first case in Hong Kong.'

Oh God, thought O'Brien. Another one of these know-alls who thinks that this is some sort of backwoods jurisdiction and will persist in telling me how things are done in England.

'Who's for the prosecution?'

'Mr Truckett. Graham Truckett, from the Legal Department. I think he had been in cases in your court before, my Lord.'

'Is he being led?'

'No, he is the leader. He has a junior, Miss Lee. Also from the Department.'

'Yes, I know Truckett. In fact, I saw him socially yesterday.' He was not going to tell even the trusted Henry that he already knew that Truckett was in the case, or what he had heard. 'So, are they ready?'

'I think so. I will bring them into court. But you would like some time to look at the papers before?'

Using an expression he had heard so often, Brett replied: 'No need.'

The courtroom was surprisingly full when Henry banged on the door and led him in. For a bail hearing he would have expected just one lawyer from each side but there were four in the barristers' row: Graham Truckett and a very attractive young woman at one end; and a Chinese barrister, whom he recognised but whose name he could not recall, and a man in his mid-forties beside him who had to be the London silk at the other; and in the solicitors' row behind, a very smartly dressed Chinese next to another European. They all bowed to the judge, and he to them, and as they straightened up he saw that it was Frank Grinder. So this *was* the case that he had mentioned. He hoped that they hadn't talked about it; he was pretty sure they had not. He nodded in acknowledgment to Frank and indicated that they should all sit down.

A large group of Chinese was in the back two rows. Several were carrying umbrellas and one or two appeared to be holding plastic pots of instant noodles. An aroma of steamed chicken drifted towards him. O'Brien leaned down towards Henry who had taken his seat below the bench.

'Who are all these people?'

'I know only the lawyers, in the front,' Henry replied.

'Before this hearing starts,' O'Brien announced,' I want to know who is in court. This is a bail application and is, therefore, in private. No members of the public may be present and nor is the press allowed. There should be a notice to that effect outside.'

Henry stood up and turned towards him.

'My Lord, there is a notice. English and Chinese.'

'Mr Truckett, do you know who they are?'

'No idea.'

'Nothing to do with the prosecution?'

'Not as far as I know,' and he added, 'my Lord.'

'Who is for the defendant? Who is appearing for him in this application, then?'

Two men in the front row stood up. Then the *gweilo*, looking confused, sat down again.

'My Lord, I am Mr Ng and I would like to introduce my learned leader who has just been admitted to the Hong Kong Bar for this case. He is a famous QC from London.' And with a flourish as if announcing the winner of a ballroom dancing contest, he added, 'This, my Lord, is Mr Jonathan Savage QC.'

Jonathan realised he should do something, so stood.

'Good afternoon, my Lord.'

'Nice to meet you, Mr Savage,' said the judge. 'Right, that's enough chit-chat. Would you be good enough to answer my question?' That ought to show Mr Toffee Nose who's in charge.

'Certainly, if I can. But I can't recall what it is.'

'I asked who are all the people at the back of the court.'

'With respect, I don't think that your Lordship did ask us that question.'

'Well, I'm asking you now.'

'Personally, I have no idea. But I will take instructions.'

Jonathan bent towards his junior, who shrugged his answer. Billy Yeung leant forward and tapped and muttered something to Dempsey who whispered to Jonathan.

'My Lord,' said Jonathan, 'would you allow me a moment whilst my instructing solicitor tries to find out who they are? He does not recognise any of them.'

Billy stood and went to the back of the court. A lengthy, animated Cantonese discussion began and complaining voices rose in volume as Billy, backing away from the umbrellas, looked anxiously at the judge and returned to speak to Dempsey, who relayed what he said to Jonathan.

'My Lord, I can confirm, like my learned friend for the prosecution, they have nothing to do with the case or with the parties. Nobody from my team recognises them.'

'Well, who are they? What are they doing here?'

'With your Lordship's permission, I will take instructions again.' Jonathan turned back to Billy.

'Oh, for heaven's sake, let's not go through all that ritual again, Mr Savage,' said O'Brien. 'Your solicitor who just spoke to them, he can tell me himself.'

'Of course, my Lord. He is Mr Young.'

'I think you'll find it's not pronounced like that.' Perhaps he had gone far enough now in putting the silk down.

'Well, Mr Yeung?'

Billy got to his feet.

'Your Lordship, I have just spoken to them. None of them are friends of the client. They say they do not know who he is.'

'Thank you, Mr Yeung. Did they say what they are doing here? They seemed to be somewhat unhappy with you.'

'Yes, they were, my Lord.' Billy turned back to look at the back of the courtroom and was met with glares and muttering.

'They are a group of pensioners on a trip from Fairview Park in the New Territories. They say they are entitled to be here because they are citizens.'

'Have you explained to them that this is a hearing in chambers, not in open court?'

'I tried, but they don't seem to understand. I told them there was a notice outside, but they say that they don't understand English.'

'It's in Chinese as well.'

'They say that they didn't see the Chinese writing.'

'Well, they are not entitled to be here,' said the judge, firmly. 'And anyway, if they don't understand English what possible interest can they have in the proceedings?'

'Because,' replied Billy, 'they are not interested. It is raining outside and so they have come to the High Court to keep out of the wet. Thank you, my Lord.' He resumed his seat. Then he rose again.

'I told them, my Lord, that they must leave.'

'But they're still here. Did they not understand you?'

'Yes, my Lord, but they say that they will not take orders from a *yao*, from a jackal.'

'A jackal?'

'Yes, they were being impolite. You can say a dogsbody.' He sat down again.

'Thank you very much for your efforts, Mr Yeung.'

The judge looked towards the back of the court.

'I am told that you do not understand English,' he said in measured tone. 'My clerk will translate this: Get out, at once, and stay out. If you don't leave immediately, all of you, I will charge you with contempt of court and you will go to prison.'

Before Henry could utter a word, there was a scream and they all rushed for the doors.

'Looks like I'm not a jackal, then. That's good to know,' said O'Brien. 'So, it's your application, Mr Savage?'

'Yes, my client is applying for bail. He has been in custody since his arrest.'

'Right, Mr Savage, but before I hear from you, I would like to know what the case is about. I assume, as the application is in my court, that I will be trying the case, but I haven't yet received any substantial papers, only the papers for this bail hearing, so I don't know anything about it. So, Mr Truckett, over to you. Give me an outline of your case.'

Graham had turned and was speaking to Pammy; he was taken aback to hear his name. He stood up and tried to temporise; he had no idea what O'Brien had said.

'Well, Mr Truckett?' The judge had seen him talking to his junior and guessed that he hadn't been listening to him.

'Er, the prosecution's position is that we, um, oppose this.'

'This what?'

'This application.'

'What application?'

'Application for bail, your Lordship.'

'That's not what I was asking you.'

'I'm sorry, your Lord, I mean my Lordship, I was distracted.'

I bet you were, thought O'Brien. 'You should pay attention, Mr Truckett. After all, I'm not a jackal. You heard that, at least, I hope.'

'Yes,' lied Graham, perplexed.

'I asked you to give me a brief outline of your case. I need to know what this case involves before I can make any real sense of a bail application.'

'Oh, I see. Well, er, it's a letter of credit fraud.'

'I know that,' retorted the judge. 'That much is clear from the bail papers.'

'And, er, it involves frauds on banks.'

'Can you think of a letter of credit that doesn't involve a bank?'

'Er, I suppose not. And, er…' Graham was floundering.

'How many banks do you say were defrauded? Was it just one or are there several?'

'Er…' Graham turned quickly to his junior who signalled to him.

'Er…more than one, I think.'

'Is he charged alone or are you alleging a conspiracy?'

Graham looked through the papers that Pammy had given him before coming into court. He found the indictment.

'No, there's no-one else facing charges, just him alone, so it's not a conspiracy.' Pammy was tugging frantically at the bottom of his jacket. 'Excuse me a moment, your Lord… Oh, it seems that we are charging a conspiracy. The other people are all underlings…'

'Dogsbodies?' interjected the judge.

'Er yes.' What's he on about? 'They are all minor employees of the defendant and they have been named in the indictment as co-conspirators. But not charged.'

'Why is that?'

'Oh, I know that one. Because they have all agreed to give evidence for the prosecution. They are immunised witness.'

'Immunised against what? Bird flu?'

'No, your Lordship, they have been given immunities against prosecution if they give truthful evidence.'

'Well, now you have injected some useful information, Mr Truckett.' Brett thought that he had probably teased him long enough, but it was not good enough having counsel in such a state of ignorance appear before him. His junior seemed to know much more about it. Well, he would throw him an easy ball.

'Mr Truckett, as this is a bail hearing, one of the relevant factors is the gravity of the case, as you know. The length of prison sentence that a defendant is likely to be facing, if convicted of course, has a bearing on whether he is likely to remain in the jurisdiction if granted bail. So, what's the quantum? How much is he alleged to have defrauded? What was the risk to the bank?'

Graham turned back again. The pretty young woman said something which, plainly, he did not catch or follow. She wrote something on a piece of paper and passed it to him. He looked at it for a moment and faced the judge.

'Look, my Lord, I've only just come into the case, and I don't know much about it. As far as I can make out, there's a lot of money involved but I can't give you a precise figure at this stage. It's not the prosecution's application and I didn't think that I would have to give you a summary of the facts at this stage.'

O'Brien tried not to show his sympathy. He, too, when at the Bar had been thrust into court without time to prepare properly, but he could not encourage slackness, even from a decent sort of man like Graham.

'Mr Truckett, I think we are wasting time. The defendant is in custody and I am not prepared to adjourn the bail hearing in order to give you more time to study your papers. If this man merits being given bail I am not prepared to have him kept in custody a day longer than necessary. So, do you object to bail? I think you said earlier that the prosecution opposes bail.'

'Yes, my Lord, we do.'

'On what grounds?'

'Er, it is my learned friend's application. He should go first and then I can answer it. My Lordship,' he added.

'No, Mr Truckett, I am asking you. I have a pretty good idea what Mr Savage's argument will be. His junior – I assume that it was his junior – has drafted a fairly full written submission in support of the application.'

Dempsey half rose, and bowed.

'So I want to know what you have to say.'

'Well, there is a lot of money involved.'

'You've already said that. Is there a risk that he might abscond?'

'Yes.'

'Why?'

'Well, because he might not want to face his trial.'

'Not many people would choose to be tried for a criminal offence, I would imagine. What grounds do you have for saying that? Has he ever tried to jump bail before?'

Graham turned to Pammy.

'No.'

'Has he threatened or tried to interfere with any prosecution witness?'

'I don't think so.'

'Has he any previous convictions?'

Again he turned and saw her shake her head.

'Your junior has answered for you, Mr Truckett. Is it inevitable that, should he be convicted, he will be sentenced to a substantial term of imprisonment?'

'I can answer that one,' replied Graham with some relief. 'I've never known a conviction for fraud in this jurisdiction where that hasn't happened.'

'Would you say that the evidence in the case is so patently overwhelming that a conviction is practically inevitable so that he might as well serve part of his sentence whilst awaiting his trial? Well, Mr Truckett?'

'Er…'

'I thought you might say that,' said the judge.

'No, I haven't said it: I haven't yet had a chance to assess the strength of our case.'

'You misunderstand me. I guessed that you would say "er" in reply to my question.'

Graham paused for a moment.

'I don't know if I can help your Lordship further at this stage,' he concluded.

'I don't know if you have helped at all.' That was too hard. 'But thank you for trying, Mr Truckett. Now, Mr Savage, I've read the written application. Were the grounds drafted by your learned junior?'

Jonathan rose.

'Yes, my Lord. But with my approval.'

'And is there anything you want to add or elaborate on?'

'Only to stress that my client is of good character, that there is no suggestion, as you have heard very helpfully from my learned friend, that he has or will obstruct his trial, that he has several properties in Hong Kong including his own home and has none outside the jurisdiction, and therefore that there is no reason to believe that he will jump bail if he is given it.'

'Thank you, Mr Savage.' He may, thought O'Brien, be a flowery London silk but at least he kept it brief. And he's right.

'The application is granted. Bail will be allowed. The sum will be one million Hong Kong dollars. There must be two sureties acceptable to the prosecution. I give the defendant until the end of the day to provide their names to the police; and the prosecution until noon tomorrow to vet them. Failing any sensible objection to them, he will be then be released on the usual conditions, and in addition he must report daily to a police station, the location of which to be agreed between the parties.'

Mr Justice O'Brien stood up, bowed briskly to the hurriedly standing lawyers and swiftly left the courtroom in a manner which he hoped would demonstrate his effectiveness.

Graham went over to his opponent.

'Well done, mate,' he said. 'Bit of a shock, that.'

'Thanks,' replied Jonathan. 'I'm sorry he was a bit unpleasant to you. Is he always like that? Have you had problems with him before?'

'No, I get on well with him, at least out of court. I think he was trying to show he's the boss. But no worries.' He gathered up his papers and left with Pammy.

Dempsey and Billy Yeung spoke to each other briefly in Cantonese.

'Client will be very, very pleased,' Billy said to Jonathan. 'He will also be very pleased with me for retaining such a powerful London silk. I told him already that you were my choice to have.'

Jonathan's smile was self-deprecating, justifiably so as he knew very well that he was only here because of Gresham Nutworthy's claret-induced unavailability.

'*Wah*,' said Dempsey. 'That was brilliant. You persuaded the judge so fast.'

'But it was your written grounds that did the trick, Dempsey. You heard him say that he had read them, and he acknowledged your work.' Jonathan was glowing, both because of the compliments and result of the hearing.

'No, he may have read them, but it was what you added that won it for us.' Dempsey was grinning but Jonathan could see a shadow on Billy's face.

'As I said, client will be very pleased,' he said. 'But maybe I am not so happy.'

Jonathan was taken aback. 'Why so?' he asked.

'Because now I will have no evening to myself. Client will call me on the phone or expect me to have dinner with him. It is safer with him in Stanley.'

Frank Grinder came round from the solicitors' row.

'Well, I think that was a very impressive performance, Mr Savage. The judge seemed to appreciate your style. Not that I know the first thing about criminal work – actually, this is the first bail application that I've seen – but it all looked very good to me. Look, I know you're probably still a bit jet lagged and might want an early night, but do you think you might fancy an early drink this evening? I'll come round to your hotel.'

陳

Henry followed his judge along the corridor and back into his room.

'So, is there anything that you want?' he asked. 'Maybe I can go now. No other work for you today and I had ask the listing office if you can take something from another judge but they say not so. So you not need me. They also say that tomorrow's list was not yet ready and I told them that you would probably go home and come back in the morning and look at the paper then. I hope that I had done right.'

'You certainly did, Henry. I really don't like hanging around for goodness knows how long just to glance through papers when, as often as not, the case turns out to be a non-starter.' Brett was already thinking about dropping into Wilson's Wines in Pacific Place; somebody had mentioned that they had a sale on for Australian wines.

'So I go now, my Lord, because you don't need me anymore?'

'Hang on, Henry. Just for a moment. Look, give me your honest opinion. Was I a bit hard on Graham Truckett, on the prosecutor?'

Henry contemplated the question.

'Because you mean that he should have won?'

'No, I meant was I a bit unfair to him?'

'By making him lose?'

'No, was I a bit short with him?'

'No, you were as long as you are always.'

'Henry, are you being deliberately obtuse?'

'That is a word I must go and look up. How do you spell it, please?'

'I am asking you for your opinion, Henry. Do you think I was ruder to Truckett than I should have been?'

'When?'

'You know when.'

'When you scolded him?'

'Yes,' said Brett. 'When I scolded him.'

'Because you want me to say whether I had thought that he deserve it?'

'Good way of putting it, Henry. Did he deserve to be spoken to like I did?'

The clerk appeared to consider the question.

'But you are the judge.'

'Yes, I know that. That is why I am sitting at my desk in this room.'

'Then, you must judge.'

'Henry, are you going to answer my question?'

'Because you are a very good judge and I think that you always make the correct decision.' Henry's face revealed nothing. 'I am just your clerk. You know better than me.'

'So, are you saying, in your circumspect way, that you think I was right?'

'That is another word that I must look up.'

'Were you trying to tell me that you agreed with how I treated him?'

'No, my Lord.'

'Well, thank you for being frank. So you think I was wrong?'

'No.'

'Henry, is it Monday today?'

'If you say so,' was Henry's response.

'Alright, I think I've got my answer, or not, as the case may be. It's no good, is it, asking you if I made the right decision in granting this man his bail?'

'Not worth, because you always make the right decision. I will go now and look at the dictionary.'

'Thanks for your help, Henry. I suppose that if I've made the wrong decision and he does a runner, it will save the Hong Kong taxpayer the cost of his trial. And, for me, the trouble of trying the case.'

'I will see you tomorrow,' said Henry.

18

Jonathan realised, with some surprise, that he was very much looking forward to meeting Frank Grinder again. They had hardly spoken to each other in the afternoon at court; indeed, apart from the formal exchanges of introduction, he wasn't at all sure that they had said anything at all until just before Frank had suggested that they have a drink together. Jonathan knew nothing about him and yet he found himself hoping that it would be just the two of them – no junior, no-one else from the solicitors' firm. He wondered what the form was, whether he should change into more casual clothes, and decided that a quick wash and putting his suit jacket back on would probably be best.

He was already sitting there, a tumbler of whisky and clinking ice cubes in front of him, when Jonathan came down to the lobby bar of the Majestic Harbour Hotel. Jonathan saw that he had been right: he was wearing a dark suit and tie, as were all the men at the other tables. Hong Kong was evidently a place of after-work formal dress. Frank half-rose in greeting and thought how tired Jonathan looked.

'How's the jet lag?' Frank asked. 'I'm sorry, I should have thought that you might still be suffering. It used to take me ages to get over it when I came out eastwards. You do begin to acclimatise yourself to it, eventually, but even then I used to get quite knocked out by it, particularly when I had to get straight to work, like you must have done. Are you sure you want to do this? Do say if you would rather we called it off.'

'No, not at all,' said Jonathan warmly. 'You're right, of course, I am feeling unusually tired after today's exertions, but I can't think of anything I would rather do just now than have a drink with you.'

Frank smiled. 'That's very flattering, but I know what you mean, I think. You want to be off-duty and the best way to do it is with another *gweilo*, another Brit. Or an Aussie or a Kiwi. Not with a Chinese.'

Jonathan was taken aback. He had not suspected such blatant racialism still to exist in Hong Kong. Had he made a mistake in so quickly taking up the suggestion for an evening drink? Perhaps the worst of colonial attitudes persisted and they might even be the norm, but he resented the implication that he would share them, that Grinder could say a thing like that and assume that it would be acceptable. He did not want to start off on the wrong foot, as they were going to have to work together, but nor could his sense of principle and pride allow it to pass. He measured his response. He was going to avoid unpleasantness, if he could.

'I am afraid you've got me a bit wrong, Mr Grinder,' he said as he sat down. 'Of course, I'm unfamiliar with how things work here. This is the first time that I've been to Hong Kong. In fact, it's my first time in the Far East. But I have to say that I am not a racist, and I don't differentiate people because of the colour of their skin. That's not simply a matter of principle with me; I also think that it is illogical to regard one racial group as inferior or superior to another. I am sorry if I offend you, but I have to say what I believe and…'

'What are you talking about?' interrupted Frank. 'Do you think that I'm a racist? For God's sake, my wife is Hong Kong Chinese. My in-laws are Chinese and live here. How can you think that I'm a racist?'

'But I thought from what you just said…'

Frank smiled. 'I'm sorry,' he said. 'Yes, I was forgetting that you are not used to Hong Kong. Look, I love my wife dearly – I'm not sure I can say that about all her family – I really do, and I have no sense of superiority other than that Hong Kong Chinese people often seem a damn sight cleverer than me, but even with Winnie, my wife, it can sometimes be a strain talking to people whose first language is not English. You're never quite certain that they've picked up the nuances of what you're saying, or realise when you are joking. When you've spent the whole working day with people whose English, excellent though it may be, is not quite the same as ours, even ever so slightly, it comes as a relief and a relaxation to be in the company of our own kind. It's not a racial thing: it would be the same if they were German, say, or French. In fact, I sometimes feel the same way with some Americans; I can't always understand what they mean or be sure that they entirely follow what I am saying. It's not the same with Antipodeans, though: they do speak the same language as us. So, I hope that that's cleared the air.'

'It certainly has,' said Jonathan, leaning across the table to shake Frank's hand. 'I'm sorry I got the wrong end of the stick. You must have found my little diatribe somewhat insulting. I apologise. Perhaps you should put it down to tiredness.'

'Forget it,' said Frank. 'But I have a question for you.'

Jonathan was, at the same time, relieved and apprehensive.

'Yes, what is it?'

'It's an important question and I think we should get it out of the way before we go any further.'

'OK.'

'Well, we are going to be working together for what might be a long time once this case gets started and I think it's essential that we get this right from the outset.'

'Well, don't keep me in suspense. What do you want to know?'

'Simply this,' replied Frank. 'What would you like to drink?'

'Oh, that. Thank you. I'll have the same as you, if that's whisky you're drinking.'

'It is, and we are going to get along very well,' said Frank as he beckoned to a waiter.

Jonathan took in the surroundings. As well as the discreetly separated tables like the one at which he sat, there was, to one side of the lounge, a semi-circular bar with high stools on which a few suited men, mostly European, were sitting. On the other side of the polished redwood counter, three beautiful young women, dressed in what he had come to recognise was the hotel's purple and black uniform, were pouring drinks and setting them out on trays. The waiter returned, noiselessly, and set a tumbler of Scotch on the rocks in front him and, almost simultaneously, replaced the half-full dish of nuts.

'I should be careful of those,' Frank warned him. 'They've got a kick like a mule if you're not used to them, or even if you are. And I don't suppose you are.'

Jonathan was feeling very relaxed. It was true, although he had not been conscious of it until it had just been pointed out to him, that in talking to Dempsey and Billy Yeung and Chan, the client, and even the hotel staff, there had been an underlying strain, an anxiousness not to misunderstand or be misunderstood. Perhaps a certain deliberation in the way he spoke, even though it was apparent that the two lawyers at least had excellent English. And another thing that he was aware of that was different with Frank Grinder: there was no element of flattery. Certainly, he'd been complimentary at the end of the hearing, but in a straightforward way and not in that overly respectful manner which, pleasant as it was to receive, had at the same time brought to mind the Emperor's New Clothes. It really was soothing to talk to someone on a level of informal equality. He took a sip, which became a gulp, of whisky, recognising at the same time how dry-mouthed he was.

'This is very nice,' he said. 'What is it?'

'It's just Black Label. Johnny Walker. Very popular here. I'm glad you like it. I did wonder whether a London silk like you would have preferred a Blue Label.'

'I've never heard of it.'

'Well, you can try it if you like but it costs over three hundred and twenty-five dollars Hong Kong a single shot in this place, so you're welcome to pay for it if you want one.'

'That's, what, about thirty pounds? For a glass?'

'Just about, maybe a little more.'

'I think I'll pass on that. This is plenty good enough for me – thank you, by the way.'

'It's my pleasure.'

The alcohol was beginning to take effect.

'And by the way, I may be a silk,' Jonathan added, 'but I'm a criminal practitioner in England. Most of my work is either legal aided defence or prosecution. Very few private cases, and there's not much money in publicly funded work. So I'm not used to drinks at that sort of price, nor business class air travel nor staying in hotels like this. I have to account for VAT and pay my very big chambers' expenses on what I earn, and there are other professional expenses like travelling and subscriptions to legal journals and so on, and then getting taxed at forty per cent on what's left. So all this is quite new to me. I don't suppose I should have told you that. Perhaps I should have kept up the pretence that I am a big-shot QC with a huge international practice. And thanks again for the drink; it's certainly making me feel comfortable at last.'

'No, I rather assumed that this was your first overseas case.'

Jonathan was taken aback. He had thought that the bail hearing had gone well, and the judge had certainly treated him with respect, in contrast to the way he had behaved towards what's his name, Trickett or something; and Grinder hadn't been at the conference with the client in that prison on Saturday morning, for if he had he would have seen how firmly he had dealt with him.

'I know that I just told you that this is my first case in Hong Kong, but how did you know that I didn't have an international practice?'

Frank took a sip of his drink and considered how best to put it.

'Well, for a start, I had never heard of you before I became involved in this case. A lot of the leading English criminal silks have been instructed in trials in Hong Kong, although, with the growth of the local Bar, it was already becoming more and more difficult to get one admitted while I was still in practice over here; but I did know the names of the ones who came out fairly regularly, as the local papers take a keen interest in the big trials. So when Billy Yeung told me he had a London silk and gave me your name, I looked you up. These websites that barristers' chambers put out have their disadvantages for you, you know.'

'Really?'

'Yes, because they say quite a lot about you, all the big cases that you've been in and your areas of practice and so on.'

'Yes, I know.'

'But they also show what you haven't achieved. I can't believe that the chambers of any silk who has been in big cases abroad wouldn't say as much on the website, or brochure.'

'Oh, I see,' said Jonathan, a touch crestfallen in spite of the whisky.

'So, that's why I know that you haven't been in any major fraud trials outside England.' And then Frank added, 'Or, for that matter, inside England.'

'I have been in fraud trials. It says so on the website, I'm pretty sure.'

'Yes, but I suspect none so big that I would have heard of them, I think.'

Jonathan was beginning to lose the inner glow he had been feeling earlier. He stared at his glass and saw that it was empty.

'Would you like a refill?' he asked Frank and he signalled to the waiter.

'Yes, thank you. But look, I'm not trying to undermine you. I have no doubt that you are bloody good and your performance in court this afternoon was very impressive. And I wouldn't dream of letting on to anyone else: everyone has to start somewhere.'

'Right,' Jonathan said, not entirely sure what this was leading up to.

'No, I wouldn't dream of it. But there is something of a trade-off.'

'What do you mean?'

'Well, I shouldn't be acting in this case. I am retired, or at least I thought I was. I used to be Billy Yeung's partner. The firm used to be Chan, Yeung, Grinder & Lam back then. I retired a while ago and went to live in Cheltenham. I only came out here because my wife wanted to visit her family. I won't go into detail, but somehow or other I found myself dragged into it as a replacement for Charlie Munsonby whose case it was. He died suddenly and Billy wanted me to take over. Apparently he has had me readmitted as a solicitor here because he thinks that's what Chan, the client, wants. But I don't know the first thing about criminal law; I was a commercial lawyer. I have never been involved in a criminal trial before, let alone a complex banking fraud. So this is going to be a first for both of us. But I would appreciate it if you didn't let the client know that I am a complete innocent in this type of thing. Also, I hope you will understand if I don't provide the sort of back-up that you would expect from your instructing solicitor. I'll do my best for you, but I can't help feeling

247

that, astonishing though it may seem when you look at me, my role in this case is largely cosmetic.'

Jonathan's relief was multi-faceted. Here was someone to whom he could turn, who knew how things worked in Hong Kong, but who nevertheless shared his inexperience. He had a rather avuncular manner which contrasted with the admiration that he had expressed in what seemed to be genuine approval of the way he had performed in court. He was a reassuring presence to have in the case. And clearly he would respect Jonathan's confidence.

'So, look,' he said, 'what am I supposed to do now? I'd quite like to get back to England and start reading the case papers.'

Before Frank could reply, a phone rang somewhere nearby. Frank reached into his jacket pocket and nodded to Jonathan.

'It's mine,' he said. 'Yes, it is. Yes. No. No. OK. Yes. What time? I think so. No. Not yet. No need. He's with me. I'll tell him. At the Majestic Harbour. OK, just assume we'll be there unless I tell you otherwise. No, no, don't come here. We're only having a quick drink. No, really, Billy, don't come here. I think he's tired and wants an early supper on his own.'

He winked across the table.

'No. Billy, don't worry, I'll tell him. No, there's no need for you to come over and tell him yourself. I'll do it. See you tomorrow.'

A sense of inevitability came over Jonathan. He had picked up enough of the one-sided conversation to understand that his early return home was under threat. He looked around the bar, vibrant with conversation, and now, with the music of a Filipino trio starting up, he realised how much he would have liked to have stayed here for an hour or so, perhaps some of it still in Grinder's company, and then perhaps a room service supper and an early night.

'Yes, I'm sure,' continued Frank. 'I'm absolutely positive. No, take my word for it, Billy, he won't thank you for it. No, really. Tomorrow, yes. Goodbye.'

Jonathan hoped that his sigh had not been audible.

'Something's up, I assume.'

'Yes,' said Frank. 'Unfortunately, Billy Yeung and Dempsey Ng went straight to Stanley after the hearing. They've told Lester Chan that he will be out at midday tomorrow. Chan wants to have a case conference at your junior's chambers tomorrow and it's been arranged for two thirty. He wants to go through the evidence against him. And then he wants us all to join him for dinner tomorrow night.'

'And there's no way of getting out of it, I suppose.'

'I don't think so. You have to bear in mind that the concept of "face" is very important to the Chinese. If you were to decline an invitation to dinner when your host knows that you are available, that would cause him a great loss of *faysee* and it would, inevitably, sour relations between you.'

'No, I'm not thinking about the dinner. I am just wondering what use there would be in my having a conference when I don't know the first thing about the case, other than what Dempsey ran through with me the other day when I was jet lagged which I have already forgotten, if I took it in at all in the first place. I can't see what it would do except expose my ignorance of the facts of the case.'

'I can see that,' Frank replied. 'But don't forget, I'm in the same boat.'

Jonathan thought for a while. In addition to wanting to go back to England to read the prosecution evidence against Chan and whatever explanation the client had put together by way of a defence to the allegations, he also wanted to have a chance to do some research and find out what, exactly, a letter of credit was, and to look up what most of the unfamiliar commercial terms, with which Dempsey had bombarded him in the park on Saturday morning, actually meant. Should he tell him that? Grinder would, at least, know all about banking practice and would have that advantage over him. He seemed to be a decent and sympathetic chap; he had conceded that this was his first major overseas case, so could he also tell him that he was, for the moment at least, in undiscovered territory? Perhaps Frank could help him with an explanation of the terminology. Or would that be going too far?

'Oh well,' he said after a moment, 'there's nothing for it. I'll just have to make it clear that I simply have not had a chance to read the case papers and that I'll need to get back to London to start working on them.' He decided not to add any more.

'Fair enough,' said Frank. 'Let's have one more drink and then I'll leave you and get back to my wife. I should think that you would appreciate a quiet evening on your own. Would you like me to collect you from the hotel tomorrow and take you to your junior's chambers?'

'No, I know the way. I've been there and I'm sure I can find it again. But thanks. And thank you for your support.'

19

The air-conditioning in Dempsey's chambers was set so low that it hit Jonathan like a cold wind as soon as the receptionist buzzed him into the lobby. The shelves of law reports and slightly shabby textbooks lining the walls and the cartoons of late nineteenth-century English legal personalities were all familiar enough, but they were curiously out of place in this steel and tinted-glass tower and in this bone-chilling temperature. He thought of the comfortable fug of his own chambers in London.

'So, Mr Savage,' she smiled brightly. 'They already all are here. In the conference room. I tell Ng *Sin-san* that you had come back.' She spoke into her phone. 'So, please sit down.'

Before Jonathan could do so, Dempsey appeared from along the corridor, both his smile and his suit immaculate.

'Hello, Jonathan. We are all here. In the conference room. My room isn't big enough, as you saw yesterday.'

Jonathan glanced at his watch. 'I'm sorry; I hope I haven't kept you waiting. I thought I was told that it was for two-thirty. Was I wrong?'

'No, no. Client and Billy Yeung have been here since client got here after he was released from Stanley. So we could talk and he could explain more about his papers. Mr Grinder had only just arrived.'

Jonathan felt a slight frisson. Were the Westerners on the team being treated differently?

'I would have been happier to come earlier, if I had known,' he said. 'I was available. You should have called me rather than keeping Mr Chan waiting.'

'No, that is not how we would do it. There were things that Billy Yeung and client wanted to discuss just with me.'

'Well, I appreciate that at this early stage there will be matters of detail that I haven't had time to take in yet but...'

'Not detail. Chan Wai-king wanted to talk about my fees. He thinks it would be impolite to do it in your presence.'

'Oh,' said a relieved Jonathan. 'I hope that it was resolved to your satisfaction.' But he could not help wondering whether that was the only matter that was not discussed in his presence.

The conference room was, if anything, even colder than the reception area. Sitting at the brushed metal and leather table were Frank Grinder and Billy Yeung, with Lester Chan at the head. Dempsey indicated the chair at the other end and sat down next to the client. Jonathan took his seat, wondering whether Chan had been home to change or whether the perfectly cut suit he was wearing had been kept for him in the prison. He waited, until he realised they were all expecting him to say something.

'Oh, it's very good to see you again, Mr Chan. So much more convenient and, er, comfortable than when we last met.'

'Yes, and it is all thanks to you, Jonathan, er, Mr Savage. You had done a very good job for the bail application. Billy told me you were brilliant. I told him he had been very good solicitor to choose you.'

'Yes, well, thank you. I am very glad to see you here.'

'So, now you have had a chance to read the papers?'

'Well, no, not really. I mean, I know a bit more about the case than when we last met, on Saturday. But I can't say that I am completely familiar with it yet. There's a lot of reading to be done. That's why, as soon as I can, I want to get back to London where I can devote myself to studying the papers.'

Chan's expression gave nothing away. If he was disappointed, he did not show it.

'That's right,' interposed Billy Yeung. 'And Mr Savage had been very busy preparing for your bail application.'

Frank thought that he should add something. He nodded sagely. 'A lot of work,' he said, 'which got the right result.'

'But I think that WK would like to discuss some of the case with you now,' said Dempsey. 'He told me earlier that there are things he wants to tell you.'

Jonathan suppressed a sigh. Although it was now Tuesday afternoon and he had been in Hong Kong since Friday evening he was still not right; waves of tiredness came at him unexpectedly and the cold in the room was doing nothing to waken him, on the contrary it was making him more aware of how uncomfortable he was. He noticed that some of the sheets of paper on the table in front of Chan fluttered in the draught of the fan. He opened his briefcase and took out an A4 writing pad.

'OK,' he said, 'what do you want to tell me? Don't go too fast and I'll make a note.'

'Well,' said Chan Wai-king, 'you know that the Department of Justice say that when I entered into the letter of credits I had nothing to back them. But that is not so.'

Dempsey Ng interrupted, 'The Prosecution's case is that there were no underlying transactions to support the applications for letters of credit; that there were no genuine goods being traded.'

'Yes, that's what I would imagine they would say. That's the usual basis for a letter of credit fraud case.' Jonathan assumed that that was a fairly safe observation to make. From the nods of agreement round the table he seemed to be right.

'So,' continued Chan, 'they are not so. They are wrong. You know the transaction which started with the Wing Bahn Bank? The one where the corresponding bank was Hanoi Commercial?'

'Er, go on.'

'Because, if you pronounce *wing bahn* in one way it can mean "always stupid". And that is right because the bank is very, very silly in this case.'

'And?'

'Well, the prosecution says that it was not about real goods. And it is right that the documents says the goods were rolled steel joists and there were not any. But there were goods. They were pig iron. It is just that they were wrongly described. So the bank is foolish when it told the police that there were not any goods.'

'Was that a clerical error, do you say?'

'Sorry, what do you mean?'

'Was it just a mistake?'

'No, no, it was not a mistake. We put down rolled steel joists on the papers on purpose. So that is my defence.'

'I'm sorry. I'm not quite following you.'

'In what way?' Chan's smile was unchanging.

'Why did you put down one thing when you meant another?'

'Because it is illegal, you see.'

'So, how is that a defence?'

'Because we cannot say that the goods were pig iron. It is illegal to import it into Vietnam. So we say they were something else.'

'But why steel joists?'

'Because we must write something.'

'But I imagine that the prosecution might say that you are making this explanation up. I am sorry to be harsh, but it is better to face the reality of what their case will be.'

A dawn of understanding was coming up: was the prosecution case likely to be that there was some kind of banking transaction whereby the client had got his hands on the bank's money on the basis of dishonestly claiming that there was some kind of deal involving commodities which did not, in fact, exist?

'Yes, I understand. But the goods did exist. Just not the ones that we said.'

'So, where are the goods? The pig iron.'

'They were at the dockside at Quang Ninh Port. In North Vietnam.'

'So if we ask the prosecution to make enquiries of the Vietnamese port authorities they should be able to be traced.'

'Not so.'

'Why not?'

'Because, they had been stolen. That is why I could not repay.'

Jonathan paused and made a scribbled note of what he thought Chan had told him. Chan waited for him to finish.

'And the charge where they say that I defraud the Dah Hing Commercial Bank and the Wing Seng Bank. You remember, that was over pork bellies.'

'No,' said Jonathan, 'I can't say that I recall it.'

'Well, anyway, that was a mistake.'

'What, you mean that the goods were described as something else by mistake?'

'No, the bank had made a mistake. That was not one of my companies. The Constantbight Commercial Trading and Good Fortune Company was the one that had done the deal.'

'And that's not yours?'

'No, mine is Constant*bright* Commercial Trading and Good Fortune Company.'

'Sorry, that sounds just the same.'

'No, not the same. No "r". That is my defence: no "r".'

Jonathan made a note of that. His fingers were turning numb.

Dempsey turned to Chan and said something in Cantonese. Chan raised his voice and then there followed what appeared to be a three-way heated conversation between them and Billy Yeung. Frank Grinder looked at Jonathan and barely perceptibly, rolled his eyes. The heavily-accented terms "advisory note", "trust receipt", "floating guarantee", "porcelain insulators", "bills of lading", "back-to-back letter" bubbled to the surface. Then it stopped abruptly.

'I am sorry,' said Dempsey. 'I tried to explain that you haven't had time to read all the papers and you can't yet know what he's talking about. So has Yeung Chi-hang. He won't listen.'

'Mr Chan,' said Jonathan, 'Mr Ng and Mr Yeung are right. I promise you that when I come back to Hong Kong I will have got to grips with the papers but, for the moment, what you are telling me is pretty meaningless. I hope you understand.'

'Yes, I do,' replied Chan Wai-king. 'But I just tell you two more pieces of thing. If that is OK for you.'

'Yes, please do.' He really was too cold to write anything and hoped that Chan would not take it as a sign of being unwilling to listen.

'So, the porcelain insulators. You know, where the Dah Hing Bank was for the beneficiary. That was a fraud.'

'What? Are you admitting it? Are you going to plead guilty to that?'

'No, I plead not guilty.'

'How can you? If you admit that you are guilty then I can't defend you on the basis that you are not.'

'No, I am not guilty. I didn't do it. It was a fraud committed by my office manager. He was trying to get some money.'

'For himself?'

'No, for my company.'

Jonathan looked down at the writing pad. 'For Constantbight, I mean, Constantbright?'

'No, different company. Constantlight Commercial Trading and Good Fortune Company.'

'So it was for the benefit of one of your companies.'

'Yes, but I did not know that he had done this. Not till afterwards.'

'Yes, I see,' lied Jonathan.

'And the Wing Seng Bank. That was the one about the timber. So, maybe I didn't sell any timber but my company did have a deal.'

'Was this a Constantbright company?' Jonathan didn't know why he had asked.

'No, no, this was Spanish Jewellery and Watches Company. They sold to Christian Channel Fashion Goods Manufacturing Company.'

'Which one was your company?'

'Both of them.'

'Well, why was a jewellery company selling timber to a clothing company? You did say timber, didn't you?'

'Yes, I said timber but it was not timber. It was cement. Fifteen thousand bags of cement. So it was there; it wasn't a fraud.'

'Mr Chan, I am sorry, I appear to be getting a bit confused. I explained to you that I haven't yet read the papers. What did the documents describe the goods as being?'

'The bills of sale said they were timber.'

'Was there any timber?'

'No, we are jewellery traders. My companies are not timber merchants.'

'I see, so why were the goods described as timber?'

'Yes, the documents said they were cured timber planks. And also some joists.'

'But why did they say that?'

'Oh, because I am not the only jewellery dealer in Hong Kong. Just one of the biggest. Also watches.'

Chan sat back and folded his arms. He appeared to think that he had answered Jonathan's question sufficiently.

'Look, I'm sorry, Mr Chan. I am not following this. What has your being in a big way in the jewellery business got to do with the wrong description being given to the goods?'

'Because it is quite easy. I did not want my jewellery competitors to learn that I am diversifying.'

'So, therefore, you described a large quantity of cement as a consignment of timber?' asked Jonathan, bewildered. 'Even though there never was any timber?'

'Ah, you are a very clever man. You already understand. Ng Dim-si told me how quickly you had pick up the case when he explain about it in the park,' and he smiled at Dempsey.

'And can I tell you about one more?' he continued.

'Yes, of course.'

'Well, you know the charge relating to those advisory notes that said gold bracelets imported to Hong Kong from Thailand?'

'Well, I haven't read about them yet, as I told you. But they sound more like your line of business.' Jonathan was not entirely sure why he had said that, other than to try to intimate that he had some idea of what Chan was talking about. He wished that he would finish soon; the cold was making him feel terrible. It was odd that none of the others seemed to be troubled by it.

'Why do you say that?' asked Chan.

'Because I thought you were in the jewellery trade. Did I mishear or misunderstand?'

'No, no. I am the Hong Kong jewellery king.'

'Well…Oh, never mind. Just carry on with what you were telling me.'

'So, the gold bracelets. I don't know if they exist or not.'

'Sorry, do you mean that you don't now or that you didn't know at the time?'

'At the time of what?'

'At the time of whatever it was you did that you are alleged to have done.'

'But I did not.'

'Did not know or did not do?'

'Did not do what?'

This is hopeless, Jonathan thought. He was getting to the stage where he would have to ask for the air-conditioning to be turned off or to bring the conference to a close; and he was now losing every vestige of what the still smiling client was trying to explain to him.

'Mr Chan, I shouldn't have interrupted you. What do you want to tell me about the bracelets.'

'It is very simple. I did not involve myself in the transaction. I had nothing to do with it. It was just that my company's name was used.'

'Was this a Constantbright Company?' Jonathan asked, in spite of himself.

'No, it was a different company. It was…'

'Perhaps you can give me the name later.'

'Yes, I give it later.'

And then Frank Grinder intervened.

'Mr Chan,' he said, 'I know that I've not yet had a proper chance to talk to you. I would have liked to have come to the meeting in Stanley on Saturday but, of course, can well understand your reason for not wanting four lawyers there at the same time.' Although that didn't seem to apply today, he reflected. 'But I would like to say something at this stage.'

If Billy Yeung and Dempsey Ng were surprised by this intervention, they gave nothing away.

'If you don't mind,' Frank added.

'No,' replied Chan. 'You are a senior *gweilo* solicitor, so anything you say would be good.'

'I'm not sure about that,' said Frank, 'but I think I can make a useful contribution.'

'It will be good, I know that,' said Chan.

'Well,' continued Frank, 'Mr Savage has told you that he has not had a chance to go through the papers in the case. How could he have done? He has just been admitted to the Hong Kong Bar and has been in Hong Kong for only a few days. He is a very well-known London QC and has already shown in court here how good he is; but even he could not possibly have got to grips with the documents and the witness statements.

'So,' he continued, 'I think that we are probably wasting his time, and your time, by going through the details before he has read them. Do you follow what I am saying?'

'Yes.'

'And also, I think he is probably still very tired. I know that it sometimes takes me a week before I can concentrate on work properly after a long flight, particularly coming eastward.'

'So long?' asked Chan.

'Yes. Maybe it is worse for us *gweilo*, I don't know. But I will tell you something else: I am used to Hong Kong, but I am finding it freezing in here. Mr Savage is not used to this sort of air-conditioning, I would imagine, so it must be even worse for him.'

'But he has said nothing about it,' objected Dempsey.

'No, and I haven't either until now because I was being polite. But what I am trying to get to is that I think that we should call it a day, that is, end the conference now.'

Jonathan tried to keep an even expression on his face, even though he could easily have hugged Frank. Billy Yeung and Dempsey spoke to each other in Cantonese. Then Billy said, 'I think you are right, Frank.'

They all looked at Jonathan, waiting for him to comment.

'I must admit that I am having some difficulty taking all this in. I probably am still tired. What do you think about our stopping now, Mr Chan?'

'I think it more better that we stop,' he replied. 'I want you to be rested. We have a big night tonight. I take you all to one of my favourite *jau-ka*.'

'Restaurant,' explained Dempsey.

'So we meet at seven,' said Chan Wai-king. 'You will collect our QC from his hotel, Ng Dim-si.'

Was that a request or a command? Jonathan wondered.

'I will take you, Frank,' said Billy.

'Why don't the four of us meet in the lobby of the Majestic Harbour,' said Frank, 'and then we can all go in a taxi.'

'No,' said Dempsey. 'My driver will take us. But let's meet at the hotel. Say, six-thirty.'

This brings back memories, thought Frank, as the car sped along the Island Corridor. The sudden night had already fallen and the illuminations on the high-rise buildings of Tsim Sha Tsui and Hung Hom glittered across the black water. He knew they were going to a fish restaurant somewhere in Lei Yue Mun, that erstwhile fishing village which lay on the narrowest point of the channel separating Hong Kong Island from the Kowloon Peninsula and which had already grown its own crop of towers and turned countryside into car parks long before he had left, but which one it was he had no idea. Winnie would have loved it if she had been permitted to join them, but he knew better than to ask if he could bring her along; men like Lester Chan preferred to dine in all male company if there was the slightest suggestion that business might be involved.

They were now at the entrance to the Easter Harbour Tunnel. The car joined the auto toll lane and eased into the lines of vehicles as they descended smoothly into the brightly-lit passage under the water. Dempsey, sitting beside the driver, turned back.

'You're used to this, Frank, I know, but have you ever seen a tunnel like this, Jonathan? It's pretty impressive, isn't it?'

'Nothing quite like this, no.'

'There used to be only one across the harbour. We've now got three of them.' Dempsey's pride was evident. 'Before that there were only the ferries, and if there was a strong wind nobody could get to work. Or back from work, and had to spend the night in the office.'

'That must have been unpleasant,' said Jonathan.

'Not necessarily,' Dempsey replied. 'A lot of babies were made that way. Now there are the cross-harbour tunnels and a lot of other tunnels and bridges, as you saw coming from the airport. A lot of it was completed around the time of the handover. So now, unless it's a major typhoon, everyone can get home. Not so much fun, I think.'

In a minute or so they were on the upward slope out of the tunnel and onto a dual carriageway, with the dark wavelets now on the right and occasional open spaces on the left. A sign pointed to Junk Bay Permanent Chinese Cemetery; Frank saw that Jonathan was staring at it as it slid past, and he wondered whether to explain it or to let him believe that resurrectionists might be at large in Hong Kong, and decided against saying anything that might cause offence in the front of the car, when Dempsey turned back again.

'Did you see that sign to the cemetery?'

'Yes, I did, and I was a bit puzzled by it,' Jonathan replied. 'Are there non-permanent cemeteries?'

'Yes, indeed there are,' said Dempsey. 'There is a great shortage of space for burials in Hong Kong and so there is a waiting list. In the meantime, bodies and ashes are kept in temporary resting places and even stored in funeral parlours. The way our ancestors are treated is very important to us Chinese. You can't just bury them anywhere; it must be somewhere propitious, preferably facing the sea and at a place with good *feng shui* – you have heard that expression? It means wind and water – and Junk Bay is a very good place. If you go out to the island of Cheung Chau there are lots of burial places there too; it's very famous for it. But there are seven million people in Hong Kong so there must be a queue and it's getting longer. The government keeps saying that it's going to do something about it, but I don't know what. We are very superstitious about things like that. But it's also not good to talk about death when we are going to a special dinner to celebrate WK's bail. Look, we're almost there.'

They had come off an elevated stretch of the road and, although there were still high-rises close by, there were some patches of trees and shrubs on the left and some buildings that could not have been more than five or six storeys high. Curiously-shaped trucks, like those Jonathan had seen on the way from the airport, vied for position with red and silver taxis. The car pulled onto a rough, concrete plot of land that evidently served as a car park, a lorry park and a marshalling yard for cement mixers. Dempsey said something to his driver and he, Jonathan and Frank got out. The heavy, damp heat hit Jonathan immediately and he was glad he had taken Frank's advice and changed into slacks and a short-sleeved shirt for the evening.

They walked round two sides of what appeared to be an inner harbour for small boats, for there was enough illumination for him to see sampans, yachts, junks and what looked like diminutive fishing vessels – Frank explained that it was a typhoon shelter – and suddenly they were in the glare of a brightly lit open passageway between rows of glass-fronted restaurants, each with a tank of live fish, ranging in size from big to enormous, squeezed in together and just about able to move. Opaque plastic pipes bubbled oxygen into the water. At the entrance to each restaurant a man loudly solicited the custom of the passers-by, almost all of whom, Jonathan noticed, were Chinese. The hubbub, bright lighting, heat and unfamiliarity and the strong smell of fish combined to give him a feeling of being detached from reality similar to that which he had experienced on that first evening after his arrival. Dempsey ignored the touts and strode ahead until he stopped at a restaurant which seemed indistinguishable from all the others they had passed. Above the entrance were four, raised, elaborate Chinese characters. They were silver-coloured, each about a foot high and quite beautiful.

'This is it,' said Dempsey. '*Ngan Lung Jau Ka*; that means Silver Dragon Restaurant.'

They went through the doorway, past the fish tanks and into a surprisingly large entrance hall.

'Now you'll see why I told you to wear sneakers,' Frank murmured to Jonathan. He looked down; the cement floor was running with water. The man at what, in any other type of restaurant, might be called the reception desk, was wearing black wellington boots with the tops turned down. Dempsey said something to Jonathan which he did not catch and, as he was about to ask him what, his attention was taken by another man, wearing a grubby singlet, faded blue jeans and similar boots and carrying a large fishing net on a pole, who escorted what must have been a customer from the dining area towards the tanks. Jonathan had never experienced anything like this before. He watched as the customer pointed to a giant fish, speckled grey with bands of a darker colour and the most mournful face, as though it was contemplating its inevitable fate.

'That is a garoupa,' said Dempsey. 'I think that WK will probably order one. Only bigger.'

He went to the man at the desk, who called over another man in rubber boots. They followed him through an archway and into the interior. If it had been loud outside the restaurant, the noise inside was astonishing. There were fifty or sixty round tables, most of them taken. More booted, singlet-wearing waiters scurried between them with precariously balanced piles of dishes, mostly laden but some empty and being taken away to some distant recess. The joyously raucous shouts of the diners pitched against the yells of the waiters. They were guided towards the centre of the room and there, sitting with some dishes already in front of them, were Lester Chan, Billy Yeung and a slim Chinese man of about fifty who was wearing an immaculately pressed white shirt and a very large green jade ring on his index finger. Beside him sat a heavily built Westerner. Chan stood up to welcome them.

'Hah, so you make it. Good.' He turned to the Chinese man. 'This is my very good friend, Law Kam-Cheung, and this is a famous barrister who acted for me once in a different case, Mr Stratford.'

'Call me Gerry,' he said, standing up to shake Frank's and Jonathan's hands.

'And you should call me KC,' said the man with the ring. 'Very few *gweilos* can say my name properly, except perhaps Gerry,' and he, too, stood up to shake hands.

Jonathan glanced at the table. He could not recognise any of the food on the plates. One dish seemed to be a pile of bleached, finger-sized pieces of jelly lying on a brownish liquid. Another contained flat grey shells from which flopped what looked like flaccid penises. There was a plate of hard-boiled eggs cut into quarters that would have been familiar except for the yolks being dark green and the whites black. And there was what appeared to be a pile of deep-fried

267

cockroaches. He gave Frank a questioning look, hoping that his host would not notice.

'I know some of these,' Frank took the cue. 'That one's sea blubber, it's a kind of jellyfish. That one,' and he pointed to the phalluses, 'that's something I have often seen in glass tanks in fish restaurants; it's some sort of shellfish. I tried it once; it's very, very rubbery, but I've no idea what it's called; that one is a hundred-year egg – hen's eggs that have been preserved in a compound of ash and other things for a few weeks – I find it a bit cloying but the ginger underneath is very nice; and that one, I've no idea what it is. It looks like insects, doesn't it, but it wouldn't be, not in Hong Kong. Bound to be some sort of seafood. Billy, what is that?'

Billy, who had taken a seat next to Lester Chan, looked at the cockroach dish. 'I think it's shellfish,' he said. 'I'll ask Chan Wai-king. *Hoi-sin mah?*'

'*Hai, hamaih,*' replied Chan. '*Ho sik.*'

'He says, yes, it's salted shrimps and very good to eat.'

'Why are you my interpreter?' asked Chan, with a broad grin. 'Don't I speak English good? Anyway, there are a lot more dishes to come, but first I must ask Mr Savage what he would like to drink. And please sit down, anywhere you want.'

Jonathan was about to suggest that he would have whatever Chan was having, when it occurred to him that he might be offered the spirituous equivalent of the food on the table, so he modified his reply.

'What do you usually drink with Chinese food, Mr Chan?' he asked.

'Me, always the same. I drink a good brandy with plenty of ice. I bring my own Rémy Martin XO. They have just taken it away to put in an ice bucket for me. Very good, very cold.'

'Oh,' said Jonathan, rather taken aback. 'I don't know if I would like brandy with ice.'

'You've got a lot to learn about Hong Kong.' Gerry Stratford was smiling at him.

'No, I know you would not like it. I had brought some whisky for you. I heard that you like whisky. I know you drink Scotch.'

'How did you know? Did Mr Grinder tell you?'

'Don't blame me,' said Frank. 'I didn't know what you drank until last night.'

'No,' said Chan, 'he had not told me. I just know things, which is why I am a very successful man. Look, here comes our bottle.'

A waiter in gumboots was carrying two ice buckets over to their table.

'I bring this too, for you. Johnnie Walker Blue Label. It cost almost two thousand Hong Kong dollars. I expect you get it cheaper in London, being so near to Scotland.'

Stratford indicated the place next to him and, without quite knowing why, Jonathan felt a moment of reluctance as he took it. Was it something in the brash manner that put him off? He hoped that he was not becoming dependent on the people he had already got to know. The waiter spoke to Chan and then put one of the buckets in front of Jonathan. Stratford leaned towards him.

'You should never have admitted that you drink Scotch,' he said. 'Old WK will expect you to finish the whole bottle.'

'What, tonight?'

'Yep.'

'I couldn't possibly. You're not serious that this bottle is just for me.'

'I'm deadly serious, mate.'

'Well, surely someone else will have some. Won't you help me out?'

'I never touch the stuff. I drink lager. A lot of it. I asked WK to order some San Mig for me. You know, Filipino, not the piss that they brew here.'

Jonathan looked at Frank, but he was deep in conversation with Billy Yeung.

'I'll have some, obviously, but not the whole bottle.'

'That's your affair,' replied Stratford. 'But WK will not like it. He'll think that it's a loss of face.'

Jonathan spoke across the table.

'Mr Chan,' he said.

Chan stopped talking to the man who had introduced himself as KC.

'Mr Chan, it is very generous of you to order such a fine whisky for me but this gentleman, er, Gerry, tells me that you might be offended if I don't finish the whole bottle. I have to say that the last thing I want to do is to offend you but I am not a heavy drinker, I think, and I simply cannot drink that much at one sitting. In fact, I am planning to fly home tomorrow to begin work on your case and I don't think that it would be a good idea for me drink too much this evening. I am very much looking forward to a few glasses but that will be it. So, please don't think that I am being rude.'

'Of course not,' said Chan with a smile. 'I had be happy for you to have as much as you want. We Chinese like to be generous hosts but not to make our guest ill. Particularly a guest who will be fighting my case.'

'Thank you, Mr Chan, that is very understanding of you.'

Chan resumed his conversation with Law.

'You're going to win this case,' smirked Stratford.

'Why do you say that?'

'Because behind all that English politeness you're a tough cookie. You know that WK is quite a big shot in HK. Not many people would put him straight like you did then. Graham Truckett is going to be no match for you. Do you know him? He's leading the case for the prosecution. He's in-house at the Department of Justice.'

'Yes, I've met him. He appeared for the Crown in the bail hearing yesterday.'

'Not the Crown.'

'Yes, he did. I was introduced to him beforehand.'

'Look, mate, you had better get used to not saying that. Since the handover, it's the prosecution. Hong Kong doesn't belong to you Brits anymore.'

'Anyway, he seemed perfectly competent to me. I rather liked him.'

'Well, we'll see. And there may be another reason why old Lester won't be convicted.'

An alarm went off in Jonathan's head. He changed the subject.

'How long have you been in practice in Hong Kong?' he asked.

'About ten years.'

'Were you at the Bar in Australia before that?'

'What? Australia? Why Australia?'

'Well, aren't you an Australian?'

'Fuck me! Can't you limeys tell the difference between Australian and New Zealand accents? It's about the worst thing you can do. I'm not from Oz; I'm a Kiwi and proud of it.'

Fortunately, more dishes started to arrive at the table and, even more fortunately for Jonathan, he was able to recognise most of them as food. A plate of roasted pigeons with their skinned heads still attached, some bright red crabs in their shells, lobsters split in half, some sliced meat, probably pork, resting on a thick black sauce, some more seafood which he could not name but which was recognisable as edible shellfish, and an enormous fish like the ones Dempsey had pointed out as they came into the restaurant. Dempsey, Billy and KC made loud '*Waahh!*' noises and Lester Chan beamed with delight. Jonathan took the opportunity to turn away from Stratford and, against the cries of appreciation and anticipation, tried to speak to Dempsey.

'There's an awful lot of food here,' he said as loudly as he could, 'for just seven of us.'

Just then the noise lessened as chopsticks and bowls were set to work.

'Yes,' said Dempsey, 'to a *gweilo*. But I think that the client will have ordered some more to come. Would you like some rice or noodles?'

'Well, there seems to be a lot of protein here and not too much carbohydrates. I love the way they do rice in Chinese restaurants.'

'That is probably in restaurants in London. At a banquet in Hong Kong or a special dinner like this, very often they come at the end of the meal if the guests are still hungry. But I shall tell him to order some rice for you now, and perhaps some green vegetables.' He spoke in Cantonese to Chan, who nodded and called over to a waiter.

'Don't eat too much rice,' Chan said to Jonathan. 'There are lots more to come. Do you like *dofu*? Bean curd.'

'I think so,' Jonathan hesitated.

'Good, because we got two sorts coming. One fried, one steamed with garlic. And we had mussels in black bean sauce and long clams and some squid and some duck and some other things, I forget what I had ordered. But maybe you should drink some of your whisky because if you don't have any at all then I shall be offended.'

Jonathan noticed that a tumbler full of whisky and ice had been poured for him. Chan put some ice cubes into a wine glass and filled it to the brim with chilled brandy. He passed the bottle round the table. Stratford and Frank had bottles of lager in front of them. Chan raised his glass to Jonathan and then to Frank.

'*Yam sing*,' he said. 'Cheers,' and he stood up, stretched across the table and clinked Jonathan's tumbler.

Jonathan took a sip from his drink and, when Chan was busy talking with KC and Billy, took the bottle from its ice bucket and offered it to Frank.

'No need, no need,' exclaimed Chan. 'I order a bottle for him. I know you both like your *wai sih gei*.'

Frank heard this.

'WK,' he said, 'that is so kind of you, but would you mind telling the waiter to cancel that? I think that you may have the wrong end of the stick when it comes to English lawyers. If I may have a glass or two from the bottle that you got for Mr Savage, that would suit me fine. I don't know if you know, but my wife is Hong Kong Chinese and she would be very cross with me if I came home drunk tonight. But what is much more scary is that she would be very angry

273

with you and I don't think that you would like that.' He hoped he hadn't said the wrong thing.

Chan's grin was expansive. He leant across the table again, took the bottle from Jonathan and filled Frank's glass.

'*Yam sing*,' he said, touching it with his glass, and then did the same to all his other guests, each taking a slurp.

The evening progressed in this fashion. More dishes arrived, Chan repeatedly rose and toasted his guests, who rose and did the same to him, and his complexion became redder and redder.

Both Dempsey and Lester Chan kept putting titbits into Jonathan's bowl and on his plate using black chopsticks to differentiate them from the white ones with which they shovelled food into their own mouths. Jonathan found, to his surprise, that even the unidentifiable food was very good, and the giant fish, which was apparently steamed simply in garlic, ginger, soya sauce and what looked and tasted like outsize spring onions, was delicious, piled onto the rice. He found that he was eating far more than he usually did and by his third, or possibly fourth, whisky and ice, he was feeling the beginnings of stupor, or would have done but for the din. Frank was talking a lot of the time to Billy, and Jonathan could no longer make himself heard across the table; in any event, much of the conversation was now in Cantonese. He was aware that it would be rude to sit there without speaking. He turned to Stratford.

'Sorry about confusing you with an Australian,' he said. 'But you're quite right, to an English ear your accents sound very similar. I didn't mean to offend you.'

'That alright, mate,' replied Stratford in what still sounded like pure Australian. 'Lots of people make the same mistake. I don't suppose that I can tell the difference between some of your regional accents.'

Jonathan did notice, in spite of the background noise, that he pronounced it "accints".

'Tell me,' he said, 'what did you mean by what you said earlier?'

'What's that?'

'About Mr Chan not being convicted. And I don't mean your flattery of me and my ability.'

'Oh, that. This is Hong Kong, you know, not England. It's a different ball game.'

'I'm sorry, I'm not following.'

'There are ways and means here,' Stratford said. 'Things aren't always what they seem.'

'What are you suggesting?' Jonathan wasn't sure whether or not he was surprised.

'Well, I'm not suggesting anything. But in the nineteen-eighties the acting Director of Public Prosecutions here was on the take. He got sent down for eight years. He was a Kiwi, like me, although I'm not proud of that. That was well before my time here.'

'But are you saying that…Look, let's change the subject. How long have you been in Hong Kong?'

'I told you. About ten years. I came out to join the Department of Justice and after a bit I left and went into private practice.'

'And do you like it here?'

'I wouldn't have stayed if I didn't.'

There was an unmistakeable terseness in his tone. Jonathan began to regret starting the conversation, but what else could he have done? Fortunately, there was a momentary lull in the immediate noise and Dempsey was speaking to him.

'Sorry, I didn't catch what you said.'

'I asked you if you were enjoying the meal?' said Dempsey.

'Oh yes, thank you. Very much.'

'I would suppose that much of it is not familiar to you.'

'Well, I recognised the rice,' Jonathan smiled. 'But not much else.'

'Sometimes with Chinese food it is better for a Westerner not to know what it is before he tries it.'

'Well, it was all excellent. I've enjoyed it. Thank you very much, Mr Chan.'

Chan rose and raised his drink to him. Jonathan did the same, leaning across the table to touch glasses.

'You're getting to be Chinese,' said Dempsey. 'But you don't need to be polite: did you really like everything?'

'Well, yes, definitely, but some things more than others.'

'Now you are being English again. What didn't you like?'

'Er, I found that rubbery thing rather, well, rubbery for my taste.'

'And what else?'

'To be honest, I couldn't manage the black and green eggs. I'm afraid I had to drop the bit that I tasted under the table.'

'Yes, I saw.'

'I hope I didn't give offence. Do you think the client noticed?'

'He was bound to.'

'Oh God, do you think I should apologise to him? I would hate him to think that I was ungrateful. It was just that it was really too rich for me. Too unfamiliar.' He avoided saying that the combination of texture and taste had made him want to heave.

'No, no need to say sorry. Just the reverse. Client told me that he saw that you ate so much and tried so many different dishes. That is very good face for him. He said that you use chopsticks very well.'

Jonathan rose of his own accord to toast Chan.

'Thank you very much for such a wonderful and unusual meal, Mr Chan,' he said.

Chan stood up again. '*Mho man tai*!' he said.

'That means "no worries". Stratford was speaking to him.

'*Mho ha hei*,' Chan added. 'And what does that mean, Gerry?'

'No idea.'

'It means something like "don't stand on ceremony", or you might say "it's a pleasure". Something like that.' This was Billy Yeung, speaking across the table.

'So everyone is now interpret for me,' said Chan. 'Even although I had spoke good English.' He staggered slightly as he rose. Then he sat down again.

'But Mr Savage doesn't understand Cantonese.'

'That's why I had speak to him in his language, in *Yingman*.'

'And that's why I think that it would be better to go home now.' This was Law.

'Yes, I think KC is right,' added Billy Yeung.

Chan raised an arm and waved unsteadily. A waiter came squelching over to him with a piece of paper covered with lines of Chinese characters. Chan glanced at it and took out a wad of yellowish-gold banknotes.

'Yellow fish,' Dempsey said quietly. 'Thousand-dollar notes.'

Jonathan tried to conceal his astonishment as note after note was peeled off and pushed towards the waiter.

Then, as if on an unheard signal, everyone at the table was on his feet and he found himself being propelled through the restaurant, which was now even more crowded, and out into the fresh air. He found Frank Grinder beside him.

'Are you OK?' Frank asked.

'Yes, I think so. Why?'

'Because if you're not used to it, these banquets can be a bit of a shock to the system. So much to eat, so many unfamiliar dishes, and all that noise.'

'Yes, I suppose so. And quite a lot to drink.' Jonathan realised that he was walking unevenly. Dempsey had joined them.

'So, I take you back to your hotel in my car. The driver is waiting. And then I drop you off, Frank. I think you said Kennedy Town?'

'Yes, but there's no need to take me home. I can get a cab from the Majestic Harbour, Dempsey. There are always taxis there.'

'No, I take you to your flat. It's better.'

'Well, if you insist. That's very kind of you.'

'*Mho ha hei*,' Dempsey said with a smile.

The conversation was beginning to pass Jonathan by. He woke when the car pulled onto the hotel forecourt. He wished them goodnight, tried not to stumble as he crossed the lobby, somehow found his key and inserted it into the slot in the lift's control panel, got into his room and out of his clothes and was asleep before his head touched the pillow.

PART THREE

20

Six weeks had passed. Frank Grinder had been back to Cheltenham, briefly and on his own, ostensibly to check that everything was in order at their house and to pick up and deal with the accumulation of mail; but his underlying, unstated, and probably unacknowledged concern was that he was troubled that Hong Kong might, again, be taking him over and that if he had no break from it he could be swallowed back into a life of social clubs, work and passing time within the perceptibly diminishing circle of his expat acquaintances. Back in Hong Kong he had been relieved to hear from Rambo that he had probably abandoned his plans to venture into business with Sicky Chan.

'My friend, he says that he can't put up any money. His father would not help. He had said that he had to spend too much money on paying lawyers for something, I don't understand what. Also, said that he cannot risk acting as guarantee, or that banks might not accept him. I don't really understand. But you are a lawyer, Frank, so how about maybe you can lend the money to us? You have plenty.' And he added, 'Old Chap.'

'But, Rambo, I'm pretty sure I told you that I couldn't, and wouldn't, act as a guarantor for a loan. And the same applies to lending you and your friend any money. I really am not in a position to do so. I'm sorry, but I don't think you should have asked me. You know that I'm retired from practice – or at least I thought that I was – and I have your sister to think about.'

Rambo looked glum but resigned.

'No, I remember, you did tell me.'

'Well, Rambo, I wasn't going to say this because I wanted you to get on in life and it was encouraging that you seemed to have a sense of direction at last but, in the end, I think it might not be a bad thing that this venture is not going anywhere.'

'Why?'

'Because I happen to know more about your friend's family than perhaps you do. And I don't think that his father is necessarily reliable. He has an odd relationship with the concept of honesty. Look, you must on no account tell your friend what I've just said, nor anyone else for that matter. You know that I rely on your trustworthiness. But I would have been very unhappy if you got your fingers burned. Do you know what I mean by that?'

'Yes, of course.'

'So, to that extent I'm pleased that you're out of it. But it does mean, I suppose, that you've still not got any prospects. No means of earning a living.'

'So, maybe I try something else?'

'Yes, give it some thought. You know that you can always come to me for advice.'

'Yes, so maybe I study to become a lawyer.'

'Yes, well, maybe.'

And all seemed to have gone quiet after that.

Brett O'Brien had had two longish murder cases practically back-to-back. The first was an attack on a pawnbroker in Causeway Bay: a gruesome affair in which the police had described the incident as "a chopping"; a heavy, rectangular-bladed meat cleaver, employed with such nimble precision by Chinese chefs and with dreadful ferocity by the minions of a Triad society, had been used. Complicated trails of mostly circumstantial evidence pointing to the three accused, and the long-windedness of one of the defence barristers, had extended the trial by about, he thought, a third of its proper length. The second was at the other end of the spectrum, but just as harrowing. A young mother, recently deserted by her husband, still grieving from the loss of her mother in a road accident, and living in a high-rise block in a housing development in Sheung Shui Wai out in the New Territories, had pushed her baby son through the only window in the apartment that could be opened. The prosecution had not accepted her plea of guilty to manslaughter on the grounds of diminished responsibility, and that trial had heard evidence from several expert witnesses on each side, giving their reasoned views of her mental health at the time of the child's death. Much as O'Brien would have approved the acceptance of the plea, he thought it right that this should be the decision of a jury, particularly as there was considerable conflict of psychiatric opinion on the issue of her state of mind. The trial had been conducted efficiently and considerately by counsel on both sides but, throughout it, the wretched young woman had sat in the dock with her eyes cast down, not appearing to understand anything of what was going on, nor to respond to the presence of the murmuring interpreter who sat beside her, translating all that was said in English. Brett had wondered whether she was under medication but thought it better not to ask in open court. Both had concluded with what he believed were the right verdicts.

During the interval between the trials, when he was dealing with short administrative hearings and a sentencing a few defendants who had pleaded guilty, Brett had received an email from Sharon telling him that she would be staying on in Sydney for a while as there was so much for her to do there. Was he managing all right without her? At about the same time, old Squires had announced his retirement, much to the surprise of many in the judiciary who thought that he must have reached the age of compulsory retirement long before and a considerable number who assumed that he had already died. A short ceremony to bid him farewell had taken place in the Chief Justice's court. Brett had attended – as it was, after all, something in the nature of a three-line whip – as had all the other High Court judges and quite a few District Court judges. He could not help feeling a twinge of pity for the old man as so few members of the legal profession had bothered to turn up. A couple of hollow-sounding, valedictory speeches had been made by the Chief and by the newest appointment to the Court of Appeal, followed by a paradigm of insincerity by the Chairman of the Bar Association; and Squires had given a surprisingly succinct and lucid reply, and then the court had risen without anything more being said. Brett found himself wondering who would come to occupy the house in

Jamaica Gardens next door to his and Sharon's – if she still considered it hers – home.

Graham Truckett had been, at least by his standards, very hard at work, allowing Pammy Lee to explain the case to him without, he hoped, revealing too much of his ignorance. William Soh, the Director of Public Prosecutions, told him that he appreciated how much there was for him to do in the preparation for the trial and had confirmed his permission to work solely on the Lester Chan case. A certain amount of grumbling by his colleagues at the Department had surfaced, but he was unsure whether it was solely because of the extra workload that had necessarily been thrust upon them or whether there was also an element of jealousy behind it; after all, he was not even an SADPP but merely a Grade Four prosecutor, and he had taken on a case which would normally have been briefed out to an SC, leading counsel at the private Bar, particularly with a London leader on the other side and particularly with such a well-known and influential defendant. In spite of his initial and, he had to admit to himself, continuing panic, he was quite proud of what he was now doing. Pammy was plainly impressed. They were seeing a lot of each other in their discussions together and in their case conferences with police officers from the Commercial Crimes Bureau. They also sometimes met each other after work since he had found the courage to invite her for a drink at the Oyster Bar at the Island Paradise, and he had been aware of the admiring glances from *gweilo* businessmen as she had walked in and joined him.

Jonathan Savage QC had spent almost the whole time back in England reading through the boxes of documents that had been delivered. Whilst still in Hong Kong he had called Eric and told him that he was not to accept any work for him until the trial was over and that he would need all the available intervening time to prepare for it. He had taken as much as could be sensibly and intelligibly loaded onto a memory stick back to his home so that he would not have to waste time commuting to central London, but he still had to go into his chambers to go through much of the hard copies and to consult textbooks in order to become familiar with the language and intricacies of banking and commercial practice. Slowly, like a shadowy, swaddled figure emerging from a Dickensian pea-souper, a discernible picture had begun to emerge. He had to admit to himself that that would probably not have been possible, or, if possible, would have taken him infinitely longer, had he not had the help that Dempsey Ng had provided in the form of his analysis of what he anticipated the prosecution's principal allegations would be and a written summary of every prosecution witness's statement cross-referenced to all the documentary exhibits. Quite what were the defendant's answers to the allegations was more difficult to discern and he knew that he would need a great deal of time with his client before the trial started to try to work out what the defence case was to be. But by the time he had boarded the aircraft at Heathrow, Jonathan was feeling both a new confidence that he had some idea of what he was doing and a sense of familiarity, not quite of an old Hong Kong hand, but of someone who had an idea of where he was going.

His arrival at the Majestic Harbour had had something of the feeling of a homecoming. He had been gratified to hear the doorman welcome him by name as he got out of the taxi, and by the time he had been swished through the glass doors and to the reception desk he was already relishing the familiar smell and sound of the hotel. This time he felt more in control of what was happening; his message that he did not want to be met at the airport had plainly got through, as had, he hoped, his request that he wanted to spend the evening on his own and would meet Dempsey Ng and Billy Yeung the following morning. He was pretty sure that Frank Grinder would know not to trouble him. And so it was that, this time, he was able to go to his room, unpack, have a shower and go down to the bar for a quiet drink on his own, relishing both the opulence of his surroundings and the solitude.

21

There was a light tap on the frosted glass panel of Graham Truckett's office door which he had come to recognise. He could see the outline of Pammy's slim figure. After all these weeks of working together, day after day, she still waited quietly until he called her to come in. Although he was beginning to find her diffidence irresistible, it was nevertheless somewhat daunting. He had found himself wondering how she might react if he went beyond touching her elbow as he ushered her to a table in a bar. Would it ruin things if he were to ask her out to dinner? He half-wished that he had met her in something other than a professional environment but he doubted whether he would have had the chance to be in her company had they not both been employed by the Department of Justice.

'Come in, Pammy.'

And then:

'You really don't need to wait outside. Just let yourself in if the door isn't locked.'

'No, I cannot do that.'

She sat at the opposite side of his desk. She was holding a thick, buff-coloured file of papers against her chest, her arms crossed.

'What's that you've got?' asked Graham. 'It's not another police report, is it?'

Still holding it, as if reluctant to let him see it, she said:

'No, you probably think that I'm foolish. But for my benefit, and in order to try to learn how to prosecute a big case like this, I have written an opening statement for this trial. I know that it will not be very good, but I thought that if I did it and if I show it to you, you will be able to let me see where I am going wrong. I thought, maybe, somehow, it could be a good exercise for me. I don't suppose that you will think much of it, and I won't mind if you criticise it. In fact, I would like you to do so. I know there will not be anything in it that you have not already thought of and there will be a lot of not good things, but if you don't mind to look at it, and if you have the time, it would be very kind of you.'

'Well, let me see it.'

Pammy slowly unfolded her arms and slid the folder across the desk. It was even thicker than Graham had at first thought.

'Look, now would be a good time for me to read it.'

'Are you sure you don't mind? And that you have the time?'

'Yes, of course I'm sure. I've always got time for you, Pammy.'

She looked down. 'I had started by explaining what is a letter of credit. I thought, maybe, that some of the jury might not know.'

'That's a good idea. I was thinking of starting in the same way myself.' Possibly he had: he had not yet properly considered the need to write an opening; it was still no more than an intimidating presence at the back of his mind. 'Look, why don't you leave it with me and I will read it in one go?'

'Would you not like me to stay with you so you can show me where I have made mistakes?'

'No, no, no,' said Graham, perhaps a trifle too hastily. 'You go away and get on with whatever else you want to do. I'll read it and make notes and then you can come back and we can go through it together.'

Pammy rose. 'Yes, of course, that it is a much wiser way. I can continue my analysis of the witness statements, which I hope you are finding helpful.'

'Very much so, thank you.'

She smoothed her dark grey skirt and left. The faintest trace of perfume lingered behind her.

Graham opened the folder. A beautifully printed document lay inside: triple-spaced and with wide margins on either side, as if Pammy had intended to make it easier for annotations and corrections. She had used the larger than normal font which he had come to expect from Chinese members of the Department. He wondered why that was; perhaps he should ask her when she came back.

He had just started reading when there was a soft tap on the door. The profile through the glass was not hers.

'Come in.'

No movement. He got up and opened the door. It was his secretary.

'Hello, Emily,' he smiled. 'Have you brought me some tea?'

'No, but I will, Mr Truckett, if you had want it yet. No, I brought this letter which just come in for you from the Judiciary Administration. The messenger said it is urgent.'

Graham put down the file and took the sealed brown envelope.

'So, maybe now you would need some tea,' and she left.

He tore it open. Inside were a compliments slip and a single sheet of paper headed: *In The High Court of the Special Administrative Region of Hong Kong*, and a case number. Beneath that it read:

HKSAR v CHAN WAI-KING, LESTER

Following an ex parte hearing in chambers this day it is ordered that:

i. *the prosecution shall, within fifteen days from today, serve on the court and on the defendant, his solicitors and/or counsel a full written opening statement, setting out all the allegations, evidence and, where appropriate, propositions of law upon which it will seek to rely; and*

ii. *the defence shall, within seven days of the service of the opening statement referred to in (i) above, serve on the court and the prosecution a skeleton argument setting out the propositions of law, if any, upon which it will seek to rely in support of any application to dismiss the charges, or any of them.*

It bore that day's date and was signed:

B. O'Brien, Justice of the High Court.

Graham dropped the order on to his desk as he felt a chill rising up his spine. He got up and looked out of the window at the thick green vegetation climbing above the buildings of Mid-Levels towards the Peak. It was a hot, sunny day. He wished that he could be in his shorts and trainers, walking the trail to Mount Collinson and on to Shek O for a cold lager. Fifteen days! How on earth was he going to accomplish a full opening in that time? He wondered whether he could make an application for an extension of time but immediately rejected the idea. There was no basis, other than that he was not up to the task. O'Brien seemed to be a decent enough sort of man but he had earned a reputation for briskness and efficiency and he plainly thought that that was a fair enough amount of time. Well, he would just have to work very long hours and hope that he could pick up the story with enough detail to produce a half-decent opening. Wasting time by looking out of the window was not the right way to start.

There was another tap on the door.

'What is it?' He had not meant to snarl.

Emily came in with a mug of tea and a plate of biscuits and put them on his desk.

'I think, maybe, you will need something to eat with your tea, Mr Truckett.' There was a look of concern on her face.

'That's very kind of you, Emily. Yes, I am going to need some sustenance, I think. And, at least for the meantime, would you make sure that I am not troubled except for only the most urgent calls?'

'Yes, I had already print out a "do not disturb" notice. I will put it on the door.'

'Thank you, Emily. Tell me, did the messenger tell you what was in the envelope?'

'No, he would not know.'

'It was sealed. You didn't look at it, did you? I wouldn't have minded if you did,' he added.

'No, it was seal, as you said.'

'Well, how…? Never mind, thanks for your concern. I had better get on with work.'

She left, quietly closing the door behind her. Graham picked up Pammy's document and began to read.

Almost immediately, a warm sense of relief started to replace the chill. This was clear, concise, well-expressed and patently well-researched; within a short time he found that he was beginning to understand the case. Some of the language was a little stilted and there was a complete absence of any human touch – written rather like the many police reports he had read in the past – but he could add that himself, he was sure, in order to make it more jury-friendly, but the important thing was that it all made sense. He had reached only the second page when he knew that this was going to be the basis, no, more than that, the structure of the opening statement. It shouldn't be too hard to jiggle it around and to introduce some of his own style of delivery. He read on for a while, writing in notes as he did so, and then paused and rang Pammy's number. She answered.

'Hi, Pammy. It's Graham. Could you come to my office, please?'

'Oh, you want me so soon?' She sounded worried.

'Yes, please.'

A couple of minutes later she was outside the door, waiting. He got up and opened it.

'Come on in. I told you earlier not to wait outside.'

She paused and then stood inside the doorway, not looking at him.

'Perhaps you want me to take it away and start again, Mr Truckett.' He had got her to call him Graham some time ago. This sounded like some sort of signal, although of what he could not guess.

'No. I certainly don't. I just wanted to tell you that, from what I've read so far, which isn't very much, it looks very, very good.'

She came further into the room and looked up at him, modestly smiling and looking relieved.

'Oh, because it cannot be so good.'

'It is,' said Graham. 'Anyway, so far it is. Of course, I've only got a short way in and I will need to read it all. But I wanted to ask you something. Have you done this on your computer?'

'Yes, of course. I know no other way.'

'Good. Then could you put it onto a memory stick or something, so that I can put it onto my computer? And so that I can add to it and change it?'

'I could email it to you.'

'Really? Would I be able to make changes and so on?'

Was she smiling at him because she was still pleased, or was it perhaps amusement? Could it possibly be a look of affectionate indulgence? No, probably she was quietly laughing at his incompetence.

'Of course. But maybe I will put it on a memory stick as well. Would you be more comfortable if I also gave you a CD?'

'Now you're laughing at me, I think. What about putting it on a floppy disk?'

'What is that? I had not heard of that.'

'Never mind. It's just some old technology from, probably, before you were born. No, an email will do. And a memory stick to be on the safe side. And thank you. Thank you very much.'

陳

'Henry,' said Mr Justice O'Brien as he picked up the papers for the next day in court, 'do you think that I was a bit too hard this morning? I seem to be picking on Graham Truckett these days.'

His clerk looked perplexed. 'But, my Lord, you did not have Mr Truckett in court today. You had spend the whole day on matters in chambers without counsel. You signed orders.'

'Yes, I know, that's the whole point. I didn't give him a chance to make any representations about the order I made in the Lester Chan case. I gave him fifteen days to serve a full written opening setting out the prosecution case.'

'Yes, I knew. I filed your order. So, I read it.'

'Fifteen days is not very long. What do you think?'

'It can be so.'

'That's very helpful, Henry.'

'I am please to help.'

'I was being sarcastic.'

'That is a word that I may not know.'

'Henry, I am asking you if you think I was unfair in giving him only fifteen days to complete the work.'

'It may be so.'

'Henry, please tell me what you think.'

'Because, I had never prepare a document for a case.'

'No, I suppose you have a point. But it's a pretty complicated case by the look of the papers and it's been set down for a longish hearing. And it's not as if Graham Truckett is hugely experienced, as far as I am aware. I wonder if I should have given him longer. It's not as if that pretty young woman with him looks senior enough to be able to offer him much help. What's her name, by the way?'

'She is Lee Sit-ming. She is a government counsel, I think at the lowest grade.'

'Yes, it is a bit hard on him,' reflected O'Brien. 'This is a difficult case for someone at his level to take on and he doesn't seem to have much by way of support. There was a rumour in the judges' lounge that it was originally due to be prosecuted by a senior assistant DPP; I heard Alfred Mak's name mentioned. Whatever happened to him, do you know?'

'He is in Canada. Running a restaurant in Vancouver. Called Double Dragon Garden. My cousin says it is not very good.'

'Do you know everything, Henry?'

'No, my Lord.'

'Anyway, do you think that I should change the order I made this morning and give him a bit longer?'

'He did not ask for longer, I think.'

'No, but that's probably because I didn't give him the chance. I made the order in chambers without counsel being present so the first that he would have heard of it would have been when it was delivered to the Legal Department. Actually, that's the first time I've ever done that: had a hearing without counsel, I mean. I wonder if it would have been fairer if I'd had counsel in.'

'But maybe, my Lord, he would say that you had given him not so much time if he need. And he has not contact us at all today.'

'Henry, that's a wise thought. Perhaps that's not a tight schedule for him. It's possible that he has already drafted most of his opening. Yes, with the help of the Police Commercial Crimes officers he may have got most of it wrapped up already. As you say, he hasn't come back and asked for more time.'

'No, my Lord.'

'And I must say, I'm quite keen to get this trial up and running. I'm due for some leave and I would like to get down to Sydney to find out what's going on. It doesn't look as if Mrs O'Brien is planning to be in Hong Kong anytime soon.'

'So, would you want me to ask the Department of Justice?'

'Ask them what?'

'If they want more time.'

'But I thought you had just pointed out to me that they hadn't come back and asked for more time and that that rather indicates that Truckett doesn't need it.'

'Yes, my Lord, but you make the decision, not I.'

'Henry, I sometimes wonder whether that is correct.'

'You may say so,' said Henry.

Brett took that as an English version of the answer *m'hai* which he had so often heard witnesses use in trials, a sort of "not yes" which they appeared to think deflected any responsibility for accuracy.

'Thank you, Henry. There's no need for you to stay. I'll see you tomorrow.'

陳

The phone in Jonathan's hotel room rang. He had just finished shaving and was looking forward to a buffet breakfast. The idea of sushi and Chinese dumplings and an enormous plate of exotic fruit was oddly appealing.

'Mr Savage,' a voice said, 'a small package has just arrived for you. Would you like it sent up to your room?'

'How big is it?'

'Not so big, a letter.'

'Ok, I'll collect it. I'm on my way down.'

He wondered who could be writing to him here. He hoped Eric wasn't sending on mail from chambers; he was enjoying dealing with just one case while he was in Hong Kong. He had rather got used to it when he was reading into this trial before he came out.

The letter was waiting for him at the concierge's desk. A white envelope marked with the red bauhinia seal and *Judiciary of the Hong Kong Special Administrative Region*. He tore it open; inside was a single document, plainly a judicial order. He skimmed through and picked up the words "…defence…within seven days…serve a skeleton argument…" He looked at the top: yes, it was his case, it had Chan's name.

'Mr Savage.' The tone of the concierge's voice indicated that he was repeating himself, that he had already tried to catch his attention.

'Yes, er, I'm sorry.'

'Mr Savage, there is also another message for you. A fax has just come in from a Mr Ng.'

'Oh, right.'

He took up the folded paper and undid the staple. It read: "Just received order from High Court. Requires discussion. Can we meet this morning? Suggest my chambers at 10.30. Yours, Dempsey."

22

Jonathan was surprised to see that the conference room in Dempsey's chambers was full when he was ushered in. He had expected to see his junior, of course, and possibly Billy Yeung but, sitting at the long table also were Grinder and Lester Chan and an elderly, wizened Chinese man whom Billy introduced as his messenger and who demonstrated that he understood no English when Jonathan tried to wish him a good morning. Apart from the messenger, everyone else was in a dark suit and tie, and Jonathan fingered his open-necked shirt in embarrassment.

'So,' said Dempsey, 'we are having this meeting because of the order that the judge has just issued. Have you seen it yet, Jonathan?'

'Yes, I got the order at the same time as your message.'

'What did you think of it?' This was Billy Yeung.

'Well, I'm not overly familiar with the way things are done here, but it seems a bit harsh. Fifteen days doesn't give the Crown much time.'

'We no longer call it the Crown,' interrupted Dempsey. 'Not since the handover in 1997.'

'I meant the prosecution. It doesn't give them very long.'

'But what do you think about giving us seven days?' Billy again.

'Well, that's not very long either; although I noticed when I re-read the order that it was seven days from the service by the prosecution of their written opening. Not seven days from now. But still not very long. But what particularly struck me was the requirement that we should serve a skeleton argument setting out any points of law that we are going to take. I've never come across that before a trial starts.'

'It happens in Hong Kong,' said Dempsey. 'Quite often these days.'

'It seems unfair,' Jonathan said. 'The defence should be able to take any valid point it sees fit to, whenever it arises and whenever the opportunity presents itself.'

'Quite right.' Lester Chan was nodding enthusiastically. 'That's why we must argue the Bill of Rights Ordinance.'

'Do you know about the Hong Kong Bill of Rights Ordinance?' Dempsey asked. 'It's much the same as the Human Rights Act in the UK. Only ours was much earlier.' There was an undisguised note of pride in his voice.

'Yes, I know about it,' lied Jonathan, 'of course. And I am very familiar with the Human Rights Act. But what has it got to do with what is, after all, a matter of timetable and procedure? It isn't a substantive issue.' That ought to impress them, he thought. 'Isn't a judge entitled to set down the timetable in his own court?'

The messenger inclined his head sagely, then turned his attention to plucking a long grey hair from a mole on his chin.

'But you are a very clever lawyer and you can make it a Bill of Rights point,' said Lester Chan. 'It seem that every week the Hong Kong Court of Final Appeal throw out a case because of the Bill of Rights Ordinance. So that is how we should proceed. That way you get the case chuck out before it got started. And I have a big party.'

'Mr Chan,' Jonathan heard himself coldly speaking, 'are you a qualified lawyer? Have you ever even studied law? At university?'

Silence held the room in its icy grip. Oh God, thought Jonathan, I've gone too far.

Then Chan roared with laughter. 'That's why I want you for my defence. You don't take shit from anybody.'

The messenger looked up and smiled his agreement. The hair had gone.

'I'm sorry, Mr Chan,' said Jonathan. 'I didn't mean to sound rude. I'm probably a bit tired still from my flight. What I meant to say is that if I find that the time we have been allotted is too short, we can make an application to extend it, but we can't really do anything until the prosecution has served its written opening because, until we've seen it, we won't know how much time we will need. And as to the apparent limit on our taking points of law, I don't think we would have any difficulty in persuading the judge that he can't stop us from making valid arguments at any stage during the trial...'

'That sounds like a Bill of Rights point,' Chan interrupted him. Jonathan ignored him.

'...and what I believe the best interpretation of the order to be, as far as it affects us, is that the judge will want a written outline of any arguments of law which we say arise from the prosecution's opening and that he has given a time limit for us to do so. In fact, there may not be anything that does arise and, if that is the case, there will be no need for us to do anything. But looked at in that way it seems to me that there is nothing unreasonable in making such an order in principle, albeit that the time allowed might turn out to be too short, in which case we would ask for longer.'

The messenger looked thoughtful but appeared to be content with Jonathan's exegesis. Then he fell asleep.

'At the moment,' Jonathan continued, 'all I have seen are the police charges. Has the indictment been served yet?'

'Yes,' Dempsey replied. 'It came in also this morning. It's much the same as the charges.'

He opened a folder and slid the document across to Jonathan.

After the formal title and case number it read:

HKSAR v CHAN WAI-KING, LESTER

Chan Wai-king, Lester is charged with the following offence:

Statement of Offence

Conspiracy to defraud, contrary to section 2(3)(b) of the Criminal Justice Ordinance and contrary to Common Law.

Chan Wai-king, Lester, on various days between the 1st day of January 2016 and the 31st day of December 2016, conspired together with…

and here there were several Chinese names which, at first reading, meant nothing to Jonathan.

…to defraud the Dah Seng Bank and Chong On Commercial Overseas Banking Corporation…and other banks and financial institutions…

and then followed the names of several other banks, some of which seemed vaguely familiar. He recalled reading about them when he was going through the papers in England: they were the issuing and the corresponding banks, he seemed to recall,

…by obtaining letters of credit purporting to relate to genuine commercial transactions when there were no genuine underlying transactions, namely…

and there followed the details of various transactions which he had first heard about when Dempsey had related them to his uncomprehending and exhausted mind all that time ago in Hong Kong Park and which he had, more or less, become familiar with in the intervening weeks of reading the papers.

As he read he became conscious that there was almost complete silence in the room and, without looking up, he could tell that the others were all watching him, with the probable exception of the messenger, who was presumably the source of the faint sound of snoring. He put the document down.

'May I keep this?' he said. 'I'll take it back to my hotel and compare it with my notes, but there doesn't appear to be any surprises in the indictment.' He hoped that this was so, encouraged by what Dempsey had said.

'So,' said Billy Yeung. 'What should we do about the judge's order? That we came here to discuss.'

'Nothing,' replied Jonathan. 'We do nothing, and we certainly don't start alienating the judge by taking Bill of Rights points. Not at this stage. We wait and see what the prosecution delivers and then we make our decision.'

Chan stood up.

'You see what a big-shot London QC we have? So we do what he says. And now I buy you all lunch. Except him.'

He spoke to Billy, who woke the messenger. It was obvious that he was telling him to go back to the office; moments later, he sat up and gathered some papers into his hands. At the door, he paused and said something to Jonathan in Cantonese and then scuttled out.

'I'm sorry,' said Jonathan to Billy. 'I couldn't understand what he said.'

'He said that he agrees with you. He thinks that you are right.'

Frank Grinder shot Jonathan an amused look. 'There you are,' he said. 'Your judgment has passed muster.'

23

Graham called Pammy on the internal telephone.

'Hi, Pammy. I've now been through your draft and I think it's excellent.'

There was silence at the other end.

'Pammy, can you hear me?'

'Yes, Mr Truckett.'

'Why the formality? Why aren't you calling me Graham?'

Again, silence.

'Pammy?'

'Because, I thought that you and I were now friends.'

'We are.' Graham restrained himself from adding that he hoped they would become something much more than that.

'Well, you are being unkind to me.'

'What?'

'You cannot mean what you say. You are mocking me.'

'In what way?'

'You cannot really think that what I did was good. I do not have your experience or your intelligence. So I just did the best I could, but it cannot compare with your work. I very much want to see what you have done so that I can learn from it. But perhaps you were just being kind to me.'

'Pammy, I wasn't being kind and I certainly don't want to mock you. I really do think that you have put together all the relevant facts very well, and you have outlined the way that a letter of credit fraud works so that a jury should easily understand it. It's set out very much along the lines that I would have followed.'

'That must be because I have been working close to you and you have taught me.' Her voice was just audible and very appealing. He felt the beginnings of a physical reaction that had to be suppressed. He also felt embarrassment that she knew much more about the case than he did, had obviously put in vastly more work than he had and because the opening was an exercise in blatant plagiarism.

'So, I have almost finished my draft and will have it sent round to you for you to look at. The reason I called you was to congratulate you on your work and to let you know, so that it comes as no surprise to you, that I have relied very heavily on the work that you have done, and have followed, pretty closely, the order in which you present the case. Obviously I've changed quite a bit…'

'Yes, well, that would have to be. You would have to correct much of it.'

'…not necessarily all that much. And I've added bits so that it is more jury-friendly. And I've changed some things around. But your work was of great assistance to me.'

'Thank you, Graham. But it is only because I made a lot of notes of what you had said to me, so if it is good, it is because of that. But I think that, maybe, you are just being a very nice person to me.'

Did she really think that? Graham was not entirely sure that it wasn't the other way round and that she knew he had needed all her help to get the opening together and was now giving him face by what she said. It was difficult to know, but whatever the truth was she was gorgeous. He found himself thinking about her rather than the task in hand, which was to add some more personal touches. Get on with it, he told himself.

24

So, next morning they met in Graham's office, and after discussion between him and Pammy, with many compliments going in both directions: Pammy's from a mix of ingenuousness, respect for a senior, both in rank and age, formulaic courtesy and a genuine desire to please; on Graham's part from admiration for all the work she had put in, both in the exegesis of the conspiracy and the factual detail, and an acknowledgment that, for all his digestible expressions and touches which were intended to make the opening sound like the creation of a fairly sharp Antipodean, without her explanation of how the fraud worked, her practical illustrations and the preparation of the schedules, not only would there have been no opening but he would probably not have been able to understand the prosecution's case as now, he was fairly confident, he did. They began to read the draft together.

Graham sat at his desk with a printout; Pammy, her laptop balanced on her knees, sat opposite him. Mostly in silence, apart from checking that they were keeping up with each other and occasionally spotting typos, which she corrected on her screen. Shortly after they started, he suggested that she bring her laptop round to his side of the desk to make it easier, and he moved her chair so that it was beside his; he soon began to wish that he hadn't as it became increasingly difficult to concentrate on the pages in front of him. She was wearing a pale blue silk top through which he could make out the outline of something lacy and, now close to him, she exuded a faintly floral perfume. Once or twice, when she turned towards him to check that he was at the right place, her knee brushed against his. After about two hours, Graham suggested that they should take a break.

'We're making very good progress,' he said, wondering how she might interpret that. 'I think we should have an early lunch.'

'Yes, Graham. I will go back to my room and maybe carry on looking for typos.'

'No you won't. I'm going to take you out for lunch. We deserve something special. Let's go to the Vineyard Café at the Majestic. And then we'll come back and finish it off. We ought to be through it by the end of the afternoon. And then, if you're free, I'd like to take you out for a drink: I think we ought to have a little celebration because we're going to able to deliver the opening well within the fifteen days.'

They came back to his room after lunch. Graham was feeling relaxed, but nevertheless aware that the second large glass of Petit Chablis with his seafood brochette might have been an error; apart from anything else, it had contributed to a bloody expensive bill. Pammy had had only mineral water and had tackled her three-course set lunch without losing any of her demure, cool sangfroid. They had, mostly, managed to avoid talking about the case.

'So,' she said, 'we are up to here.'

She leant in towards him and turned the page in his draft, her elbow brushing his shirtfront. Her perfume was, he thought...alluring, that was the word. Probably the sort of fanciful name under which it was branded, but it really was. He told himself to concentrate on the task, but he was side-tracked by the thought that he might be the only man in legal history who felt a stirring in his trousers whilst reading through the prosecution's opening statement in a letter of credit fraud.

They worked on. The typos seemed fewer now and the picture clearer; they were up to the point where it was dealing with the documents relating to the supposed shipment of porcelain insulators, and the assurance the jury would not have to go into all the dry details at this stage of the proceedings but that an expert witness, an accountant, would be giving evidence and helping to explain the schedules. And then they were finished.

'Do you think, Graham, that we should attach the schedules to this document when we serve it?'

'Well, no,' he replied. 'That would make them part of the opening itself. But we should serve them at the same time as we serve the opening, on the judge and on the defence.' He wasn't sure that he knew what the difference was but there might be a subtle distinction somewhere. Indeed, he wasn't at all sure why he had not just said 'Yes'.

'That is good,' she said. She had that admiring look again. Did she really think that he was wise and intelligent?

'Have you had a chance to check the schedules?' he asked.

'Oh yes, because I thought that you might want to attach them, so I have read them through and they are all correct for each of the false transactions. Do you wish to go through them with me?'

'No, no,' Graham replied, perhaps a bit too hurriedly. 'Just number each one in date sequence, as far as possible, and we'll serve them as a separate bundle.'

'I had already numbered them in that way.'

'Great,' said Graham and, without considering what he was about to do, leant over and kissed her cheek.

She appeared not to be flustered, but said, 'So, I will get the opening printed out and send them by email and printed copies by messenger to the court and to the defence solicitor.'

'And a printed copy for me, too, please.'

'Yes, of course.' Had she even registered what he had just done?

'And then we will meet back here at, say, six o'clock and go off for a little celebration,' he added.

25

And this is the prosecution opening statement they produced. The reader is encouraged, at least briefly, to try to follow this, if only to empathise with what the jurors would have to go through. You may even learn something.

HKSAR v Chan Wai-king, Lester

Prosecution Opening

The defendant, Lester Chan Wai-king, is charged with conspiracy to defraud. The fraud was practised on banks, and the means of doing it was by using letters of credit which he and his co-conspirators had applied for by unlawful means. Letters of credit are a very useful aid to commerce, particularly in international trading, because when they are used properly they are a means by which a bank, acting for the buyer, will guarantee that the seller will be paid. But they also and regrettably, not infrequently, can be a vehicle by which dishonest, and therefore criminal, people try to enrich themselves at the expense of a bank. That is what the prosecution says has happened in this case.

Of course, a genuine application for a letter of credit presupposes one very important thing: that there is, in each case, an underlying commercial transaction, with a real buyer and a real seller and genuine commodities which are being traded.

So, the letter of credit is a letter from a bank guaranteeing that one party, the seller, will receive payment on delivery of the goods if certain conditions are fulfilled. It is the purchaser who applies to his bank to issue the letter of credit; he is called the applicant and he makes arrangements with the bank for the necessary funding, either by having his own credit line extended or by transferring the money from his existing resources. The seller, who is going to receive the payment from the bank, is called the beneficiary.

Sometimes different banks are used: the issuing bank, which provides the letter of credit, and the corresponding or collecting bank, to which the funds are transferred and which then pays the beneficiary. This is particularly useful in international trading. Sometimes the whole transaction goes through the same bank, though often through different branches which reflect the locations of the two parties.

The principles are not particularly complicated, although the details and documentation can be. How it works is that the party which is going to have to pay for the goods, that is, the buyer, applies to his bank to issue a letter of credit in favour of the beneficiary who is the supplier of the goods. The bank will agree to do so on evidence of a genuine commercial transaction and further agrees to release the money to the beneficiary, directly or to the corresponding bank, on evidence that the transaction has been completed. In that way, both seller and buyer know that the buyer has put up the money and that the seller will not be paid until the goods have been received by the buyer.

The sort of documents that the bank will want to see as proving that there is a genuine transaction will be written sale and purchase contracts, despatch notes, bills of lading (a legally binding document issued by the shipper or other carrier describing the goods and their quantities and packaging), delivery notes and commercial invoices all describing the goods and showing what is happening.

So far, so straightforward. However, letters of credit can be used as a vehicle for fraud. Sometimes a company wants to raise money for itself but, for a variety of possible causes, cannot do so. One reason might be that it is insufficiently creditworthy or does not have sufficient assets as collateral for a bank to be prepared to take the risk of lending it money. Nevertheless, the company has a pressing need for some more cash. It might be that it knows of a very attractive investment opportunity in something which it sees as likely to make it a profit in the medium or long term but does not have money available to buy; it might need to pay off some of its debt to trade suppliers or other creditors who are pressing for their money and threatening to cut off further supplies or to start proceedings, in either case, resulting in the company being unable to trade and going out of business; or it may see the opportunity to buy and sell something quickly and at a profit, in other words, a fast buck; it may want to have some ready money available so that it can play the stock market or take advantage of different short-term rates of exchange between international currencies. Or the purpose might even be as simple as this: to use credit facilities with the bank to create a large payment to a fake beneficiary and then to catch the first available aeroplane to some exotic, palm-fringed resort which is located in a country which does not have the inconvenience of an extradition treaty.

There are, of course, many other reasons why a sudden pot of cash would be very appealing. We can, all of us, dream of being presented with, say, HK$100 million and being told that we do not need to pay it back for, say, a week and that we can keep any interest or other profit that we can make in the meantime. So, if there was a way to get hold of the money, and pay it back, without anyone knowing what we had done with it in the meantime, it might make a very attractive proposition. But two questions might occur to you here: (a) How could anyone manage to do that to a bank?; and (b) What is wrong with doing that if all the money gets paid back? After all, you might ask, you appear to be outlining the prosecution case in a fraud trial, so how can it be a crime?

To answer (b) first. What is wrong lies in the word "if". If all the money is returned to the bank. You might not be able to repay it. Your big idea may be written in sand; you might not, for instance, be able to sell what you have bought at net profit or even to cover your costs. Or your attempts to pay off your creditors, so that you can keep trading, might be unsuccessful and you rapidly go bust. Or the exchange rate that you thought you could take advantage of might plummet overnight and the wrong currency goes up whilst the other goes down. In a nutshell, you are taking a risk that you are not going to be able to repay the bank, a risk that the bank knew nothing about when it advanced the money to you and which it would not have been prepared to underwrite if it had known the truth about what you were proposing to do. It is a bit like believing that you have a sure-fire winner for the evening meeting at Happy Valley; but, knowing that your favourite uncle wouldn't lend you the stake money if he knew what you were going to do with it, you persuade him to part with it by saying that you have mislaid the key to your safe at home, in which you put a large sum of cash, and you need to have a temporary loan so that you can pay a locksmith to come out and open it for you. Of course, you hope and even expect your horse will be first past the winning post, that you will clean up and that you will be able to repay your uncle and also buy him a nice box of chocolates from your winnings as a little thank you for helping you, as he believed he was doing, to get the safe unlocked. Similarly, the commercial fraudster no doubt hopes, in many instances, that he will be able to repay the money advanced to him before anyone finds out what has happened. But the fact remains that, even if he does repay, he has been taking a risk with someone else's money, a risk to which they would not have consented if they had known the truth. Any right-minded person would know that such conduct was dishonest.

An analogy can be found in the term "robbing Peter to pay Paul". Of course, it isn't robbery, the money is obtained by theft or by deception, but the basic principle remains the same. Even if the aim is to pay off the debt to Paul so that you can keep afloat financially in the hope that you will eventually be able to repay the money you have taken from Peter, the fact is that Peter did not know what you were doing and would not have consented, if he had known, to his money being used to pay your debt to someone else.

And here is another example, which is much closer to the facts of this case. Suppose that you are in business in a very big way and that involves your company or companies borrowing huge sums of money, so much so that the Monetary Authority, which is the regulator responsible for the conduct of banks, is alarmed at the size of the bank's exposure to your companies and threatens to intervene and prevent the bank lending you any more, either by advancing more cash or by allowing any more interest to accumulate on your existing debts. That would be pretty bad for the bank but disastrous for your companies because the flow of money is the bloodstream of business. What a neat – and thoroughly dishonest –solution it would be if you could get the bank to provide more money in a way that neither was nor appeared to be a further loan or an extension of credit so that you could pay that money back into the bank and thus appear to reduce your existing borrowing and thus get the Monetary Authority off the case, at least for the time being.

A very attractive, if unscrupulous, solution to the problem; but what of the first question that I posed? How can it be carried off? How can you make use of letters of credit to achieve this? The answer is: by sheer dishonesty, by pretending that there is an underlying and genuine commercial transaction when none exists. No goods. No separate parties. Just you, disguising yourself as both seller and purchaser. Of course, as I said earlier, the banks, both before agreeing to an application for a letter of credit and before paying out to the beneficiary, would want to see the documents which prove that there is a contract to buy and sell the goods and that they have all been despatched and delivered. What are you going to do if there is no transaction? Simple, you just fake the lot.

The essence of the fraud, therefore, is that the bank or banks are led to believe that, in the course of their normal business, and under the terms of the letters of credit, they are paying out money as part of a commercial transaction between independent and separate entities, on behalf of the applicant, the buyer, to the beneficiary, the seller. Moreover, the bank will not have known that there was any risk to itself in doing so because, under the terms of letters of credit, the bank has title to the goods until the buyer has paid into the bank in full and the goods have been delivered. Sometimes the bank, in full knowledge that the buyer has not yet satisfied his obligation to the bank, will nevertheless release the *goods to him so that he can trade them. This is called a trust receipt. But the important thing is that the bank still owns the goods until the buyer has paid the bank for them. So, what is happening in a fraud of this nature is that, as there is no genuine transaction, there are no commodities and, although the bank thinks that it has title to valuable goods, it, in effect, owns thin air, and the whole purpose of the operation, unknown to the bank, is that the applicant for the letter of credit is raising an unsecured loan for himself.*

Occasionally – who knows how often? – the bank will never find out what has happened because the dishonest applicant for the letter of credit will have managed to put the money raised to profitable use and so be able to put the money back, so to speak, intact. But it still is fraud because the bank has been exposed to risk, without knowing it, by advancing money to an uncreditworthy adventurer who cannot satisfy the principal condition, which is to ensure the repayment of the money that has been advanced.

Often, it all comes to light when the bank tires of waiting for the debt to be repaid, very often because payment under the trust receipt is overdue, and so the bank tries to exercise its rights (a) to detain the goods which are supposed to be at the buyer's premises or (b) to get back the goods which have been released and purportedly then traded on by the buyer, and it sends off its investigators, only to find that there never were any goods and that all the documents were false.

You quite often find that a letter of credit fraud is, in fact, a conspiracy involving various people who are connected with and acting for the so-called buyer and seller of the goods to give the impression of independence from each other, when, in fact, they are all taking instructions from one person. Very often they are members of the staff of his company or business, and sometimes they involve others in the provision of false documents, such as people working for haulage companies or the wharfing master at the port where the goods are supposed to lie. Sometimes, they limit the numbers of outsiders and simply fake the documents, such as bills of lading, in-house. But astonishingly, occasionally the conspirators include in their numbers junior officers of the bank which is the intended victim of the fraud.

How does that come about? Well, an obvious explanation is greed and corruption. If enough money is at stake it might be worth the applicant for the letter of credit greasing a few palms so that the relevant members of the bank's staff do not look too closely at these transactions. But sometimes there is another explanation. The prosecution cannot prove whose idea it originally was. In conspiracy cases it is often the case that the identity of the person who first came up with the idea cannot be established; that is not important because all we have to do is establish that there was a conspiracy and that the accused was, knowingly, part of it; and we can prove that this defendant, Chan Wai-king, was a participant in the conspiracy, that he was the one to benefit most, that he controlled, directly or indirectly, all the companies which were used in the scheme and that, even if we cannot prove that the idea came from him in the first place, there is an overwhelming inference that it could not have got off the ground without his knowledge, approval and active support.

Let us suppose that a bank's customer, let us call it Constantbright Commercial Trading and Good Fortune Company Limited, for that is indeed the principal company with which this trial is concerned, is in so much debt to the bank that the bank is seriously overexposed, that is to say, at risk of going under and causing a catastrophe to its other customers, its shareholders and its creditors, and that the Monetary Authority, if it were to find out the true position, might intervene to prevent the bank from lending any more money to Constantbright and to insist on a scheme of arrangement requiring Constantbright to start repaying its existing debt immediately. That could have a number of consequences: the cutting off of any further credit, the likelihood that Constantbright would be put into administration and, with it, the chance that the bank itself might be taken over, with the almost certain consequence that the bank's officers who have allowed the debt to get dangerously out of control will lose their jobs. So, it might even be they who first came up with the idea of paying off the immediate and pressing debt, and making it appear that they are getting Constantbright to behave responsibly, by generating funds from false letters of credit purporting to be from the sale by Constantbright of valuable goods to an overseas, and quite fictitious, buyer. Of course, that must be done with the complicity of the person or persons who run Constantbright, which is hardly surprising as it is for their benefit, and this inevitably means with the cooperation of the company's accounting and bookkeeping staff.

Amongst the false documents which are intended to show that a transaction has taken place are: the cargo receipt, which is a standard form showing that the vendor has delivered the goods to the shipper; and the bill of lading, which is a form of receipt of shipment and accompanies the goods as they travel and is signed by the carrier, the shipper and the consignee and is a legally binding document which shows all the details of the vessel, the goods, the shipper, the sender and the receiver, including their names and addresses, and it records the date of the shipment, a description of the consignment, how it is packed and its weight and its value. It is a standard and standardised form in the shipping industry.

It sometime happens that the ship referred to in the cargo receipt and the bill of lading could not have made the passage because, for instance, at the date shown in them, it was on the other side of the world on other business or was under repair in a dockyard; that would go a long way to proving that the transaction shown in the documents was bogus and that something was afoot but, decidedly, not afloat.

The hallmarks of a letter of credit fraud are:

i.   A large number of letter of credit transactions. This is because it is much easier to slide a large number of relatively small transactions past the scrutiny of senior bank officials and regulatory *authorities than if you appear to be raising a very large sum for a single transaction. It is also much more difficult to see discrepancies and factual impossibilities if they are hidden in a snowstorm of documents than if, for instance, there was just one bill of lading which was being used as evidence to support a very big extension of credit to the applicant. For that reason, it is usually necessary to employ the names of a large number of different companies which are, purportedly, the sellers in the various transactions. Very often you find that there as many as twenty-five letters of credit to create funds for what is, in reality, one attempt to raise money from the bank. I use that number because that is precisely what happened in this case.*

ii. *For that reason these companies are closely associated with and under the control of the buyer, that is, the applicant for the letters of credit. This can be established by a painstaking examination of the shareholding of the companies. Very often, intermediary companies are used but, in the end, it can be shown that the shares of the so-called sellers, the beneficiaries of the letters of credit, are directly, or more often indirectly, controlled by the purchasing company which applies for the letters. And very often this comes down to one man, who is the chairman and principal shareholder of the applicant company. So, if you can trace that line of control, it points very strongly to one entity, whether it is an individual or a group of individuals or a limited company, under the guise of entering into commercial transactions with different companies, apparently buying commodities from itself. In this case the prosecution can prove that the so-called sales and purchases were all made by companies owned or controlled by Constantbright and that the majority shareholder in Constantbright was none other than Lester Chan Wai-king. It will probably come as no surprise to you that the subsidiary companies avoided having Mr Chan as a director. In fact, they avoided doing anything because not one of them appears to have done anything in the way of trading or any other business apart from the bogus transactions which were the bases for the applications for letters of credit in this case. No other activities of any kind; and all of them recently purchased "off-the-shelf" companies. Their shares were all owned either directly by Constantbright, or indirectly by one of its subsidiaries whose shares were owned by Constantbright. Of course, Chan Wai-king could not afford to be seen on the records as a director of any of these newly acquired companies but we can prove that those people shown as directors were connected to him. To take one example, the Perpetual Happiness Make Dollar Company Ltd* *appears, on the documents, to have sold a large quantity of rolled steel joists to Constantbright; the two registered directors of that company were Chan's personal driver and one of the ladies who cleaned the office at Constantbright. And another, Always Good Heaven Typewriter Company Ltd, is interesting. It purportedly sold one hundred thousand porcelain insulators, which were dockside at a port in Vietnam, to Constant Light Company Ltd, which was one of Constantbright's subsidiaries. The price was pretty substantial, shown on the purchase contract as HK$1500 a piece, which seems a bit pricey as you can buy them retail in Honk Kong at around HK$200. It is a puzzle that this company managed to acquire these goods bearing in mind that company searches reveal that it had been lying dormant and was not acquired by the shareholders and directors until the day after the insulators were purportedly sold to Constant Light; but, aside from the date, it would be interesting to know what commercial experience the two directors and shareholders had, as they were Lester Chan's wife's ninety-seven-year-old grandmother and a Nepalese former Ghurkha soldier who had, only three days earlier, acquired Hong Kong Permanent Resident status and who happened to be employed by the security firm which provided the doormen for the apartment block in which Mr and Mrs Chan lived.*

iii. The flow of funds. In a genuine letter of credit transaction you often find that the seller is the manufacturer or the stockholder of the goods being traded, in which case, you would not be surprised to see the funds moving quickly, because X wants to buy them from Y and Y has them readily available and so there should be no delay in performing the terms of the contract, which is to supply them and have them paid for. If, still assuming a genuine transaction, the seller is not in possession of the goods but is merely acting as a factor or broker, you would expect him to have to obtain them from other sources, which could entail some delay as he might have to negotiate a price and arrange delivery and might well have to look to several different sources before he could satisfy the demands of the buyer. But if it can be shown that the seller is neither a manufacturer nor a holder of stock but, nevertheless, the funds were credited to the seller immediately on the bank's agreement to issue a letter of credit and before the seller could possibly have arranged for the supply of the goods, then that is a powerful evidence that there never was a genuine transaction between the applicant and the beneficiary and that the funds were, in reality, being raised at the bank's risk, for some other purpose, and without the bank having the comfort of the security of temporary ownership of the goods. That is precisely what we can prove happened here in some of these transactions; and, of course, if the whole thing is a fraud, the purpose of which is to get the applicant's hands on a large sum of money so that he can make use of it as quickly as possible, well then, he will want to do so without delay and have the funds credited to the beneficiary immediately so that they can be recycled back to him. Because of the complexity of this kind of fraud and the commensurate anxiety to get the money, the so-called applicant sometimes slips up and examination of the documents shows that the seller appears to have released the goods before the letter of credit has been issued. If that can be shown to have happened, it is one more sign of there never having been a genuine transaction. All these things happened in this case.

I mentioned earlier that often the motive of a letter of credit fraud is to enable a company to keep afloat. A company is in debt and its credit lines are overstretched. In order to keep trading, it requires both to access credit from the bank and to pay off some of its debt to other creditors in order that it will continue to supply goods and/or refrain from starting proceedings against it, with a view either to getting payment by forcing the debtor to sell some of its assets or to putting the company into administration. So it applies for letters of credit merely for the purpose of generating some funds, pays off some of the existing debt and, for the time being, is able to keep going. So it is, in effect, stealing money from the bank in order to pay its trade creditors. Let me give you an example, and that concerns trust receipts, which as I mentioned earlier are a means whereby goods over which a bank has a charge, for instance because they were the subject of a letter of credit, are released to the buyer so that he can trade them. But the applicant for the letter of credit, the buyer, has to pay the bank for them within a specified time, and this is known as "retiring" a trust receipt. Well, if the buyer has no money, even though he has sold the goods, so that the trust receipts are overdue for payment, and he is dishonest, an easy way out is for him to apply for more letters of credit, in the way I have indicated, and in a manner which disguises the true identity of the seller, because the truth is that there are no goods, there is no seller and therefore no genuine transaction. So what he is doing is fraudulently raising money from the bank in order to pay off some of his debt to the bank as well as his trade suppliers. As you probably are aware, Chan Wai-king is in the jewellery business in a very big way. He is sometimes called Hong Kong's jewellery king. The evidence will show that, prior to this conspiracy coming into effect, his trading company, Constantbright Sparkle Ltd, was in a prolonged and very serious debt both to its main suppliers and to its bank.

It is the prosecution's case that all these things that I have outlined so far applied in this case. The documents were all fake and therefore there were no underlying transactions and, accordingly, the letters of credit which were applied for and granted and under which the bank paid out money were used solely as a dishonest means to generate funds for the business run by the defendant, with the assistance and full knowledge of his co-conspirators. It might be suggested that there was no intention to defraud the banks and that there was some sort of honest purpose, although it is difficult to see what that could be. But if that is to be the defence case, you will have to ask yourself: why all the dishonest conduct which led the banks to take risks that they would not otherwise have taken?

There is only one defendant in the dock, Chan Wai-king, even though the charge is one of conspiracy. That is because the other conspirators were his employees or nominees or were doing his bidding. Some of these people will be prosecution witnesses, and it is only fair to tell you that they are giving evidence under an immunity from prosecution; they are called "immunised witnesses". That means that they might well have been charged but for their preparedness to assist the prosecution. When you have heard all the evidence you may well come to the conclusion that I foreshadowed earlier that some of the bank officials did not have clean hands either. The principal banks upon which the fraud was practised were Dah Seng Bank and Chong On Commercial Overseas Banking Corporation, the two first banks named in the indictment. They were the issuing bank and the corresponding, or collecting, bank in each of these fraudulent letters of credit. There will be several other banks and financial institutions referred to in the evidence, and this will establish a pattern of conduct to show that this fraud was carried out on a *large scale and on other banks – what we call "similar fact evidence"– and to counter any suggestion that there may have been an innocent explanation for what happened, but these were the two which were the main victims and which the prosecution has chosen to rely on in framing the charges. It is not going to be part of the prosecution case that any of the bank employees must have deliberately involved themselves in the conspiracy but it may be thought that some of them must, at the least, have been less than conscientious in fulfilling their duties because they allowed the scheme to develop: all these letters of credit, without any alarm bells going off earlier than they did. Some of the banks' officials will be prosecution witnesses and it might be suggested that some of them were induced to turn a blind eye; you might even come to that conclusion without the defence even making the suggestion. But if that were said to be the case, the prosecution's response would be: so what? All that would mean is the conspiracy may have involved more people than those who are specifically named in the indictment. It would not provide any sort of defence to the charge. But in fairness, it is only right for the prosecution to point out that some of them may, like the immunised witnesses, have their own axe to grind and you should bear that in mind.* (Doesn't that make me sound decent? Truckett had thought as he had inserted this, although most of the jury will have probably fallen into a stupor by this stage).

Now, I appreciate that this may have been something of an ordeal for you (but you can have no idea what it was like for me having to try and understand the

331

case, even with Pammy Lee's terrific draft) *listening to all this detail. So, rather than going through all the documents and all the supposed transactions with you now, I have decided that the easiest way would be to produce written schedules which will show all the relevant material relating to each one in a fairly digestible form and to have them explained to you by the expert witness, a forensic accountant, who prepared them.*

26

The anteroom outside Courts 31 and 33 on the sixteenth floor of the High Court was an eclectic blend of architectural styles, but Hong Kong municipal predominated. On every storey of the high-rise building, with the exception of the entrance hall, the layout was identical: four grey metal sliding doors in a sombre lift lobby, and then a large, rectangular open area, on one side of which could be seen, and frequently smelt, the male and female conveniences and on two other sides were the entrance doors to the courtrooms. The fourth elevation consisted of floor-to-ceiling, grey-tinted plate glass, looking down to the busy traffic on Queensway, and beyond that, through gaps between the towering office blocks, to the harbour, with Kowloon-side not very far away. Cross-harbour ferries, casino ships, ponderous tugboats towing heavily laden barges, police patrol vessels and the occasional small fishing sampan bobbing queasily in the murky water, all in constant movement.

In a corner, opposite the window and tucked away beside the entrance to the men's lavatory, was a small door marked "Private" and equipped with a numeric security pad.

Behind it lay a corridor where the judges' private rooms were, and across from them were the doors through which they were led into court and to their seats of power. The windows of the judges' chambers looked out onto the steep wooded hillside stretching up to the Peak. Brett O'Brien stood, gazing out at the clumps of wild ferns with fronds bent almost at right-angles and at the plants that he had always thought of as giant rhubarb immediately below, and ruminated, as he had often done, on the contrast between this impenetrable, pathless forest on this side of the building and the pulsating streets and crammed pavements on the other. He had taken off the jacket of his suit and, using his reflection in the glass, was fiddling with the studs which attached his stiff wing collar to the neckband of his shirt, before tying the tapes of the white linen bands which, like the barristers', were part of the robes which he had to wear in court. There was a soft tapping on the door.

'Come in, Henry,' he called without turning away from the hillside. Behind him the door opened and then closed.

'I hope you haven't brought me any more papers,' he said; 'there's going to be quite enough to do this morning. Damn, why are these bloody studs so awkward?'

A woman's cough.

'I haven't brought you any papers, you old fart.' It was Sharon. He turned.

'What the…'

'I know, I know. I should have told you I was coming. But I thought that if I turned up without warning, I might just catch you at it, Brett. So I caught the overnight flight and got in at seven this morning. I went to straight to the house, but you'd already left.'

'What do you mean "catch me at it"?'

She did not look as if she had just arrived after an eight-hour flight. Her auburn hair was smooth and shiny and she was wearing a pale grey linen skirt and jacket which showed no creases or crumples. Her lipstick was a less obvious shade than she had sometimes taken to wearing in the weeks before she left for Australia.

'Ah, come on, Brett! I've been away longer than I should have and I haven't exactly been a dutiful little wife to you, have I? I thought that perhaps you might have had a little dalliance on the side; couldn't altogether blame you if you did. But I hope not. Anyway, I'm back now.'

She paused for a moment and then added quietly, 'If you want me.'

Brett was unsure how to take this or what to say.

'No, I have not had any "dalliance", as you call it. But what about you? You've not exactly been keeping me up to speed with what you've been doing.'

'You need have no fears on that account,' she replied. 'I really have been spending a great deal of time on the house in Parramatta. I don't think I realised how much time it was taking up, and then I...'

There was another discreet knock at the door and Henry put his head round.

'Oh, good morning, Mrs O'Brien. I heard that you had came back. Do you want me to leave, my Lord?'

'No, no, we've got work to do. So, shall I see you this evening, Sharon?'

'Yes, but you're not getting rid of me so easily: I want to come into court and watch. I've heard that this is a big case – it even made *The Sydney Morning Herald* – and I have a feeling that there's a place in the Court of Appeal waiting for you if you get it right.'

'How did you know that the trial was starting today?'

'I have my methods,' she replied with what she hoped was an enigmatic smile. 'And I've not been completely out of touch with my friends in Hong Kong. Social media can be a wonderful thing.'

'I'm not so sure about that. And,' he added, with a touch of bitterness, 'it seems that you've been keeping them more informed about yourself than me. I hope that you've been careful about what you've said.'

'Perhaps I come back later,' said Henry.

'No, no, you stay. Well, perhaps you could organise a couple of cups of coffee for us. I take it that you still drink coffee, Sharon.'

If that stung, she showed no sign of it. Henry went out.

'Sharon. I'm glad you're back.'

Along the corridor, on the other side of the security door, the anteroom was beginning to fill up and people were sitting in the double rows of seats in the centre. There were smoked-glass fronted conference rooms, two of them between the entrance to the courtrooms. In one could be seen Jonathan in his QC's robes, Dempsey in a barrister's black gown, both with wing collars and white bands and wigs (This could be in England, Jonathan had thought), Frank Grinder and Billy Yeung sitting at three sides of the table, Lester Chan at the fourth.

Graham came out of the lift and into the anteroom with Pammy, both in robes, each carrying their wigs in one hand

and a briefcase in the other. They walked towards the giant window, Graham slightly ahead. A woman's voice called from behind him.

'Hey, prick-face!'

He turned. Charlie and Liz, in dark suits, were sitting next to each other at the end of the row of seats.

'You're not in this case, are you?' Graham had not been told how many juniors from the Hong Kong Bar the London silk would have, but he knew of cases in the past where wealthy defendants had wanted show that they could afford an abundance of lawyers. He didn't think that he could take several weeks of these two and their abuse.

'No,' replied Liz or Charlie. 'No such luck. Wouldn't have minded getting into Lester Chan's piggy bank, though.'

'No, we wouldn't,' said Charlie, or was it Liz? 'No, we've come to wish you luck and to support you. We'll be in court today and in your corner. We thought you might like a bit of backing.'

Graham smiled in surprised appreciation. 'That's very kind of you, er, guys.'

'Not that our wishing you luck will be much use to you,' added one or the other. 'You'll need a lot more than that with a London silk against you. Not to mention the judge. He's an old toughie; doesn't like time-wasters. Gave me a very hard time when I appeared in front of him a couple of weeks back.'

'Or perhaps he doesn't like…' Graham recalled their behaviour on the junk trip, but thought it better not to continue.

陳

From inside the conference room, Frank Grinder thought he saw a familiar figure in the burgeoning throng on the other side of the glass. He stood. Yes it was.

'Excuse me,' he said to Chan and to Jonathan. 'I've just got to go and speak to someone.'

He got up and went outside.

'What on earth are you doing here?' he exclaimed.

'It's part of my new job, old man,' said Rambo.

'What new job?'

'Because, I had definitely taken your advice not to go into business with Sicky. I know his dad's not a good egg. Also, that he might be going to prison soon. And so, I had decided that, maybe, it is more better to think of something different.'

'What do you mean by that, Rambo? Do you know who is sitting over there in that room, on the other side of the glass?' and he pointed with his thumb over his shoulder towards the discussion that was going on.

'The room you had just come from?'

'Yes.'

'No.'

'What do you mean, "No"?'

'Like, no I don't know who's in there. Looks like another *gweilo* with some lawyer's clothes on and a local who dress like him with the same thing on his head and some other locals.'

'One of the locals is Lester Chan. You know, Chan Wai-king. The father of your friend Sicky. And I am one of his lawyers.'

'Yes, Older Sister told me that you were going to court today in a very big case. So you must be the boss man.'

'No, I'm not. I am just… Never mind. The question is: what are you doing here? What new job?'

'Well,' and Rambo paused, thinking how best to explain it to his brother-in-law. 'Well, old chap, I decide that, after all, I want to be a lawyer like you. But not quite like you. Work for the government; that's more steadier. And so I think that I would train to become the top man. The Director of Prosecution.'

'What!'

'Yes, so I get myself a job in the Legal Department, you know, the Department of Justices.'

'Good heavens. As what?'

'I start as an office clerk and work myself up.'

'When?'

'Oh, should take a couple of years, maybe three, before I become top man.'

'No, I mean when did you start. It's news to me. Winnie didn't say anything.'

'This morning, I start this morning. This is my first case.'

'Your first case? What have you got to do with anything?'

'The case in this court. This is my first case,' and Rambo grinned with pride.

'Doing what?' asked an incredulous Frank.

'Very, very important. I bring important things for our *gweilo*.'

'Rambo,' said Frank, trying to be as patient as he could, 'what do you mean by "our *gweilo*"? Who are you talking about?'

Rambo pointed towards the glass wall overlooking the harbour.

'That man over there. The one next to the *ho leng* girl, the very pretty lady. The one with the lawyer's head thing in his hand.'

'Do you mean the one with those two women talking to him?'

'Yes, him. That is our *gweilo*. I've got some writing papers for him. And a pen.'

'Do you mean Graham something, er, Graham Truckett?'

'Yes, that's who.'

Frank inhaled loudly.

'Rambo, that is counsel for the prosecution in the case where I am one of the lawyers for the defendant, Lester Chan. I'm sure it's him: I saw him when we had the bail application. Oh shit!'

'Had you done something wrong, Frank?' said Rambo sympathetically. 'Never mind, we all make mistakes. You know that you can always tell me about it, old man.'

'No, I have most definitely not done anything wrong. But you, Rambo, have put me in a difficult position. Why on earth didn't you tell me that you were going for a job in the Department of Justice?'

Rambo looked hurt. 'I thought that you would be please,' he said.

'Well, I am, in a way. I am glad that you have, at last, got some sort of real work. But don't you see? We are related by marriage and working for opposite sides in the same case.'

He thought for a while.

'Look, Rambo, I really am happy for you and I wish you well in your new job. I can't prevent you from carrying out your, um, important new duties, but I think it best if you don't tell anyone that you're my brother-in-law.'

Rambo nodded sagely, as if he understood.

'But I can't stop here, talking to you. I'd better go back in,' and he returned to the conference room.

'I'm sorry about that,' he said as he closed the glass door behind him. 'I saw somebody I know and I had to speak to him.'

'About my case?' asked Lester Chan.

'Well, yes. Look, I'd better be frank.'

'You are Frank,' said Chan.

'Yes, I know that. Did I tell you,' and he addressed the whole room, 'that my wife is local? That she's a Hong Kong Chinese? I'm much older than her and she has a younger sister and a younger brother.'

A polite silence.

'I had a bit of a shock when I saw her brother in the hall out there.'

Curious silence.

'That's why I had to go and speak to him and find out what he was doing here.'

The curiosity was growing.

'And it turns out that he's got a job with the Department of Justice, at a very humble level, I'm glad to say. He was bringing some stationery for Mr Truckett.'

'I see,' said Jonathan reflectively; 'that might cause some embarrassment. Does he live with you and your wife?'

'Fortunately not. But we do see him, and he and the rest of his family came over to Cheltenham to stay with us some time, well, not that long, ago. And he is constantly popping in to our apartment now that we're back in Hong Kong. I can see that this might make things awkward. I can assure you all that I had no idea that he was even considering applying for this job, let alone that he had got it. This is the first I've heard of it, just now.'

'I see,' said Jonathan. 'I don't think that any rules have been broken; in fact, I know of a case in England where husband and wife barristers ended up appearing on opposing sides in the same case, although that did raise a few eyebrows. And it's not as if your young brother-in-law is in any position of influence. I don't believe that warrants mentioning it to the judge – what do think, Dempsey? No? Good. But it would probably be sensible if I had a word with prosecuting counsel and asked him to make sure that, what is his name…?'

'Rambo,' said Frank. 'Well, of course, that's not his real name – that is Wong Chi-king – but that's what he calls himself.'

'Really? That's a bit odd, isn't it?'

'Not at all. When you've been in Hong Kong a bit longer, you'll realise that that's quite reasonable compared to some of the names that people give themselves. There's a Symphony and a Superman out there and even a Vagina.'

'What! Well, I'll go and have a word with Truckett and explain the position and suggest that, er, Rambo is kept away from this case and this court whilst the trial is going on. Do you agree, Dempsey?'

'Yes, that sounds like a good solution,' said Dempsey.

'And you, Billy, er, Mr Yeung?'

'Yes, of course. Whatever you two say. You are the counsel.'

'Thanks,' said Frank, somewhat relieved.

'But,' Jonathan went on, 'the person most concerned is the defendant. I have to say that I don't think that there is the remotest chance that the case would be stopped, or even delayed, because of this, but it is your decision, Mr Chan, whether or not you wish me to go any further than I have just suggested. Would you like me, for instance, to let the judge know?'

'What, you mean you phone the judge and tell him what to do?' Chan was impressed with his London QC's authority and influence. 'You make a private call to him?' The possibilities seemed to be very attractive.

'No, of course not. I mean would you like me and counsel for the prosecution to ask if we can go and see the judge together? In his chambers.'

'No,' replied a crestfallen Chan. 'No, you leave it as you said. Or, how about maybe, you don't say anything to Mr Bucket?'

'I think that I must at least explain the relationship between Mr Grinder and Rambo. Why don't you want me to?'

'Because,' said Chan, his confidence returning, 'it is good to have a spy in their side.'

'Mr Chan,' said Frank forcefully, 'that is not going to arise. There is absolutely no possibility that I would use young Rambo to obtain information or to try to influence the other side. In fact, I will tell him that we are not going to talk about this case until it's all over. I hope you understand.'

'Mr Grinder is, of course, quite right,' Jonathan said, and Dempsey nodded. Billy said something to Chan in Cantonese.

'So, if you say so,' he replied, smiling to himself.

Outside, in the antechamber, Liz and Charlie got up and started towards the lift lobby.

'Bye,' one said. 'Better get back to work. You don't really want us in court, watching you, do you?'

'Perhaps not,' said Graham. 'But I appreciate you coming.'

They left.

'Hello, it is Graham, isn't it?'

He turned and saw an immaculately dressed man. A Westerner, with a dark, sharply-tailored suit of an obviously top-of-the-range material, gleaming white shirt and an impeccably knotted and discreetly patterned silk tie that obviously, but quietly, proclaimed that it had come from one of those exclusive, uncrowded shops in the Landmark or the ICC or the top floor of Pacific Place, where the sale of one item would probably pay the rent for a week. A dark blue silk handkerchief drooped with studied nonchalance from his top pocket.

'Erm, hello,' said Graham, conscious of the expanse of grubby shirt showing beneath his court jacket. 'I know that we've met…'

'It's David. David Cockcroft. We were on a junk trip together. KC Law's junk. Sandy, my wife, was there.'

'Yes, of course, sorry I didn't immediately remember where we'd met. You're a solicitor, aren't you?'

'Yes, that's right. I'm a partner at Luck &Egg.'

'Of course. I'm a bit distracted. I've got this big trial that I'm about to start.'

'Yes, I've heard about it.'

'But, hang on, you're not involved in it, are you?'

A slight shudder disturbed Cockcroft's flawless demeanour.

'No, no,' he replied hastily, 'our firm does not get involved in criminal law.'

'Well, what are you doing here? You've not come to wish me luck, too, have you?'

'Well, I will if that might help. But no, I have a mention in Court 33. It's a company matter. Rather important. We act for a very, very big multinational conglomerate.'

An almost palpable aura of condescension surrounded Cockcroft. There was something about many of these sleek corporate lawyers – not all of them, but a lot – that galled Graham. Criminal cases, it suggested, were grubby and beneath the consideration of these high-earning solicitors. Perhaps, he conceded to himself, he was jealous of the huge fees that they commanded, but he was, nevertheless, happy that he could sink a few bottles of Filipino San Mig with some mates at a pub in Wanchai, something that you would never see these tossers do.

Cockcroft turned and started towards the doorway of that court.

'So, *bonne chance*,' he said and absorbed himself instantly into his far more important business.

Graham turned back to Pammy.

'There's something about that bloke that makes me want to nut him. Perhaps it's his type rather than the man himself, but they really do get up my jacksie.'

'I am sorry, Graham,' she said. 'I don't understand what you mean.' Did she not understand the word or the sentiment? Her face gave nothing away.

'Oh, I mean they're all so bloody superior.'

But he had more to worry about than that. Perhaps an overreaction caused by nerves.

'My goodness, what are all these people doing here?' A quavering voice behind him.

At his shoulder was a slight, dusty figure in an elderly black suit. Watery, pale eyes and thinning grey hair combed from a side parting like a faded echo of a school photograph from long ago.

'Oh, hello, Judge,' said Graham. 'I didn't expect to see you here.'

'Why are they all here?' responded Mr Justice Squires querulously. 'This is the judges' corridor. They've no right to be here. You're Trickett, aren't you?'

'Graham Truckett, Judge. But I think that you might have made a mistake. This area is open to the public. It's the anteroom to Courts 31 and 33. These people, myself included, are mostly waiting to go into court. To Mr Justice O'Brien's court.'

'Goodness me, I must have come through the wrong door. And I'm on the wrong floor. I'm in Court 11, not these courts.'

'That's several floors down.'

'I know that,' said Squires testily. 'I know which floor my court is on. But how am I going to get to my chambers from here?'

'Can't you go through the security door, over there?'

'Of course not. Be sensible. You can't get through from the public area; otherwise all sorts of riff-raff could get in.'

'Well, all I can suggest is that you go down in the lift to the entrance lobby and then leave the building and come back in again through the judges' entrance. Would you like me to show you where the lifts are?'

'Please don't treat me like a geriatric,' snapped the judge, 'but which way is it?'

Graham pointed the way to the lifts and the old man hesitantly threaded his way through the throng. Old man, he thought. Why old man? The retirement age is sixty-five. He must have been born elderly.

More and more people were coming in. Graham noticed the urbane figure of KC Law, the owner of the junk, whom he had met at the yacht club. He was standing outside the conference room, deep in conversation with Gerry Stratford. He noticed, sitting on one of the seats near them, a man with, even visible from a distance, an extravagantly long growth of hairs sprouting from a mole on his cheek, who was absorbed in wolfing down noodles with his chopsticks from a polystyrene box. A trolley, piled high with cardboard bankers' boxes, leant against the seat beside him.

Jonathan Savage caught sight of Graham Truckett through the tinted glass.

'Come on, Dempsey,' he said, 'we'll just go and say hello to the opposition.'

'Good move,' said Lester Chan. 'Good tactic. Keep them sweet.'

Jonathan said good morning to the messenger as they came out of the conference room, but he was concentrating on his noodles and did not respond.

'He's considering the merits of making a stay application,' said Dempsey. 'Or maybe he is considering whether we can challenge the indictment on some technical ground, like insufficient particularisation.'

'Or,' laughed Jonathan, 'he's just wondering how long he will last before he needs another meal.'

They walked across the crowded room towards the window.

'Ah, g'day,' Graham said, transferring his wig to his left hand as Jonathan extended his right. 'I thought that you Pommy barristers didn't shake hands.'

'Oh, that's just a tradition, it's not a rule.' Jonathan thought of adding that it didn't apply to colonials and that he was used to shaking hands with convicts and their descendants, but decided that that wasn't very funny.

'You remember my junior, Pammy Lee?'

'Yes, we met at the bail hearing.' He was hardly likely to forget her. 'And you know Dempsey Ng, I suppose.' He still struggled with pronouncing it.

'Yes, we've known each other for quite a while. How are you, mate?'

'I'm fine, thanks,' Dempsey replied.

Jonathan brought an end to the niceties. 'So, what's the procedure? Presumably we start by empanelling the jury, the same as a trial in England.'

'Yep, just the same as in Oz as well,' said Graham. 'Except for a couple of differences.'

'Oh?'

'Yep. There are only seven on a jury here.'

'Really?'

'Although the judge might order a nine-member jury if he considers that the case merits it. It's a safeguard in a very long trial; it's a buffer against jurors getting ill or being discharged, and going below the minimum that you can continue a trial with.'

'Which is?'

'Five.'

'That's a surprise to me. I've never been in a trial which didn't start with twelve jurors, although sometimes there are casualties and we're left with eleven or ten. What's the other difference?'

'Well, actually, there are two. The first is that you'll find that they tend to be brighter than the average we're used to in Australia and, probably, the UK. As jury trials are above all still held in English, they have to have attained an educational level so that they can be sure of following it. So they're all pretty bright. The other is the excuses they give to try to get out of a serving on a jury, particularly if they know it's going to be a long one. They've all got jobs where they're indispensable or they're running their own business – which is usually true – or they are about to take some very important examination, or get married and go on honeymoon or all of the above.'

'So, how do you get a jury together?'

'Apart from the ''going on honeymoon'' cases, the judge can order that we sit what's called "Carrian hours".'

'What's that? I've not heard of that before,' said Jonathan.

'No, I think it's only in Hong Kong. The jury is in court from eight-thirty in the morning to two-thirty in the afternoon, with a couple of short piss breaks.'

'That sounds hard.'

'That's not the half of it, mate. Once the jury has gone, to get back to their businesses or to study for their Civil Service exams, we have another short break to grab something to eat and then come back to court to argue any points of law which would normally be done in the absence of the jury. So it means that you have to have all your arguments highlighted and ready in advance as the judge won't usually agree to a request to send the jury out during the hours when they are slated to be in court.'

'What happens if something arises while a witness is giving evidence before the jury? Say an unexpected question of the admissibility of part of his evidence comes up; my experience has always been that the jury is sent away while the defence and the prosecution argue the point and the judge gives his ruling and then the jury comes back and then the witness continues with his evidence with or without the part that the judge has ruled on. Surely you can't prevent that happening.'

'All I can say is that sitting Carrian hours tends to concentrate your mind. The defence usually knows, from the written statements, what the witness is likely to say and has to raise any objection before the witness gets to that part, and after the jury has gone home for the day.'

'So, how long does the court sit after the two-thirty break to deal with legal arguments and so on?'

'Any time till about five o'clock.'

Jonathan had not realised how demanding a case in Hong Kong might be. During a trial it was usually necessary to put in several hours of work both before and after the day in court.

'Let's hope he doesn't order these hours, then,' he said.

'You can say that again, mate.'

Jonathan was on the verge of politely requesting his opponent kindly not to call him that, but thought better of it. Antagonism at this stage, or at any stage, was best avoided, and he always found that it improved efficiency if a degree of cordiality could be maintained. They were, after all, fellow professionals. His musing was interrupted by Dempsey.

'What about the boy?'

'What boy?'

'Jonathan, you said you were going to mention it to Graham.'

'Oh God, yes. I almost forgot. Look, Graham, there might be a bit of a problem. There's a young chap, a Chinese chap, who has just got a job with your Department and he has some sort of connection with this case.'

'What do you mean? Is he a witness or something?'

'No, no. He comes to court to give you some sort of assistance.'

'He carries paper,' explained Dempsey.

'Well,' Jonathan went on, 'the coincidence is that he turns out to be the younger brother of the wife of one of the solicitors in the firm instructing Dempsey and me.'

'Brother-in-law,' elucidated Dempsey.

'And it's only because that solicitor is here today – he's the grey-haired Englishman with heavy glasses, over in the conference room – and saw him, that he got to hear that his wife's young brother had got this job. My client doesn't have any objection and I can't foresee any problem with it, but you ought to know.'

'Ah, thanks, mate. No worries. I don't think it's going to fuck the odds.'

'No, I thought you'd say that. Well, not in those words. But I had to mention it to you; perhaps it would be best if he didn't come into court though, after today, and you got someone else to do your fetching and carrying.'

'Well yeah, I'll try. But the Legal Department is not exactly overflowing with spare parts.'

'Mr Truckett, I mean, Graham,' said Pammy, 'I can carry and fetch for you if you need. How about I do that?'

'No,' said Graham, 'bugger that. I mean, certainly not. I want you by my side.'

Hardly surprising but, again, Jonathan kept his thought from his lips.

'Thank you. We had better be getting back to our client,' he said. 'But just before we go, can I take it that the prosecution has no objection to his bail continuing throughout the trial?'

'In my opinion, he shouldn't have got bail in the first place, but nothing has changed, has it, since O'Brien decided to grant it, so no, no objection – unless something happens during the course of the trial. You can tell the judge that. Are you going to kick off this morning with a defence application that bail should continue? That's the usual course in Hong Kong.'

'Thanks, yes. In England, too. I'll tell him that you don't oppose bail.'

When Jonathan and Dempsey returned to the conference room, Lester Chan was very eager to find out what had happened. He half rose from his seat and leaned across the table as they sat down.

'I was watching you,' he said. 'You appear very masterful. You got something good?'

Jonathan paused for a moment.

'I think that we have established a good relationship. We seem to get on alright, so far.'

'Very clever,' said Chan. 'Very useful.'

'And he said that the prosecution won't oppose an application for your bail to be enlarged, that is, to continue during the trial.'

Chan sat back in his seat, his eyes widening.

'*Wah!*, that is good. You are some powerful lawyer, Mr Savage. You make him see the sense in what you say. Very, very strong,' and he looked at Jonathan admiringly.

'It wasn't exactly difficult.'

'No, no, you are too modest. You are a very clever man. Powerful. So I am very happy that Ah Yeung, that is, Mr Billy, he persuade you to come over and do this case for me.'

Dempsey was looking at his slim, elegant Chopard wristwatch. 'I think that we should all go into court now,' he said.

They all rose and started to leave the conference room. Frank looked up and was startled to see his wife walking across the lobby towards him. She was wearing a red, slim-fitting, tailored suit of some linen-like material which he could not remember seeing before.

'Winnie,' he said, 'what are you doing here?'

'I came to bring you good luck,' she said, and she kissed him, shyly, on the cheek.

'Mr Chan, this is my wife. I don't think that you've met before.'

'No,' Chan replied. 'But thank you, thank you, *doh-jeh lei*.'

'Hello, Winnie,' said Billy Yeung. 'So, you have come to support us?'

'*Doh-jeh, doh-jeh*,' Chan repeated. '*M'goi sai. Lei ho ho*.' He grasped her hand and shook it vigorously.

Jonathan took Dempsey aside. 'Is he saying thank you?'

'Yes.'

'He's overdoing it a bit, isn't he?' Jonathan said quietly. 'What's so special about the wife of one of the solicitors coming across to court?'

'That's because of what she's wearing.'

'Seems fairly ordinary to me. She looks very nice in that smart suit, but it's just a suit. And matching shoes.'

'No,' explained Dempsey, 'it's not the suit. It's the colour. Red will bring him good fortune; at least, that's what traditional Chinese believe. And you never know, it might.'

As the group moved towards the entrance to Court 31, a large figure in a dark suit came towards them.

'I've come to wish you all the best,' he said.

'Thank you,' said Lester Chan. 'You are very kind. But who are you?'

'Don't you remember me? I'm Gerry. Gerry Stratford. I appeared for you a while ago in that civil case. In this building. And I was at your dinner party with KC at Lei Yue Mun a few weeks ago. Don't you remember?'

'No.'

'Anyway,' he went on, apparently undeflated, 'I'm here with KC Law. You surely remember him.'

'Yes, of course. He is a friend. But please, I must go into court with my law team. I have a very famous London QC.'

27

Like all the courtrooms in the High Court Building in Supreme Court Road, number 31 had no natural light. Its walls were lined with pale yellowish wood, giving it something of the impression of the interior of an enormous sauna. Three rows of dark red tip-up seats for the barristers and solicitors faced a low wooden wall separating from the rest of the court the raised area on which were the judge's desk and chair. On the wall behind it was a roundel with a bauhinia emblem and, written in English and Chinese: *Hong Kong Special Administrative Region.* You could just make out, behind it, the shadowy outline of the lion and unicorn which had been in its place until July 1997. The entrance was in one of the two walls which lay at right-angles to the judge's section and, on either side of it, were seats for the public and the press. Facing them, and up against the other wall, were two enclosed rows of seats for the jury. Below the judge's seat and in front of the partition, piled with court papers, bibles, textbooks and assorted stationery, was a large table for the court clerk, the interpreter and other officials. The dock was behind the lawyers' row, enclosed in the same wood and topped with sheets of toughened glass; it had enough seats for several defendants and officers of the Correctional Services Department.

The public and press rows were already filling up when Billy Yeung led Lester Chan in and pointed to the dock. They spoke briefly in Cantonese; Chan shrugged his shoulders and went towards it. A CSO officer, in his olive-green uniform, opened the door at the back and let him in.

Jonathan moved into the front row followed by Dempsey who indicated that they should move to the other end.

'In Hong Kong,' he said, 'it is usual for the defence counsel to sit nearest to the jury.'

'Really, why?'

'Because it is always done that way. It is thought to be fair to the defence.'

'I would prefer to be further away,' said Jonathan. 'I think that you can be more forceful when there is some distance between you and the jury. And also, it is difficult for us to talk to each other if there is a chance that they may overhear. And if that's the witness box,' and he pointed to what looked like an upended half of a pale yellow coffin with cushioned ledge inside between the jury and the clerks' table, 'it makes cross-examination less effective if you are right on top of the witness. Would it cause any problem if we were to stay where we are?'

'I don't know,' said Dempsey as Frank Grinder and Billy Yeung came into the row behind them.

As Jonathan sat down and was beginning to arrange his papers, notebook and pens, he was aware that someone was standing in front of him. He looked up. It was Graham

Truckett and he now had his wig on and, over that oddly cut court jacket, he was wearing a barrister's gown of exactly the same material as Jonathan was used to in England, similarly torn and worn – the supposed hallmark of experience.

'Are you going to stay there?'

'Yes, unless there's a problem. I prefer not to sit close to the jury.'

'No, I'm alright with that. Come on, Pammy.'

He went along the front of the raised partition to the other end of the row. A door beside the judge's chair opened and out came a bespectacled figure in his late forties.

'Hello, Henry,' Graham called. 'How are you?'

'I am well. The judge want me to check that everyone is in court. Mr Chan, yes, you are in the dock. You are ready, Mr Truckett? And you, Mr…?'

'Savage, Jonathan Savage,' sounding a bit, he thought, like James Bond.

'Yes, I know you from the last hearing. So, all ready. Good.'

He went back through the door. A moment later it opened again. Taking the cue from the barristers, solicitors and the CSO officer, the whole court rose to its feet. An elderly woman in overalls and carrying a bucket appeared and got her mop caught in the door jamb. She muttered something as she disentangled it and then looked up.

'*AIEEYAAAH!*' she screeched, shouted something in Dempsey's direction and fled back. There was a roar of laughter.

'What did she say?' Jonathan asked.

'She said that she was in the wrong court. That she thought it would be empty. I would be sorry for her but she used some very bad language. She cursed me for misinforming her.'

'You? Why you?'

'Ah, I suppose she mistook me for someone else. All we Chinese in barrister's wigs look the same, you know.'

The court subsided. The door, which the cleaner had left open in her flight, closed again. A few moments later there were a couple of loud raps from the other side, and they were all on their feet again. It opened and through it came the judge's clerk, who went through a wicket gate down into the well of the court; then appeared the Honourable Mr Justice Brett O'Brien, in the same red robes, stiff wing collar, white linen bands and judge's wig as would be worn by a High Court judge trying a criminal case in England. He bowed to the court and sat down, as did the others. Jonathan remained standing.

'Yes, Mr Savage,' said O'Brien.

'My Lord,' he said, 'I am speaking from this position because it is more convenient for me. But I gather that it is conventional in Hong Kong for defence counsel to sit at the other end of the Bar row. If your Lordship is not happy with this arrangement my junior and I will change places with Mr Truckett and his junior, but I have not been told of any practice direction that requires any particular seating arrangement.'

'Mr Savage,' said the judge, 'as far as I am concerned you may sit where you like, within reason, that is. And I am very pleased that you didn't try to lecture me on what the practice is in England. We humble colonial judges get quite a lot of that from visiting QCs from London.'

'No, of course not, my Lord. And whilst I am on the subject of seating arrangements, I sometimes find that, in complex criminal cases, where the solicitors are having constantly to take instructions from the lay client as the evidence progresses, that it is often more convenient if the defendant does not have to sit in the dock but can sit alongside his solicitor.'

'No,' O'Brien said. 'Your client will stay in the dock while the court is sitting, like all other defendants.'

'And may I raise the question of bail?'

'You may.'

'Your Lordship, as you know, bailed him to appear for trial. He has done so, as you can see.'

'Yes, my eyesight is pretty good.'

'Then, I apply for his bail to be enlarged throughout the trial and on the same terms. The prosecution has indicated that it has no objection.'

'Is that right, Mr Truckett?' asked the judge.

Graham nodded, without getting up. He did have an objection, because Chan should not have been granted bail in the first place, but it was no good arguing it now.

'Very well,' O'Brien said, 'bail will be continued on the same terms, whatever they are, to include the lunch breaks – as you will, no doubt, want to talk to your client – and up to the jury's retirement or unless I make a further order.'

Brett sat back in his well-cushioned chair. That's set the tone, he said to himself. A similar reflection went through Jonathan's mind: He doesn't waste time, does he? Graham thought, Brett, you can be a bit of a bastard with your efficiency drive. Oh shit! I never got round to speaking to him again about the incident with Gerry Stratford on the junk trip. Too late now.

'Very well,' said Brett. 'Are we ready to start empanelling the jury?'

Graham stood up.

'No reason why not, your Lordship. Except…'

'So, are you about to give me a reason why we shouldn't?'

'Ah, no, except, er …'

'Well?'

'You haven't indicated whether you want a nine-man jury in this case.'

'"Nine-person" is, I think, the correct expression now.'

'Alright, nine-person. Do you want to have a bigger jury?'

'Are you making an application?'

'Well, it might be a good idea. This trial might take quite a while.'

'It's listed for six weeks, I believe.'

'Yeah, but, you know, these fraud trials can go on longer than they're listed for. Especially with an expensive London silk defending.'

Jonathan was not sure he had heard that correctly. He got to his feet.

'I hope that my learned friend is not implying that I am likely to draw the case out for an improper motive. Or, indeed, at all.'

'Mr Savage,' said the judge, 'you beat me to it. I was about to ask what Mr Truckett meant by that. I hope you were not suggesting that because of his, no doubt substantial, daily fees he would try to draw the case out.'

'No, not at all,' Graham replied. 'I, um, merely meant that they have a reputation for, er, thoroughness and he might take a lot of points. My Lord,' he added.

Jonathan resumed his seat. 'Nifty footwork,' he said quietly to Graham.

'No, this looks like a straightforward letter of credit fraud trial,' said the judge, 'with one defendant, one counsel cross-examining, one defence case and one defence speech. I don't see why the case should take longer than its estimate. Indeed, I think it likely that we will finish before then. So we will have a jury of seven. And I agree, that was smart footwork, Mr Truckett. Bring in the jurors in waiting.'

The clerk nodded to the usher who opened a door which Jonathan had not noticed before. It was set into the wooden panelling, just to one side of the jury box. A few moments later a group of about twenty somewhat bewildered-looking people came through, all of them Chinese apart from a plump European woman aged about fifty, with uncontrolled brown hair and a troubled expression. They moved in silent single file, at the direction of the usher, towards the back of the court.

'Good morning, ladies and gentleman,' the judge addressed them. 'As you know, you have all been called for jury service. As is the practice, more of you are here than will be eventually needed. That is because there may be challenges to some of you and so we must have extras if any of you have to be replaced. Also, I have to tell you that this case concerns the defendant, Chan Wai-king, also known as Lester. He owns a number of jewellery shops, so if any one of you either knows him or knows someone who works for him, could you say so now.'

There was silence.

'Right, that's good. Now, I have to tell you that this case is estimated to last for six weeks. It might take a little more and it could take less; no-one can predict its exact length. If any of you have compelling reasons why you cannot serve on the jury for that long I might be prepared to excuse you. But it is a civic duty to sit on a jury, and if you don't do it someone else will have to. Inconvenience is not an excuse. So it would have to be a really strong justification.'

Silence again. Then a forest of hands.

'Alright, this is what we will do. Your names will be picked from the ballot, that is, at random, as is normal. Then, if your name is called by my clerk and you think that you have a good reason not to serve on the jury, let me know. Alright, Henry, pick the first name from the box.'

'Dawn Walsh.'

The obvious owner of that name took a step forward and half raised her hand.

'What's your difficulty?' asked the judge.

'I'm a teacher. I teach English at junior secondary level. At the Blessed Bernadette and the Bleeding Heart School.' She had a trace of a Liverpool accent.

'Is that, by any chance, a Catholic school?'

'It is, sir. I mean, Judge.'

'And what's the problem? Your pupils are not about to take the Diploma of Secondary Education.'

'No, but six weeks is a long time and it would thrust a burden on the other staff if I weren't there.'

'But teachers do serve on juries, even in long cases. In fact, they make a very positive contribution. If you were ill, the other teachers would have to cover for you. Is there anything else you want to say?'

She shook her head and lowered her hand.

'No, Ms Walsh,' said O'Brien, 'you are not excused. Please go and take your place in the jury box.'

Crestfallen, she followed the usher's direction and sat down.

'Next,' said the judge.

'Ko Yee-choi.'

A puny, balding man with a straggle of hair combed over the crown of his head and wearing a cardigan stepped forward. He raised his hand.

'Mr Ko, you wish to be excused jury service? Why?'

'Because, Sir Judge, I am also a schoolteacher. But I am teaching senior secondary level. So, maybe, approaching diploma exam.'

'And what is it you teach?'

'Because, also English. And physic. And also physical education.'

'At what school?'

'Pardon me?'

'Where do you teach?'

'Please?'

'What is the name of the school where you teach diploma-grade students? Remember, we can check up.'

'I now think I will be on the jury.'

'Good. Take your place.'

There was laughter from the back of the courtroom.

'Poon Man-tin, Martin.'

A smartly dressed man, aged about thirty, stepped forward.

'Excuse me,' he said.

'Look,' said the judge, 'I haven't invited everyone whose name is called to come up with an excuse not to sit on the jury.'

'No, sir, I have a question: whether you think I should be on the jury.'

'What's the problem?'

'I am happy to serve, but my wife is the manager of one of Chan Wai-king's jewellery stores. I have met him several times when he has held banquets for his senior staff and their husbands and wives. So, I began to think that maybe you would not want me to be in this case.'

'You are quite right to tell us, Mr Poon. It is obvious to me that you cannot be on this jury. You can go, but you may be needed in another court.'

The jury selection continued fairly smoothly. There was, indeed, a wedding and honeymoon booked, which the judge allowed, and two employees who claimed to be indispensable to their bosses, which he didn't. One woman said that she had to care for her elderly and ailing mother and that she could manage a short trial but could not count on her neighbours to help out for as long as six weeks; after a series of searching questions about the availability of other members of her family, Brett softened. This woman's life is probably stressful enough without my making it worse, he thought, and her readiness to serve in a shorter trial weighed in her favour. He excused her from this trial. And then, relatively effortlessly, there was a jury of seven men and women sitting in the jury box. Twelve or so people still stood at the back of the court. Brett addressed them.

'Although we have now a full complement for the jury, I must ask you to remain where you are for the time being. You see, the prosecution and the defence have a right to challenge jurors when they come to take the oath or to affirm, and if any are challenged and have to step down we will need some back-up.'

But the jury were sworn in without challenge and Graham was faced with the chilling reality that the trial was about to begin. He stood up, with his opening note in his hand.

'One moment, Mr Truckett,' said O'Brien. 'We haven't discussed the sitting hours. Members of the jury who have just been sworn in, the normal sitting hours in the High Court are ten till one for the morning session and two-thirty till about five for the afternoon. You will notice that there is an hour and a half for lunch and there is an excellent canteen for the jury in this building, so you need not worry that you won't have a chance to get plenty to eat. In addition, I usually allow a short break in the middle of the morning session and another in the afternoon. In some cases, which are expected to run for a long time, we can sit different hours, starting much earlier and finishing earlier. This is to allow for people who are, for instance, running their own small businesses. But it means that there won't be a break for lunch.'

There was a palpable frisson of alarm in the jury box.

'So, if I may ask you to have a quick discussion and let me know what you want to do.'

Shaking of heads and muttering as the three in the front row turned to three of the four in the back. The real teacher sat silent. Then there was nodding and Ko Yee-choi, the putative teacher, stood up in the back row.

'Mr Judge, we all agree. Normal hours, please.'

'Very well,' said Brett. 'I take it that that suits all counsel. Good.' He wondered, briefly, whether to inform the jurors that the correct mode of address was "my Lord" but decided it was better not to be pompous, or at least not appear to be. There was a great deal to be said for establishing a good relationship with the jury from the outset.

'Then, we'll get on,' he said. 'Oh, and the jurors in waiting whose names have not been called may go.'

There was a confused shuffling until the usher pointed to the door, and then the court was silent.

Graham stood up once more and made an extravagant turn towards the clock which was fixed on the wall behind the public seating. Brett wondered why it was that barristers always looked at the clock when they were about to mention something to do with the time. Can't they afford a watch? He guessed what was coming.

'My Lord, it's just gone half-past twelve.'

'Yes, I see it is.' He looked at his wristwatch. 'Yes, that clock is right.'

'Well, my Lord, it's going to take me quite some time to open the case for the prosecution.'

'Yes.' Brett tried to keep his face expressionless.

'Well, er, I was thinking that it might be better not to start till after lunch.'

'What's your view, Mr Savage?'

Jonathan half-rose.

'I'm neutral, my Lord.'

'Is there anything that we can usefully do in half an hour, Mr Truckett? Any points of law or administrative matters that don't require the presence of the jury?'

'No, I don't think so.'

'Well, I don't want to waste court time. Alright, we'll rise now and you can start this afternoon. But earlier than normal. You are ready, I suppose.'

Graham thought that unnecessarily barbed. So, on refection, did O'Brien.

'So,' he said, turning towards the jury, 'today you can have an early lunch and beat the rush. Please be ready to be back in your places by two. Two o'clock.'

He stood up briskly and made for the judge's door before Henry could get there. When he got to his room Sharon was not there; but he had not expected her to stay. It would have been nice, though, to have had lunch together.

28

Graham was all afternoon opening the case to the jury. He tried not to go off script but he found it impossible to avoid throwing in the odd explanatory aside as he watched the jury's reaction to what he was saying. He was determined to avoid giving the impression that he was reading from a script as if he were merely reciting what someone else had written, which, he hoped, only he knew was pretty much the truth. From time to time he shifted his weight from one foot to the other, leaning on his wooden lectern, and occasionally referring to copies in the bundles of exhibits which had, at his request, been placed before the jury by the usher. The short pauses during which they found the documents gave him snatches of relief from speaking; he also found that the occasional diversion, such as when he asked them not to flick through the papers but to follow him as he went through them, provided momentary breaks from the monotony of his recital. Once or twice he went on a little explanatory aside as he appreciated more the significance of the passage he had just come to, dealing with a particular aspect of the prosecution's case. As much as he could, without staring too obviously, he tried to watch the reaction of the jurors to what he was explaining to them. Some, from time to time, nodded as if to indicate that they understood; some were impassive and it was impossible to tell whether they were at all on his side at this early stage of the trial. One or two, in particular the comb-over Mr Ko, simply looked bored.

He was beginning to get backache. He was also finding it quite warm; he knew from experience that the air-conditioning fans in this court were idiosyncratic and if he had been at the other end of the row he would almost certainly be feeling too cold. He glanced at his wristwatch: it was half-past four. Another thirty minutes to go

'Mr Truckett.'

It was the judge.

'Mr Truckett, I hesitate to interrupt your flow but, like Mr Savage, I have the advantage of having a copy of your opening address to the jury.'

'Yes, my Lord. I'll try not to go off-piste too much.'

'No, it's not that. This isn't a criticism.'

Graham was relieved.

'No,' continued Brett, 'I can see that you have still got a long way to go and – am I right? – there's no real possibility of your being able to finish by five.'

He was even more relieved. 'No chance,' and just in time he stopped himself from adding "mate". 'No, my Lord,' he said.

'Well, I think that it is a lot for the jury to take in. And I am conscious that there is quite a lot of physical strain on you.' That will show the jury what a considerate judge I can be, he thought.

'So, if you would like to find a convenient moment, we will rise early for today.'

'Now would be a good time,' Graham replied. 'I was just about to turn to a different topic.' And, Brett, you're human again.

'Right,' said the judge. 'Ten o'clock tomorrow, ladies and gentlemen of the jury,' and he was up and making his way through his door before Henry could get there. Sharon had not come into court, after all. It would be wonderful if she were waiting in his room.

But she wasn't there. He looked out of his window at the gloomy hillside climbing up toward The Peak. It was beginning to drizzle and water dripped off the dark green gunnera plants, which crowded the bent leaves of fake pineapple ferns, almost it seemed within touching distance. It would not be too long before the sudden, short dusk would come down; lights in a few of the windows in the apartment blocks in Mid-Levels were already on. Already there was that dull, comfortable sense that he often experienced at this time of day when Sharon was away, the evening was approaching and he had no work to occupy him. He went to his desk and sat down, waiting for his clerk to arrive.

There was a tap. For a moment, his spirits rose. But it was Henry, after all, opening the door in that cautious way he always used.

'So, my Lord.'

'Yes, Henry.'

'Yes, my Lord.'

'Yes, what?'

'I said yes because you had.'

'Had what?'

'You had said yes.'

'Henry, what are you talking about?'

'About what you had said.'

'Henry, let's cut this short. Has the listing office added anything for tomorrow morning?'

'No, my Lord. I told them that this is a big and difficult case and that you will have much work and reading and writing to do while it is running and that they should not add to your burden. Except urgent.'

'That was very thoughtful of you, Henry. As it happens, we haven't yet reached the stage when I have to work every evening. That won't happen, I imagine, until the evidence starts. That's when I'll have to make notes of what the witnesses say so that I can work on my summing-up as we go along. But you know that. And I very much appreciate your concern for me. But as they haven't added anything for tomorrow, unless there is anything else that you want to mention, it looks as if I shall have a free evening. Er, I don't suppose my wife gave you any message for me?'

'No, but she had write a note for you.'

'Did she?'

'Yes, I put it on your desk. Oh, the cleaner came in. Here, it is under your newspaper which came today.'

Henry moved the weekly edition of *The Australian* aside, and there was a pale blue envelope. In Sharon's distinctive handwriting it read "Personal. To the Hon. Mr Justice Fart".

'Thank you, Henry. I won't need you any more today. Would you let my driver know that I will be ready to leave in ten minutes?'

He waited until Henry had gone and then opened the letter. Inside was a slip of paper: "I popped into court this afternoon but you were too busy looking bored to notice your wife. See you at 6.00 at the Admiral's Bar? XXX".

29

Graham Truckett spent almost the whole of the next morning completing the opening of the prosecution's case. The jury seemed to be paying attention, or at least listening to him without too many signs of boredom or distraction, and even Mr Ko has stopped fiddling with his watch. Some of them were, from time to time, taking notes. Dawn Walsh seemed to have overcome her initial disappointment at having to be there and occasionally nodded attentively, perhaps even empathetically, as he pursued little avenues of explanation to illustrate a point that he had just made. It was all quite encouraging, but the morning break, when it came, was welcome.

He and Pammy went down in a crowded lift to the lawyers' restaurant where she insisted on finding a chair for him and ordered coffees for them both.

'It's very tiring, standing and talking all this time,' he said.

'But you are doing a wonderful job,' she replied admiringly. Was that also adoringly? No, get a grip, Graham told himself, she's just being nice, that's all, and he took a sip of the scalding, black, bitter coffee that had been filled to the brim so that there was no room to cool or weaken it with milk. Every time he had coffee in this place it always came like that, and he regularly resolved to avoid it. It was so hot that there was never enough time to drink more than a mouthful before the recess was over, which was probably just as well as it was always disgusting and tasted as if it had been made from mud and concentrated Vegemite. Chinese tea would have been much better and probably what Pammy would have got for herself if he had not been with her. More soothing for his throat too, he imagined.

After a few more sips, he stood up.

'You can stay for a bit longer, but I think that I had better go on up. I don't want to risk being late. I've no idea what mood O'Brien is in today.'

'No, I will come with you. I think that the judge is in a very nice mood; he seems to like you. He is listening carefully to what you say.'

'Well, he's not interrupting me. That's one good thing.'

Back in court the defence team was already there. Perhaps they hadn't left. No, Graham noticed that they had fancy cardboard cups which must have been brought in from an outside coffee shop. They all took what had already become their established places, the judge came in and then the jury was brought into court. Graham waited until they had settled down, glanced at the judge for his nod of approval, rose to his feet and continued with his address. The jurors, for the most part, still seemed to be attentive to what he was saying. He carried on until just before ten to one, saw with relief that he was on the last page and concluded.

'So, that's it, members of the jury. That's an outline of the prosecution case,' he said and sat down, relishing both that he was no longer on his feet and that he had managed to get through the opening without any mishaps. He turned to Pammy, who was looking anxiously at him. That was disappointing; he had hoped for one of her engaging smiles.

The court was silent. Then the judge spoke.

'Yes, Mr Truckett?'

Graham stood up wearily.

'I've finished my opening address, my Lord.'

'Yes, I realise that.'

'Well, that's all I've got to say,' said Graham, puzzled. 'Your Lordship,' he remembered to add.

'Well, are you not going to call any witnesses? Because, if you're not, I imagine that Mr Savage will have something to say. Perhaps he'll make an application for me to enter a verdict of not guilty on the basis that the prosecution has offered no evidence.'

Jonathan tried not to smirk at his opponent's discomfiture. He turned slightly towards Dempsey, who was smiling.

Oh shit!, thought Graham but, just in time, managed not to say it aloud.

'Yes, of course, my Lord. Of course, I will be calling evidence. The first witness will be PW1, Alfonso Lam, the manager of the Dah Hing Commercial Bank. Do you want me to start the evidence now?' Again in an exaggerated gesture, he looked at the clock on the wall and then at his watch.

'No, you can start to call your evidence at two-thirty,' said the judge. 'Members of the jury, please be back and ready to start then; have a good lunch. Mr Chan, you will please be back in the dock ten minutes earlier, that is, by two-twenty. That should help avoid accidental contact with jurors or witnesses. Don't think that I am being hard on you by cutting your lunch break; that is the usual practice in trials.' He rose quickly and, once again, was at his door before Henry could get there.

Lunch for Jonathan Savage was the first in a pattern that established itself that day, and which he would have done anything to avoid except be rude to his client, for Lester Chan had reserved a large table in a restaurant in nearby Hong Kong Park. Jonathan would have valued the chance to chat to Dempsey and, perhaps, Frank Grinder, or even to go off with his own thoughts and a sandwich by himself; but he assumed that eating with the lay client and the whole of the legal team was the convention here, so he made no demur and was led, still wearing his wing collar and bands and his QC's black, sleeved waistcoat with its cloth-covered buttons and ridges of piping, along with Dempsey and Frank and Billy Yeung and the messenger and, of course, Chan, to a long table where they were plied with pre-ordered dishes of noodles, rice, meat, fish and vegetables. He declined Chan's offer of beer or wine.

'So, because you keep your head to be clear,' he said approvingly. 'You are very wise,' and he sat Jonathan down next to him. Frank cast a sympathetic glance and took a small bowl of noodles. Once again, Jonathan was struck by how impervious the Hong Kong Chinese seemed to be to any feeling that they had, perhaps, had enough to eat. Lester Chan used his chopsticks to shovel in mouthfuls of food whilst maintaining a commentary on how he thought the trial was going so far. Out of politeness rather than a real interest in having a conversation, Jonathan made anodyne responses, mostly to observe that, at this very early stage, it was not possible to draw any conclusions and that the prosecution's opening speech contained no surprises, as they had seen it, in written form, and had been able to study it. Chan would reply by saying that that showed what a very clever London QC he was. Then he said,

'I think the judge like you much better than the prosecutor.'

'Why do you say that?' said Jonathan.

'Because, at the bail case, he scolded the prosecution lawyer.'

'Well, that was because he hadn't got himself ready for the bail application. That was quite a while ago; he seems to have prepared his case pretty thoroughly since then.'

'Yes, but yesterday, the judge still seemed cross with him.' Chan spoke with an air of certainty that the trial was going his way and, putting his chopsticks down on the tablecloth, leant back in his chair. 'You see, I am very good at looking at character: that is how I made a success of my businesses.'

'It's early days yet, Mr Chan,' Jonathan said. 'You really can't form an opinion yet. But, much more importantly, it's the jury that matters. It will be the jury that decides the case.'

'Ah, yes, but the judge, he can influence them. He can make them follow his wish. I know this.'

'That might, perhaps, have been the case once, but I don't think that applies anymore, not in my experience. And I shouldn't think that it's any different in Hong Kong these days.'

'But I know the judge does not like Mr Bucket. I know that he has a reason.'

'Honestly, Mr Chan, I don't think you should speculate on this. Do you know what I mean? You shouldn't try to guess what is in the judge's mind.'

'I know, already, what is in his mind. And I can see that he respect you.'

'Hang on a minute. Do you mean that you know about something that might influence the judge's attitude or are you just making a comment about what you have seen in court?'

'I told you that I know.'

'Mr Chan, if there is something that might affect the integrity of the trial, I think you had better tell me what it is. You realise, don't you, that I am bound by rules of professional conduct? What is it that you know?'

Lester Chan smiled, picked up his chopsticks and, while shovelling noodles from his raised bowl into his mouth, was somehow able to convey an air of intrigue.

'What I know, I had been told by a lawyer, a barrister. Not Chinese. I know him from a different case. He is a friend of a friend of mine. He tell my friend that the judge does not want to be in this case because it takes too much of his time. Too long. My friend says that the lawyer told him that the judge is angry with Mr Bucket because there was a way to make this case very short but the prosecution would not do it. That is what the lawyer tell my friend.'

'Mr Chan,' said Jonathan, 'that sounds like nothing but gossip and I can't believe that it has any substance. I really think that you should not take any account of what your friend told you.'

'I see. But, Mr Salvage, my friend KC Law is reliable. And you can see that the judge has been cross with the Mr Bucket.'

'First of all, his name is Truckett. More importantly, you should not read anything into what went on between the judge and him. Judges often get impatient when they think a barrister has made a mistake. So, let's just conduct your defence normally.'

'You may say that,' replied Chan, mystifyingly.

'Alright, Mr Chan. Look, if you don't mind, I would like to get back into the court now. I must have a look at some papers I left in there, with my wig and gown. Don't forget that you have to be there by twenty past two. If you're late, your bail might be stopped.'

'No, I won't be late. I would not spoil all the hard work you did for me in getting me the bail.'

'Right,' said Jonathan, 'I'll see you in court.' He had always wanted to say that.

30

Back in court, with everyone in their now accustomed places, Graham Truckett began to call his evidence, starting with prosecution witness number one, the exotically named, or possibly Macanese, Alfonso Lam, who was the first of the many bank officials to be called to the witness box.

Now, dear reader, this was a trial that was estimated to last for six weeks and we have only got up to the first day and a half. It is a common enough perception that criminal trials, if not high drama, are at least interesting; and that may be reasonably true of some murder cases. There are, of course, many proceedings where there are instances of humour and, occasionally, of theatricality and tension, but that is about it; those moments are just that, sporadic oases in an arid and seemingly infinite desert. The truth is that most criminal trials comprise long stretches of pulverising boredom for those not actively engaged in them (and even, often, for those who are), and fraud trials of any kind are particularly prone to numbing tedium; and the letter of credit fraud outstrips all the others in its dreariness for the disinterested observer. So, if this tale were now to continue with a recital or even a résumé – or what lawyers are fond of calling an adumbration – of the evidence that was called as the days turned into weeks, you would, before long, be unable to resist the urge to consign this book to the recycling bin, or put it in the pile on the bedroom floor with all the others you have abandoned part-way through with a half-meant intention to pick it up again if you were struck down with some debilitating illness that confined you to your bed; or possibly, and if you were sufficiently mean-spirited, you might gift-wrap it and give it as a Christmas present to an unloved, elderly relative from whose estate you had absolutely no prospect of any inheritance.

On top of all that, there has to be some prospect that, before too much of the rainforest has been sacrificed for its pages, a book will eventually come to its conclusion. So, you will be relieved to hear that you will not now have to plough through all the evidence that Graham Truckett and, on the odd occasion when a witness's testimony was unlikely to be complicated or controversial, Pammy Lee called in support of the prosecution's case before the jury: not their evidence-in-chief or the cross-examination by Jonathan Savage, who would have liked to have allow his patently competent junior, Dempsey Ng Dim-si, to question a few of them but who had been quietly alerted by Frank Grinder that their client would not take kindly to it because Billy had told him that his increasing admiration for Jonathan did not mitigate his instinct to get value for money. As Billy put it, 'He thinks that, as he is paying top dollar for a top London QC, no-one else should do your work.'

And so, the trial progressed, day in and day out, from Mondays to Fridays. Witness after witness was called and documents detailing the letter of credit transactions were put before the jury; and every evening, after the court had risen and the jurors had gone home, Brett O'Brien spent a couple of hours or so in his chambers, writing a condensed version of the day's evidence and the issues that had arisen, in preparation for his summing-up. In court, when the prosecution had finished asking each witness questions, Jonathan would rise and either point out the occasional inconsistency or apparent discrepancy in their testimony or in the paperwork they produced or, from time to time, would suggest to the witness that the truth was different and would put the case, which he now understood, and which he had failed to absorb all that time ago when he had first come out to Hong Kong; could it really only have been a couple of months earlier?

So, although it would be egregiously tedious to recite all the evidence, you need a flavour of what went on in court and here it is:

Jonathan put to the bank officials from the Wing Bahn Bank and the Hanoi Commercial Bank that there were genuine transactions but that a mistake had been made in the documentation, resulting in their being described as rolled steel joists when, in fact, they were consignments of pig iron, so that the goods did exist, and that the inspectors would have found them in storage at the dockyard if they had known what to look for.

'You may so, but *m'hai*, it is not yes,' replied the Wing Bahn official.

He suggested the same explanation to the man from Hanoi Commercial Bank. The Vietnamese interpreter said, 'His reply is: that cannot be true.'

'How does he know?'

'He says that it was he who went to check on the goods after the letter of credit had been arranged.'

'Yes, but was he looking for rolled steel joists?'

This was interpreted to the witness.

'Yes, he admits that he was.'

'So all that he recorded was that there were no rolled steel joists?'

'That is correct. There were no steel joists.'

'He was not looking for pig iron and, in any event, would not have expected to see pig iron.'

'That is correct.'

'Because, at the time, it was illegal to import pig iron into Vietnam?'

The witness thought for a moment and then answered, through the interpreter, 'It was not wholly against the law. There was, at the time, a restriction on the amount of pig iron that could be imported. I think the importer would have to have a special licence. But it did not apply, I think, to bonded goods in transit. Or so I believe.'

'Alright, but, Mr Interpreter, please put this to him: You only would have made a note of the existence, or absence, of the commodity that you expected to find.'

'He says that is also correct.'

'He was not looking for pig iron and would not have made a note if that's what he had seen.'

'You may say that.'

'Please, I want an answer: yes or no.'

'Yes, he says that is so.'

'So, if he made no note, he cannot be certain that there were no goods underlying the transaction.'

'He says that is not so.'

'Why not? If there had simply been a misdescription of the goods in the bill of lading and the other documents relating to the transaction and if, therefore, he was looking for the wrong commodity, how can he be sure that there were no goods at all and, therefore, no underlying transaction?'

An animated discussion in Vietnamese took place between the interpreter and the witness.

'My Lord…' Jonathan addressed the judge.

'Yes, Mr Savage, I know just what you are going to say. Mr Interpreter, please tell the witness simply to answer the question and not get into a debate with you.'

'My Lord,' replied the interpreter, 'he wants me to tell him how to answer the question without disappointing the lawyer.'

'Just tell him to answer truthfully and not to worry about anything else. Put your question again, Mr Savage.'

'Mr Nguyen,' Jonathan said to the witness, 'I suggest that you cannot be certain that there was no underlying transaction to the letter of credit because you were looking for rolled steel joists in the warehouse and, if there had been a misdescription of the goods and the deal was really about a consignment of pig iron, you would not have been looking out for pig iron; all that you noted was that there were no goods fitting the description in the documents that you had.'

'He says that you may suggest that,' said the interpreter.

'Yes, I know I may,' replied Jonathan, a trifle more testily than he intended. 'Just answer this question: Were you sent to see if there was a consignment of rolled steel joists?'

'Yes.'

'Were you looking for anything else?'

384

'No.'

'And you found no steel joists?'

'There were none.'

'And you recorded that fact?'

'Yes, I wrote it down when I was there.'

'But you did not record the presence of any other materials in the warehouse?'

'I did not.'

'So, if there had been a consignment of pig iron, it would have been of no interest to you at the time and you would not have made any note of it?'

'That is so.'

'Good,' said Jonathan. 'Now we're getting somewhere. So, what I am putting to you is that, assuming that there may have been an error in the documents, you cannot say for certain that there were no goods and therefore there was no genuine underlying transaction, as the prosecution claims.'

A short exchange started again between the witness and the interpreter.

'Mr Nguyen, please. The judge has previously told you just to answer the question. I don't want to have to go through it all over again. Do you understand the questions that I have just asked you?'

'Yes.'

'Then, please, what is your answer?'

'His answer is that it is not so.'

'How? After what you have agreed to, how can you possibly say that you are sure that there was no real transaction?'

The witness paused and looked embarrassed.

'Come on, Mr Nguyen. Please answer.'

The interpreter scribbled a few notes and then said, 'He says that he is sorry to make you lose face. But he can be sure because when he got to the place where the bill of lading, the cargo receipt and the copies of the correspondence with the Hanoi Commercial Bank said that goods were stored – the rolled steel joists – he found that the warehouse looked derelict, and when he asked around at the dockyard he was told that it had closed many years before. He even looked through one of the broken windows and there was nothing inside.'

'May I have a moment, please, my Lord?' Jonathan turned back towards his instructing solicitor to see if there was anything else he needed to go into. Billy Yeung shook his head slightly. In the dock, Lester Chan was smiling and giving him a thumbs-up sign.

When the manager of Chong Hing Commercial Bank was called, Jonathan cross-examined him.

'Mr Sin, I believe that you speak English fluently, as your correspondence would suggest.'

'Yes, I do,' he replied, in English.

'Then may we continue in English, rather than having my questions translated into Cantonese and your answers into English? It might save a great deal of time.'

'Yes, of course.'

'Thank you. Now, your evidence has been that you entered into a letter of credit agreement with the Wing Seng Bank.'

'Yes.'

'Your bank was the corresponding bank and Wing Seng was the issuing bank.'

'Yes.'

'And the transaction was said to be a consignment of pork bellies. You recall that?'

'And that is also what the documents show.'

'Yes, I accept that. But, Mr Sin, would you please look in the bundle of exhibits at page 1,043. You will be shown it by the court clerk.'

Henry hurriedly pulled the relevant file from the stack in front of him and opened the page for the witness.

'Yes, I have it.'

'That is, I think, a bill of lading.'

'Yes.'

'And would you please glance through the pages that follow.'

The witness turned a few pages.

'They are,' continued Jonathan, 'other documents relating to the same transaction are they not? The sort of thing that you are, no doubt, very familiar with in letter of credit transactions.'

'Yes, they are. And, as you say, I am familiar.'

'And the company whose name is shown in the application for the letter of credit relating to the transaction and shipment of the pork bellies is Constantbight Commercial Trading and Good Fortune Company Limited.'

'Yes, that is so.'

'Well, I suggest to you that that company has nothing to do with my client.'

'Pardon?'

'Mr Sin, you would be very careful, as the manager of the corresponding bank, to get the details of the applicant company exactly as you had been informed of them by the issuing bank, would you not? That is essential in this sort of banking arrangement, is it not?'

'Of course.'

'So you have no doubt that the company you were dealing with was called Constantbight.'

'No doubt. That is what the documents say.'

'So, if Mr Chan Wai-king had nothing to do with a company with that name, he could not have been involved, if there was indeed a fraud practised on your bank in respect of this transaction. Would you accept that?'

'Yes, of course.

'Thank you, Mr Sin. I have no further questions, my Lord.'

Without turning, for it would have been an ostentatious gesture to do so, Jonathan could almost sense the glow that was coming from the dock in his direction.

The prosecution called Wai Man-tin, the manager of the Wing Seng Bank, and he gave evidence through the interpreter, dealing with his bank's side of the pork bellies transaction.

Jonathan cross-examined him.

'Mr Wai,' he said, 'can you also give your evidence in English?'

He replied in Cantonese.

'He prefers not to,' said the interpreter.

'Very well, I know that it is your right. Just look at the bundle of documents which the previous witness, as well as you, has been explaining to the jury.'

'Yes.'

'Your bank was the issuing bank in this letter of credit transaction, you have told us, have you not?'

'That is so.'

'And as such, the application for the letter of credit would have been made to you?'

'That is so.'

'And you would have been very careful to get the name of the applicant correct?'

'That is so. Always.'

'Now, please look at the exhibit at page 1,019.'

There was a rustling in the jury box as they turned the pages of their bundles and the witness found it in his.

'That is the letter of application to your bank, is it not? It is in English.'

'That is so.'

'And what is the name of the company shown on the letterhead. You can, of course, read English, can't you? Please, read what it says.'

Mr Wai looked at it for a moment and said, 'Constantbight Commercial Trading and…'

Jonathan interrupted him.

'Don't worry about the rest. Constantbight,' he said. 'Not Constantbright.'

'That is so.'

'And that is the name you passed on to the corresponding bank, Chong Hing Commercial?'

'You may say so.'

'Thank you. No further questions.'

Pammy had been whispering anxiously to Graham, who rose to re-examine.

'Mr Wai,' he asked, 'tell us about your bank. What is your client base?'

'Mostly Chinese private clients and fairly small Chinese companies. No, actually, they are all Chinese-run.'

389

'Local Chinese or mainland, PRC?'

'Hong Kong.'

'And in what language do you normally correspond?'

'Chinese.'

'Would it be normal for you to receive an application such as this one written in English?'

'Not normal. I would say very unlikely.'

'What about this document?'

'No, this is a translation. It is a certified translation, I think. The letter I received is the next one in the bundle, written in Chinese.'

'Thank you. And could you read out what the first two characters of the company's name say in Chinese.'

'The first is "Wing", same character as my bank. The second is "Ming". It says Wing Ming.'

'And for the benefit of my learned friend, would you say what that means.'

'*Wing* means eternal, or always or ever. *Ming* is the sun and moon together in one character. It means bright.'

'So, without going through the interpreter, how would you translate the first part of the name.'

'I would say "Always Brightness", I think.'

Graham was deflated. He could not lead the witness into what he hoped for as an alternative.

'Or,' said Mr Wai after a pause, 'it could be Constant Bright. Yes, that's it; I remember thinking at the time that this could be one of the famous Mr Chan Wai-king's companies. Yes, it looks like someone made a mistake in translating the application letter after we got it.'

Jonathan and Frank turned at the same time to look at the dock. Lester Chan was sitting there smiling contentedly.

When the prosecution, in due course, turned to the evidence concerning the letter of credit for the purchase of an enormous quantity of porcelain insulators which were supposedly sold to the Constantright Commercial Trading and Good Fortune Company Limited, the funds being transferred through Dah Hing Bank, Jonathan rose and said:

'My Lord, my learned friend may lead the witnesses who deal with this transaction.'

'Thank you,' said Graham.

'Really?' said the judge, intrigued. 'Is there no dispute on this issue?'

'No,' replied Jonathan. 'The evidence from the banks is not in dispute. In fact, in this instance, the defence does not challenge the prosecution case that a fraud was committed on both the issuing bank and Dah Hing, the beneficiary's bank.'

There was a sudden moment of silence in the courtroom. Some of the jury leant forward, as if to suggest that they were not certain that they had heard correctly.

'Your client admits that, in this instance, there was a fraud?' asked the judge.

'Yes, my Lord, those are my instructions.'

'Well, I await your case with anticipation.' At last this is getting interesting, thought O'Brien.

When the witness, Lo Shun-tak, the chief cashier of Chung King Bank gave evidence that Constantright Commercial Trading and Good Fortune Company had applied for the issue of a letter of credit to fund the purchase of insulators from Always Good Heaven Typewriter Company Limited, the vendor to be paid by Dah Hing Bank, Graham took advantage of the invitation.

'Mr Lo,' he asked, 'did you make enquiries about that company, Constantright?'

'No need,' replied Lo. 'We had done business before with this company. Over the purchase of jewellery.'

'And did you know who owned the company?'

'Yes.'

'And were all the shares in it beneficially owned by another company called Constantlight International?'

'Yes.'

'And was the owner of Constantlight the defendant, Chan Wai-king?'

'Yes, that is correct.'

Once Graham had taken Lo Shun-tak through all the intricacies of the letter of credit for the purchase of the insulators, Jonathan again rose to cross-examine.

'I thought you said that none of this is in dispute,' the judge interjected.

'That is correct, but would you allow me to question the witness, as I am entitled to do? I wish to elicit some important information…' Jonathan paused, before adding, 'my Lord.'

That's me stuffed for interrupting, thought Brett. This bloke's got some backbone. But "elicit", that's a bit poncey.

'Mr Lo, you had charge of this transaction from the bank's point of view, did you not?'

'That is so.'

'All your dealings were with Li Hong-tat, who was the office manager at Constantright Commercial. He is also known as Patrick Li.'

'He used both names in correspondence.'

'Yes, we have seen that in the exhibited documents. And did he also have meetings with you in connection with this transaction?'

'Yes,' replied the chief cashier, 'he came several times to my office.'

'Always him?'

'Yes, always Mr Li Hong-tat.'

'No-one else?'

'No, just him.'

'My client, Lester Chan, Chan Wai-king, he never came to see you?'

'No, I have never met him. Have heard of him, of course.'

'Nor did he write any letter to you?'

'No.'

'No fax or email?'

'No, none.'

'And you never spoke to him on the telephone?'

'No.'

'So, from all that you saw, Mr Chan had no dealings in this transaction.'

'Not from what I saw. But I do know that he owns the company.'

'Yes, I accept that. But you went through all the relevant documents when you were answering the prosecutor's questions, didn't you?'

'And before then also, because I collected them and gave them to the police from the Commercial Crimes Bureau to use in their investigation.'

'Thank you, Mr Lo. That is a very helpful observation. So, we can be sure that you are very familiar with every one of the relevant documents, can we?'

'Yes, I know them all.'

'And I am right in saying that there is not a single letter, internal note or commercial document that even mentions Mr Chan's name?'

'Yes.'

'And, therefore, if I were to suggest to you that, from what you have seen, there is nothing at all to connect Mr Chan, as opposed to the manager employed by one his companies, with this fraudulent transaction, what would you say?'

'I would say that you are right.'

'Thank you,' said Jonathan. 'I have no more questions.' He resumed his seat.

This man Savage is a smooth operator, thought Brett.

Oh fuck, thought Graham.

Jonathan glanced back. Lester Chan was giving him two thumbs up.

An urgent, whispered discussion was taking place between Graham and Pammy.

'My Lordship, I mean, my Lord.' Graham had risen.

'Yes, Mr Truckett.'

'I think that it would be appropriate, in the light of the cross-examination, if my next witness were to be called out of the batting order. I was going to call him later but…'

'You think that it would be better to call him now when the issue is still fresh in the jury's minds.'

'Yes, and he is Patrick Li Hong-tat, PW29. He is one of the people named in the indictment as a co-conspirator. He will be giving evidence under an immunity from prosecution.'

'Well, Mr Truckett, it's up to you. You call your evidence in any order you like. It's not my decision. Do you have some sort of application?'

'I do, your Lordship. It's now half-past three and there is no prospect of getting him here before the usual time for the court to rise. I did not anticipate that he would be needed today; otherwise I would have asked the police to make arrangements for him to come to court. So, might I ask that we rise early?'

'Well, Mr Truckett, I suppose that some might say that you should have been prepared for this turn of events and had the witness waiting,' said the judge, trying to look neither too severe with Truckett nor too pleased with the chance to have an early day. Turning towards them and smiling, he added, 'I don't suppose the jury would mind an occasional early day. We'll rise now.'

The following morning, when the court had re-assembled and Henry had brought the judge back in, a crestfallen Graham stood up.

'My Lord, the police have not been able to find the witness. They have made enquiries and their intelligence is that he has gone off to somewhere in Indonesia, without telling them. He was told to keep in touch with them regularly for the duration of the trial, so we can only assume that he has deliberately made himself scarce. He has probably had some inducement to keep out of the way.'

Jonathan was on his feet like a rocket.

'That is a wholly improper comment. Unless Mr Truckett is prepared to call evidence to substantiate it, I insist that he withdraws it. If he is suggesting, as he appears to be, that my client, or someone on his behalf, has made an improper advance to the witness, I challenge him to prove it.'

'Well, Mr Truckett?' said the judge.

'Er, um, the witness is under an immunity and would have had explained to him the possible consequences of not giving evidence when called on.'

'That is as may be,' replied the judge. 'But do you have any evidence to support the implication that he has been offered an advantage not to give evidence?'

'Or a threat,' interjected Jonathan.

'Yes, quite so. Do you have anything to support your comment, Mr Truckett?'

'Er, no, my Lordship. Just a guess.'

'Well, that will not do. Members of the jury, it is unfortunate that the prosecutor said what he did in your presence. You will, please, disregard it. All that we know is that a witness, who may well have reasons of his own, has not made himself available. You must not, I repeat not, hold that against Mr Chan. You will try this case only on the evidence and nothing else. So please put it out of your minds; unless, of course, Mr Savage has something to say about it in due course.'

With the wind blowing his way, Jonathan thought it best to remain seated and say nothing. But a moment later he stood up again.

'My Lord, may I please have a moment? I gather from my instructing solicitor that Mr Chan wishes to speak to me. I don't believe that I need ask the court to rise.' He squeezed past Dempsey and went to the side of the dock.

'What is it, Mr Chan? Don't speak too loudly.'

'I had just want to say,' said Chan quietly, leaning forward, 'that you are very brilliant. I am very pleased I have you as my QC. And, like I tell you before, you see the judge is cross and scold Mr Bucket.'

'Thank you, my Lord,' said Jonathan, returning to his place.

'Are we ready to continue, Mr Truckett?' asked Brett.

'Yes. I will now start on the evidence concerning the timber transaction which was a fake.' And he decided to take a cautious approach, 'I mean, the prosecution case is that it was false.'

Graham called several witness to show that the letter of credit had been obtained from the Wing Seng Bank of Macau for the sale and purchase of a container load of mostly kiln-dried railway sleepers and a small parcel of wooden joists, shipped from Willagong in Australia and lying in Container Terminal Number 11 at Kwai Chung in Kowloon. They testified that there was no such consignment to be found at the terminal. They also proved, through an examination of the records held at the Hong Kong Companies Registry, that both the vendor, Spanish Jewellery and Watches Company, and the purchaser, Christian Channel Fashion Goods Manufacturing Company, were companies which were closely linked with each other because Lester Chan owned ninety-five per cent of the shares of both.

Jonathan, in cross-examination, attempted a similar exercise to that in the case of the rolled steel. He put to the first witness that there might have been a mistake; and that, in fact, there had been a misdescription in the bill of sale; and that there had been a genuine underlying transaction but it was concerned with bags of cement: fifteen thousand bags, to be precise.

'Not so,' replied Mr Remedios, the manager of the bank.

'How can you be sure? Did you come to Hong Kong to carry out the inspection personally?'

'There was no need for me to do that,' replied the manager, a suave Macanese with a slight Portuguese accent. 'No need at all, sir.'

'Why do you say that?'

'Well, first of all, there are no container ships plying between Willagong and Hong Kong. Secondly, my bank has, in the past, issued letters of credit for cement transactions, and I know two things from that. You could not fit such a large quantity of bags into a single container and, also, all the relevant shipping documents, the bill of lading, the cargo receipt and so on, make it clear that there was only one container for the load. You have to be very careful and very specific about the number of containers on the documents, otherwise you risk extra handling and dockage fees and, in some countries, penalties. And thirdly, cement is a very vulnerable material. For obvious reasons, bags of cement must not be exposed to moisture otherwise they will go off and become valueless. So, the terminals where they are to be unloaded must be able to store them in dry conditions. I know that Number 11 has no such facilities.'

Jonathan thought for a moment. This was a seemingly very competent witness and he had no material to challenge what he had said. The only possibility was to try to put his credibility in doubt.

'Mr Remedios, your witness statement does not refer to bags of cement. It is concerned only with timber, or the lack of it. I raised the possibility of cement with you for the first time, just now, in cross-examination and yet you appear to have come to court ready-armed to answer questions about bags of cement. May I ask you: have you been discussing your evidence with anybody and, in particular, any other witness?'

'Well, sir,' replied the unperturbed witness, 'I did, of course, discuss my evidence with the Hong Kong police when they took my statement. But I have certainly not talked about my evidence with any other witness in this case.'

'Well, you see, Mr Remedios, I did raise the question of a mistake in the documents with a previous witness and I mentioned the possibility of cement to him. Are you sure that you haven't been putting your heads together?'

'I'm sure.'

'Then how do you explain your apparent state of preparedness for the questions that I just asked you?'

'Because, Mr Savage, when the bank was first approached over this letter of credit I thought it a bit odd that a jewellery company should be in involved with a clothing fashion company over a shipment of timber. I wouldn't say I was suspicious, just a bit curious. I happen to have met Mr Chan Wai-king on a couple of occasions before because he has an account at our Macau head office, and I called him to ask him about it as I had been told that he was the principal shareholder in the two companies concerned in the transaction. It was he who told me that he was trying to keep his diversification into other lines of commerce from the eyes of his competitors in the jewellery trade and he mentioned then that it probably was cement and not timber. So that's why I knew. But there was no timber and no cement.'

'One moment, please, my Lord,' said Jonathan. He turned to Dempsey and quietly asked him if Chan had ever told him that. Dempsey shook his head and shrugged. Jonathan looked back enquiringly at the dock, where Chan was still smiling broadly. He wondered whether his client had any conception of how badly this was going. He was not going to risk it getting any worse.

'I have no further questions,' he said.

The trial dragged on. Graham called more witnesses to establish that many other letters of credit had been applied for on the basis of documents relating to the sale and purchase of a wide range of commodities; that, in most cases, the banks had paid the vendor company before discovering that they were phantom transactions; and that, in almost all cases, the link between the selling and buying companies was so strong as to indicate that it was the same person who was controlling them, that person being Lester Chan. Jonathan was able to make a few more inroads into the prosecution case. In the Thai bracelets transaction he put to the witnesses that there was no evidence that Chan Wai-king had any connection, directly or indirectly, with the control of any company registered in Thailand and that the name of the company on the vendor's side of the transaction, Constantsmiling PTLC, did not appear in the Thailand Register of Companies and seemed to have been made up. The witness agreed and also conceded that the use of that name made it at least possible that someone had deliberately taken advantage of the brand name that Chan

400

had created. Jonathan pinpricked occasional instances of discrepancies in the documents so that, for instance, the description and quantities of the commodities in the bills of lading were at variance with the cargo receipts. But he also had several serious rebuffs; and when he put to two of Chan's office staff that they had been conducting a fraud for their own benefit and without the knowledge of their boss, neither would be shaken: they admitted that they knew it was wrong to apply for the letters of credit when the transactions and the documents were bogus but insisted that they were acting under the instructions of Mr Chan because they knew that he wanted to raise some short-term capital, and they benefitted from it only in that he gave them a reward for what they had done.

陳

And then, almost as if without warning, the last witness was called and cross-examined and briefly re-examined and left the witness box and the prosecution case concluded. Graham, this time remembering not to take himself by surprise, used the expression that had been relied upon by generations of prosecutors, relieved that they had come this far.

'That is the case for the prosecution,' he said and sat down.

'Thank you, Mr Truckett. Yes, Mr Savage?' Brett placed a mental wager with himself that the Pommy QC would ask for more time.

'I am ready to start now,' replied Jonathan. 'However, I don't think that we could get much usefully done before your usual rising time,' and, just as Graham had done earlier, he looked deliberately at the clock. Brett sighed inwardly and then reminded himself that that was just what he used to do when he was a barrister.

'Yes, you have a point there, Mr Savage, and I imagine that you will want to take some final instructions before you start you case.'

'Yes, I would appreciate the opportunity.'

'You see,' said the judge, turning towards the jury and trying to conceal his mischief, 'you've heard me tell the witnesses for the prosecution that they must not talk about the case to anyone else until they have finished giving their evidence. Well, the same applies to *all* witnesses, including the defendant, Mr Chan. So, once he has started, he won't be able to discuss his case with his barristers or solicitors, or anyone else for that matter. So it is, I think, only fair that Mr Savage and his team have this last opportunity to talk to their client. Has your client decided whether…?'

Jonathan shot to his feet.

'My Lord, may I please stop you there? What, doubtless, you have in mind is something upon which I need to take my client's instruction. Not, if I may say so with respect, a matter for public debate.' What is the matter with this chap?, he thought, but he had not meant to sound so abrupt.

Brett coloured for a moment. Then he thought how right Savage was to stop him.

'You're quite right, Mr Savage. We'll rise now and you can let me know what is happening when we all meet again tomorrow.'

'Thank you, my Lord. I appreciate that.'

'Good,' said the judge, still nevertheless determined to lay a mine. 'You are not yet in a position, I take it, to let the court know how much longer the trial is likely to run?'

Jonathan considered his response for a moment and decided to say nothing.

'Well…' said Brett.

'Good afternoon, my Lord,' said Jonathan, slamming a metaphorical door.

Outside the courtroom Jonathan took off his wig and gown as Dempsey sent the messenger back in with the trolley to collect the files that he thought would be needed.

'What was all that about?' Jonathan asked him.

'What do you mean?'

'What on earth did the judge think he was doing, asking me in front of the jury whether or not our client would be giving evidence?'

'Did he? I didn't hear him say that,' said Dempsey.

'No, not in so many words, but what do you think he meant when he asked about taking instructions and whether Chan had made a decision and how long the case was going to last?'

'Oh, I see. I hadn't thought of it like that. And you told him that he should not talk of it in front of the jury.'

'Yes. He knew perfectly well what I meant but he wouldn't leave it alone.'

'But, Jonathan, I have to say that I do not really see what is wrong with it if he did.'

'Well, let's suppose that Chan does decide to give evidence. There was the judge raising the possibility that he might be better off not testifying.'

'Yes, I see. I think I see.'

'And supposing he decided not to and the jury were told. What would happen?'

Dempsey looked bemused. 'I don't follow,' he said.

'Well, we wouldn't have gone straight into closing speeches this evening. So the jurors would go home and tell their families and friends that the case was going to be shorter because the defendant was not going to give evidence in his own defence and they would all tell them that that was because he was guilty, and the jurors would sleep on it and come back tomorrow morning with their minds already made up.'

'Yes, I see what you mean. But the jury would have to find out eventually if he isn't going to go into the witness box.'

'Of course, but that would be tomorrow morning. Truckett would then have to go straight into his closing speech – which I bet he hasn't prepared – and he would not, as you know, be allowed to make any adverse comment about our client's not giving evidence: I assume that the law here is the same as it is in England. Is it? Yes, I thought so. And then it would be our turn to address the jury and we can minimise the impact as much as possible by stressing the point that the defendant never has to prove his innocence in the common law system, which is something the judge will be required to say also when he sums up the case; so, by the time the jury retires, they will have got used to the idea that a defendant can be acquitted even if he does not give evidence on his own behalf. Of course, unlike the prosecutor, the judge is entitled to make some comments about the absence of the defendant's evidence, but it has to be balanced. Gone are the days when a judge in England told a jury that a trial without the defendant's evidence was like a performance of *Hamlet* without the Prince of Denmark.'

'Well, you certainly put O'Brien in his place,' Dempsey replied, perhaps a little reservedly. 'But the client seems pleased.' Lester Chan had been released from the dock and was coming through the double doors towards them with a wide grin and an outstretched thumb.

'So, Mr Savage,' he said, 'you had show the jury that you are the boss and that you not afraid of the judge. They definitely will do what you tell them now.'

'That's nice of you, Mr Chan,' said Jonathan. 'I had to do something as I didn't want the judge to put us in a difficult position, but I just hope I didn't go too far.'

'No, no. You said it just right. So, now we have a meeting, and then afterwards I take you and Ng Dim-si and Yeung Chi-hang out to dinner. And Mr Frank.'

By now, Billy Yeung and Frank Grinder had joined them.

'Thank you, Mr Chan,' said Frank, 'but I promised to take my wife out tonight. So I'll leave you after our conference.'

'Me too,' said Billy in English. 'I'm busy tonight.'

Jonathan looked anxiously at Dempsey. 'Let's see how long we are in our meeting,' he said.

31

They all went back to Dempsey Ng's chambers. The conference room did not seem quite as cold as previously and Jonathan idly found himself wondering whether he was becoming attuned to it or whether, because this meeting had not been arranged in advance, there had not been time to bring it up to the full level of ostentation. They sat round the long table, the messenger taking his place at the head with a notebook open in front of him. Jonathan sat across from Lester Chan.

'Alright,' he said, as the others settled down, 'now, Mr Chan, we come to the point where you have to make a very important decision.'

He had been preparing himself for some time for this. It was always the duty of counsel for the defence to discuss with the lay client the question of whether or not he would testify. Sometimes the choice was obvious: the defendant would be likely to make an impressive witness or, more often, without his evidence there would be nothing to gainsay the prosecution's case. On the other hand, occasionally even the client could see that he would make a devastatingly bad witness and his evidence in cross-examination would greatly strengthen it. He had had to explain this so often to defendants of varying degrees of intelligence that he had developed what was almost a formula. He had to tailor it to fit the facts of the case and the strength of the opposing evidence, but always he said that if his client did not give evidence, the prosecution was not permitted to comment on it in its closing speech, but that he could in his, and the judge could and almost certainly would in his summing-up, which would, of course, be the last address the jury would hear before it retired. He told the defendant that, whilst the judge could not go overboard, he was entitled to say that, where there was a dispute of fact, the jury had heard evidence to support only one side of it. He emphasised that, whilst he could advise, and would advise, neither he nor any of the other lawyers could make the decision for him and that the choice was the client's alone. At this point, the messenger inclined his head gravely and stared at Chan.

The defendant sat in silence, smiling agreeably, as Jonathan went through all these important preliminaries. Then Jonathan said,

'Let's just look at the evidence, briefly. I won't go through it all, but I think you will agree that the prosecution has laid out quite an impressive case; and whilst I think it safe to say that we have made a few dents in it, there is a substantial amount that is left and which the jury will probably think requires an answer.'

He then took Lester Chan through various parts of the evidence which supported the argument for Chan's implication in the conspiracy to defraud. Chan said nothing throughout all of this until Jonathan began to wonder whether he was taking it in or even listening; his expression remained unchanged. When he had finished Jonathan asked him whether he had understood what he was saying.

'Of course,' said Lester Chan.

'Is there anything else you want me to explain to you? Or Mr Billy Yeung, or Mr Ng or Mr Grinder?'

Frank jumped slightly, but reassured himself that as Chan had asked him nothing from the moment they had first met he was unlikely to ask his views on criminal law at this stage. He was right.

'No,' said Chan. 'I understand all. I had already think about this.'

'Well,' continued the QC, 'don't you want to know what my advice to you is?'

'Alright,' said Chan, still smiling sweetly. 'So, tell me.'

'Right, then,' said Jonathan. 'In a nutshell, my opinion is that you should give evidence. If I thought that you would make a terrible witness I would tell you so: it would be my duty. I may, of course, be wrong, but I don't think you will. You are an intelligent man; you must be to have built up the business empire that you have. And I have also to form a judgment of our opponent and, whilst he seems to be a decent man and a reasonably competent operator, I am bound to say that I have not formed the impression that he will be a devastating cross-examiner. So I don't think it likely that he will come up with anything that will take us, that is, you or me, by surprise and that we haven't already anticipated in the daily case conferences that we have been having since the trial began.'

'Yes, I see.'

'There is, of course, always the possibility that you won't stand up well in cross-examination. And I can't anticipate every point that our opponent might make. And, when it comes down to it, although the jury will be told by me and by the judge that it is not a balancing act and that they cannot convict unless they are satisfied so that they are sure that you are guilty, and that suspicion is not enough, well, there is always the chance, not to put too fine a point on it, that they simply won't believe you. We cannot rule that out. There are cases where, when the defendant gives evidence, he strengthens the case against him but, as I say, I don't think this is going to be one of them. You do understand what I am saying, don't you?'

'Yes,' Chan replied. 'You put it very clear.'

'But let's just see what the others think. Dempsey?'

'Yes, I agree with what you say,' said Dempsey.

'Mr Yeung?'

Billy said something to Chan in Cantonese.

'I told him that he should listen to your advice,' he explained.

Frank was hoping that Jonathan would not include him in this, his previous experience of this problem being zero.

'Mr Grinder?'

'I agree with you all,' he said, adding, 'but, of course, Mr Chan, you know that my practice has not been in criminal trials. But my gut feeling is that he will be able to look after himself in cross-examination. And also, in some of the examples, such as Remedios of the Wing Seng Bank and where our case is that the office staff were carrying on a fraud for their own benefit and without Mr Chan's agreement or knowledge – I know that I am not a criminal lawyer – but it seems to me that, unless he goes into the witness box, the evidence will be all one way, that is, the prosecution's way. I imagine that the judge will have to tell the jury that, in those instances, the defence has called no evidence to contradict what the prosecution alleges.'

'That's a very good point,' said Jonathan.

The messenger said something, stroking his chin hair and loudly clearing his throat.

'He says that he agrees with his boss,' Dempsey explained.

'OK,' said Jonathan to Lester Chan. 'We all seem to be of the same opinion. But, as I said earlier, the decision is not ours; it is yours and yours alone.'

'Yes, you had explained it well. And my decision is that I will not give evidence.'

Jonathan was taken aback. This was the first time, as far as he could recall, that that had happened, that the client had rejected his advice.

'Mr Chan, I stress that it is not for us to decide for you, but I am a bit surprised. Would you like some more time to think about it? You can consider it overnight if you would like to.'

'No need, I had been thinking for a long time.'

'Really? When did you start thinking about it?'

'Oh, months. I thought about it when I first met you and saw that your earlobes were very good.'

'What?'

'Yes, I thought then that you look what we call auspicious. That is the word we use. And I take advice in the Wong Tai Sin Temple. I shake the *kau chim* sticks and the fortune teller had explained that you will win the case for me without me needing to do anything except pay you. He said just to watch and I will see how good you are, and he was right. You are very good and I don't want to spoil my chances.'

'Mr Chan, I have to say that that is not the basis for you to make a decision as important as this.'

'But you tell me that it is my choice and, whilst I do not want to seem to disagree with you, that is the decision that I have made.'

'And is there no prospect of you changing your mind if you have more time?'

'No. I am only sorry that the case will be shorter so that you will not earn so much fees. But I will make up your fees.'

'Mr Chan, please, my fees have nothing whatsoever to do with the advice that I have given you. I would have been delighted for you if the charges against you had collapsed before we got to the end of the prosecution's case; but they haven't and we are faced with an important decision and, I must admit, I am not at all happy that you are making it on the basis of something as irrelevant and inappropriate as these sticks, whatever they are called, and the advice of a fortune teller.'

'They are called *chim* sticks. They have writing on them and you shake a jar of them and you take the ones that come loose to the interpreter to be read. That is what I believe in. And that is my choice and you will not change it. And so, shall we have dinner soon?'

32

Next morning Henry bustled in to the judge's chambers. Brett was already there, robed except for his wig. The sun was shining and the sky, untroubled by the polluted mist that usually hung in the air above the Admiralty District, was unusually clear and blue, so different from what he had, in the past, described as the Land of the Midnight Smog. His mood matched the fine weather, as Sharon had told him over dinner the previous evening that she intended to stay in Hong Kong until he retired and that she hoped he would eventually agree to go back to Sydney with her. She had not explained why it had taken so long for her to tell him what he had been craving to hear and he wasn't going to ruin things by pressing her for an answer.

'Good morning, Henry.'

'You are early today, my Lord.'

'Yes, I thought I had better clear my desk and make some notes. I have a feeling something is going to happen today.'

'Yes, my Lord?'

'Indeed. Are you a betting man?'

'I am from Hong Kong.'

'Of course, silly question. Tell me, do you think that Chan is going to give evidence?'

'I don't know, my Lord. I have heard nothing, except that I had spoke with Mr Truckett about the timetable yesterday and he said that he thought that the defendant would have to give evidence as there was so much for him to answer. He told me that he had prepared his cross-examination and that he thought that he would be in the witness box for at least a week. He also say that he got the impression that Mr Chan would call some other defence witnesses. He say that he had believe that from the way that Mr Savage had put some of his questions. But the defence had not told me anything.'

'No, I can see why they wouldn't, but I'll tell you something in confidence: my guess is that he won't give evidence.'

'Really, my Lord?'

'Yep. Do you want to put a small bet on it? Say, a hundred bucks?'

'Oh, my Lord, no, I only bet with my friends and at Happy Valley. I did not think that it would be correct for me to bet against you.'

'You're probably right. It might not look right if it got out. Not that I don't trust you completely. But you mark my words. I've seen too many of these trials to be taken by surprise. These *tai-pan*, these big shots, think that a combination of their fame and their lawyers' skills will be enough to get them off and, often enough, they are right. I also think that there is an element there that they don't want to be seen to lose face by having their credibility challenged directly.'

'Would you like me to remain here while you sort out your papers?'

'No, you go and have your morning tea. There's plenty of time. Just come back when it's about time for the court to sit.'

Henry did that curious shuffle-run favoured by shop girls in Hong Kong, anxious to retrieve some goods and not lose a customer, and left. Brett got up from his desk and went over to the window. Until Sharon had come back from Sydney and, to an extent, until last night, he had not fully appreciated how much a sense of uncertainty had been quietly eating away at him. In fact, if he was honest with himself, he had not put his finger on the insecurity which had become, in recent months, so much part of his life; nor how much he needed her to be with him. Without consciously planning for the possibility or even allowing it to settle in his mind, he now realised that he had, from time to time, found himself wandering to the thought of living on his own in the house in Jamaica Gardens until he reached the statutory retirement age and then, after that, to the choice between staying on or going back, on his own. Was that, he wondered, why he had increasingly found himself short-tempered in court and intolerant of long-windedness and what he perceived to be incompetence? That chap, Savage, seemed to be able to stand up for himself but he recognised that he had, on a couple of occasions, been too hard on Truckett, who was doing his reasonably adequate best in the difficult circumstances of being outgunned. But now his mood had lifted and he could contemplate the view and the future with equal satisfaction. The vegetation on the hillside seemed to sparkle in the bright sunshine and there was just enough breeze gently to ruffle the foliage. It was oddly satisfying to try to identify the houses up on the Peak; the Secretary for Justice's official residence was easy because he had been there for dinner, and some were the homes of hugely wealthy society figures and were recognisable from the pictures in the local magazines, and some were where the consuls of foreign countries lived, flying their flags from tall poles, but others were difficult to place even though their size and obvious opulence marked them out as being significant.

There was a knock on the door and Henry came in.

'My Lord, the court is assembled. The defendant is in the dock. Mr Truckett and Mr Savage had said that they are ready.'

Brett moved away from the window and picked up his wig from his desk. He gathered a few papers and his notebook.

'Good, let's go in and see if I have won my non-bet.'

He went in to face, as every day, a crowded, standing courtroom. Henry pulled the chair out for him and he sat down, followed by everyone else except the English silk.

'Yes, Mr Savage?'

'Thank you, my Lord.'

A pause, perhaps a trifle too long and touching on the histrionic.

'Mr Chan will not be giving evidence and nor will there be any other defence witnesses. I call no evidence.'

Brett looked down at Henry who, with bent head, seemed to be filling in a form of some kind.

'Thank you, Mr Savage. So, that is your case concluded.'

'Yes, my Lord.'

'Then, Mr Truckett, it's your closing address now, I believe.'

Graham stumbled to his feet, not having expected to have to do anything, except to listen, for at least the day.

'Ah, my Lordship, this has come as…'

'No,' Jonathan muttered sharply. 'Don't you dare say anything.'

'What? I mean, I mean… May I have a word with my learned friend?' He bent towards Jonathan.

'What's the matter, mate?'

'You were about to say that I had taken you by surprise,' said Jonathan in the same fierce whisper. 'You can't do that in the hearing of the jury. My client is perfectly entitled to choose not to give evidence, as you well know, and you are not entitled to advance notice of his decision. To suggest otherwise implies some sort of underhandedness on the part of the defence and I resent that. Do you want to abort the trial?'

'No, of course not,' Graham replied in a suitably hushed voice. 'Look, I'm sorry. It's just that I need a bit of time.'

'Then you'd better tell the judge, but don't say that you have been taken by surprise.'

Brett could guess what was happening.

'Yes, Mr Truckett?'

'Er, my Lordship, I mean my Lord, I don't quite know how to put this. I, um…Look…'

'Members of the jury,' the judge addressed them with an apologetic smile, 'I know that you came into court only a few minutes ago, but I think that it would be a good idea if you took your coffee break now. I believe there is something that learned – he tried not to make that sound too sarcastic

– counsel wants to raise with me and it is probably one of those matters that have to be discussed in the absence of the jury. So, off you go; I'll make sure you have another short break later this morning. But let's say twenty minutes now. Thank you.'

The jury obediently got up from their seats and filed out. Graham watched them go. Did he imagine it, or was that a glance of sympathy that the English schoolteacher shot at him as she left?

'Well, Mr Truckett?'

'Er, it's like this. My learned friend didn't warn me that his client would not be giving evidence or that there wouldn't be any other defence witnesses.'

'Was he supposed to? If so, that rule is a new one to me.'

'No, there isn't any rule. It's just that sometimes, out of courtesy…'

'Mr Truckett, this is a criminal trial, not a tea party.'

Jonathan got up. 'I don't know what Mr Truckett is implying, but I hope he isn't suggesting that I have done anything improper. But, as a matter of observation, your Lordship rose early yesterday to give me the opportunity to take instructions from Mr Chan and it is both normal and obvious that that would include the question of whether he would go into the witness box. So, even if I had wanted to, I could not have told him what was going to happen earlier than this morning when we all met at court. So I don't see what he is complaining about, if he is complaining, that is.'

'Well, Mr Truckett?'

'Er, no, I'm not making a complaint.'

'So, why have we sent the jury out? What is it that you want to say to me?'

'Well, it's like this…'

There was a painful pause.

'Look, I'm not saying that Mr Savage has done anything wrong. It's just…'

'Just what?'

'Just that I wasn't expecting this to happen. I thought that the defendant would give evidence. And, and I haven't prepared the prosecution closing speech.'

'So, you are asking for more time?'

'Yes, please,' Graham replied, grateful that O'Brien could see his difficulty. He'd probably been in a similar position when was in practice at the Bar.

'Do you have anything to say, Mr Savage?'

'No, my Lord.'

'Right, Mr Truckett. I'll give you some time. We'll extend the current coffee break to half an hour. That should give you time to marshal your thoughts. Anything else? No? Then we'll sit again thirty minutes from now.'

The judge rose and left the court. Graham remained standing, a chilled panic creeping down his spine.

'Oh, Graham.' Pammy moved closer to him. 'Let's go to the canteen. I'll buy you a cup of coffee. I know that you will make an excellent speech.'

They had to wait for the lift. Downstairs, Graham stared at the cup she had put in front of him. What the hell was he going to do? He had managed to get through to the end of the prosecution case without anything going too badly wrong, but he had assumed that he would have enough time to put his closing speech together, relying heavily on his junior's input. He had envisaged, or at least had hoped for, a full weekend when he and Pammy could work together; it would have been pleasurable, he in his jeans and a short-sleeved shirt, she in slacks probably, and one of those demur, soft silk tops, sitting side by side at his desk and, maybe on Saturday afternoon when the air-conditioning had been turned off in the building, his suggesting that they go back to his flat to continue working on what he was going to say to the jury. He closed his eyes for a moment; when he opened them he saw that nearly ten minutes had already gone by since the judge had risen, and she was saying something to him which he had not taken in.

'I'm sorry, Pammy, I didn't catch what you said. I was a bit distracted.'

'I said, how about that you make a very short speech? Without notes. Just tell the jury that on what they have heard they must convict. I am sorry, it is not my job to tell you what to do, but you are a very good advocate and I think that they will listen to you. But you know best.'

'That's it! Pammy, you're brilliant.'

Kissing her in the lawyers' crowded canteen would not have been appropriate. They finished their coffees at a leisurely pace and then took the lift back to the sixteenth floor. Jonathan and Dempsey were already in the courtroom; in fact it looked as if they had not left, as they had drinks in Ocean Coffee paper cups which someone must have brought in for them. Jonathan looked over at Graham and shrugged his shoulders as if empathising with his predicament.

'Sorry about this,' he said. 'I've been caught off guard in the past, myself. But you understand, I have to look after my client.'

'Yes, of course I do,' Graham replied and added, deliberately, 'mate. But don't shed any false tears on my behalf. I'm prepared.'

'Yes, I thought you might be. When I'm prosecuting, I usually make some notes for my closing speech as I go along. How long do you think you'll be?'

'Ah, that's hard to say. But I'll probably be finished by the end of the day. It's still not eleven o'clock.'

'Thanks,' said Jonathan, 'that's helpful.'

The jurors came back and took their places. The judge's door opened, Henry came through, looked around and retreated. A moment later there was a loud knock on the door and he came out again, leading the judge, who bowed briefly to the court and sat down.

'Mr Truckett.'

Graham rose.

'Yes, my Lord.'

'Do you have any application to make?'

'No, my Lord. Should I?'

'Are you ready to start?' Brett half-smiled in surprise. Over the break he had been thinking of the position that Graham was in. In his place, he would have pressed hard for some time. He had decided that, if he asked for it, he would almost certainly give him more time, probably the rest of the day at least.

'Yes, I am ready.'

'Well, off you go, then,' said Brett and sat back in his chair to listen.

Graham turned towards the jury. They all looked attentive and, yes, that was a kindly look that Dawn what's-her-name was giving him.

'Members of the jury,' he said, 'I haven't checked to see precisely how many days you have been sitting on this case.' And he added, significantly, 'I haven't had time. But it has been several weeks, as you know, and the one thing that has been obvious to all of us on this side of the court is the attention that you have paid from the very beginning and throughout the trial. You listened with care, and I saw that many of you were making notes, when I opened the prosecution case to you all that time ago, and you have shown equal interest in the evidence of the witnesses and the documents that the prosecution has put before you. So, my closing address to you is going to be very short and that is for two reasons. The first is that you don't need any further explanation or elaboration from me. You have listened, you have taken it all in and I think that it would be insulting to you if I went over it again, point by point, when there is obviously no need for me to do so. The second reason is this: you will, in due course, when the judge sums up the case to you, be told that you must not convict Mr Chan, or any accused for that matter, unless you are satisfied so that you are sure of his guilt. That is the expression which is used and that is the law. That means that it is the prosecution's job to put the evidence before you that makes you feel sure, and you must assess that evidence. It is no part of my duty to try to persuade you to convict if you are not, by this stage, ready to do so. So, all I am going to say to you now, members of the jury, is that you have heard all the evidence that there will be in this case; that that evidence is all one way; and that, bearing in mind the oath or affirmation you each took when you were sworn in, to return a true verdict according to the evidence, the only verdict that is open to you on this charge of conspiracy to defraud is one of guilty. Thank you.'

He sat down and looked at the clock. Two and a half minutes. That will teach that Pom a lesson. He felt his hand being squeezed.

'That was wonderful,' Pammy whispered. Her dark eyes were shining.

'Thank you, Mr Truckett,' said the judge. 'Yes, Mr Savage.'

'My Lord, Mr Truckett has been commendably brief but, if I may say so, unusually so. I would be grateful if...'

'Are you making an application for more time?'

'Well, yes, my Lord.'

'I believe,' said Brett, 'that the expression "what's sauce for the goose is sauce for the gander" originated in your part of the world.'

'I've no idea, my Lord. But I need some time to take instructions from my client.'

'What could he possibly give you instructions on at this stage, Mr Savage?'

For the first time since the trial began, Jonathan felt discomfited. 'Well, perhaps not so much to take instructions from Mr Chan as to have an opportunity to discuss the contents of my closing address with my learned junior, Mr Ng, and with my instructing solicitors.'

'You can have five minutes. I'll rise to let you get your papers in order and to get your lectern in a comfortable position. No more.' The judge stood and swept out.

Jonathan looked back towards the dock. Lester Chan was signalling, trying to catch his attention, so he walked to the end of the row and went over to him.

'What is it, Mr Chan? I haven't got much time.'

His client winked and gave him a knowing grin.

'You are doing bloody good job,' he said. 'Wonderful.'

And he shook Jonathan's hand vigorously.

33

When the judge came back, Jonathan had moved his lectern nearer to the jury and had put beside it the printed summary of the prosecution witnesses' evidence which Dempsey had produced as the trial progressed and had managed to find just when Jonathan needed it. He had, at first, considered a filibuster, waffling along until the lunch break when he could use the time to sort his papers into some sort of order; but a combination of professional pride and confidence in both his memory and his eloquence discounted such a course. And anyway, from what he had heard about Hong Kong juries and from what he had seen, it would be recognised for what it was: a mere tactic. He would just start and see where it took him.

'Any further applications, Mr Savage?'

'No thank you, my Lord.'

Muttering to Dempsey to make a note of the topics that he touched on, Jonathan turned towards the jury.

'Members of the jury,' he said, 'Mr Truckett is to be congratulated for making such a short and unusual closing speech.'

Worryingly, several of the jurors nodded.

'But,' he went on, 'you will have observed that he did not deal with any of the issues that have arisen in the course of the trial. He did not give you his insight or explanation on the many instances when his witnesses did not support his case or when cross-examination disclosed a quite different picture from that which he had painted when he addressed you at the beginning of the trial. You will, therefore, have to forgive me if I take considerably longer than he did. I will have to remind you of where the witnesses did not come up to scratch or where they, in the end, said something that was entirely different from what he had, no doubt, hoped they would say. My position is quite different from his: I cannot be cavalier, that is, take the easy way out. I am defending a man for whom the consequences of conviction would mean the loss of his good character and much else besides, and it is in the interests of justice that no man is wrongly convicted, as well, of course, as his interests that his defence is put forward thoroughly.

'And first of all, I must come to something which is staring us all in the face; the elephant in the room.'

One or two jurors looked around the court with puzzled expressions; he must try to avoid English colloquialisms.

'What I am referring to is the fact that Mr Lester Chan did not go into the witness box; he did not give evidence. Well, I am going to deal with it straight away. The learned prosecutor was quite right when he told you that it is for the prosecution to prove its case. It is never the other way round. In our legal system no person ever has to prove that he or she is innocent. Quite apart from the fact that giving evidence when you are accused of a crime must be a tremendous ordeal which no-one in his right mind would look forward to, every accused person has the right to say that it is up to the prosecution to make its case out and that he or she is not going to let them try to create a case by cross-examining the defendant. It must not be held against a defendant if he chooses not to give evidence, if he relies upon a careful analysis of the evidence of the prosecution witnesses to show that the case has not been made out to the standard required by the law, what used to be referred to as "beyond reasonable doubt" and is now more conventionally expressed as "satisfied so that you feel sure", which, to my mind, amounts to the same thing. So that is what I am going to do. Mr Chan has exercised his right – his right, members of the jury – like many other defendants in these courts have done, and I am going to show you how, in spite of the way that this case was opened to you and in spite of the sparse words of Mr Truckett's closing address, you cannot feel sure that he is guilty and you must, therefore, acquit him, that is, find him not guilty.'

Glancing down from time to time at Dempsey's note, Jonathan began a summary of the flaws in the prosecution evidence. When he needed to refer the jury to a document, his junior always seemed to be able to indicate the correct page in the bundles which the jury had; and Jonathan, to his relief, was able to remember the inroads he had made when cross-examining the witnesses who dealt with them. Time was taken up with the jury retrieving and opening the right bundles, and the clock crept round until it was twelve-fifty.

'My Lord, I am about to turn to a different topic which I won't complete in ten minutes. Would that be a convenient moment?' Jonathan used the hackneyed phrase employed by all English barristers when what they meant was: let's take a break.

'No, you tell me if it's convenient,' said Brett. 'If you want, we can rise now.'

'Thank you.'

'Well, you can have a bit longer for lunch, members of the jury. Back at two thirty.' And he was, again, through the door before Henry dashed over to open it.

Jonathan, for the first time since the trial had started, declined the disappointed Chan Wai-king's invitation to lunch, explaining that events had compelled him to start on his closing speech earlier than he had expected and that he needed the break, with Dempsey, to go over the points he was to make. Sensing that this might alarm his client, he explained that he had a pretty good idea of what he was going to say but just wanted to polish it.

'But, no need,' said Chan. 'You had won the case already, I think. And you must eat lunch.'

'No, no, this is what I always do when I am in the middle of addressing a jury. And Mr Ng will send out for sandwiches, I'm sure.'

Dempsey nodded and spoke to the client in Cantonese. Frank heard his name being mentioned and resigned himself to yet another visit to the restaurant in the park, this time without the dilution provided by the presence of Jonathan and Dempsey. He hoped that Billy would speak in English, but he doubted it. Leaving their wigs and gowns on top of their papers, the two barristers went down in the lift and across to Dempsey's chambers.

After the lunch break Jonathan, revitalized by the intense and productive session with his junior, resumed his closing address. He analysed the essence of the charge and the evidence by which the prosecution had sought to prove it, laying emphasis on the parts where he was pretty sure that he had made an impact and glossing over rest. He dealt at length with the evidence of Mr Sin in the pork bellies transaction and the probable mistake over the company's name; and he placed much stress on the way that an injustice could have occurred until he had elicited from Mr Lo of Chung King Bank that he had, in fact, always dealt with someone else and never with Chan Wai-king. As for Mr Nguyen and the rolled steels joists and the derelict warehouse, he said, merely, that there was always room for mistakes and passed quickly onto another, more rewarding, topic. Always watching the jury to make sure that they were paying attention, pausing from time to time to let some of them make notes, throwing in the occasional humorous aside if he thought that it was getting too tedious, he kept up his peroration as the afternoon wore on.

At four o'clock, the judge intervened.

'I am sorry for interrupting your flow, Mr Savage. Have you got much longer to go?'

'I won't finish by the usual rising time, my Lord,' replied Jonathan, relieved and guessing what was coming.

'Right. If you had thought that you might conclude your address at a reasonable time today, I would have encouraged you to continue. But as you don't, I think that the jury could do with a break. They have been listening to speeches since mid-morning and there is only so much they can take in. How much longer do you think you'll be? And I am not hurrying you: it's been a pleasure to listen to you.'

428

'Thank you. I imagine that I will be finished within about an hour and a half tomorrow. Having some time to consider matters overnight usually results in a reduction.'

'Yes, I agree. So, you hear that, members of the jury. If we have an early end today it might make the case shorter. So, tomorrow morning, please. Would you leave now, as there is something I want to discuss with counsel.'

The jury left and the judge waited until their door had closed behind them.

'Gentlemen,' he said, 'once Mr Savage has finished his speech, are there any matters that will be raised before I start my summing-up? Any questions of law to be discussed?Do you want to agree a definition of conspiracy to defraud?'

Graham was nonplussed. 'Er…' he said.

Jonathan stood.

'My Lord, I think that the definition of the charge of conspiracy to defraud is now well-settled. It has been established in the common law by decisions in England, Australia and, of course, Hong Kong.'

That is what he said. What he meant was: you're not going to trap me into nailing my colours to the mast. You're the judge, you tell the jury what the law is and if you get it wrong my client will have a good case on appeal.

'Oh. Anything to add, Mr Truckett?'

'Um, no, my Lordship. I agree with Mr Savage.'

'Right then, ten tomorrow,' and this time he waited for Henry to get to his door.

'Right, let's go back to your chambers and run over what's left,' Jonathan said to Dempsey. 'I'll leave it to Billy to explain to the client that you and I need to work together this evening. Do you mind, Mr Yeung, doing that? I am afraid that you and Frank might have to put up with Mr Chan's hospitality without our assistance.'

Graham started to gather up his files but was then struck by the happy thought that he did not need to. He had finished all the out-of-court work for the trial. All that was left for him was to sit and listen to the rest of the defence speech and to the summing-up and then wait for the verdict..

'Pammy,' he said, 'we don't have to take any papers back with us this evening. Nothing. We've got nothing else to do. Isn't it marvellous? We've got through without any disasters. Honestly, I can't thank you enough for all the help you've been.'

She smiled and cast her eyes down demurely, irresistibly. How, he thought, could anyone look so sensational in a horsehair wig?

'I have done nothing,' she said. 'But I have learned much about advocacy from you.'

'Nothing? You don't know how wrong you are. And I am going to take you out for a drink to celebrate and to thank you. Let's just go back to the Department to see if there are any messages.'

They left court together and squeezed into a packed lift next to each other. The air outside the building was clear and warm and the sky still blue. Sensing that the case was coming to an end, a pack of journalists and photographers clamoured by the doors in the hope of catching a shot of their prey, the famous but now vulnerable jewellery king. They pushed through them and took the escalator up to the lift lobby of the government building.

As soon as they arrived on the ninth floor, Graham could sense that something was happening. Instead of the usual passage of lawyers and clerical staff moving along the corridors on their way in and out of the Department, there were small groups of people talking to each other, and loud laughter. They walked along the corridor to his secretary's room and Graham looked in.

'We're back, Emily. Any messages?'

'No, Mr Truckett, but Mr Brown wants to speak to you. He is waiting in your office. I had just let him in.'

Andrew Brown was from back home. They had come to Hong Kong at about the same time, though Graham was a year or two older, and they had remained friends; and there was no apparent resentment even though he had not yet been appointed to Grade Four in spite of, in the view of many, Brown being the better qualified. Probably wants to meet for a drink this evening, thought Graham, but he was going to have to disappoint him. He was sitting in the easy chair.

'Hi, Andy. What can I do for you? You know Pammy, of course.'

'Of course. I wondered if you're up for a drink this evening, mate.'

'No, sorry, can't do it this evening.'

Andrew glanced briefly at Pammy.

'No, I can imagine not. But I was hoping to tell you something over a beer or two. I'll have to tell you now. Everyone's talking about it.'

'What?'

'It's pretty hot news. It concerns your mate, Gerry Stratford.'

'He's not my mate, Andy. I don't particularly like him and I definitely don't trust him.'

431

'I thought you'd been on a junk trip with him.'

'I did, once. And that's why I don't trust him.'

'Just as well. He's been arrested in the Pines.'

'In the Philippines? What's he doing there?'

'Money laundering, apparently. And he didn't get bail. So I don't think we'll be seeing him for a long time.'

34

Jonathan was right. Frank had not been able to conceal his irritation as Billy came over to him and told him that Lester Chan was insistent that they have dinner together. It seemed that he was very disappointed by the barristers' refusal as he simply could not understand why they would need to do any more work on the case, particularly as the judge had made it quite clear that he was on their side; and, Billy felt, it would be a serious loss of face if they, too, declined his invitation; the messenger had already told Chan that, of course, he would accept.

'Alright,' said Frank with resignation. 'But please tell him that I can't go straight out from here. I must go home first. What with one thing and another, I haven't had a chance to have a chat with Winnie for some time.'

'He won't think that that is a very good reason. I'll tell him that you have some important business that you have to deal with.'

'Thanks, Billy. Just give me a call and let me know where and when to meet. But not before seven o'clock, please.'

So, for the first time for weeks, Frank was home by five. Yes, it was "home"; he had come to enjoy living in the apartment in Kennedy Town. Almost every day Winnie had added another appealing touch and it really was a very convenient and pleasant area to live in. She was not yet in when he got back, but she would not have been expecting him so early. Probably over at her parents' or on the way back. He sat down in an easy chair. Perhaps too early for a drink? Maybe, just a beer.

The sound of a key turning in the front door, and she was there, in a light blue summer dress, carrying a folded parasol.

'Oh, I had not expect you so soon. I had not cooked our supper yet. Howabout we go out for dinner?'

'I can't, love,' said Frank, ruefully thinking that he would like nothing better. 'I've got to go back into town to have dinner with Lester Chan. But at least it looks as if things are moving towards the end. We're on the defence speech now, and then the summing-up and waiting for the verdict. And,' he added, 'possibly the sentence. No, I came home to be with you for a bit.'

'That is good,' she replied. 'I had some things to tell you.'

'OK, what about? Come and sit down here.'

She pulled up a dining chair and sat next to him.

'Well, the first is I think that I should go back to England.'

'Why? Why now?'

'Well,' she said slowly, 'it had been a long time since we both were there, apart from your very quick trip, and even longer since I came out. So, I think that I should go back to Cheltenham to see that the house is good.'

434

Frank realised with something of a jolt that he had hardly thought about their house. Somehow, without noticing it, he had slipped back into the very agreeable life of a Hong Kong expat. She was right, of course: it was far too long for her to have left their home in England. But he wondered what the true reason was. Could it be that she needed a break from her family?

'Is this anything to do with your relatives? You've been seeing them almost every day since you got back to Hong Kong and I don't suppose that that can always have been easy.'

'No, not my family. Except…'

'Except what?'

'Well, the other thing is Rambo.'

Frank sighed.

'Not him again. What is it now?'

'Well, he now decide that he don't want to be a judge.'

'A judge? I thought that he wanted to be the director of public prosecutions.'

'Maybe that. Anyway, he does not want to anymore.'

'So, what does that have to do with you?'

'He's my younger brother,' said Winnie, offended.

'Unfortunately, I know that only too well. But I still can't see…'

'So, he decide that he want to go back to college.'

'Well, I suppose that's something. What does he want to study.'

'It's something called Creation Study, I think.'

'What? Rambo? Doing a bible course?'

'No, not about religion. About being a writer.'

'Do you mean creative writing?'

'Ah, yes, that's it, I think.'

Frank was intrigued.

'Where can he study that in Hong Kong? I thought all the universities here tended to go for the more traditional academic courses.'

'No, not in Hong Kong.' Her hesitant manner sent out an alarm signal to Frank.

'You don't mean in England, do you?'

'Yes, my darling man,' Winnie lowered her eyes. 'He found a course in Gloucester. But my daddy and mummy both think he should not go to England to live on his own. They think, maybe, that there is a chance that he will get into trouble there.'

'A chance? It's an absolute certainty! Look what happened when he came to visit us last time. Do you remember how he got my naive young nephew into such a mess?'

'Of course,' Winnie replied demurely. 'But my parent had found that Gloucester is near Cheltenham.'

'So they think that you should go back home so that you can be near enough to his college to be able to keep an eye on him? That's a bit of an imposition, isn't it? To make you go back before we were intending to leave. It's not as if we shall be here much longer. As I told you, the case is coming to an end soon and my work will be finished. In about a couple or three weeks, I would guess. When is this course supposed to start?'

'Before that, I think. On Monday. He already has his flight. *Daddiah* pay for it.'

'Glad to see the back of him, I should imagine. So, you have to leave me and go home simply so you can be near him. I don't think that that is very fair on either of us.'

'Not so, F'ank.'

'Sorry, but I think it is. Surely the warden, or warder, or whatever he is, in charge of the college where he will be staying will be able to keep watch on him. Even though you are his older sister, you can't reasonably be expected to be his guardian.'

'No, that is not right.'

'Winnie, it is right. It is quite unfair for your family to expect it of you.'

'No, not right. Younger Brother will not stay in the college. They want him to live in our house. That is why I must go back.'

Frank was flabbergasted. He could think of nothing to say. His phone pinged with a message from Billy and he glanced at it.

'I have to go out soon. I'm meeting Billy Yeung and Chan Wai-king in half an hour,' was all he could manage.

陳

Jonathan and Dempsey walked over to Dempsey's chambers together.

'Tell me…' said Jonathan on the way, 'and please, I don't mean to be offensive, but do you genuinely enjoy going to the sort of dinner that Chan organises?'

'Oh no,' replied Dempsey. 'I loathe them. But it is part of life in Hong Kong. Don't misunderstand me, I love our food and it can be a lot of fun going out to a big restaurant with friends who let their hair down. And, of course, it's good to eat with family. But going out with big shots who insist on paying for everything to try to impress you with how rich and important they are is usually appalling. I did wonder at the time, when the client hosted that dinner at Lei Yue Mun when you were here last time, what you thought of it.'

'Well, it was certainly an experience and I don't regret having been to it. But there was rather a lot of food, wasn't there? And I think there are fewer fish in the aquarium at London Zoo.'

'But that was the whole point: he wanted to impress you. Unfortunately it is expected of barristers and solicitors in Hong Kong that they should endure their clients' lavish entertainment. I sometimes think that we should charge for our time; I certainly wouldn't choose to spend my free time like that. At least, that time, we pretty well managed to stop him from speaking to you and Frank about the case. Billy Yeung and I weren't so lucky.'

'I'm sorry; I had no idea. He was talking in Chinese quite a lot, as I recall.'

'Sure. That was all about the case. The way he thinks is: I'm paying for dinner so I've bought your time. That's why I was so pleased when you declined on our behalf today. Here we are.'

They went up to Dempsey's chambers and, once again, into the conference room. Again, it did not seem quite as wintry: perhaps Jonathan was getting used to it. No, the papers laid out on the big table were not fluttering in the artificial wind anywhere nearly as much. A clerk came in with two cups of jasmine tea as they sat down.

'So,' said Dempsey, 'these are the notes I made, as you requested, of the points you have so far covered.'

'Up to lunchtime?'

'No,' Dempsey was puzzled. 'Up to four o'clock. Up until the judge sent the jury away.'

'How have you done that? It's only just gone four-thirty?'

'That's what I thought you wanted me to do.'

'Yes, I did, but I didn't expect…How on earth…?' Jonathan was reluctant to expose his ignorance of IT. 'Well, thank you very much, that's perfect.

He glanced over the pages.

'Yes, you seem to have got everything.'

'Yes, I think so. Is it good enough?'

'It's wonderful, it really is. It's going to save us a lot of time this evening.'

Together, they went through all the points that Jonathan had so far, dealt with and discussed what arguments were left to be covered. Jonathan, somewhat embarrassed, made a note of them using a ballpoint pen and a block of writing paper; if Dempsey was amused or perplexed by this outmoded way of proceeding, he did not show it. Within a couple of hours, they had finished. Jonathan stood up and stretched.

'Thank you, Dempsey, that was extraordinarily helpful. I'm going to go back to the Majestic and try not to think about the case for the rest of the evening. I usually find that, if I switch off, I perform better the next day.'

'Oh, that's a useful tip to come from a London silk; I must try to remember that. But not always so easy, here in Hong Kong. But that's another reason why it was better not to have dinner with the client. I will try to use that as an excuse in future. I will say that that was your advice. But would you like a drink before you go back to your hotel?'

'I've got a better idea. Why don't we do that, and then let me go back and drop off these papers and have a wash and then have an early dinner somewhere, just the two of us?'

'I would really like that. As long as it isn't somewhere that Lester Chan would want to go to.'

'No chance of that,' said Jonathan. 'Somewhere simple, and European. And please, do me a favour and let me pay.'

35

'Thank you, my Lord.'

Jonathan turned to the jury.

'Last lap,' he said.

Only Dawn the schoolteacher smiled. The others seemed not to understand; perhaps another colloquialism that should have been avoided.

Refreshed by his time with Dempsey in his chambers, by their light Italian meal together, by the early finish and, above all, by his having put his mind in neutral for the rest of the night, Jonathan felt on top again. He was able to cover the topics remaining from the previous day with scarcely a glance at his notes, and he felt that he had introduced an air of confident realism as he summarised the main points that he had dealt with, without seeming to be repetitive. He introduced two or three light touches, half-jocular comments, which, he noted with relief, brought smiles to almost all their faces, and then brought them back to earth by reminding them that Lester Chan was on trial on a very serious criminal charge. Turning briefly towards the clock, he concluded.

'So, that's it, ladies and gentlemen. Just after eleven o'clock. I told you yesterday that I wouldn't be too long, and I have now finished. You will remember, I am sure, that the most important thing that I have said is that you must not – you *must* not – bring in a verdict of guilty unless the prosecution has proved its case to that very, very high standard, which I know the learned judge will remind you about. Surely it is obvious to you, now that I have been through all the flaws in their case and have demonstrated the possible – and *very* real – alternative explanations for what happened, that the only – *the only* – verdict that is open to you is "not guilty".'

He smiled and resumed his seat, drained. Dempsey patted him twice on the forearm. He deliberately avoided turning to look back.

'Thank you, Mr Savage.' It was the judge.

'Members of the jury,' he said 'we are getting towards the end of the trial. It now remains for me to sum the case up to you, that is, to remind you of the evidence and to tell you what the law is. You've been listening to speeches almost all day yesterday and for part of today, and I think that it would not be fair on you if I went straight into my summing-up. So, although it is only mid-morning, I am going to rise now and give you the rest of the day off and we'll resume tomorrow morning.'

So, thought Jonathan, it's definitely not sauce for this male goose. The possibility of enquiring whether O'Brien wanted some time, to use another expression originating in his part of the world, to take a gander at his notes was quickly dismissed; he knew that he was both exhausted and elated at having, at last, finished, and recognised how easily a serious misjudgement could be made in that state.

'There is a matter I want to raise with counsel,' the judge added. 'I won't need to detain you.'

The jury picked up their belongings and, some looking pleased others puzzled, they left.

'The question of bail arises, gentlemen.'

'Your Lordship's order, as I recall it, was that bail would be continued until the jury retires,' said Jonathan.

Graham rose. 'That's what you said,' he said.

'That is part of what I said,' the judge responded. 'The rest was "or unless I make a further order", and the time to consider that is now.'

Jonathan looked back at the dock. Did Chan understand what might be happening? He was smiling contentedly as if he did not.

'My Lord,' said Jonathan, 'my learned friend for the prosecution has not asked for a revocation or a variation of the bail.'

'Maybe not,' said the judge, 'but that doesn't stop me reconsidering the matter.'

Jonathan thought, What on earth is he doing? Is the implication that my closing speech was so inadequate that the client will be likely to do a runner?

'My Lord,' he said, 'I appreciate that you can vary or revoke bail without any request from the prosecution. But nothing has happened to justify such a course. Mr Chan has, throughout the trial, honoured all of the conditions of his bail. He has always arrived at court in good time, he has never given any indication that there is a risk of his absconding and there is not a shred of a suggestion that he has tried to interfere with prosecution witnesses – a possibility which, in any event, is now over. It would, in my respectful submission, be unjust and unwarranted to deprive him now.' And he reflected how sensible he had been not to make the gander jibe.

'Well, Mr Truckett?'

'My Lord, I am not making any application. I can't disagree with Mr Savage.'

That's enough, thought O'Brien, not now entirely sure why he had raised the matter. Perhaps he had meant to worry the defendant, who did not seem to understand what was happening for he still had that idiotic grin on his face. What was his game?

'Very well, bail continues on the same terms for the time being. Mr Savage, please ensure that Mr Chan understands the importance of his turning up on time.'

'Of course, my Lord.'

Brett stood up, bowed briefly and was off to his room. His clerk followed him in.

'Is there anything that my Lord had wanted?'

'No, thanks, Henry. Well, yes: would you mind getting me a cup of coffee? A decent one from outside, not the horrible muck from the judges' restaurant. I'm going to stay in my room for the rest of the day, working on my summing-up. Once you've got it, as far as I am concerned you can go. I won't need you at all; in fact, you know me well enough by now, I would appreciate not being disturbed. What I need is a few hours with no interruptions.'

'So, perhaps you would want me to leave your coffee outside the door?'

Brett was never entirely sure whether Henry had any sense of irony; his face gave nothing away.

'No, Henry, you can bring it in. I won't start work until you've brought it. Knowing your efficiency, I will probably not have got my robes off before you're back.'

'Thank you, my Lord.'

'No, thank you, Henry.'

In his shirtsleeves, with the sunshine streaming onto his desk, Brett started to make his notes for summing the case up to the jury. He decided that he would follow his usual practice and first of all outline the law that applied to the charge. Although he had laid it out scores of times before, he made a note to tell the jury of the burden and standard of proof: that it was for the prosecution to prove the case and that they must be satisfied so that they feel sure of the defendant's guilt before they could convict him. As in every previous trial, what he said about that was no more than a repetition of what they had just heard from the defence, but he knew that if he merely said that counsel was right, that would not fulfil his obligation: he must spell it out himself. It was important to get all the law right and not to risk having a conviction overturned by the Court of Appeal. This was not the time to mess up.

He then wrote out his exegesis of the offence of conspiracy to defraud, explaining that whilst the jury may have heard that conspiracies were now governed by statute (this was put in to flatter them, as the chance of any of the jury being aware of, or interested in, it was remote, although in these days of internet knowledge, who could be sure?), section 159A of the Crimes Ordinance made an exception of conspiracy to defraud, which remained an offence against the common law. He also pointed out that the indictment correctly referred to section 2(3)(b) of the Criminal Justice

Ordinance. What difference did it make to the decision that the jury had to take? None. Why was he telling them this? Because, he admitted to himself, he wanted to ensure that his summing-up was bomb-proof. He explained what constituted the element of fraud and distinguished it from forms of deceit that did not amount to a crime, taking as an example the "white lie", such as keeping the true extent of someone's illness from him. He pointed out that a good intention did not necessarily provide a defence to a charge, and added that a hope to reinstate the victim and even to pay him back with a profit to him did not excuse risking his property or money, so that even had this defendant expected to put the money back into the various banks without any loss to them and before anyone had found out what had been going on, it would still be a fraud. He made a note to stress that what was important was the question of dishonesty: if the prosecution had not proved that, then there could be no conviction, but if they had, and if all the other elements of the charge had been proved, then they must find him guilty.

He wrote that dishonesty was a perfectly simple word which they would all understand, but that, nevertheless, because there had been some doubt that everyone saw it the same way, the appeal courts in England and in Hong Kong had decided to give a legally binding definition, and that was that the conduct must be considered according to the standards of ordinary decent people. He was tempted to add the comment that it was difficult to see how a jury could distinguish between those standards and their own and, therefore, it was a fairly pointless exercise, but refrained; it would be better to wait until he was on the bench of the Court of Appeal before he sounded off like that.

Then came the question of territorial jurisdiction. Hong Kong juries were, generally, pretty intelligent and some of them might wonder if the fact that some of the activities had taken place outside Hong Kong – the insulators transaction in Vietnam and the jewellery in Thailand came to mind – meant that the case should not have been tried in Hong Kong. The defence had not taken the point and the prosecution had not chosen to justify it, and he did wonder whether he needed to deal with it at all; but it was better to be cautious, for no conviction had ever been overturned by the Court of Appeal on the grounds that the trial judge had accurately explained all the relevant law. So, tedious though he knew this would probably be, he noted that it was covered by the Criminal Procedure Ordinance and by sections 2(3), 5(a) and (b) and 6 of the Criminal Jurisdiction Ordinance, which stated that, even if part of the activities took place outside the jurisdiction, if the principal activities were in Hong Kong, then the case could properly be tried in these courts. Even if the jury was by now comatose, it was worth getting all this in because it would prevent any point being taken on appeal that he had not done so; because it would show what a good lawyer he was; and, above all, because it would enhance his reputation as a hard-worker.

By comparison, what was to follow would come as light relief. Henry had come with the coffee and gone, and now it was cold. And it was lunchtime. Brett got up, stretched himself and went over to the window. There was a tap on the door.

Henry slid in.

'You now need to eat, my Lord. I have brought you some sandwiches. And some fruit. And soup also. And a doughnut and coffee. And a bar of the chocolate that you like. Because this is just a snack. Maybe you would have a proper lunch when you go home.'

Thanking Henry briefly and trying to send him home for the day – who knew what duties his clerk could conjure up for himself to avoid appearing to be a slacker? –O'Brien ate one of the sandwiches at the small table near the window and then, taking the cardboard cup of cardboard coffee back to his desk, brought up on his computer the summaries that he had, at the end of each working day of the trial, been making of the evidence of the witnesses who had testified that day. It was a practice that he had adopted soon after being appointed to the bench and he was now particularly glad that he had done so. It was all there, on the computer: a brief account of what the witnesses had said, a note of the exhibits they had produced or referred to, the transactions they had spoken about, a cross-reference to other witnesses dealing with those transactions, and the significance of what they had said. He had taken the files on a memory stick home with him every evening so that he could check the accuracy of the work he had done earlier in his chambers, and so all that was needed was to print out the summaries for easy reference in court, and to make sure they were clipped together in the right order.

Finally, he came to evidence of the officers of the CCB, the Commercial Crimes Bureau, who had arrested the defendant and conducted the interviews under caution. That could often be an onerous part of the preparation of the summing-up, having to link what was said by the police to the prosecution's allegations at the trial, and to relate what the accused had said in interview to what his evidence had been in court, so that he would then have to help the jury to see whether those answers were compatible with what he later said in the witness box and whether or not they might draw the conclusion that he had lied somewhere, or whether he had been consistent. But in this case it was easy; Chan had said nothing when he arrested, other than "no comment", which suggested that he had been expecting his arrest and had consulted his solicitor and, doubtless on the advice of the same solicitor (hadn't he heard somewhere that that pompous, overweight, doubtless very expensive and now deceased Charles Munsonby had been representing him?) had persisted with that answer throughout all the interviews, so Brett had, consequently, been saved a great chunk of work. He must remember to manifest his gratitude, in the event of a conviction, by lopping some time off the sentence.

He stacked all his notes in a large, ordered pile and was about to pack them into his briefcase, when he paused. What was the point of taking them back home? He had done everything that he could and he wasn't going to make it any better by going through them again; and there was a great deal to be said for leaving well alone and taking a rest from the work. He would switch off his mind and his computer and spend a relaxing evening with Sharon. Perhaps they would go out for a drink in the Club and for a meal somewhere. He must get used to this upturn in his life. He looked at his watch; it was four-thirty. He had done a long enough day, even though it was earlier than he had been leaving recently. And his back was aching.

He picked up his empty case and was about to call down to the administration office to see if any of the other judges was going back to Jamaica Gardens and could give him a lift, when there was a soft tap on the door. Henry came in.

'My Lord, because I think you probably finish work for the day,' he said, casting a disapproving look at the uneaten food, 'I had told your driver to get the car ready and he is now waiting downstairs.'

'Thank you, Henry, that was very thoughtful, but how did you…?'

Henry smiled like an indulgent nursemaid.

'And, my Lord, I do not think that you need to take your case home with you.' He prised it gently from Brett's hand. 'You had done enough work.'

As so often before, Brett resigned himself to his clerk's judgment.

'Alright,' he said, 'I'll do what you say. But if I'm going home so must you.'

'Not yet, my Lord. I must first clear away the food. You had eaten almost nothing of your lunch. So, will you promise me that you will have a proper meal for your dinner?'

'Yes of course, Henry. You know best.'

36

'Members of the jury, we really are coming to the end of this long trial now and all that is left is for me to sum the case up to you, explaining what the law is and reminding you of all the important parts of the evidence. What I tell you about the law is what you must follow because, as in every criminal trial with a jury, it is I, the judge, who makes that decision. But, and this may come as a surprise to you, I am not the only judge sitting in this court today. There are eight judges: for you seven members of the jury are the judges of the facts and you are the only judges in that area. It is you who decide who and what you believe and what has and has not been proved, and it is you who measure the importance of the various aspects of the evidence, the witnesses and the documents. So, when I summarise the evidence for you, you must always keep in mind that what I am trying to do is to help you in your recollection and no more than that; so, if I mention a piece of evidence that you do not think is important, then you must ignore it, and if, on the other hand, I do not mention something that you do think matters, then you must give it what weight you think fit. And if you think that you detect in what I say about the evidence any indication of what I think about it, well then, all I can say is that you would be wrong, for it is not my job to tell you who to believe, or what part is more relevant. Just like it is no part of my function to tell you what the verdict should be, for it is you, and you alone, who decide whether to convict or to acquit.'

That ought to be appeal-proof, thought Brett. Or anyway, the judges of the Court of Appeal are not going to criticise me for that or accept any argument that I have not sufficiently explained what the function of the judge and jury are. He was feeling very – how best to describe it? – very content. He had had a lovely evening with Sharon as he had got back in time for them to go to bed together before going back to the Club to have a quiet drink and dinner; and they had managed to get a table on their own so that they could talk and allay all the minor doubts they both admitted to having about this new phase in their marriage. The sun was still shining this morning and he had the agreeable sensation that came from having completed all the hard work that was required of him, leaving nothing for him to do but coast along, using the notes he had made. And, he admitted to himself, he did like the sound of his own voice, in that he took pleasure in a well-modulated delivery and clearly-expressed explanation. Everyone had turned up to court on time and he had been able to start at ten o'clock and, from the attentive way that all the jurors were looking at him, and from their note-taking and occasional nods and slight smiles, he knew that they were following what he was saying. This was one of the pleasures of the job and he felt entirely in command.

He continued with his summing-up, sticking closely to the pattern he had laid out on the previous day. He finished his explanation of the law by saying that the failure of Lester Chan to give evidence could not be taken as strengthening the prosecution's case but, on the other hand, the jury was entitled to conclude from it that there were questions which might have been answered had he gone into the witness box and which were left unanswered; and also that where a prosecution witness had said something which Mr Savage said the defence did not accept, there was no evidence which might have contradicted that witness. He then moved on to his analysis of the prosecution case and his summaries of the evidence that had been given. From time to time, Henry left his place in the well beneath him and made such a show of trying to do so quietly and not to create a disturbance that the jury's eyes followed him as he went out of court and followed him again as he came back.

He told the jury that their morning break would be longer than usual because he knew how hard it was to listen to a single voice; and when it came to lunchtime he gave them another extra ten minutes. And at four o'clock he told them that he thought that they had probably had enough for one day and that he would resume his summing-up at ten tomorrow and that he was confident he would conclude in sufficient time for them to be able to retire quite early to consider their verdict.

After the jury had left, he remained seated: a tacit indication to counsel that he wanted them to remain behind.

'Mr Savage.'

Jonathan rose.

'As I indicated, I anticipate that the jury will be retiring fairly early tomorrow as I have almost come to the end of my summing-up. Two matters arise.'

He's surely not going to revoke bail now, thought Jonathan. Not after what was said yesterday. What is the matter with the man? Has he got judge-itis?

'Firstly, the question of bail. He can have bail overnight on the existing terms, but once the jury retires I propose to alter the terms. It is my practice, when a defendant is on bail, to restrict it to the confines of the court building whilst the jury is out. That is what I usually do and I can see no reason to depart from it in this case. Do you have any observation?'

'No,' said Jonathan, mentally apologising to the judge. 'Except that it is not impossible that the jury will be out overnight.'

'We will discuss it further if it should come to that. Mr Truckett?'

Graham stirred from the torpor that had come over him since lunchtime when, assuming that he would have nothing else to do except turn up to court, he had had a couple of VBs in the Legal Department mess. He had not taken in what the judge had said.

'Oh, your Lord, I mean, my Lordship, er, I've got nothing to say. Thank you.'

'About what?'

'Sorry, your Lord?'

'What have you got nothing to say about?'

'About what you just said.'

That's enough, thought Brett. Leave him be. He probably doesn't realise that I've seen him nodding off throughout the afternoon.

'The other matter is this: I have dealt with the law that the jury must apply and I think it unlikely that I will return to it tomorrow. So if either of you have any observations to make – if you disagree with anything that I have said, or think that I have omitted anything – now is the time to make your representations to me and I will consider them.' That's always a good tactic for the Court of Appeal. Let them see that I have given them the chance to correct me if they think I am wrong.

'Mr Truckett?'

'What? Oh.'

Graham whispered hurriedly to Pammy.

'Er, no, thank you. Nothing.'

'Mr Savage?'

'My Lord, I would like to consider the question overnight. Nothing occurs to me at the moment, but my learned junior has been making a careful note of what your Lordship has said so far and I would welcome the chance to go over it with him to see whether we need to make any representations to you.'

'No, Mr Savage, I want it done now. I don't want the jury to be delayed tomorrow morning.'

'With respect to your Lordship,' said Jonathan, try to combine courtesy with firmness, 'it is surely not unreasonable to give us some time to go over fairly complex directions in law. As to timing, we could sit, say, half-an-hour early tomorrow, before the jury arrives. And I would suggest that it would have this advantage: I am not familiar with the practice here in Hong Kong, but in England, where there are potentially difficult areas of law, the judge often shows counsel, before he starts his summing-up, his written note of what he is proposing to say about the law and invites them to make representations then. You have not chosen to do that in this case.'

Ouch, thought Brett. He's right; perhaps I should have done that.

'But sometimes the judge waits until he has all but completed his summing-up and then sends the jury away so that he can discuss any potential issue with counsel before the jury retires. Either way, those are practices of which the Court of Appeal of England and Wales has approved. If your Lordship were to do what I now request, it would have the advantages both of fairness to the prosecution and the defence and of avoiding having to send the jury away only to come back for the last few sentence of the summing-up before going away again.'

Shit, thought the judge, this guy is a smooth operator. I get the message about the Court of Appeal.

'Very well, that is what we will do. Nine-thirty tomorrow.' And as he rose he added, 'Try not to work too hard overnight, Mr Truckett.'

陳

The next morning, with sun shining frustratingly outside, they were back in court.

'Yes, Mr Truckett?'

'Nothing I want to raise with your Lordship.'

'Mr Savage?'

'My position is this: my learned junior and I have not found anything that we think that we need to raise with your Lordship at this stage. However, you have not, of course, concluded your summing-up. And more importantly, I would not wish any appellate court to regard itself as bound by our failure to make representations at this stage. Further consideration may make us, or any counsel who might replace us, form a different view.'

'So,' said O'Brien, not attempting to disguise the irony, 'I have your permission to carry on, do I?'

Jonathan sat down, affecting not to have heard.

'Very well,' said the judge, 'we will resume with the jury at ten.'

When he had left, Jonathan went back to the dock with Dempsey and the two solicitors. Chan stood up and leant over the rail.

'Did you follow what was going on just then, Mr Chan?' asked Jonathan.

'Yes, yes, of course. You certainly show the judge who is boss. But what was the talk about replacing counsel? I didn't understand.'

'Well, obviously, we want to continue to act for you. But if you were to be convicted you might want to change to different barristers, or at least a different leader, for the appeal. I was anxious that any future defence team would not be bound by anything that I said in court today.'

For the first time, and only momentarily, Lester Chan's smile slipped.

'But I would not want to change you. I have faith in you. Because, anyway, there is no need to talk of conviction. I can see how well the case is going. The judge is being very fair.'

'Alright, Mr Chan. Look, you've got time for a coffee or tea if you want. Make sure you're back in time. Mr Ng and I will come and have a proper chat with you after the jury retires; there's something I need to talk about with him now.'

As they walked out of the courtroom, Dempsey asked him what it was. Jonathan told him that he found Chan's optimism disturbing.

'Has he no sense of reality, do you think?' he asked.

'Oh, he probably has. My guess is that he is just one of those old-fashioned *tai-pans*, big bosses, who think that there would be a loss of face if they ever admit to the possibility that things may not be going their way. On the other hand he may be what we call *cheun choi*.'

'An idiot?'

'Precisely.'

They strolled around the anteroom together, watching the sun glittering through the skyscrapers on the bustling harbour and the endless traffic on the streets below them. Even at this height they could hear the sound of a siren as a fire engine rushed in to view and out again. Jonathan could see that the client was watching them and smiling approvingly, doubtless assuming that they were machinating some clever tactic on his behalf. Dempsey signalled to him by pointing at his wrist, and he and Jonathan went back into court. The jury was already there, and Lester Chan came in and went into the dock. Then the judge came back in.

'Good morning, members of the jury.' They all nodded and smiled at him. 'Thank you for, once again, being on time. Not far to go now.'

He reminded them that they must convict the defendant only if they were sure that he was guilty, and that if they were left in any real doubt then they must acquit him. He told them again that, as this was a charge of conspiracy, they would also have to be satisfied that at least one other person was involved and that that person would have to have acted dishonestly, albeit that his or her role may have been subservient and acting under the direction of another or others; and he pointed out that they might have little difficulty on that score as some of the office staff had admitted that they had taken part in something they knew to be dishonest by submitting documents which they knew to be bogus, that it to say, fraudulent. And finally, he told them that they should try hard to reach a unanimous verdict but if, after a suitable period had elapsed, they could not do so then he would be prepared to accept a majority verdict, that is, six to one or five to two. He told them that if they had any questions they should put them in writing so that he could discuss them with counsel before having them back in to court to answer them. He said that they must not feel under any pressure of time or anything else. Finally, he added that they had undertaken to return a true verdict according to the evidence and that they must let neither sympathy nor animosity influence them. And he had finished.

Henry swore in the ushers as jury bailiffs, and O'Brien asked the jury to retire and consider its verdict.

It was quarter to eleven.

After the judge had performed his cursory bow to counsel and left court, Jonathan beckoned to Lester Chan to leave the dock and the whole defence team followed him out of court and into one of the glass-sided conference rooms. Billy Yeung spoke briefly to the messenger, who replied angrily in machine-gun Cantonese and left.

459

'What's the matter with him?' asked Jonathan, removing his wig and gown.

'Oh, I told him to go out and get some coffee for us all but he thinks he should be present if we are discussing the case. He says that you value his opinion. I told him that he was better at hot drinks. He is cross with me now and he scolded me.'

'Well, we can benefit from his opinion when he gets back,' said Jonathan. 'Let's all sit down. Mr Chan, this is always a difficult time, waiting for the jury to come back.'

'Yes, I guess it must be for you, although you should be used to it.'

'True, it is not the nicest part of my job. But I meant that it is hard for you; I am always conscious of the stress that an accused person must go through at this stage of the trial.'

'Not so bad,' said Chan, seated with his elbows on the table and his hands clasped close to his lips. 'How long do you think they will be?'

Dempsey glanced at Jonathan.

'Chan Wai-king, *sin-san*,' he said, 'it is no good asking Mr Savage that. You never can tell how long a jury will take. Sometimes they can be very quick, others they take a long time. It's not unusual for them to be overnight. I've known that happen several times. There is accommodation for them in the court building.'

'Really?' said Jonathan. 'In England the jury no longer has to stay together if they can't reach a verdict by the end of the day. They used to be sent off to a hotel under the care of the jury bailiffs, but that doesn't happen anymore; now they are sent home with a warning not to try to contact each other.'

'No, we still sequestrate the jury,' said Dempsey. 'They are given a meal and bedrooms and the judge tells them not to discuss the case until they get back to the jury room and are all together. I think that that could happen in this case: it's been a long trial and they have a lot to get through.'

'I do not think so,' said Chan. 'I do not think that they will be too long. Maybe a couple of hours or perhaps three. Because you had done such a good job for me, Mr Savage.'

'Thank you, but it wasn't just me. Mr Ng was invaluable to me, and Mr Yeung and, of course, Mr Grinder have done excellent work in preparing the case. But my purpose in getting you in here with the others – apart, of course, from the messenger – is to see if there is anything you want to discuss with us. Do you have any questions? Now is the time to ask us.'

Chan's smile expanded as he put his hands down. He looked round the table.

'I have one question,' he said. 'Although perhaps we should wait till the messenger get back with the coffee so he can say what he think.'

'No, let's not wait for him,' Jonathan grinned, impressed by the fortitude of his client. 'Put your question to us now. We will try to answer it without him.'

'OK, if you're sure. So, my question is: where would you like to go for our celebration dinner this evening?'

The door was pushed open and the messenger returned carrying a tin tray with several flimsy disposable plastic cups. He had evidently merely gone down to the canteen so that he would not be away from the discussions for too long.

'Ah, here's the coffee,' said Jonathan. 'May we postpone the talk of a celebration until we know the verdict? You know, Mr Chan, you mustn't assume that we will get the right result. There's no certainty in any form of litigation, as you know, and that is particularly true of criminal trials.'

Chan's smile hardly shrank.

'But after the way you defend the case, yes, we will win. And because there is another reason why I know.'

'Look, Mr Chan,' said Jonathan, 'unless there is anything else that we can usefully talk about…'

'Yes, what do you think of the judge's summing-up?'

'Well, I thought that is was pretty fair. He went straight down the middle when he was summarising the evidence and I think that his directions on the law were accurate, although that is something that Mr Ng and I will want to discuss together. In fact, now would be a good time for us to start as it will be useful for us to make notes in case there is an appeal.'

'What, do you think that the prosecution might want to make an appeal?'

'No, Mr Chan. Look, unless there is anything else you want to ask, I think it best if Dempsey and I went across to his chambers now and started looking at the summing-up. I take it that we can be called if the jury have any questions or…'

'Quite usual,' Dempsey interrupted. 'The court clerk has my mobile number, and judges here don't mind if counsel leave the building.'

'Good,' said Jonathan. 'We'll do that then but, Mr Chan, remember that your bail has changed now and that you must stay within the building. So no lunch in the restaurant in the park today.'

'But I had kept the table. Maybe we go there if jury are back by lunchtime.'

'Maybe,' Jonathan replied.

There was no message from the jury and, at just before one o'clock, Brett told Henry to contact counsel and to announce in court that he would not take a verdict before two-thirty so that everyone could go off to lunch, except, of course, the defendant. For the first time, a look of despondency flickered across Chan's face. Frank noticed it. He reminded him that he could not leave the building and told him that he knew that there was a very good public dining room downstairs. He wondered whether it would breach any local rules if he invited him to the lawyers' restaurant, balancing the risk that he might earn the opprobrium of the profession as well as having to endure an awkward lunchtime with someone whom, he realised, he had almost never been alone with since the start of the trial, indeed, since he became involved in the case, against the common decency of not leaving him to cope on his own at such a stressful time.

'I'll tell you what, Mr Chan,' he said. 'I'll go out and get some sandwiches and coffee and we can eat them together, perhaps in one of the conference rooms, if there's one free.'

'That is very good. So, perhaps you would get me a lot. I am very hungry. And perhaps orange juice. But are you sure? You don't want to go to a restaurant for your lunch? That is very kind. Thank you.'

'*Mo ha hei.* Don't mention it.'

'So you speak Cantonese? I did not know.'

'A little. I used to live here.'

'Oh, I thought you were a London solicitor, like Mr Savage is a London QC.'

Frank was struck by how little Chan knew about him and, indeed, how little he had contributed to the defence case other than by fitting the client's requirements of having grey hair and being a *gweilo*.

'No, I don't live in London but I used to work in Hong Kong, with Billy, you know, Yeung Chi-hang. And my wife is from Hong Kong. Anyway, I had better go out and get us something to eat.'

陳

As he came back with the food, Frank could see Lester Chan through the tinted glass of the conference room. He was still sitting where he had left him, upright and alone. It was difficult not to admire his stoicism. Frank had never before experienced a client facing a serious criminal charge and waiting for a jury to come back. He wondered how he would feel if he were in that position and decided that he would rather not think about it. Chan continued to be courteous; indeed, his smile hardly ever left him. Perhaps he was a Buddhist and was prepared to accept, with equanimity, whatever fate had decided for him and to take an advantage from diversity by proving to himself that he could remain calm in circumstances where others would be agitated. The smile broadened as Frank came in to the room.

'Thank you, you are very kind,' he said as he unwrapped the four sandwiches that Frank slid across the table to him.

'So, it is good that you get just a little. We must save room for our celebration party tonight.'

'Yes,' replied Frank. It was difficult to know what else to say that would not, at least to himself, sound crass.

'Look, Mr Chan. Why don't you eat all the sandwiches? I have to make a couple of phone calls. One is, er, private. Will you be alright on your own for a bit?'

This is cowardice, he thought.

'Yes, sure, I will eat what I can and perhaps have a little sleep. Thank you again for bringing me some snack.'

Frank went out into the anteroom and then across to the lift lobby, where he could not be seen from the conference room. He called Winnie's phone but there was no reply. Perhaps she was playing mah-jong with some of her lunchtime friends and couldn't hear above the clatter as the tiles were slapped down. He felt strangely agitated and wanted to hear her calming, sensible voice. He pushed a button and took the lift down to the entrance hall and went out into the sunshine, by the circular fountain. Press photographers were still at their station by the glass doors. He wondered why there were fewer of them than before and then a thought struck him. He went over to the pavement at the edge of the turning area and looked down towards the roadway; there they were, the rest of them, clamouring around the prison van exit. He stepped back, barely avoiding a hooting taxi which was driving away from the doors, unsure what was causing his palpitations. He went over and sat on the low wall surrounding the fountain and tried Winnie again.

'*Wai?*'

'Oh, hello, love. It's me.'

'Yes. I see your number on my phone.'

'Then, why did you answer in Cantonese?'

'Because I was not sure it was you.'

'Well, who else would it be, using my phone?'

'Well, somebody might have stole it, and it wouldn't be a *gweilo*. That's why I spoke in Cantonese.'

'Or could the reason be that you are with your friends and forgot to speak in English?'

'Can be.'

'Anyhow, I just wanted to talk to you. The jury are out and we are waiting for them to come back. It's a new experience for me and it's a bit nerve-racking. You're alright, aren't you?'

'Yes, of course.'

'Well, I just wanted to say that I've no idea how long the jury will be. And I don't know what the practice is in criminal cases; I don't know how late the court will sit waiting for them or what happens. So I have no idea what time I'll be home. I'll call you again as soon as I know something.'

'Do you want me to come and keep you company?'

'No, but thank you. That's lovely of you. But I thought you would be busy packing for your flight tonight.'

'No, already packed. How is Chan Wai-king?'

'He seems fine. He seems to be convinced that he will get off.'

'He is, maybe, calmer than you are?'

'There's no maybe about it. Anyway, I'd better go.'

He ended the call, wondering why they still used the expression "hang up". There was scarcely anyone old enough to have used one of those old telephones where the receiver hung on a bracket. Come to think of it, why do they still "dial" a number; it must be thirty years or more since phones with dials disappeared.

A slight breeze had started in his direction and he was getting covered by a fine spray from the fountain; refreshing though it seemed, he was not altogether keen on having a shower in dilute botulism. He stood up and walked back to look down again to the roadway. There was the usual constant stream of traffic on Queensway and, to the left, the group of photographers seemed to have grown. A feeling of uneasiness came over him and he decided there was little he could do, standing outside the court building. He walked into the park, past the restaurant where he had had so many awkward, time-wasting lunches over the last weeks, and down to the artificial lake. He sat on a bench for a while but the sun was very hot and it became uncomfortable, even with his jacket off and tie loosened. He got up again and went towards the old colonial barracks building and into the shade of its verandah, but he felt uncomfortable just standing there being stared at by parties of schoolchildren on their way to the Museum of Tea Ware that lay inside. He put his jacket back on and went back and into the lawyers' restaurant. It was almost empty and he took a table by the window, overlooking the giant ferns. A waiter came up with a menu; he waved it aside and asked just for some Chinese tea. His stomach was knotted and he did not want anything to eat. He sat sipping the scalding, pale green tea and looked at his watch. He had better go back to Lester Chan as soon as he had drunk it: he was probably still on his own and might need someone to talk to.

When he got back to the court floor, Frank saw that Lester Chan was not on his own. He was still in the conference room, but Billy Yeung was with him. He went in.

'Oh, hello again,' said Chan, cheerily. A pile of empty sandwich bags lay on the table in front of him.

'I came over,' said Billy, 'because the court clerk called and told me that the jury have sent a message. They have a verdict. We've still got ten minutes before the judge said that he would take it. I have spoken to Ng Dim-si, and he and Jonathan are on their way over. Oh look, there they are.'

Jonathan and Dempsey were walking from the lift lobby, with their gowns on and wigs in their hands. They came into the room and sat down.

'How are you, Mr Chan?' said Jonathan, anxiously. He hated this stage of a trial. In all his years at the Bar he had never found a way to avoid the stomach-fluttering stress that preceded the verdict and had often wondered what it must be like for the client. Some old lags took it in their stride, part of the baggage that went with being a career criminal, but for a man like Lester Chan it must be an agony.

'Oh, I am fine, thank you; just thinking about our dinner tonight.'

'I think that Mr Ng and I ought to be getting back into court. I saw that the door was open as we came across. I'd like to get my papers in order.'

'Mr Savage?'

'Yes, Mr Chan.'

'Do you think that it is a good sign that the jury are ready now?'

'Well, it's fairly quick, after a long trial.'

'But that looks good?'

'Impossible to say. Don't stay here too long. It's important that you are back in court before the judge comes in.'

Jonathan and Dempsey went back in and made a play of shuffling their papers. Then they saw Billy escorting the client back to the dock. The court began to fill up with journalists and various other people who Jonathan had noticed from time to time during the trial. His heart was thumping. There was a loud knock from the other side of the judge's door and Henry appeared and looked round.

'All rise.'

Brett O'Brien came in and sat down.

'Mr Savage, Mr Truckett.'

They rose.

'I understand that the jury has a verdict. Is there any reason why they should not be brought into court?'

'No, my Lord,' they both said. Jonathan was conscious that his voice was quieter than normal.

'Very well. Jury bailiffs, please bring the jury back into court.'

37

Billy asked Frank to stay behind. He thought it would not be right to have four of them go see the client, so he, Jonathan and Dempsey went through the dock and down the stairs to the cells. They waited at the door at the bottom until they were let in by an officer of the Correctional Services Department. They were led to a small, glass-walled room where Lester Chan was sitting at a table. He spoke rapidly in Cantonese to Billy, who wrote down some notes and what appeared to be telephone numbers.

Chan got up and shook Jonathan's hand.

'Mr Chan, I am so sorry.'

'No, you did everything you can. And the sentence is not too bad.'

'Actually, I thought five years was quite severe, quite hard. But the judge did ask whether we wanted sentencing to be adjourned so that we could get reports and testimonials. I was a bit surprised when you instructed us to say no.'

'No, I want to get on with it. It won't be long, I think, till our appeal is heard, I think. And in the meantime it would give me a chance to meet up with some old friends.'

'People you met when you were in Stanley on remand?'

'A few. But quite a lot of my friends are businessmen serving sentences. I haven't seen some of them for a few years.'

Jonathan wondered whether it would be the right time to remind him that all his lawyers had advised him to give evidence, but recognised that there might be an element of blaming Chan, and not himself, for the case going the wrong way. He said nothing.

'So, I would like to thank you and Ng Dim-si for your very good work for me, and of course Mr Yeung Chi-hang. It was not your fault that I did not get acquitted today.'

'Well, that is very generous of you, Mr Chan. You are a lot more composed than many defendants in your position would be. In fact, if I may say, surprisingly so. You seem to be as cheerful as ever, which is very impressive in the circumstances.'

'Oh, that is because you and Mr Ng and Yeung Chi-hang *sin san* will do my appeal for me, I hope.'

'Of course, if you still want us.'

'I do. And we will win in the Court of Appeal. And if not there, then in the Court of Final Appeal. The fortune teller at the Wong Tai Sin Temple could not be wrong.'

Billy Yeung and Lester Chan spoke briefly in Cantonese. Dempsey listened without saying anything. Jonathan watched them, uncomprehending.

'He wants to know,' said Billy, 'whether he should apply for bail while he is waiting.'

'You mean bail pending appeal,' said Jonathan.

'Yes, that is the term.'

'I have to say that it is very rare in England. I always feel that it is unfair on a defendant who later gets out on an appeal to have spent time in custody, but the Court of Appeal takes the view that, unless there is a very strongly arguable ground that can be shown to be likely to succeed, it is better for a convicted defendant to start serving his sentence straight away. But that has a lot to do with the length of time it takes to get an appeal heard. What's the position in Hong Kong, Dempsey?'

'Much the same here,' Dempsey answered. 'It hardly ever happens unless a Court of Appeal judge can be persuaded that the full court is probably going to overturn the conviction. I have known it happen, but not very often.'

'So, what do you think, Mr Savage?' Chan asked. Did Jonathan detect a flicker of anxiety?

'Well, Mr Chan, of course I haven't had the opportunity to go over the judge's summing-up in detail – we'll need to see a transcript to do that – but I do not recall any outstanding and obvious errors which we could point to in an application for bail.'

'No, I agree with that,' said Dempsey. 'And the fact is that if a convicted defendant is on bail, there is not so much urgency in listing the appeal for hearing. So, without bail, the appeal will probably come on earlier.'

Chan's smile was restored. 'So, quicker to prove the truth of prediction of the *kau chim* sticks,' he said.

38

After Chan had been taken down to the cells, Brett thanked
the jurors for the care and conscientiousness they had shown
during this fairly long trial. He considered, for a moment,
excusing them from future jury service, as so many judges
did at the end of a complex case, but then thought it
would be better to keep these, mostly sensible and efficient,
people available for future trials. He thought of adding
that he believed they had come to the correct conclusion,
but decided against that, too. It might provide an appeal
point if he said something which could be interpreted as
showing partiality to the prosecution and, anyway, he had
been at pains to point out that the decision was theirs and
not his and some might say that his views as to what the
verdict should be were irrelevant. Then he extended the
conventional judicial courtesy by thanking counsel on both
sides for their assistance to the court, rose and went back to
his room.

As he was removing his wig and robes and unbuttoning
his winged collar, he didn't know why, but he recalled

something that Graham Truckett had said, something about wanting to talk to him. Perhaps he should send him a note, now that the case was over, inviting him to come and see him. He could perhaps add his congratulations; at first he had thought that Truckett was well out of his depth but, in the end, he had done quite an efficient job and he had, after all, got the right result. Anyway, that could wait until they were all clear of the court building. It wouldn't look right if he were to be seen sending a personal letter to the prosecutor before the dust had settled. And first of all, he must call Sharon and tell her to meet him at the Club later so that they could go out to dinner together. He assumed that, the jury having come back so quickly, and when they could well have wanted to have another day's deliberation, the listing office would not have given him any work for tomorrow, so that there would be no papers for him to read this afternoon or evening.

There was a quiet tap and Henry put his head round the door.

'My Lord. Because there is a message. Please call the Administrator?'

'Oh shit! Er, I'm sorry, Henry. I didn't mean to swear. But, for heaven's sake, won't they leave me alone? It's been full on with this case for weeks, and they couldn't possibly have expected it to end today. Can't I have any let-up?'

Henry smiled indulgently, like an *amah* whose charge is having a minor tantrum but will soon be pacified.

'No, not the listing office. The message was from the Judiciary Administrator. He wants you to call him.'

His smile broadened. It was almost a grin.

'Henry, do you know what this is about?'

'No, of course not, my Lord.'

'Henry, you are not a very good Chinese. You're not inscrutable.' Perhaps he should not have said that, but his clerk was still smiling, so probably no harm done. 'Come on, out with it.'

'Well, my Lord, I thought that you had been tired and so I save you the trouble and telephoned the Administrator to ask what he wanted.'

Brett was somewhat taken aback. He had never before known Henry to do anything indiscreet.

'And did he tell you?'

'Yes, he said that he had been having a discussion with the Chief Justice and that the Chief wants you to go and see him tomorrow at nine-thirty. So I had arranged with his clerk that you will be there.'

'Well, you had better tell the listing office not to put in any early applications for me tomorrow.'

'No need. They already know. They tell me the Judiciary Administrator had already said that they should not put any more cases in your list until you had told the Chief Justice whether or not you accept.'

陳

Still in their robes, Graham and Pammy walked across from the court building to the escalator leading to the lobby of the government building which housed the several floors of the Department of Justice. They stood close to each other in the crowded lift, saying little. Someone at the back called, 'Well done, you two,' but he did not see who it was. They got out and walked along the corridor to his room.

Pammy's shining black hair was tousled from wearing her wig. Graham could not say why, but it increased her gamine look and made her even more attractive. He was about to say something when Emily came in.

'Mr Truckett, Mr William Soh has just called you. He says that he is in the Bar mess and is waiting to buy you both a drink. Maybe, perhaps, you should go now.'

The mess was one floor up. It was a large room, with windows overlooking the harbour. Its walls were hung with plaques from overseas prosecution departments and framed photographs of various sports teams, mostly made up of long-retired members of the Legal Department, many going back to the days before the changeover, when it was the Attorney General's chambers. In one corner was a small bar area, with stools and an array of bottles and glasses on shelves. It even had optics for the spirits and looked, except for the absence of a barman, like a small-scale pub. Sitting on a shabby leather settee near the opposite wall was the Director of Public Prosecutions. He had a glass of fruit juice on the worn and scratched glass-topped table in front of him. There were two equally elderly easy chairs at either end.

'Ah, Graham, and Sit-ming,' he said as he rose to greet them, 'my congratulations. That was a very good result. I knew that I could trust you to deliver, Graham. Let me get you both a drink.'

'Ah, look,' said Graham, 'Pammy was tremendously helpful. Couldn't have done it without her.' That, he thought, is something of an understatement.

'Well done to you, of course,' Soh said, turning towards her. 'You make an excellent team.'

Graham could see that she was, in equal proportions, terrified by the DPP and impressed by Graham's easy manner with him.

'So,' said Soh, 'what can I get you? Sit-ming?'

'Oh, I'll have what you are having. An orange juice, perhaps, please.' She was scarcely audible.

'And you, Graham?'

'Just a beer. A VB, please.'

'Nonsense,' said the DPP.

Graham was all too conscious of how worn and scruffy his suit was compared to Soh's immaculate and beautifully cut dark grey two-piece.

'No, if you had lost the case, I might, possibly, have got you those drinks. But you won, and convincingly: the jury was unanimous and were back in a pretty short time. This calls for champagne.'

Graham would have loved a thirst-slaking Australian beer but knew he could say nothing. Pammy looked at her hands.

'And, please, take a seat,' said the DPP as he went behind the bar, signed a book and took a bottle from the drinks chiller. He came back holding it and two glasses.

'I'm afraid it's only The Widow,' he said, as he put the bottle of Veuve Clicquot Brut down on the table. 'There doesn't seem to be any vintage champagne. I'll have a word with the committee.'

'Only two glasses? Aren't you joining us?'

'No, Graham. I have to get back to work. I have a meeting with the Secretary for Justice shortly. I don't think he would approve of my smelling of alcohol. But you two, take your time and then call it a day. I wouldn't expect either of you to do any more work today. Well, I had better go. And, again, well done.'

William Soh smiled, touched the knot of his already perfect silk tie and walked towards the lifts.

'Well,' said Graham, 'that's a nice surprise. Bit early in the day for me to start on fizz, but it would be criminal to waste it.'

He stood to remove the foil and the wire and prised the cork from the bottle. Then he sat down on the settee where the DPP had been.

'Come and sit next to me,' he said as he began to fill the two glasses, carefully so that they did not overflow. Pammy sat down, straightening her skirt. Her legs were at an angle so that her feet were inclined away from him and her knees towards him.

'Well, cheers,' he said. They both drank, or rather, he swigged and she sipped.

'Ah, look, Pammy, I can't begin to thank you enough for all the work that you have put into this case.'

He turned towards her and topped up their glasses.

'I don't think,' he continued, 'that we would have got this result without your help.'

She looked into her glass and then at him. Was she blushing, or was it the effect of the drink?

'You are very kind to me, Graham. But you did all the hard work and you took control of the case in court. I am so grateful because I learned a lot from you. About advocacy and about case preparation.'

Graham considered confessing that it was her work that had made him understand the case, but decided that it would be wrong to disillusion her. He wondered if she remembered the embarrassingly acid comments that the judge had directed at him. This time she had taken a bigger swallow and there was more space in her glass as he topped them up.

'We have to finish it,' he said. 'You can't put the cork back in a champagne bottle.'

'Oh really?' she said. 'I did not know that. You see, you continue to teach me.'

'Yeah, it's true. So, here's to our win. And here's to having finished this case.'

He raised his glass and touched hers with it. A small splash fell onto her lap. She looked down and ignored it. They both drank and he refilled the glasses.

'Ah, Pammy,' he said, aware of the affect the drink was beginning to have on his inhibitions, 'let's not talk about the case anymore, except that, I have to say, it has been a real pleasure working with you all these weeks.'

She looked directly and openly at him. My God, he thought, she's so attractive. He was conscious of an awkward stirring and he shifted his position slightly.

'Thank you,' she said. 'It has been wonderful for me.'

'Look, Pammy, I can't help myself saying this. You've come to mean a lot to me. I think you're terrific. I mean, I think you're gorgeous.' He couldn't think of how to put it less clumsily. 'What I want to say is…Oh God, I'm sorry, I shouldn't…'

But her face brightened.

'Oh, Graham,' she said, 'I thought that you were not interested in me. I thought that you were being very kind to me because I know so little about being in a big trial like this and you were not scolding me. I am so happy that you like me.'

He looked down at the bottle: only about a third left. He poured more into their glasses.

'Actually, Pammy, what I wanted to say is that I think I love you. I've felt that way for a while, but I didn't want to say it. Er, I am sorry. That's probably not appropriate, me being your senior and everything.'

She put down her glass, took his from him and held his right hand in both of hers.

'No, I am glad you did.'

'So, are you free this evening?'

She nodded and smiled, still looking at him.

'Good, let's go and have a celebratory dinner somewhere.'

He paused, wondering whether he dare; then said it.

'So, to save you having to go home and then meeting up somewhere, would you like to come up to my flat? You can, er, freshen up and, um, relax there and then we can head off out together.'

'That would be very nice,' said Pammy.

The plane roared down the runway and took off, climbing into the night sky. Jonathan, sitting in a window seat, watched the streams of condensation streaking the Plexiglas. He could not help thinking of Lester Chan, in a cell somewhere, in amongst the tilting curve of the lights below as he flew home, free to do as he chose. He wondered how much this case had cost Chan; all that money spent and he had lost. Maybe he would have stood a better chance if he had gone into the witness box to explain his version of events, although it was possible that the sentence would have been longer if the judge had taken into account that he had been disbelieved on his oath; at least he could not be accused of having perjured himself. He wasn't sure what principles applied in Hong Kong. It was a pretty long sentence, by English standards, but he had been warned that Hong Kong sentencing policy was very harsh, particularly in fraud cases. Chan had seemed pretty stoical about the result and had been very courteous. Perhaps that was all it was: courtesy. His promise that he would retain him and Dempsey for the appeal could evaporate when he spoke to other prisoners, and he might well decide that it was better to have different barristers or, at least, to change leading counsel. He had not been the instructing solicitors' first choice: that was Gresham Nutworthy, who was far better known than he was. Perhaps Nutworthy had recovered and would be fit enough to take on the appeal. Or, having spent so much money on accommodation and flights for him, Chan might want to retrench and take on a local silk. Jonathan continued to look down at the diminishing nightscape below until the plane veered sharply and the lights disappeared altogether. Goodbye, Hong Kong.

Further back in the same compartment Frank Grinder was looking forward to going home and joining Winnie. He had not realised that he and Jonathan were booked on the same flight until they had seen each other in the airline's business class lounge. They had had a couple of glasses of wine together and some finger sandwiches and had made small talk. Even though they had taken a liking to each other at an early stage, both had been too absorbed in their own affairs during the trial to have had much to do with each other beyond the commitments of the case and the client's lunches and dinners. That drink they had together in the bar at the Majestic Harbour had not been repeated. And flights that left just before midnight were not particularly conducive to chattiness. Neither of them had made any suggestion of changing seats so that they could travel together.

Frank had found his unexpectedly extended time in Hong Kong surprisingly satisfying. He had been able to meet up with many old acquaintances and had enjoyed renewing the luxury of the Club and living at a standard which was very different from that in the highly-taxed UK. There was so much to enjoy – that wonderful day out in Lamma, for instance, and all those Cantonese restaurants with Winnie in control; and he had grown to love the apartment in Kennedy Town; but with Winnie gone, it was not the same. Moreover, all that eating and drinking was beginning to have an effect on the waistband of his trousers and the collar of his shirt, so he had probably had enough, at least for the time being. But Hong Kong did have one priceless advantage: Rambo was in England. Much as he wanted to be back in Cheltenham with Winnie he did not know how he was going to cope with sharing their home with her younger brother. Every minute, every mile that the plane sped westward brought him closer.

Suddenly, the answer appeared. He had made a lot of money, unexpected money, being the token grey-haired *gweilo* solicitor in the defence team. He could easily afford to rent a room for Rambo, somewhere in Gloucester. He and Winnie would be near enough to satisfy their consciences and at least claim that she was discharging her duty as an older sister to keep an eye on him. It could not cost much and, anyway, it was unlikely to be for very long as he would almost certainly be thrown out of the college within a term or two.

Frank reclined his seat contentedly and was soon asleep.

 Matador

For exclusive discounts on Matador titles,
sign up to our occasional newsletter at
troubador.co.uk/bookshop